FOR MORE
THAN GLORY

WILLIAM C. DIETZ

ACE BOOKS, NEW YORK

This is a work of fiction. Names, characters, places, and incidents either are the product of the author's imagination or are used fictitiously, and any resemblance to actual persons, living or dead, business establishments, events, or locales is entirely coincidental.

FOR MORE THAN GLORY

An Ace Book / published by arrangement with the author

PRINTING HISTORY
Ace hardcover edition / October 2003
Ace mass market edition / October 2004

ISBN: 0-441-01214-0

ACE®
Ace Books are published by The Berkley Publishing Group,
a division of Penguin Group (USA) Inc.
375 Hudson Street, New York, New York 10014.
ACE and the "A" design are trademarks belonging
to Penguin Group (USA) Inc.

PRINTED IN THE UNITED STATES OF AMERICA

10 9 8 7 6 5 4 3 2 1

continued . . .

This book is for my daughters Allison and Jessica,
both of whom know the meaning of "grit."

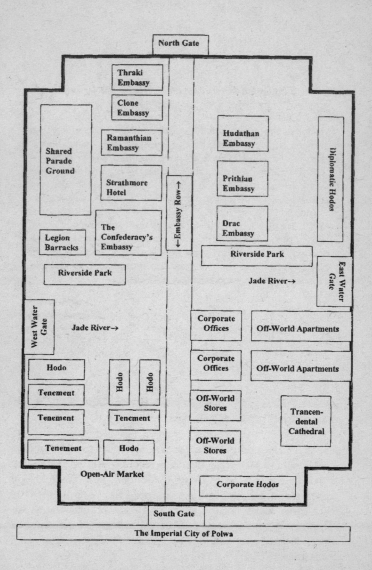

1

War remains an art and, like all arts whatever its variation, will have its ending principles. Many men, skilled either with sword or pen and sometimes with both, have tried to expound those principles. I heard them once from a soldier of experience for whom I had a deep and well-founded respect. Many years ago, as a cadet hoping some day to be an officer, I was poring over "The Principles of War," listed in the old Field Services Regulations, when the Sergeant-Major came upon me. He surveyed me with kindly amusement. "Don't bother your head about all them things, me lad," he said. "There's only one principle of war that's this. Hit the other fellow as quick as you can and as hard as you can, where it hurts him most, when he ain't looking."

Sir William Slim
Defeat Into Victory

ABOARD SYNDICATE BASE 012, ON A MOON NICKNAMED "FLOATER," IN ORBIT AROUND RIM WORLD CR-7893

The soft but insistent beep of the alarm served to summon Captain Frank Moy from the deep, alcohol-induced slumber to which he had gradually become addicted. His eyes felt as if they were glued shut and a sustained effort was required to force them open. Finally, welcomed into the darkness of his cabin by the smoke alarm's Cyclops-like red eye, the ex-naval officer ordered the beeping sound to "Stop, dammit," and, thankfully, it did.

Then, rolling out of the rack the same way he had for more than twenty years, Moy managed to stand. The only light came from the smoke alarm and the LEDs embedded in the console next to his bunk. Seven of them were green but one glowed red. That was bad, very bad, but so was the pressure on Moy's bladder. He took a step toward the head and swore when pain stabbed his brain. The light over the stainless-steel sink came on as Moy lined up on the toilet and gave his body permission to let go.

Finally, once the pressure was relieved, the ex–naval officer turned to the mirror. What he saw made Moy wince. Much of the once thick black hair had disappeared and what remained was heavily shot with gray. The blue eyes were faded now, as if the light behind them had dimmed and might soon go out. A field of black stubble covered cheeks so gaunt it appeared as if the skin rested on bone. A far cry from the bright-eyed young stud who had graduated from the academy more than two decades before.

Moy shook his head in disgust, considered the possibility of shaving, and remembered the red LED. Something, a sizable chunk of spaceborne rock was the most likely culprit, had entered the volume of space that defined the moon's defensive zone and triggered a number of alarms. Odds were that the clowns in the control center had dealt with the matter hours before and chosen to let him sleep. Still, once the situation was cleared, the LED should have turned green.

Moy used half a glass of water to wash the foul taste out of his mouth and the other half to help him swallow a couple of tablets. Then, gritting his teeth against the pain, he made his way into the middle of the cabin. "Open com. Moy to control center . . . who's the OD?"

There was no reply. Either the com was down, something that occurred with disturbing regularity, or the C&C crew were screwing off. A punishable offense in the *real* navy—but a joke in the so-called Syndicate. Just one of the many problems that plagued the organization.

Propelled more by the bone-deep sense of duty the navy had instilled in him rather than any particular loyalty to the organization he was now part of, Moy turned toward the hatch. There were no uniforms, not since the "members" had voted them out, so it didn't matter what he wore.

Moy entered the main corridor, turned right, and followed the B ring in toward the station's core. Having been constructed during the early days of the rebellion, immediately after Earth Governor Patricia Pardo and Legion Colonel Leon Harco had usurped Earth's government, the outlaw habitat was well put together. And a good thing, too, because discipline had slipped a lot since then, and maintenance was abysmal.

All manner of graffiti covered the bulkheads to either side, trash littered the deck, and it seemed as if every third or fourth light fixture was burned out. The life-support systems continued to receive a fair amount of attention but even that was starting to slip. So much so that Moy had given serious thought to leaving. But for what? The Confederacy wanted to put him on trial for mutiny, murder, and miscellaneous "crimes against sentient beings," life out on the Rim was hard, and nobody wants to hire an alcoholic.

Moy palmed a lock, waited for the hatch to hiss open, and entered the station's control room. It smelled of sweat, alcohol, and ozone. Screens flickered, air whispered through vents, and the computer nicknamed "Bitching Betty," spoke via the overhead speakers. "Incoming targets, one, three, and four are continuing to close. Target two is stationary, repeat, stationary, but well within range. Recommend that all station personnel don space armor, report to assigned battle stations, and prepare for combat. Screens, *ready*. Electronic countermeasures, *ready*. Weapons systems, *ready*. Downloading firing solutions now."

Moy swore, stormed up onto the command platform, and looked for someone to kick. Ex–Naval Lieutenant Tosko had passed out in the command chair, the com tech was facedown on the deck, and the weapons officer sat with her forehead resting on the control panel. The injector tube, which was still clutched in her hand, told the officer everything he needed to know.

Back during the rebellion the Syndicate had "liberated" any number of naval vessels, not the least of which were the *Ibutho* and the *Guerrero*, both of which had taken on stores and departed roughly six hours earlier. In spite of specific prohibitions against taking part in the typical bon voyage celebration, it appeared that the control room crew had ignored regulations and partied anyway. Now they were going to pay for their laxity, for *his* laxity, because the navy had taught him that the responsibilities of command reach everywhere even into one's sleep.

Tosko felt something hard connect with his leg, jerked in response, and opened his eyes. "What the hell? Who kicked me?"

Moy looked grim. "I did . . . and I'd kick your ass if you weren't sitting on it. Look at those screens."

Tosco looked, swore, and slapped the general alarm button. Klaxons sounded, weapons came on line, and groggy crew members stumbled down corridors.

Betty, oblivious to what her owners did, continued to chant. "Targets one, three, and four are launching what appear to be short-range in-system spacecraft having target profiles consistent with CF Dagger 180s, CF-10 assault boats, and CF electronic countermeasure (ECM) decoys. Tracking, tracking, request permission to fire."

Everyone in the Control Center knew that the letters "CF" stood for Confederacy Forces and what would happen if they were captured. Tosco, his eyes wide with fear, flipped a protective cover up out of the way. The button glowed green. He mashed it. The verbal command came a fraction of a second later. "Fire!"

The station's Class I weapons, those which were computer controlled, burped coherent light, spit missiles, and launched torpedoes. The speakers rattled with ECM-induced static as com calls began to flood in, and the station fought back.

"Damn," Tosco said, his eyes glued to the screens. "Where the hell did they come from?"

"From our past," Moy answered grimly, "from our past."

Legion General Bill Booly III and Navy Admiral Angie Tyspin sat in the *Ninja*'s Command and Control Center and listened as Big Momma, the ship's primary C&C computer, provided her own low-key narration for the assault. "Fighters launched . . . Assault boats launched . . . Lead elements taking fire. Units F-5, F-6, and A-3 destroyed. Units F-9, A-9, and A-12 damaged. Enemy fighters launching, repeat launching, profiles are available screen right."

Booly glanced at the profiles, confirmed that all of the Syndicate's fighters dated back to premutiny days, and nodded. "I don't see anything new, that's good."

Tyspin, who had known Booly for quite a while by then, and fought at his side through two major campaigns, looked into the steady gray eyes. The lines that extended away from them cut deeper now, dividing his skin into white deltas, before disappearing into what remained of his youth. Some gray had crept into his close-cropped hair. "Yes," the naval officer agreed, "the prerebellion stuff is bad enough. Lord help us if they get their hands on any of the *new* fighters."

The possibility caused Booly to grimace. The new fighters, the 190s, were equipped with cloaking technology obtained from the Thrakies, and were very dangerous indeed. However, assuming all went well, the Syndicate would be broken long before the criminals were able to lay their hands on a 190. "Roger that. Fortunately, judging from how long it took them to respond, we caught the bastards napping."

"True," Tyspin replied grimly, her eyes on the screens, "but F-5, F-6, and A-3 won't be coming back. That's a high price to pay for a bunch of deserters. Maybe we should nuke 'em."

"I'd be tempted," Booly responded levelly, "if I knew where the *Ibutho* and *Guerrero* were. How many raids are they respon sible for? Twenty-six at last count? Intelligence claims there's some sort of harbor inside that moon . . . Maybe they're in there, like fleas on a dog, or maybe they aren't. We need to know."

Tyspin knew that the other officer was correct but hated to take the casualties. Especially from mutineers, whom she saw as the lowest form of life in the universe.

The legionnaire saw the pain in her green eyes and nodded. "I know how you feel Angie, honest I do, and I'll do everything I can to keep the engagement short."

Booly stood. He wore a full-combat rig, including body armor and a sidearm. The grin was genuine. "Keep the coffee on . . . I'll be back shortly."

Like the rest of Booly's staff, Tyspin thought it was foolish for him to participate in the assault, even if it was in wave three, and took one last shot at dissuading him. "This is a mistake, sir, and your wife will blame me."

Booly laughed. "If you don't tell her, then neither will I."

Tyspin thought about what it would be like to notify Maylo Chien-Chu of her husband's death, and was just about to answer, when Booly disappeared.

The control room was fully staffed by then, as were the rest of the station's various departments. Having claimed the command chair for himself, Moy touched a control and allowed the power-assisted seat to swing left. A large diagram filled most of the wall, and rather than the lines being green the way they should have been, one end of the habitat was red. It had taken the navy less than two hours to silence most of the habitat's weapons systems and land the marines. All of which was little more than a diversion since Moy knew that the harbor located below his feet was the *real* objective. Neither the *Ibutho* nor the *Guerrero* happened to be in port, but the navy didn't know that, and hoped to trap them.

So, the ex–naval officer thought, *what should I do? Surrender? So they can try me for mutiny and lord knows what else? Or die for the Syndicate?* Neither alternative seemed especially attractive.

Others must have been thinking similar thoughts because that's when the weapons officer stood, removed her headset, and dropped it on the control panel. "I don't know about you," she said, her eyes sweeping the room, "but I'm outta here."

"What?" Moy asked sarcastically. "No vote of the membership? No valiant defense of the Syndicate?"

"Screw the Syndicate," the weapons officer replied. "There's only one way off this turd ball and it's through the harbor. We go now, or we don't go at all."

The others agreed with her. Moy watched in silence as the rest of his staff stood in ones and twos, averted their eyes, and made their way toward the lockers that lined the room's back wall. Once in their space armor they would drop through the tubes, seize whatever vessels they could lay their hands on, and run like hell.

The weapons officer faced him, hands on hips. They'd been lovers once, many months ago, and she still felt something for the gaunt-looking man who sat slumped in the chair. "So," she said, "are you coming?"

"No," the ex–naval officer heard himself say. "I don't believe that I am."

"Then I'll see you in hell," the weapons officer said, "or wherever people like us go."

"Yes," Moy agreed thoughtfully, "I'll see you in hell."

Floater hung like a silvery ball against the backdrop provided by the planet designated as CR-7893, a brownish sphere, heavily marbled by white clouds. Now, as assault boat A-12 drew closer, Booly looked out over the pilots' heads and to the scene beyond. The faceplate restricted his total view but not the area straight ahead of him. The Syndicate's habitat looked like a barnacle on the surface of a rock.

Down farther, roughly midway between the satellite's poles, a black hole was visible. Small minnowlike spaceships, none larger than a shuttle, darted out of the tunnel and sped away There were dozens of the small craft, which suggested that those who could were trying to escape. And that was fine with him. After all Booly reasoned, once the officers ran, the troops were likely to follow.

Thanks to his status as CO, Booly had access to all radio traffic and listened in satisfaction as Tyspin's fighters took off in hot pursuit. Each of the departing vessels would be intercepted and called upon to surrender. Those who complied would face trial. Those who refused would die. *That* part of the operation appeared to be a complete success.

But where were the battle cruisers? Why hadn't they emerged to give battle? *Because the bastards aren't there,* Booly thought to himself, *because they already left.*

The tunnel yawned in front of them. Dozens of red beacons, still blinking their endless warnings, guarded the passageway's enormous circumference. The tunnel was huge, more than large enough to accommodate the *Ibutho* and the *Guerrero,* and a testament to the Syndicate's initiative during earlier times.

There was no way to know what sort of object had struck the moon's sunward side, but whatever it was had been *big,* and judging from the amount of debris thrown up around the point of entry, moving at a high rate of speed.

The rest of the work, including the last few miles of tunnel, and the facility at the moon's rocky heart, could be credited to the Syndicate's engineers. Men and women who had turned against the Confederacy with disastrous results. Thousands of lives had been lost, the Confederacy had been weakened and forced to fight the Thrakies. A sad affair indeed.

Booly's thoughts were interrupted as something exploded, an enemy scout ship flashed by, and the assault boat veered to port. The pilot swore, brought his boxy little vessel back on course, and apologized over the intercom. "Sorry about that, folks . . . the port engine is going to need some maintenance, but the starboard unit is fine. Lieutenant Chang and I hope you enjoyed your flight—and hope you have lots of fun on Floater. Check your harness. We're two minutes out."

Lights streaked past to the left and right as the pilot fired his retros, and the assault boat started to slow. Unlike the station on Floater's surface, where argrav generators provided something like Earth-normal gravity, conditions within the harbor approached zero gee. But there was *some* gravity, something both pilots and computers needed to compensate for, and that meant things could go wrong. Booly saw an assault boat, its bow crushed, tumble past.

Then, as the external blur resolved itself into a rock wall, the A-12 coasted out into an enormous cavern. In spite of the fact that the concepts of "up" and "down" didn't mean much within the confines of the globular "harbor," Booly found it useful to assign such values in order to orient himself.

The legionnaire said, "Map, Floater," and watched the HUD morph into a line diagram of what intelligence believed the layout to look like. The map shivered as real-time supplementary input was entered by pathfinders included in the first wave of troops.

Now, as Booly awaited permission to release his harness, the HUD displayed a macro view that included the outline of the moon itself, the limpetlike habitat that clung to the service, tubes that dropped straight down into the moon's core, and the outlines of the harbor itself.

Then, morphing to a tighter perspective, the officer saw that the surface tubes terminated on what he thought of as the "left" side of the inverted U, while shelflike landing platforms projected out from the center wall, and three enormous berths occupied the space to the "right." All of them were empty. Silent confirmation of what Booly already knew. The battle cruisers had escaped.

There were other features, many of which could be seen through the viewscreen. A globular traffic control center floated at the harbor's epicenter, wrecked assault boats drifted like flotsam on a bay, and space-armored bodies pinwheeled through open space while an enormous reader board flashed the same unintentional epitaph over and over. "Remember . . . security first."

Thanks to the A-12's high-priority VIP status, the assault boat's pilot was able to put his vessel alongside the "upper" landing stage without entering the long queue. Booly felt a distinct bump, followed by a second bump, and heard the pilot make his announcement. "All right, folks, most of the docking area has been secured, but watch for snipers. There's a severe shortage of gravity out there, so be sure to 'look and hook.' The harbormaster and her team have enough to do without chasing floaters all day."

Booly released his harness, felt his suit start to rise, and grabbed a handhold. Then, turning toward the stern, he followed his bodyguards back toward the port hatch. Because the marines wore space armor, and had an ongoing need to deass their transportation as quickly as possible, the assault craft were not equipped with locks. That made it easy for the general and his staff to push-pull themselves through the open doors.

Though not as comfortable in space, Booly's Naa bodyguards were naturally athletic and managed to look reasonably competent as they swam out through the hatch and found ways to anchor their feet and themselves in place.

Like them, Booly had been raised on Algeron, a planet with mountains so high that they would dwarf Mt. Everest. But, the fact that Algeron's equator was 27 percent larger than Earth's, combined with the fact that the planet's polar diameter was 32 percent smaller than Terra's, meant the equator was nearly *twice* the diameter of the poles. The massive Towers of Algeron weighed only half what they would on Earth.

Facts Booly learned during a childhood when nearly all of his Naa playmates could run faster, jump higher, and generally outperform him in every way. So, given their warlike natures, and his respect for them, who better to include in his bodyguard?

The thought caused Booly to smile, an expression the officer waiting to greet him thought unusual given the circumstances, and would tell his friends about later on. "There we were, still taking the occasional round from snipers, when the general blows himself off his boat, grabs a monkey bar, and asks how the kids are. The guy's smiling! Can you beat that?"

Booly listened to the major's reply, slapped him on a well-armored shoulder, and said, "Glad to hear it! I don't have any children of my own, but the wife wants some. Just a matter of time I suppose . . . So, it appears that the *Ibutho* and the *Guerrero* both got away. How's it going otherwise?"

The marine major, an officer named Koski, delivered a concise sitrep. Initial resistance had decreased rather dramatically as the Syndicate's officer corps piled into ships and took off. Now, with hundreds of prisoners in the bag, the marines were dealing with a mere handful of holdouts. Within an hour, maybe less, the opposition would be neutralized. It was great news, *fabulous* news, except that the real objectives were still on the loose.

Booly nodded. "Thanks, Major. You and your troops did one helluva job. I'll tell the admiral that when I return. In the meantime, knowing how generals tend to get in the way, I promise to maintain a low profile. I would like to take a look at their control center, however—assuming that's convenient."

Koski nodded. "No problem, sir. Gunnery Sergeant Benton! Take the general topside, show him the control center, and tell our people not to shoot him."

Benton grinned through his visor. "Sir, yes sir! Follow me, General and I'll take you up."

The noncom used steering jets to guide his suit away from the harbor and in toward a long bank of lift tubes. As Booly followed he noticed the scorch mark on the marine's left shoulder. Not the sort of burn that a hand weapon would cause, but a deep gash indicative of something heavier, like a crew-operated weapon. A clear indication that some of the bad guys had come damned close to bagging a jarhead.

If Benton knew how close he had come to death, there was no sign of it in his cheerful demeanor. "The argrav generators are out of service, along with lift grips, but the tubes are clear. Just dive inside, aim for the top, and fire your jets."

The marine led the way. As Booly entered the vertical passageway he noticed that there were handholds, or "lift grips," all linked to a continuous chain. Now, motionless as a result of battle damage, they functioned like markers.

The officer, closely followed by four bodyguards, propelled himself upward, fired his retros at what he judged to be the right moment, felt the suit slow, brought his boots up over his head, and used his feet to bounce himself off a wall. Then, gliding free of the tube, he gave thanks for the miraculously clean exit.

Benton yelled, "Attention on deck!" and half a dozen marines, all anchored via foot rails, came to attention.

Booly nodded, said, "As you were," and followed Benton into a passageway. The visitors used suit jets to propel themselves down the hall, through a blown lock, and into the C&C. The screens were on, the facility's computer continued to deliver information that no one cared to listen to, and all manner of debris drifted through the room. A hat nodded agreeably, coffee droplets orbited around their mug, and a stylus turned cartwheels in front of an air vent.

The place was deserted, or that's the way it seemed, until Booly rounded the command platform and caught sight of the station's duty officer. For some inexplicable reason the mutineer wore no space armor, and the sudden loss of pressurization had practically ripped him apart. He was smiling though, as if in response to a private joke, and wore a tag which read FRANK MOY.

Booly winced, wondered what was so funny, and continued his tour.

PLANET HIVE, THE CONFEDERACY OF SENTIENT BEINGS

During his travels throughout the Confederacy, Senator Alway Orno had seen many planets but none more beautiful than Hive. Now, as the pilot prepared to dock with one of twenty-four heavily armed space stations that orbited the Ramanthian home world, Orno took a moment to gaze out through the viewport.

Thanks to the special contact lenses, which the representative routinely wore off-planet, the multiple images produced by his compound eyes came together into a single picture. The planet, for which Orno had sacrificed so much, seemed to hang in space. The north pole, the only one that was visible, was so white it seemed to glow. Lower down, below the cold, inhospitable, subarctic regions, the land appeared to be brown. That was deceptive however since the diplomat had walked those gently rolling plains, had gazed on seemingly endless fields of grain, and listened to the rhythmic grunting sound that the herds of domesticated animals made.

South of there, spanning the planet like a thick green belt, lay the equatorial jungle. An important source of oxygen and the place from which his people had risen to sentience and still regarded with reverence. *Yes,* he concluded, *here is a treasure worth defending.*

The view changed suddenly as the ship skimmed along the station's sunward flank. Built to defend the Ramanthian home world against the possibility of Hudathan attack, the massive platform bristled with energy projectors, missile launchers, heat deflectors, landing platforms, antenna arrays, and all the other paraphernalia required to defend the planet below. The look of the structure, the psychological *heft* of it, was sufficient to make the diplomat feel proud.

The ship slowed, banked to the right, and entered one of the cross-station passageways reserved for passenger traffic. Orno felt a bump as the ship touched down, a second bump as the lock-to-lock contact was established, and a subtle change as the space station's argrav generators overrode those on board the spaceship. A tone signaled the fact that it was safe to stand and move around.

The diplomat touched a control, waited for the saddle-style seat to lower itself out of the way, and turned to depart. Confident that his luggage would be dealt with and that someone would be there to meet him, the senator left through the lock. A low-ranking functionary bowed, escorted Orno into the deceptively titled Detox Center, and promptly disappeared. Though far from pleasant, no one was allowed to bypass the ensuing process, no matter how senior they might be.

As with most of the Confederacy's many races, the Ramanthians wanted to make sure that no alien microbes or other organisms made it to the surface of their home world. But the detox centers on the four stations to which off-worlders had access were intended to protect against much more than that.

First it was necessary to ensure that Orno was who he said he was rather than a cleverly engineered cyborg, a surgically altered traitor, or a nano-generated construct.

Then there was the need to cleanse the diplomat of artificial contaminants, including robots smaller than the dot on an "i," bioengineered spores that could be tracked given the right equipment, and tiny biometric devices that might have been introduced into his food or drink.

Not a pleasant process, but necessary if the race hoped to not only maintain the sanctity of their most important world, but protect the secrets hidden there. All 5 billion of them, since that was the number of eggs scheduled to hatch during the next year—forcing the Ramanthians to make massive preparations lest Hive be overrun by the very race it had nurtured.

That's why Orno dropped his robes and allowed himself to be herded past three banks of highly sophisticated sensors, marched into then out of two chemical baths, and swabbed for DNA. After that his retinas were scanned, his voice was sampled, and the whorls on his chitin were compared to those already on file.

Then, certain that the diplomat was who he claimed to be, and amazed by the total number of intelligence-gathering mechanisms they had either destroyed or removed from his person, the technicians allowed the senator to dress and enter the station proper. Unlike the so-called commercial platforms, on which off-worlders were allowed to buy and sell goods,

Orbital Station-12 was "race restricted," meaning that no one but a Ramanthian could board or conduct business on it.

That being the case, Orno was not only spared the often objectionable sights, sounds, and smells associated with alien races, but took advantage of the opportunity to exercise his priority status and claim a seat on the next shuttle.

The crowd included a significant number of commercial functionaries, but there were warriors, too, off duty or on their way to another assignment. The very sight of them, and his home through the viewport beyond, was sufficient to trigger feelings of sorrow.

Like all Ramanthians, the diplomat was part of a three-person unit which was chemically bonded prior to birth. Each grouping included a functionary such as he, a warrior, and a female who required both males to fertilize her eggs.

More than that, the adults needed each other in order to achieve vis, or balance, lest they become emotionally unstable. But now, ever since the War Orno's death on the surface of Arballa, there could be no vis, a fact that ate at him like the drops of acid used to recondition criminals.

Making the situation even worse was the knowledge that it was *his* scheming, *his* manipulations, that led to the duel in which the War Orno was killed. But given the fact that there was no way to bring the War Orno back, the diplomat tried to suppress such thoughts in the hope that time would heal what nothing else could.

The shuttle departed on time, bucked its way down through the upper layers of Hive's atmosphere, and leveled out over the gently rolling plains. Here, clearly visible through the side ports, was the beauty Orno had only imagined up in space.

Thanks to the common vision embraced by three successive queens, not to mention the aesthetic natural to the Ramanthian race, a great deal of thought had gone into the way the surface appeared.

Unlike worlds like Earth, where undisciplined humans had allowed scabrous cities to spread across much of the planet's surface, Hive was a place of perfection. In fact, were it not for rivers that looked like canals, fruit trees that stood in uniform ranks, and crops that grew in perfect circles, Hive looked largely untouched.

That was because the cities in which Ramanthians lived, the power plants upon which they relied, and the factories that produced their goods were all underground.

First, because underground living came naturally to the insectoid race, second because it allowed them to optimize the use of their arable land, and third because an underground culture is less vulnerable to attack than one that dwells on the surface. An important consideration in an age of faster-than-light (FTL) travel.

So, while the beauty visible through the viewport might have been by way of an unintended consequence, it was a source of considerable pride, and still another reason for living below Hive's surface.

The shuttle swept in over what appeared to be a gently rounded hill, dropped into a well-manicured park, and was immediately lowered into the ground.

In spite of the quick rate of descent the trip still lasted for the better part of ten standard minutes. Finally, after a gentle bump signaled the end of the ride, Orno rose and made his way outside. The combination train-air terminal was crowded but not oppressively so. Because there was no need for windows or doors, public structures were open on all sides. Fractal art graced what few walls there were, green plants grew in lavishly decorated pots, and the air was warm and balmy.

The diplomat followed a group of warriors across the tiled floor and out into the sunlight which Ramanthian engineers had funneled down from the surface. Galleries rose to all sides and were generally accessed via ramps, although the younger members of the race still had the ability to fly, and could flap from one building to the next.

The city was called The Place Where The Queen Dwells, and as such ranked as one of the most important habitats on the planet. Orno was not only proud to live there, but to occupy quarters adjacent to the eggery, from which the Queen mother continued to rule.

Now, before he could go home for a much-delayed reunion with the Egg Orno, the diplomat had to make the requisite courtesy call, especially in light of the fact that the Queen had almost certainly been informed of his arrival and would take offense were he to go elsewhere first.

There were no private vehicles within Ramanthian cities, a policy that not only served to conserve the space that would otherwise be dedicated to driving, repairing, and storing them, but reduced air pollution. Something that holds special interest for any race that lives below ground.

As befitted Orno's rank, a government ground car waited at the curb. The politician approached the rear of the vehicle, waited for the hatch to hiss up out of the way, and slid onto one of two saddle-style seats.

The driver waited for Orno to settle in, turned the handlebar-mounted throttle, and merged with traffic. There was no need for the politician to provide a destination since the driver already knew where he was going.

The car swept along busy arterials, through an open-air market, and under a heavily reinforced arch. Orno knew that above the arch, ready to fall, was a thick blastproof door. The Queen, not to mention the billions of eggs stored in the climate-controlled vaults located directly below her, lived within a containment so strong that it could withstand a direct hit from a subsurface torpedo.

The vehicle was forced to stop on two different occasions so that guards could scan the driver, the passenger, and the ground car before it was allowed to proceed through the royal gardens, along a gently curving ramp, and up to the eggery itself.

The carvings that decorated the facade were said to be more than three thousand Hive years old. When viewed from right to left, and without benefit of contact lenses, the panels told the story of the first egg, the first hatching, and the glory to come. A future that Orno would not live long enough to see but for the fulfillment of which he bore a great deal of responsibility.

The car eased to a stop, an entire squad of heavily armed warriors crashed to attention, and Orno backed out of his seat. Then, his heart pounding, the diplomat entered the royal residence.

The Queen, her huge, grossly distended body supported by the same birthing cradle that her mother's mother had used during the last tricentennial birthing, waited for her visitor to appear.

Her feelings toward Orno were decidedly mixed. Though fallible, and overly given to scheming, the diplomatic functionary was dedicated to betterment of his race. A quality the Queen valued so highly that she had seen fit to ignore the manner in which some of his most recent schemes had failed.

Now, as Orno returned from time spent with the Confederacy's Senate, what sort of news did he bear? The fact that she was trapped, unable to move, was a constant source of frustration. No more than a year in the past, she'd been blessed with a normal body and lived a normal life. Well, not exactly normal, since members of royalty do have certain privileges, but relatively *free*. Freedom she made use of to travel off-planet, experience everything that she could, and prepare for the obligation ahead.

Now it was upon her, and the Queen's body, which everyone treated like some sort of factory, had become her prison. Yes, there were times, more and more of late, when the Queen wished she could have been a common everyday female with only three eggs to produce and a lifetime in which to enjoy the results.

But for reasons that only the gods of evolution could explain, her race had been gifted with a *second* means of reproduction, a birthing so huge that earlier hatchings sometimes led to war and famine. Meaningless where nature was concerned, so long as the race survived, but cruel and degrading for those who suffered through it.

That's why Orno's work was so important and why his plans had to succeed. Because to fail, to bring 5 billion Ramanthians into the world without having the means to house, feed, and educate them would be nothing less than a disaster.

The ramps that led up to the cradle had switchbacked three times before Orno passed between a final pair of guards and was free to approach the Queen. More than a dozen brightly robed attendants, medics, and advisors stood to one side and pretended to speak with one another as the diplomat passed.

In spite of the fact that the diplomat had been in the royal presence before, the sight continued to amaze him. The Queen's head, which amounted to little more than a bump when compared to her monumental pregnancy, jutted forward. Her voice was unexpectedly soft. "Welcome home."

Orno bent a knee. "Thank you, Majesty. It's a pleasure to be here."

"I was saddened to hear of the War Orno's untimely death. Please convey the full depth of our sorrow to your mate."

Orno bowed his head. "Thank you, Majesty. I will gladly do so."

"So," the Queen said, eager to learn the latest news, "how do events arrange themselves?"

Orno, who was well aware of the fact that the Queen had other sources of information, some of whom were members of his own staff, was careful to stick with the facts. "Events appear to be propitious, Majesty. My staff and I continue to negotiate for the rights to six of the planets that were depopulated during the Hudathan wars. However, as Your Majesty knows, our true objective is to secure but two worlds, both of which are located in a system adjacent to our own. Once certain adjustments have been made, both planets will offer habitats comparable to Hive."

"Negotiations are one thing," the Queen said tartly, "but progress is something else. What progress have you made?"

"*Good* progress," Orno answered honestly. "By supporting other races in their claims against the Hudathans we have what should be a more than sufficient number of votes."

"I'm gratified to hear it," the Queen replied, "especially in light of earlier failures. And the ships required for transport? What of them?"

Orno swallowed. The mention of his earlier failures, especially with others in attendance, was no accident. The Queen was delivering notice. There would be no leniency where future mishaps were concerned. "Efforts to secure all or part of the Sheen fleet via political means have met with failure."

The Queen fastened Orno with the Ramanthian equivalent of a frown. Her attendants listened intently. "So, functionary Orno, how *will* my eggs arrive on the planets you hope to acquire? Will the Qwa carry them home?"

The retainers laughed. Not only had all of the birdlike Qwa been killed off millennia before, they ate Ramanthian eggs, and could hardly be trusted to carry them from one place to another. Orno struggled to keep his voice level. "Political means having failed, it's my intention to *steal* the ships and bring them to Hive."

The Queen looked as surprised as she felt. "Won't the Confederacy object?"

"Yes," Orno admitted, "they will. But that's a risk we have to take. Given the number of ships lost during the recent war, and production delays, we have very little choice."

"You astound me," the Queen said thoughtfully. "It appears that the Ramanthian representative to the Confederacy is either a genius or a fool."

"I prefer the former, Majesty," Orno put forward, "if the Queen will pardon me for saying so."

The Queen, who was not known for her sense of humor, laughed anyway. "Assuming you obtain those planets, and assuming you deliver those ships, I will forgive anything you might think, do, or say. Do I make myself clear?"

Orno bent a leg. "Yes, Majesty, *very* clear.

PLANET HUDATHA, THE CONFEDERACY OF SENTIENT BEINGS

The Valley of Harmonious Conflict had been created by a meteor strike many thousands of years before. Cliffs, some of which played host to clumps of gray foliage, circled the valley like arms of stone. Nestled within the ancient crater, protected from the worst of the unpredictable winds, was a Hudathan military base.

During feudal times the huge depression had been the site of many battles, culminating in the horror known as the Harvest of a Million Heads. A slaughter in which thousands of aristocrats died, leaving many clans without effective leadership.

It was in the wake of that battle that a single government was born, a tripartite structure consisting of three individuals, each representing a group of clans, each having a single vote. Now, with one of the positions having been open for the better part of a year, it was time to name a replacement.

Snowflakes circled the valley as if unsure of where they should land, dusted thousands of onlookers, or joined the crust that already covered the ground. A trumpet blew, and the simple rise and fall of the notes sent a chill down Hiween Doma-Sa's spine as he and the venerable Ikor Infana-Ka looked out over the silent multitude and waited for the newest member of the triad to join them on the raised platform.

Boots crunched through snow and leather squeaked as Horo Hasa-Ba made the symbolic journey from the ranks of his ancestral clan, through the passageway that separated civilians from the military, and across the openness beyond. A file of soldiers, each representing a different clan, marched behind. The fact that they were there, at Hasa-Ba's back, signaled mutual trust. No small thing in a society where paranoia was the norm.

Doma-Sa, who harbored grave reservations regarding the triad's newest member, watched the processional with something akin to dread. Like most Hudathan males, Hasa-Ba was big, about three hundred standard pounds, and extremely strong. His skin, which would turn white when exposed to high temperatures, was currently gray, and with the exception of the leather straps that crisscrossed his chest, and the clan cape that fell back from his shoulders, he wore nothing above the waist.

In contrast to his body, Hasa-Ba's head was unusually small, which when combined with prominent dorsal fin that ran front to back along the top of his skull, gave rise to the nickname "Hatchet Head," gifted to him by his playmates, and which the newest member of the triad had never been able to shake.

Regardless of appearances, however, Doma-Sa knew that Hasa-Ba was a force to be reckoned with. First he was strong, having risen through the notoriously competitive ranks of the Hudathan military machine to achieve the rank of War Commander in less time than it had taken Doma-Sa, which was no small accomplishment.

Then, in contrast with many of his peers, Hasa-Ba was smart, something he had proven not only at the Hudathan War College, but later, when as the leader of a task force sent to attack a Thraki outpost, he used some of their own transports to land unopposed. That required imagination—not something Hudathan officers were known for.

But of most concern, to Doma-Sa at least, was the fact that Hasa-Ba was ruthless, a quality generally admired by Hudathans, but one which in combination with a raging xenophobia had resulted in two disastrous wars and a period of enforced isolation from which the race had only now started to emerge.

It was that, combined with Hasa-Ba's incessant calls for "full autonomy," by which he meant restoration of the Hudathan navy, and a return to the truculence of the past, that gave Doma-Sa reason to worry.

Not only did he fear the possibility of another self-destructive war; Doma-Sa was concerned lest Hasa-Ba's radicalism divert energy away from efforts to deal with the *true* enemy, which was the solar system into which the Hudathan race had been born.

Hudatha's sun was 29 percent larger than Earth's and locked into a Trojan relationship with a Jovian binary. The Jovians' centers were only 173,600 standard miles apart, which when combined with other planets in the solar system, caused Hudatha to oscillate around the following Trojan point, causing a wildly fluctuating climate.

Even now, as the newest member of the triad mounted the platform, the weather had begun to change. The clouds seemed to melt away, the sun came out, and the ground started to steam. Seen from the platform it appeared as though thousands of souls had emerged from the blood-soaked ground to take their places among the living.

Now, as Hasa-Ba stood in full view of the globe-shaped cameras that floated over the crowd, it was time for the formal investiture.

Ifana-Ka, still suffering from a wound sustained more than fifty years before, was too frail to stand. His body seemed smaller now—as if years of suffering had consumed part of his substance. But there was no denying the strength of the personality that projected itself through the old warrior's eyes. The speech was short, characteristically conservative, and to the point. "We live in troubled times. Adversity threatens from every side. If there is a single word that could be used to characterize our race that word would be 'strength.' Mental strength, physical strength, and moral strength. All attributes that the newest member of the Hudathan triad is known for. The people have spoken through the clans—and a decision has been rendered. It is my pleasure to welcome Horo Hasa-Ba to the highest office any Hudathan can aspire to."

Had the audience been exclusively military, the traditional cry of "Blood!" would have been heard. But, given the crowd's mixed makeup, a chant took its place. "Hasa-Ba! Hasa-Ba! Hasa-Ba!"

Pleased by the response, and eager to impose his personality on the Hudathan people, Hasa-Ba took two paces forward. The cameras rose, refocused, and beamed his image to satellites. They relayed the pictures to millions around the world.

"Thank you," Hasa-Ba said, his heavily amplified voice echoing off the surrounding cliffs. "There is no greater honor than to serve the Hudathan people, no better time to serve them than in their greatest hour of need, and no greater purpose than the full restoration of their honor and freedom."

The crowd roared its approval. In spite of the fact that the majority of Hudathans approved of the more moderate policies pursued by Infana-Ka and Doma-Sa during the last year, and appreciated the extent to which membership in the Confederacy had improved the quality of their lives, the "strategy of accommodation," as it was known, still rankled. A sentiment that Hasa-Ba was well aware of and hoped to exploit.

Surprised by both the speed with which the newcomer had launched his attack, and by the sheer effrontery of the other Hudathan's effort, Doma-Sa remained silent as the mob continued to cheer.

Meanwhile, high above, the clouds reappeared. The sun, its warmth diminished, suddenly disappeared. A wind pushed in from the north, snow started to fly, and a shroud fell over the land. Below, their bones locked in ice, a million warriors continued to sleep.

2

There's only one thing worse than diplomacy, and that is war.

Moolu Rasha Anguar
Second President of the Confederacy of Sentient Beings
Standard year 2622

THE INDEPENDENT PLANET OF LANOR (CR-9765)

There was no fast way to get from the Legion's headquarters on Algeron to a Rim world like LaNor. Not for a "zero-gee" second lieutenant like Antonio (Tony) Santana, who had no pull whatsoever.

Not only that, but given the fact that there was little more than a handful of legionnaires on LaNor, the navy had no reason to send more than the occasional transport there. That left the officer to make his own way using what the regs referred to as "appropriate civilian transportation," which in this case turned out to be a berth on a decrepit tramp freighter.

The *Rim Queen*, as her crew of misfits called her, had been old back before the first Hudathan war, and now, more than seventy-five years later, it was a miracle that she could still complete a hyperspace jump. However, thanks to round-the-clock maintenance and a seemingly endless supply of good luck, the old lady was still in service.

Though normally quite curious, especially where a new posting was concerned, the impromptu farewell party had gone long into the second watch, and the legionnaire was tired. For that reason he slept through the first part of the trip down to LaNor's surface and was still in dreamland when a hand touched his shoulder. "Hey, Tony, time to wake up. Welcome to LaNor."

Santana opened his eyes, found himself looking up at the *Queen*'s first officer, and remembered the last time he'd seen her from that particular angle. She'd been naked then, her pink-tipped breasts surging up and down as her thighs clamped the outside surface of his hips. The lovemaking had been good, *very* good, and the highlight of an otherwise unremarkable trip. Her name was Cass, Molly Cass, and she could read his mind. "Yeah, that was fun wasn't it? Too bad you have to play soldier. I wasn't done with you yet."

Santana raised an eyebrow. "No? Perhaps a going-away present would be in order."

Cass shook her head and backed away. "Sorry, Tony, but you have a reception party waiting outside, and I have cargo to off-load. Maybe next time."

Santana knew there would be no "next time," and that it was her way of putting some distance between them. He nodded agreeably and yawned. Then, having released the four-point harness, he stood. The legionnaire was six-two, reasonably well built, and attired in one of his best uniforms. It fitted his body like a glove and bore the razor-sharp creases expected of a professional officer. Cass liked it. She waved, ducked into the control room, and closed the door.

Carry-on in hand, the legionnaire made his way forward, stepped out through the lock, and felt the sun hit him like a hammer. It was just shy of noon in the foreign city of Mys on a hot summer day. The bright sunlight, combined with what could only be described as a pervasive stench, caused him to pause. The smell, which was one part coal smoke, one part raw sewage, and one part mystery, hung heavy in the unmoving air.

The officer had just started to scan his surroundings, when

a noncom marched up from the right, stopped with a flourish, and executed a smart left-face. The salute was perfect. He wore the Legion's traditional white kepi, a khaki uniform, and the cap badge that denoted membership in the First Foreign Cavalry Regiment, or First REC. His face was hard and lean, his eyes were bright, and his skin had a leathery look. "Corporal Dietrich, sir, welcome to LaNor."

Santana returned the salute, made his way down the short flight of roll-up stairs, and said, "At ease, Corporal, glad to meet you. So, where exactly am I?"

Dietrich, who had rather high standards where officers were concerned, liked what he saw. Most second lieutenants were green as Earth grass, spent half their time looking scared, and the other half looking stupid. But this one wore six ribbons over his left shirt pocket. A single glance was sufficient to inform the noncom that Santana had seen combat during the mutiny, had fought the Thrakies, and won a medal. Not just *any* medal, but Medal for Valor (MFV), the third highest decoration the Confederacy had to give.

So, why was the incoming officer a second louie? Anybody with that kind of time in, plus an MFV, should be a first lieutenant by now. There had to be a reason, and Dietrich was determined to find out what it was. "We're in the city of Mys, sir. *That's* the Confederacy's embassy, *that's* the parade ground, and *that's* the Legion's barracks."

Santana followed the legionnaire's finger from point to point. A small part of the parade ground was visible through a formal arch and shimmered in the sun.

The barracks were a good deal larger than he would have expected and made of the same stone as the embassy minus the architectural details.

The fact that Dietrich had ignored the formal garden off to the right, an outdoor pavilion, and any number of other structures to focus on the features most likely to interest a soldier was both amusing and promising.

Given the ribbons Dietrich wore on his chest, the corporal

had seen combat in the last war, and given the fact that there wasn't so much as a trace of green among the multicolored rectangles, it was clear than none of them were for good conduct. The officer nodded. "That's a good beginning, thanks. Where do I report?"

"Over at the barracks, sir. Major Miraby is over at the embassy—but Captain Seeba-Ka is in his office."

Some of the Hudathans who had been integrated into the Legion to fight the Thrakies had resigned at the end of the war, but a surprising number had elected to stay. Although Santana had never served under a Hudathan, he *had* served under a Ramanthian, and lived to regret it. Careful to keep his face expressionless, he nodded. "Good enough . . . any idea where my gear might be?"

Dietrich stuck two fingers into his mouth and produced a loud whistle. Santana heard metal squeak and turned just in time to see a heavily loaded wheelbarrow round the shuttle's stern and come his way. The conveyance was propelled by a frail-looking LaNorian of indeterminate age. The porter was dressed in a conical hat, a sweat-soaked singlet, and baggy trousers.

Not having seen a LaNorian before, Santana was interested to see that the native had a high forehead, eyes set diagonal to his face, six opposing nostril slits, and a thin-lipped mouth. His ears, which stuck straight out from the sides of his head, gave the LaNorian a sort of elfin look. However, rather than being made of cartilage, they consisted of stiff featherlike structures.

The LaNorian brought the wheelbarrow to a halt, came to rigid attention, and produced a serviceable salute. Dietrich grinned. "This is Daw Clo, sir. We all chip in to pay his salary."

Santana had reservations about the use of civilians, especially *indig* civilians, in and around a military barracks, but was careful to keep his mouth shut. The situation at every command was different, and it was always best to carry out a reconnaissance prior to attacking the status quo. He returned the salute. "Glad to meet you, Daw Clo. My name is Santana, Lieutenant Santana."

It wasn't clear if the LaNorian understood standard, or was responding to the officer's tone, but the result was the same. The porter grabbed the handlebars, aimed the one-wheeled conveyance at the barracks, and set off. The squeak came at regular intervals.

Santana, with Dietrich at his side, followed. Had he turned to look back over his shoulder, the legionnaire would have seen Cass standing hands on hips at the center of the shuttle's main lock. But he *didn't* look back, so Cass turned away. There was work to do . . . and damned few people to do it.

Captain Drik Seeba-Ka, holder of the Confederacy's Distinguished Service Order (DSO), and the second-ranking legionnaire on the surface of LaNor, was sitting behind his massive desk trying to wade through the administrative crap that Miraby loved so much when there were three raps on his door. "Enter!"

The door opened, a second lieutenant appeared, took three steps forward, and snapped to attention. "Sir! Second Lieutenant Antonio Santana reporting for duty, *sir*!"

Seeba-Ka looked to see if the human was wearing an academy ring, saw that he wasn't, and found that interesting. Most ring knockers, especially the junior ones, wore their rings by way of a status symbol. Not good, not bad, but interesting. "At ease, Lieutenant . . . and welcome to LaNor."

Though somewhat sibilant, Santana noticed that Seeba-Ka had an excellent command of standard. The junior officer moved his left foot eighteen inches to the left and clasped his hands behind his back. Many officers, hell most officers, would have invited him to sit down. Seeba-Ka hadn't. Why?

The Hudathan stood. An old-fashioned fan hummed in a corner but only served to move the air rather than cool it. Thus, the officer's skin was white. The prominent supraorbital ridge, deep sunken eyes, and tightly stretched skin were intimidating enough. The sheer size of his body was even more so. His uniform looked as if it had been sprayed on. That, plus the service ribbons, and his general demeanor all added up to the same thing: The captain was a tight-assed, locked-down, by-the-book cavalry officer. But Santana knew that appearances can be and often are deceiving. All he could do was wait and see.

The Hudathan used an enormous finger to tap the olive drab field comp that rested on the surface of his desk. "We don't get a lot of ships out here, but the message torps arrive on a regular basis. Your P-1 arrived a week ago. It made for some interesting reading. You went to the academy, graduated just in time to fight the mutineers, and took part in the assault on the Noam Industrial Complex.

"During that engagement you were wounded, but in spite of that wound went out under heavy fire to retrieve a Trooper II's brain box, and successfully brought her out.

"Subsequent to that battle you were awarded the MFV and promoted to first lieutenant. All very commendable."

Seeba-Ka turned at that point, walked to the open window, and looked out through the peace arch to the parade ground beyond. The Clones were out there, yelling cadences and running through their daily physical training (PT). The fact that the Hudathan could stand there, with his back fully exposed, testified to the manner in which the officer had been assimilated into the Legion. His comments seemed to be addressed to the entire world. "So, having distinguished yourself on Earth, you were assigned to lead the second platoon of D Company, Second Battalion, First REC, just before it landed on Clone World Beta-018, then occupied by the Thrakies.

"Subsequent to that landing, D Company, then under the command of a Ramanthian officer named Hakk Batth, was ordered to march overland and attack an enemy outpost designated AD-14.

"Once in position, Captain Hakk Batth ordered you to take your platoon to the east side of AD-14, dig in, and hold. His call sign was 'hammer.' Yours was 'anvil.'

"The plan was for the First platoon, under Batth's command, to engage the enemy, drive them out of their fortified position, and into your arms. At that point you were to call upon them to surrender, and failing that, to engage."

The words took Santana back in time. He could feel the snow give under his boots, see the puffs of lung-warmed air in front of his face, and hear the rattle of automatic weapons as the First platoon opened up on the Thraki compound.

AD-14 consisted of a small cluster of prefab domes, weapons emplacements at each corner, and a ten-foot-high defensive wall that circled the perimeter. Numerous repairs had been made, and it was blackened where fighters had hit it from the air, but the structure still stood.

However, assuming the spooks at Battalion HQ knew what they were talking about, the most important stuff was hidden away below the surface. No one knew what the "stuff" was, only that intel wanted it, and that Dog Company was supposed to bring it in.

The ground shook as the Trooper IIs loosed their shoulder-launched missiles, a weapons emplacement took a direct hit, and blew with a loud *whump!* Not far away, on the other side of the enemy compound, there was another flash as a hundred-foot-tall antenna toppled toward the north.

Then, per Batth's plan, the Thrakies started to bail out. A gate opened, Thrakies spilled out onto the snow-covered field, and the second platoon opened fire. But something was wrong, that's the way it looked in any case, and Santana yelled "Cease fire!" into the boom-style mike that curved in front of his mouth.

No sooner had the second platoon obeyed his order than another voice came over the company push. "Hammer Six to Anvil Six . . . the enemy is trying to escape. Fire!"

Santana raised the electro-binoculars up to his eyes, and the Thrakies seemed to leap forward. "Anvil Six to Hammer Six. Negative enemy troops, repeat, *negative enemy troops*. I see females and cubs. None of them are armed."

The reply was nearly instantaneous. "Hammer Six to Anvil Five . . . Thraki females fight alongside their males. Weapons can be concealed. Relieve Anvil Six and engage the enemy. That's an order."

Santana's number two, a sergeant named Withers, turned to his platoon leader for instructions, saw the officer shrug, and looked apologetic. Then, consistent with the regs that had governed his every waking moment for the last seventeen years, he gave the necessary order. The biobods opened fire, the T-2s followed suit, and fifty-three noncombatants died.

"So," Seeba-Ka said, turning back toward Santana, "there was a court of inquiry. Not a court-martial, because the newly formed alliance was too fragile for that, but a military court of inquiry. Batth was reprimanded for his failure to use good judgment—and you were broken to Second lieutenant for your refusal to obey a direct order. A rather lenient finding give the statement you made in which you referred to your superior officer as 'a psychotic *bug*'."

The Hudathan advanced on the more junior officer until he was only two feet away. Santana, still at ease, kept his eyes centered on the wall beyond. A plaque hung there. It read: "*Legio Patria Nostra* . . . The Legion Is Our Country."

"So tell me," Seeba-Ka said, his breath warming the side of Santana's face, "if your previous CO was a bug, then what the hell am *I*? *A shovel head*? *A lizard*? *Or a slope*?"

It was a direct question and Santana had no choice but to answer. "Sir! The captain is a captain, *sir*!"

Seeba-Ka, who fully expected Santana to classify him as a *Hudathan*, and would have accepted that finding, was silent for a moment. Then, his eyes boring into the human's head, he said, "That's affirmative, Lieutenant . . . The captain *is* a captain. And, should you ever be so stupid as to disobey one of *this* captain's orders, he will rip your head off and shit into the hole. Do you understand?"

"Sir! Yes sir!"

"Excellent. You may sit down."

Seeba-Ka returned to the chair behind his desk as Santana took the only seat. It was hard and uncomfortable. The Hudathan leaned back and brought his thick, sausagelike fingers together to form a steeple. "Now that we have that out of the way . . . let's talk about the present rather than the past. We may be part of a cavalry unit, but that doesn't mean jack shit out here. LaNor is a Class III planet. That means we can't put any weapons in orbit, we can't make use of any aircraft other than shuttles, and we can't land any armor over and above Trooper IIs and a few utility bots. Not a lot of hardware for legionnaires who like to ride everywhere they go.

"The good news is that the company is at full strength, a rarity on the Rim, but with one reservation. After I add your name to the table of organization (TO) I'll still be one officer short. Lieutenant Beckworth commands the second platoon. That means you'll take the first while First Sergeant Neversmile continues to handle the third.

"We have responsibility for the embassy's security, a certain amount of ceremonial bullshit, and trying to keep our private parts from getting caught up in Major Miraby's wringer."

In spite of the "tune-up" Seeba-Ka had administered at the beginning of the meeting, Santana was impressed by both the Hudathan's command of standard and his forthright manner. "Sir, yes sir. How 'bout the locals, sir? The folks on the *Rim Queen* said there had been some trouble."

The Hudathan nodded. "That's correct. Soon after a survey ship stumbled across LaNor, every race you can think of started to flood in. The Confederacy came in early, but that didn't stop the Prithians, Ramanthians, Drac, Hudathans, humans, and human clones from wanting direct representation. Accordingly, anyone who could walk, swim, or fly dropped hyper, opened an embassy, and started to take meetings with the locals. A whole shitload of corporations followed, all vying to grab concessions, secure mineral rights, and build factories.

"Then, faster than you could pull the pin on a grenade, the business types started to build railroads, introduce steam age technology, and hawk off-world luxuries. Throw in a bunch of missionaries hell-bent on trying to convert the LaNorians to off-world religions, and the poop makes contact with the fan. As things stand now the workers who were displaced by off-world technology are angry, the ruling class feels threatened, and a group called the Claw is busy trying to take advantage of the situation. But what the heck," Seeba-Ka finished lightly, "at least we won't get bored."

"Sir, no sir," Santana replied.

"Good," the Hudathan said, rising from his chair. "There's more, a lot more, but that can wait. It's time to settle in. Corporal Dietrich can take you to your billet, help draw some gear, and put you in touch with First Sergeant Hillrun. Two months have passed since Lieutenant Bora-Sa rotated out—and the platoon is starting to lose its edge. See what you can do."

Santana knew a dismissal when he heard one and came to his feet. "Yes sir."

The junior officer came to attention, delivered a salute, and got one in return. Then, just as Santana was about to execute an about-face, Seeba-Ka spoke. "Lieutenant . . ."

"Sir?"

"There's one more thing. There was another Santana on Beta-018. A real hard-ass named Sergeant Major Antonio Santana. A relative perhaps?"

A lump formed in Santana's throat, but he managed to swallow it. His father, better known to his troops as "Top," had been killed during the first hours of the assault on Beta-018. "Yes sir. My father."

Seeba-Ka nodded. "The entire company respected him, and so did I. If you are even *half* the soldier your father was, then the first will be in good hands. Dismissed."

Santana said, "Sir! Yes sir!" did an about-face, and left. Dietrich was waiting in the hall. His face was expressionless, but Santana wondered how long he'd been there—and how much he might have heard. But there was no way to know and little he could do beyond following the enlisted man down the highly buffed corridor, past the portrait of Captain Jean Dan-jou, and into the Legion's well-ordered universe. His tour of duty had officially begun.

NEAR THE VILLAGE OF NAH REE, ON THE INDEPENDENT PLANET OF LANOR

The high-tech prefab Bliss Industries Hab Dome boasted its own Soro Systems—manufactured computer system, which according to the company's multitudinous marketing literature "came complete with its own high-quality security system."

Now, as a small body triggered one of the motion detectors, and other sensors verified the intruder's presence, an alarm began to beep. But the sound, which Bethany Busso had intentionally set low because loud noises bothered her, failed to wake anyone up.

Finally, after the mandatory ten seconds had elapsed, the mission's artificial intelligence (AI) chose to intervene. The Bussos, who ran their family like a small democracy, had chosen a female persona for the computer, and the children named her Trudy after *Aunt* Trudy, who remained back on Earth. The voice was soft but insistent. "Security Zone Three has been violated . . . Security Zone Three has been violated . . . Security Zone Three has . . ."

Frank Busso slapped a button on the console next to his bed, sat up, and swung his feet to the floor. Bethany, conscious of the movement, rubbed her eyes. "Frank? What's wrong?"

The missionary stood, grabbed his robe, and headed for the door. "The security alarm went off . . . Some sort of critter most likely. Go back to sleep."

The vinyl floor, which was soft rather than hard, gave beneath the missionary's feet as he left the master bedroom and padded down into what his children called the pit but the Bliss product literature referred to as "a spacious sunken living room."

The pit was circular, like the hab itself, and was centered

on a large white console. Though designed to look like a modernistic coffee table, the structure housed the majority of the dome's electronic equipment, including Trudy's central processing unit (CPU). Busso dropped into his favorite seat, threw his feet up onto the console, and addressed the cleverly concealed microphones. "Okay, Trudy, what's the problem?"

The AI's voice seemed to come from nowhere and everywhere all at once. It was soft but firm. "An intruder penetrated Security Zones Three, Two, and is entering One. His/her body mass and heat signature is consistent with that of a LaNorian adult."

"Gee, what a surprise," Busso said dryly. "Here we are on LaNor, and LaNorians are skulking about."

Trudy, who was inclined to view the world in a much more cynical light than Busso was, chose to ignore the comment. "At this point the intruder has circled around behind the residential hab and is approaching the rear entrance."

There was a soft buzzing sound as someone pushed on the doorbell. Busso shook his head in amusement. "Polite burglars . . . what will they think of next? Video, please."

Trudy made a connection, and a three-dimensional holo bloomed over the console. Busso saw a frightened-looking face and recognized it as belonging to one of his flock. Nuu Laa had a narrow face, large, soulful eyes, and carefully tended ear fans. Busso came to his feet. "She's one of ours . . . Let her in."

Trudy did as she was told, and Busso was there by the time the door opened. The missionary was good at languages and, like his wife, had a good mastery of LaNorian. "Nuu Laa . . . what's wrong?"

It was hot and muggy outside, but the LaNorian female shook as if from the cold. "The Claw came to our home. They told my husband that we must pay money to come here or something bad will happen."

Bethany Busso, who had been unable to go back to sleep, chose that moment to arrive. "You poor thing! Come, have a seat while I make some tea."

Nuu Laa didn't want any tea—but was too polite to say so. She continued to tremble as Bethany bustled around the kitchen. "Your husband," Frank Busso said, "is he all right?"

"Yesss," Nuu Laa said nervously, "but only if we stay away. I came to say good-bye."

"Good-bye?" Busso asked. "Why would you say that? If the Claw wants money, give it to them. We'll complain through the embassy in Mys, and the government will force them to stop."

"Yes," Bethany Busso added, placing a cup of tea in the female's three-fingered hands, "Frank's correct. In a few weeks, a month at most, the so-called Claw will be a thing of the past."

Nuu Laa took a sip of tea, discovered that it had a calming effect, and considered what the humans had said. Though notoriously fickle in her pronouncements the sixty-five-year-old Dowager Empress Shi Huu *had* issued a number of edicts aimed at suppressing the Claw—and the off-worlders were powerful. Evidence of that could be seen in their flameless lanterns, pictures that moved, and medicines that made people feel better. There was one problem, however, and she was hesitant to mention it. "Yes, all that you say makes sense, but I must still say good-bye."

"But *why*?" Busso demanded, his patience starting to fray.

"It's the money, isn't it?" Bethany Busso said, her eyes on Nuu Laa's face.

The LaNorian looked down at her lap. "Yes," she said, her voice very small. "I'm sorry, but my husband and I cannot afford to pay to them."

"Is that all?" Frank Busso said, coming to his feet. "Well, we can fix that."

"We certainly can," Bethany Busso beamed as her husband left the room. "We're all part of one big family . . . the Transcendental family. You let us take care of the money."

"Here you go," Busso said, emerging from his study. He held three lengths of cord, each heavy with LaNorian coins.

"You pay with these, Bethany and I will turn up the heat on the folks in Mys, and we'll see you on five day."

Nuu Laa accepted the rope coins, slipped them over her head, and concealed them beneath her clothes. "Thank you . . . I should go now . . . before the sun starts to rise."

Coins clinked as Busso ushered the LaNorian out through the back door and locked it behind her. Bethany yawned. "Those Claw people are starting to get out of hand."

"Yeah," her husband answered, "they sure as heck are. I'll make a call in the morning. In the meantime let's go to bed."

The Bussos returned to their room, told Trudy to turn off the lights, and soon fell asleep.

Meanwhile, the AI, who could "see" well beyond the limits of Security Zone Three, watched the LaNorian depart. Two *additional* heat signatures, both of which were larger, followed behind. Interesting but not relevant since their actions posed no danger to mission or its occupants. Consequently, the AI processed the electronic equivalent of a shrug and placed itself on standby.

Outside, beyond the dome's walls, a pair of blood red moons rose, a momentary breeze ruffled the kas grass, and the Gee Nas River murmured toward the sea.

THE FOREIGN CITY OF MYS, ON THE INDEPENDENT PLANET OF LANOR

It was dark inside the crate, *very* dark, not that a lack of light was much of a problem for a being like Chien-Chu. The onetime president of Chien-Chu Enterprises, ex–navy admiral, and the man that some people referred to as the Father of the Confederacy awoke. Chemicals flowed and systems came on-line as the machine that cradled the industrialist's brain moved to a higher state of readiness.

Chien-Chu thought the word *vision* and "saw" through the vid cams mounted behind his bright blue eyes. It was pitch-black inside the shipping container, which was to be expected. He thought the word *time* and was rewarded with a digital readout that appeared in the lower right quadrant of his vision: 0400. It was time to go to work.

But first, prior to his "arrival" in Mys, the cyborg decided to make sure that his ship, a small but highly sophisticated vessel named after his wife, had arrived in orbit. A radio was activated, code was sent, and an acknowledgment was returned. When and if he needed the *Nola,* she would be ready to respond.

Satisfied that everything was as it should be, the cyborg raised a power-assisted arm, felt the packing material give way, and punched his fist through the side of the crate. Something his *original* body, the one that died from a massive heart attack many years before, would never have been capable of.

Another blow followed, and another, until the lid popped open. That was the moment when the things that were warm mapped themselves onto Chien-Chu's infrared vision and the industrialist could see. He took three steps forward and paused to look around. This particular body, the one he had chosen for the trip to Mys, resembled a rather muscular human. Anyone there to see it would have been confronted by what appeared to be a twenty-five-year-old male with blond hair and a woodenly handsome face. A rarity at one time but more and more common of late. So much so that lots of civilian borgs were out of work. A problem that played into the mission he was on.

The warehouse, just one of thousands of such structures that Chien-Chu Enterprises owned on various worlds, was relatively small. The building's power plant was marked by a blob of green luminescence. Power lines glowed, a fan motor shimmered, and a small lime-colored animal darted across the floor. A rat or the local equivalent.

The purpose of the facility was to receive, process, and store supplies destined for the subsea exploration platform located offshore. There had been allegations, rumors really, concerning Thomas Boad, the engineer in charge of the platform, and Chien-Chu was on LaNor to check them out. An activity that both wife and niece frowned on, but he considered to be absolutely necessary. It was his experience that it's easy for a company to be hijacked from within. All it took was one bad person. They hired more bad people, who hired *more* bad people, until the cancer spread throughout the entire organization.

Now, having just spent the last few weeks in a packing crate, stowed in the *Rim Queen*'s number two hold, the industrialist knew that at least one of the allegations lodged against the local platform manager was true. The cost of transporting new employees to Mys came out of Boad's budget, and rather than pay full-fare passenger rates, as he was supposed to, the station boss forced cyborgs to travel as cargo and pocketed the difference.

So, given the fact that Board already had his hand in one till, what else was he up to? Only time would tell. Later that day someone would come for "Jim James" and take him out to the platform. Once there he would have ample opportunity to observe the operation.

In the meantime the industrialist knew there was a very real possibility that Board was "losing" equipment, which he could then sell on the black market. In order to counter that Chien-Chu planned to take a full inventory of the warehouse before the staff arrived for work. A boring project but an important one.

The cyborg went to work, the nar rat scuttled out through a hole, and the first rays of sun appeared in the east.

Santana waited for the sounds of reveille to die away, nodded to Platoon Sergeant Quickfoot Hillrun, and watched the noncom enter the long, narrow room. Except for the soft sleek fur that covered their bodies, some slight differences in dentition, and the absence of fingernails the Naa were very humanoid.

Of course anyone who had spent time on Algeron, or been stationed with Naa nationals, knew they could smell things that humans couldn't, sense heat through the soles of their feet, and run most earthlings into the ground. All of which meant that they were among the best troops the Legion had to offer. Santana felt fortunate to have a noncom with Hillrun's experience as his number two . . . and some Naa troopers to boot.

The door banged against the wall, Hillrun yelled, "On deck!" and went to work with the NCO version of an alarm clock. Santana thought it was amazing how much noise could be generated with a garbage can—and how much verbal abuse could be hurled in return. A folding partition served to separate the men from the women, but it was far from soundproof, and Hillrun's wake-up call was sufficient to reach them as well. The platoon's squad leaders added to the din by shouting orders and shaking racks.

Sixty seconds later the partition had been opened, the biobods were up and standing at attention. And that's where they were, each soldier at the foot of his or her rack, when Santana walked in. Like Hillrun, the platoon leader was dressed in Legion T-shirt, shorts, and running shoes. Most of the troops wore their skivvies although a couple sported silk pajamas purchased from LaNorian merchants.

Santana paused, said "At ease," and walked the line. Each footlocker had a name stenciled on top of it, which made it easy for the officer to put a face with the entries on his roster. Santana said each name out loud both as a form of acknowledgment and a mnemonic device. Not counting Hillrun the platoon included thirty biobods plus two Trooper IIs, who were quartered elsewhere.

"Albro, Bays, Chan, Davis, Dietrich, Fareye, Fosky . . ." and so it went until the officer had walked the length of the room and back again. He nodded. "My name is Santana, *Lieutenant* Santana, your new platoon leader. Captain Seeba-Ka tells me this a *good* platoon, and based on what I've seen so far, he's right."

The last part was a lie, but a harmless one, and calculated to build a sense of pride. "Over the next few days I'll find opportunities to get acquainted with each one of you, learn more about your various backgrounds, and review your training requirements.

"In the meantime Platoon Sergeant Hillrun and I would like to invite you on a morning run. The *first* run in what will become part of our daily routine.

"Then, after some PT, you'll be free to hit the showers and go to chow. Squad leaders should check with Sergeant Hillrun regarding activities for the day."

Santana allowed his eyes to drift from one face to the next. "In case you're wondering about the emphasis on physical fitness, consider this: In spite of the fact that the First REC is a cavalry outfit, the nearest armored personnel carrier (APC) is thousands of light-years away."

Some of the platoon chuckled, and others nodded.

"So," Santana continued, "if we're going to *look* like an infantry outfit, we'd better be able to move like one. You have ten minutes to get your running gear on and meet me at the arch. The first two legionnaires to arrive will spend the evening in the native quarter. I haven't been there, but Sergeant Hillrun tells me that when it comes to some first-rate R&R, that's the place to go. Dismissed."

The platoon seemed to explode in every direction.

Fifteen minutes later Captain Seeba-Ka heard a voice calling cadence and looked out through his window in time to see Santana lead his platoon out onto the parade ground. Even the T-2s were there . . . bringing up the rear.

The Hudathan watched for a moment, uttered what might have been a grunt of approval, and turned back to his work.

The staff meeting, which was scheduled for 8 A.M. sharp, started the way it usually did, with the Foreign Services Specialists (FSSs), secretaries, and the like arriving first, Foreign Service Officers (FSOs) wandering in next, and the ambassador himself arriving fifteen minutes late.

Christine Vanderveen, a lowly FSO-5, the second lowest rung on the long multitiered ladder, arrived with the secretaries, said hello to everyone, placed her coffee mug on the conference room table, and took her favorite chair. It was positioned in the southwest corner of the aptly named Sunset Room and looked out over the neatly kept gardens, the peace arch, and the parade ground beyond. A detachment of troops could be seen there, and thanks to the presence of the hulking T-2s, there was no doubt as to which contingent of off-worlders they belonged to.

The embassy's computer specialist, a young woman named Imbulo, saw the direction of the FSO's gaze and winked. She had an infectious smile, mocha-colored skin, and a body that men liked to look at. "He came in on the *Rim Queen*. Everyone says he's 'hot.' "

Vanderveen raised a well-plucked blond eyebrow. " '*He?*' And who might '*he*' be?"

Imbulo laughed. "Lieutenant Antonio Santana. He has medals and everything."

The FSO stood as if intent on getting a better look, peered out the window, and sat down again. "You must be joking . . . The lieutenant has a face like the back end of a razbul."

The computer tech laughed again. "You've been out here too long. I *saw* the man, and he can march into my fort anytime."

The conversation was interrupted as servos whined and Ambassador Soolu Pas Rasha entered the room. The high-tech exoskeleton fit over and around his frail, sticklike body like a form-fitting cage. A neural interface served to connect the diplomat's nervous system to the machine's microcomputer. Not especially pleasant, but necessary, if the Dweller wanted to leave his low-gee home world and pursue a career among the stars.

As was Pas Rasha's habit, he sat at the far end of the long bana wood table from Vanderveen, treated the entire staff to a frown, and cleared his throat. "Good morning, everyone . . . Harley, let's start with you."

Harley Clauson, an FSO-2, was in charge of the Political

Section, which, given the embassy's rather modest staff, included Christine Vanderveen, two off-world FSSs, and a half dozen locals he liked to refer to as Information Specialists but were actually spies. Clauson was fifty pounds overweight, had a tendency to sweat even when the air was cool, and loved the sound of his own voice. He squinted at his comp and spoke without looking up.

"Thank you, Mr. Ambassador . . . Based on reports from my Information Specialists it sounds as if Claw forces continue to stage what they call spirit rallies in the outlying provinces. According to eyewitness accounts they spend most of their time leaping about, yelling various kinds of nonsense, and playing host to various spirit beings that allegedly render them invulnerable to all manner of projectiles. They also print and distribute leaflets. Christine, if you would be so kind."

Vanderveen rose, circled the table, and provided each staff member with a facsimile of the original leaflet along with a full translation. They read: "The foreign devils continue to open missions, erect telegraphs, build railways, deny the sacred doctrine, and speak evil of the gods. Their sins are as numerous as the hairs on their heads. The people are commanded to burn the missions, cut the telegraph wires, and rip up the railroads, for such is the will of heaven."

Pas Rasha looked up from the document in front of him. "Do you think they're serious? Or is this more wild talk?"

Though fat, and a bit pedantic at times, Clauson was competent. "I think they mean it. Do you remember the Bussos? The TC missionaries near Nah Ree? Well, Frank Busso radioed early this morning. It seems that the Claw started what amounts to a protection racket. Local members of the Transcendental Church have to *pay* in order to attend services. Busso wants you to lean on the Empress.

"And that's not all. My people say that the Claw have entered Polwa itself and are calling for 'a cleansing by blood.' I think we should expect a full-scale uprising."

Pas Rasha frowned. "Let's avoid the tendency toward hyperbole. There's no need to exaggerate."

Clauson, never one to defy authority, was about to apologize, when Vanderveen cleared her throat. "No offense, Mr. Ambassador . . . but Harley is correct. Take a stroll through the market in Polwa. You'll find that the price of knives has *tripled* over the last two weeks."

The ambassador allowed one of his thin, nearly invisible eyebrows to rise incrementally. "Interesting . . . but far from conclusive. If the textbooks mentioned a positive correlation between the sale of cutlery and civil unrest, I failed to notice it."

Vanderveen made no attempt to defend herself, but Clauson shot her a grateful look, and Imbulo grinned approvingly.

Major Homer Miraby, the Legion's ranking officer on LaNor, cleared his throat. He shaved his head every morning, and it gleamed under the overhead light. Bushy eyebrows hung over brown eyes, a large nose, and a handlebar mustache. It twitched as he spoke. "I suggest that we issue a directive to staff advising them to be especially vigilant where their personal security is concerned, send similar notification to citizens living outside the walls, and reinforce security."

Pas Rasha nodded. "Thank you, Major, it's always better to be safe rather than sorry."

"And the other embassies?" Clauson inquired cautiously. "What about them?"

"Put it on the agenda for the next round table," the ambassador replied easily. "Let's see what they've heard. Who knows? Maybe we can agree on something for once."

Vanderveen knew that the ambassador faced any number of challenges, not the least of which was the fact that the Ramanthians, Hudathans, Prithians, Thrakies, and Drac had all elected to send their own diplomats to LaNor rather than allow the Confederacy to represent them.

Surprisingly, in spite of the fact that their government remained outside of the Confederacy, the Clones were the easiest beings to get along with.

Clauson nodded, made a note, and the meeting continued.

Marcy Barnes, a thin, rather severe woman who some staffers referred to as the stick, went next. The Agricultural Service, for which the FSO-4 had responsibility, was something of a backwater since the studies that might eventually enable the LaNorians to import and export food products had not even been started yet.

That didn't stop the agriculturist from delivering a fifteen-minute lecture on the wonders of kas, the grasslike plant from which the LaNorians harvested most of their grain, and upon which they were dependent for most of their food. The FSO claimed it was better than rice, could be used in hundreds of ways, and urged the staff to try it. Most of the staff already had, but Barnes insisted on downloading select recipes to their comps and urged everyone to provide her with feedback.

A big bear of a man named Yvegeniy Kreshenkov went next. He was in charge of the Science and Technology Section, and, with help from Willard Tran, the FSO having responsibility for Economics, had written a report titled: "The La-Norian Wheel Tax."

Pas Rasha raised an eyebrow as the title page appeared on his comp. "What is this? Some sort of joke?"

Kreshenkov, who was well-known for his sense of humor, shook his shaggy head. He had green eyes and they seemed to dart from face to face. "No, sir. The fact that LaNor is a Class III world, and should have developed into a Class IV by now, has everything to do with the wheel tax. As you know the Imperial government derives a significant portion of its annual revenues from a rather high tax which is levied on each wheel that an individual owns regardless of size or purpose.

"Each wheel is taxed at a flat rate of twenty plaks per year or approximately one-fifth of the average per capita income. That's why there are millions of wheelbarrows, thousands of two-wheeled carts, and hundreds of four-wheeled wagons in Mys and Polwa combined. All of which drives a lot of other things. That's why Willard and I decided to examine the tax's deeper implications."

Vanderveen listened intently as the other FSOs took turns explaining their thesis. The essence of their argument was that the imposition of the rigorously policed wheel tax resulted in numerous unintended consequences.

The first of these was the creation of a large, top-heavy bureaucracy dedicated to tracking how many wheels each person owned, collecting the requisite tax, and punishing those who attempted to cheat.

In fact, based on Willard's calculations, it appeared as though the organization created to enforce the wheel tax spent one-third of all the revenues collected on salaries and expenses.

The second problem was the manner in which the wheel tax slowed pretelegraph communications, acted to inhibit trade, and fostered regionalism.

The third difficulty, and the one that caused Kreshenkov to become visibly angry, was the way in which the wheel tax acted to inhibit technology overall. "Imagine an old-fashioned pocket watch from the late 1800s," the technologist said passionately. "Each and every one of those suckers included a crown shaped like a wheel, an escape wheel, a balance wheel, and half a dozen gear wheels. Under LaNorian law each and every one of those wheels would be taxed at the rate of twenty plaks a year. Nobody could afford one, so why attempt to build it?

"But that's not all," Kreshenkov continued earnestly. "The ability to measure time lays the groundwork for hourly wages, accurate navigation, advances in medicine, and Lord knows what else. And that's just *one* application of the wheel, remembering that there are thousands more."

"So," Willard continued, "here's the so what of all this . . . We suggest that the Political Section attempt to educate the Empress and her key advisors regarding the negatives associated with the wheel tax—and put forward the following alternative: By removing the wheel tax, and switching to a sales

tax on non—food-related items, the government could stimulate innovation, *increase* the amount of revenue they collect, and
not put anyone out of work. Not for a while at any rate.

There was silence for a moment, Vanderveen started to clap,
and even Pas Rasha joined in. Both Kreshenkov and Tran
beamed. There were times, rare though they might be, when
being a diplomat actually felt good.

APPROXIMATELY TWENTY-TWO STANDARD MILES WEST OF THE FOREIGN CITY OF MYS, ON THE INDEPENDENT PLANET OF LANOR

It was a long hard ride from the foreign city of Mys to the
ancient ruins of Tankor, which meant that Ambassador Regar
Batth was tired by the time he finally arrived. Tired and sore
since the Ramanthian diplomat was not accustomed to riding
on anything more exotic than a conference room bench.

The diplomat's party included one of Regar's two lifemates,
the military officer known as Hakk Batth, or the War Batth,
along with six heavily armed warriors. They passed between a
pair of ancient columns and followed an overgrown road toward the shattered building beyond. The structure's base was
intact if somewhat overgrown, but the dome, or what remained
of it, resembled a broken eggshell. A single tree had grown up
through the hole, night birds circled above, and insects
hummed.

The Ramanthian thought the place was empty at first, and
was starting to wonder if the long arduous journey had been
for nothing when his mount uttered a characteristic "Reeep!"
and was answered from deep inside the ruins.

Then, as the off-worlders neared the temple complex itself,
LaNorians seemed to materialize as if summoned from the soil
itself. They made no attempt to interfere, but stood where they
were, eyes following the Ramanthians like so many gunsights.
The feeling of antipathy was so intense that a chill ran through
the ambassador's nervous system and he questioned the decision to come.

A drum stared to pound, and the rhythmic *thump, thump, thump* matched Hakk Batth's heartbeat. The War Batth heard a series of telltale *clicks* as his warriors released the safeties on their weapons and murmured into his headset. "Steadddy . . . They want to intimidate us. Don't give them the satisfaction."

The ambassador heard the instruction via the earphones fastened to both sides of his thorax, took comfort in the knowledge that his mate was there to protect his back, and focused on the scene before him. The more he could observe, the more he could take in, the more successful the mission would be.

All of the Claw, for that's what the Ramanthian ambassador knew them to be, were male. They wore red turbans, red sashes around their waists, and carried a wild assortment of weapons. Swords were common, as were spears and muzzle-loading muskets. Less common, but present nonetheless, were a scattering of only slightly outdated assault rifles, grenade launchers, and at least one shoulder-launched missile (SLM).

The more modern armaments appeared to be of human manufacture, and it seemed safe to assume that the weapons had been acquired from what the soft bodies referred to as the Syndicate.

The Ramanthians passed through the space once occupied by a pair of massive gates into a passageway lined with inward-facing loopholes, then out into a circular area once protected by the dome. The right side, the spot where the roof had collapsed, was littered with shoulder-high mounds of rubble. They had a uniform appearance, as if someone had sifted through the debris, taken whatever it was they were after, and left the rest. A member of the Claw stood astride one of the piles, the barrel of his assault rifle pivoting along with the razbul mounts, his eyes like chunks of coal.

The drum was louder now as the Ramanthians turned to the left, circled a large heap of stones, and entered the Claw encampment. There was a large open area, swept clean by the look of it, and a fire around which the gloom had started to gather. A chair sat beyond and might have been occupied, though it was difficult to see through the flames.

A half dozen LaNorians came forward, struck each razbul behind the front left knee, and watched with unabashed curiosity as the insectlike aliens backed off their mounts. Then, once the Ramanthians had dismounted and their mounts had been led away, one of the Claw gestured for Regar Batth to follow. Hakk Batth and his warriors had little choice but to remain where they were.

The Ramanthian embassy had a generous budget where matters of intelligence were concerned, which meant that Batth already knew a great deal about the tall austere figure who rounded the fire to greet him. Born to minor nobility but orphaned during the plague still referred to as the great darkness, Lak Saa came under the authority of a paternal uncle who, in his role of guardian, had "given" his nephew to the Imperial Court and thereby acquired title to the youngster's estate.

By long tradition most of the Emperor's closest advisors and functionaries were eunuchs, voluntarily sacrificing their sexuality in return for the power and wealth available to those within the Imperial Court.

There were exceptions, however—especially where "gifts" such as Lak Saa were concerned. At the age of ten the youngster was forcibly castrated, enrolled as a page, and thereby inducted into the dangerous world of Imperial politics.

Eventually, having risen through the bureaucratic ranks on the strength of his intelligence and guile, Lak Saa became one of the Emperor's most trusted advisors. A position which the supreme one's first concubine, later to become the Empress Shi Huu, was quick to resent. Not only did her views vary from Lak Saa's, but she was jealous of his power and afraid of what he might eventually do to her.

So, when the Emperor died, and power devolved to Shi Huu, one of the first things she did was to send assassins against Lak Saa.

But the eunuch, who was a master of the martial art called Tro Wa (the Claw) killed the assassins with his bare hands, sent their heads to Shi Huu, and left Polwa for the countryside where the movement known as the Claw was born.

Nor was "the Claw" a purely figurative term, for as Batth drew closer to the rebel leader he saw that the nails on each of the LaNorian's middle fingers had been allowed to grow into six-inch-long hooks or "claws," which, having been reinforced with thin strips of carefully layered animal bone, were said to be strong as steel.

The Ramanthian had doubts about that, but could certainly see how lethal such weapons could be, and was impressed by the sacrifice involved since the claws would make it difficult for the Tro Wa master to use his hands. The claws remained at Lak Saa's side as he bowed from the waist. He spoke good if somewhat accented standard. "Greetings and welcome to the temple of Tankor. My name is Lak Saa."

The diplomat bent a knee in the Ramanthian equivalent of a bow. "It's a pleasure to meet you, Minister Lak Saa. My name is Regar Batth. I represent the Ramanthian people."

"I no longer hold ministerial rank," Lak Saa said matter-of-factly, "but serve my people as a 'gudar,' or advisor."

Batth had reason to believe that Lak Saa's ambitions were a good deal more lofty than the title of "advisor" but kept such thoughts to himself. Now that he had been in close physical proximity to the rebel leader for a few minutes he could detect the harsh acidic smell of urine. An odor he had experienced on previous occasions while in the company of Imperial eunuchs. It seemed that their surgeries, most of which were quite brutal, left many of them at least partially incontinent. Still another payment for position and power. The Ramanthian bowed for the second time. "Thank you for clarifying your status. The LaNorian people are fortunate to have such an extremely well qualified advisor."

Lak Saa bowed in acknowledgment, a turbaned follower rushed to fetch a chair, and Batth was interested to see that while crude, the chair was a good-faith replica of the Ramanthian bench-style seats back at the embassy. How did they know? The answer was obvious, and the diplomat made a mental note to dismiss all of the LaNorian help.

Batth slid onto the chair, allowed it to take his weight, and watched his host settle himself into the large thronelike chair. The drum had fallen silent, the fire crackled wildly as a Claw warrior dumped more wood on it, and a bird called from somewhere beyond the wall. Much to the diplomat's surprise Lak Saa came straight to the point. "I understand that representatives of your race have established factories south of here."

Batth inclined his head. "Yes, that is correct."

Lak Saa raised his left hand. One of the Tro Wa approached. He held a bundle in his arms. A single snap of the LaNorian's wrist was sufficient to send four objects tumbling onto the hard-packed earth. "What," the rebel leader asked, "are they?"

Once again Batth was struck by the extent to which the Claw had penetrated off-world affairs all the way down to furniture they used and the types of products they chose to manufacture. The Ramanthian pointed to each item. "That's a can of wing wax. Members of my race rub it onto their wings in order to keep them supple. The concave pumice stones are used to smooth our exoskeletons and remove irregularities. Once the surface has been prepared we apply the substance contained in that tube to remoisturize our chitin and make it shine."

"And the last item?" Lak Saa asked, pointing to a tool with a curved tip. "What is that used for?"

"Our young molt," Batth replied patiently, "meaning that they shed their exoskeletons as their internal organs grow. The process can be uncomfortable. Molt picks are used to remove sections of chitin that refuse to come off on their own."

"So," Lak Saa said thoughtfully, "let's see if I understand. Having developed the ability to travel among the stars, the Ramanthian people make use of it to reach LaNor, where they proceed to manufacture molt picks. You will excuse me if I say that this seems *very* strange."

A lump had formed in Batth's throat, but he managed to swallow it. In two lightning strokes a Rim world primitive had sliced his way to within inches of the great secret. With some 5 billion new Ramanthians on the way, his race would need *everything* including 5 billion molt picks. Certain things, electronics for example, had to be fabricated by the Ramanthians themselves. So, with no excess production capacity to call on, it was logical, not to mention less expensive, to manufacture everyday utensils off-planet. He couldn't say that, however, not without revealing more than he should, so a partial truth would have to suffice. He offered the equivalent of a shrug. "It would be necessary to pay a Ramanthian twice as much to make the same products."

It was Lak Saa's experience that profit was a strong motive, and he raised a languid hand. "Thank you for your honesty. I suspect that the pay differential is a bit larger than you indicated but take no offense. Merchants, *successful* merchants, must guard such information.

Batth inclined his head. "Thank you. The gudar is most perceptive."

"So," the LaNorian said, switching to the Imperial "we," "now that we understand *what* you are asking our people to manufacture and *why*, it's time to discuss *how*.

"Life is rife with peril. Workers fail to show up, supplies go astray, and factories burn down. All of which have a negative effect on profits."

Batth gave a small sigh of relief. It could have been worse. The LaNorian was running what amounted to a protection racket. Annoying but well within the parameters of what he was prepared to deal with. "Yes, the gudar is correct. Such occurrences can be most disruptive. I wonder what, if anything, he would advise?"

Though prepared to kill the Ramanthians, and bury their bodies deep, Lak Saa liked Batth. The off-worlder demonstrated an almost LaNorian understanding of graft and was possessed of a polite and circumspect manner. Virtues rare among off-world devils. Consequently, the rebel leader decided to move ahead.

"My people have a saying . . . 'Friends are the best insurance that one can have.' Friends share information, friends defend each other from harm, and friends look to the future."

The Ramanthian listened carefully. It appeared that the LaNorian wanted to exchange intelligence, obtain more off-world weapons, and lay the groundwork for a potential alliance. "We're of a mind," Batth replied firmly. "An ongoing exchange of information is one of the hallmarks of friendship, as is a commitment to mutual defense. In fact, if the gudar allows, it would be my pleasure to present him with a gift of friendship."

Pleased by the graceful phraseology, and by his guest's adherence to LaNorian etiquette, Lak Saa inclined his head.

Though prohibited from landing outside the confines of Mys, the Ramanthian assault boat had been present throughout the conversation, ready to pounce should the diplomat require assistance.

The whine of engines was heard as the ship arrived from the west, produced six blindingly bright spotlights, and lowered itself toward the ground. Dust swirled, sparks twisted up out of the fire, a flock of birds took to the air as the skids touched down.

There was a loud *bang!* as one of the Claw fired a musket, and the air was filled with the sound of squalling mounts as the razbuls charged from one end of their pen to the other.

Lak Saa felt fear stab his belly as the aircraft appeared out of the darkness above, knew he had underestimated the opposition, and resolved never to make the same mistake again. Apparently unmoved, he raised a claw. His subordinates saw the movement, realized their mistake, but were unsure of what to do. Many continued to aim their weapons at the spacecraft.

Metal creaked as the full weight of the assault boat settled onto the skids, the engines cycled down, and the main hatch swung open. Ambassador Batth slipped back off his chair. "With the gudar's permission, my military attaché would like to demonstrate one of our gifts."

Lak Saa had little choice but to give consent. Together, the strange twosome walked over to the spot where a crate had been off-loaded onto the ground. Heat continued to radiate off the black matte hull, and metal pinged as it cooled.

One of Hakk Batth's warriors managed to pop the top off the crate, allowing his officer to reach deep within. The weapon he withdrew was a Ramanthian-made Negar III general-purpose assault rifle converted for LaNorian use. It could fire six hundred rounds per minute (cyclic) using thirty-five-round magazines, with a muzzle velocity of twenty-four hundred standard feet per second. Far from the best that the Ramanthians had to offer but a sturdy weapon that had proven itself on more than one backward planet.

The War Batth checked the action, slammed a magazine into the slot at the bottom of the receiver, and managed to pull the charging lever back in spite of the fact that it had been shortened for use by LaNorians. The bolt made a clacking sound as it rammed a bullet into the firing chamber, and the weapon was ready to fire.

Then, making use of the translator snapped to the front of his combat harness, the Ramanthian spoke. "Please choose a target . . . Anything within the temple."

There was no reason for Lak Saa to make the task easy, so he didn't. The LaNorian pointed a talon toward the far side of the plaza, where a male stood among the shadows. "Shoot him in the thigh."

The rebel in question gave a start, fought the temptation to run, and came to something like attention.

The War Batth recognized the unfortunate individual as the same person who had fired his musket without permission, turned to the Batth for permission, and saw the diplomat nod.

Though modified for LaNorian use, there was no denying the fact that the weapon was of Ramanthian design. The stock fit his shoulder to perfection, his tool hand caressed the un-protected trigger, and the target swam into the center of the sight. The warrior took a deep breath, let it out, and touched the trigger.

There was a sharp cracking sound as the slug whipped across the courtyard, blew a hole through the offender's leg, and dumped him on the ground.

Then, flicking a lever to full automatic, the officer fired one long thirty-four round burst. Dirt geysered all around the prostrate body, but not one of slugs actually struck it.

Once the magazine was empty, the War Batth sent it clattering to the ground and slammed another into place. Then, performing a smart left-face, he took two steps forward and presented the rifle to the LaNorian leader.

It was the Ramanthian diplomat who spoke. "Please accept this rifle plus those that remain in the crate as evidence of our friendship."

Lak Saa took the weapon, sampled its heft, and passed it on to an assistant. The weapon was clearly quite superior to those purchased from the Syndicate gunrunners, and the rebel was impressed. A fact which he was careful to conceal. "Not bad for a clearly outmoded weapon. Please join me for some tea."

The better part of two hours had passed, and the teapot had been refilled on numerous occasions by the time negotiations were finally complete. In return for assurances that nothing untoward would happen where the Ramanthian factories were concerned, Batth had agreed to deliver a constant flow of information regarding affairs within the foreign city of Mys, ten thousand assault rifles, 2 million rounds of ammunition, a supply of surface-to-air missiles (SAMs), plus an adequate number of spare parts.

Both sides felt good about the outcome and parted company with a heightened sense of respect for the other. The Ramanthians spent the night, rose to find that the Claw had disappeared, and rode toward the east.

And so it was that the sun rose, insects circled a pool of dried blood, and thirty-five brass casings lay scattered on the ground. Still, it was but one more day in the temple's long tumultuous life, and barely worth notice. It dozed in the heat.

3

All warfare is based on deception. Hence, when able to attack, we must seem unable; when using our forces, we must seem inactive; when we are near, we must make the enemy believe we are far away; when far away, we must make him believe we are near. Hold out baits to entice the enemy. Feign disorder, and crush him. If he is secure at all points, be prepared for him. If he is in superior strength, evade him. If your opponent is of choleric temper, seek to irritate him. Pretend to be weak, that he may grow arrogant. If he is taking his ease, give him no rest. If his forces are united, separate them. Attack him where he is unprepared, appear where you are not expected.

> Sun Tzu
> The Art of War
> Standard year circa 500 B.C.

THE FOREIGN CITY OF MYS, ON THE INDEPENDENT PLANET OF LANOR

When the Imperial troops came they did so with a great deal of fanfare. Cannons boomed, firecrackers popped, gongs rang, trumpets blew, flags snapped, and what seemed like an endless stream of orders were shouted as an enormous column of soldiers approached Mys from the north. The formation was twelve troopers wide and appeared to be at least three miles long. Once the phalanx drew within a quarter mile of the North Gate it split into two columns. One went east, and the other went west, both following the thirty-foot-high defensive wall south toward the Jade River.

There were shacks there, along with all manner of less permanent shelters, and pens filled with animals. These were leveled by a force of heavily armored razbuls that preceded the main infantry column and laid waste to everything in their path.

Santana was shaving when the alarm rang and still had patches of foam on his face as he grabbed his jacket and followed Corporal Dietrich out through the back of the barracks, up a steep flight of stone stairs, and onto the walkway that ran along the top of the twelve-foot-thick wall. In spite of the fact that it was only 0713, the prevailing winds had pushed Polwa's eternal light brown haze north to Mys, where the locals supplemented the pollution with their own coal-fed cook fires.

The Imperials were sweeping down along the west wall by then, the solid *thump, thump, thump* of their open-toed hobnailed boots pulverizing what remained of precious food stores, tiny well-kept gardens, and miscellaneous household items.

Representatives from all of the various embassies had mounted the wall and could do little more than watch as the squatters, most of whom were able to escape with little more than their lives, screamed and ran away from the walls. Their animals, those lucky enough to survive, squealed, squawked, and grunted as they hopped, dashed, and flapped in every possible direction.

The Jade River bisected Mys from east to west and might have offered something of an obstacle had it not been for the sturdy barges tied end to end in an effort to form temporary bridges on both sides of the city. Boots thundered on wood as the LaNorians crossed the tributary, arrived at the point where the northern part of Polwa abutted the southern extension of Mys, and came to a ceremonial stop.

Santana discovered that he had a towel in his hand and used it to wipe the rest of the foam off his face. The second platoon was on duty and first Lieutenant Mary Beckworth materialized at his side. She had wide-set eyes, a no-nonsense mouth, and wore a single earring, which dangled from her left ear. It was in the form of a circle and torch—the emblem of the First REC. The Class B khaki uniform had lost some of its creases during the long humid night but still looked professional. Santana liked her and hoped the feeling was mutual. "Good morning, Mary, what's going on?"

The other officer grimaced. "An Imperial messenger rode in an hour ago. They had to get Pas Rasha out of bed in order to receive him. It seems the Empress is worried about our safety and sent some of her household troops to protect us."

The conversation was interrupted as the flow of troops stopped, trumpets blared, and the entire column performed a well-coordinated right-face thereby creating countless six-person files. Then, responding to orders from their officers, the soldiers marched exactly one hundred paces to the west, did an about-face, and faced Mys. There was no way to see what was occurring off the east wall, but Santana figured it would look about the same.

"So," the legionnaire said, "assuming the soldiers were sent to protect us, how come they're facing *in* rather than out?"

"That's a good question," Beckworth replied. "A damned good question indeed."

The trumpets sounded again, clouds of dust rose as a long train of two-wheeled carts appeared from the north, and split at the same point the troops had, following the walls south toward Polwa. The barges bucked like live animals as the first heavily laden carts rumbled over the Jade River, reached the end of the line, and turned toward the west. The whole thing was well executed and obviously meant to impress.

"It looks like they plan to stay for a while," Beckworth observed dryly.

"Yes," Santana agreed. "It sure as hell does."

It took two days for the Imperials to settle in, establish their various encampments, and discover the obvious. The plain was a miserable place to camp. The sun baked the soldiers during the day, insects bit them during the night, and boredom eroded their morale. But that was where the Empress wanted them—and that's where they would stay. The dry season deepened and time seemed to slow.

NEAR THE VILLAGE OF NAH REE, ON THE INDEPENDENT PLANET OF LANOR

In spite of the fact that the Busso family was a long way from their comfortable little house back on Earth, they still did many things the same way. Bethany Busso typically went to bed an hour earlier than her husband and therefore got up first. By the time Natalie, ten, and Mark, thirteen, had finished their showers, and her husband had pecked her on the cheek, breakfast was ready.

Sometimes Bethany served sponsor-supplied Mission Rations (MRs), which Mark liked, and the rest of the family hated. But that was rare since the Bussos had gradually become accustomed to their own versions of LaNorian fare. The menu that morning included fried kas cakes, molo fruit, and half a protein bar each. Frank said grace, and the meal began.

Despite Bethany's best efforts to slow them down, the children had a tendency to eat quickly so they could go outside and play before school started. That particular day was no exception. Natalie finished first, thanked her mother, and dashed out the back door. Mark gobbled his fruit, used a napkin to wipe his mouth, and was close on his sister's heels.

Frank Busso had just taken a sip of carefully rationed coffee, and was about to comment on the day ahead, when he heard Natalie scream. The missionary came to his feet and headed for the door. His mug fell, coffee splattered onto the floor, and Bethany rushed to a window.

The screams had stopped by the time Frank Busso arrived in front of the mission. Natalie sobbed as her brother put his arm around the little girl's shoulders and guided her back toward the kitchen. His face was white and there was a tremor in his voice. "It's Nuu Laa, Dad . . . I'll tell Mom to stay where she is."

Uncertain of what he would find, the missionary rounded the front of the dome, saw the twenty-five-foot-tall T that marked the mission for it was, and realized something had been added. There, at the foot of the Transcendental T, a cluster of poles had been planted. Each supported something round, but from a distance Busso couldn't tell exactly what they were. As the missionary moved forward he felt a cold clammy hand grab his stomach and squeeze. Then he was there, just beyond the line of demarcation for Security Zone Three, and close enough to see what his children had seen.

Each gore-drenched stick bore a LaNorian head, all of which had been arranged so they appeared to be looking upward, as if worshiping the off-world symbol that towered above them. Frank Busso recognized Nuu Laa, her mate, and all three of their children.

A strange inarticulate noise issued from deep within Busso's throat, his stomach rejected the recently consumed breakfast, and the missionary puked on his own feet. Finally, having nothing more to give, Busso used a sleeve to wipe his mouth. Then, with his back to the dome, he scanned the surrounding area. The sun seemed unnaturally bright. The air was heavy on his skin. The ground seemed to roll beneath his feet. Way off in the distance, on the road to Nah Ree, a rider could be seen. He or she watched for a moment longer, wheeled, and rode away.

Suddenly, for the first time since he and his family had landed on LaNor, the human felt truly afraid.

ABOARD THE CHIEN-CHU ENTERPRISES' SUBMERSIBLE PLATFORM *SEADOWN*, APPROXIMATELY FIVE HUNDRED MILES DUE EAST OF POLWA, IN THE OCEAN KNOWN AS THE GREAT WET.

The cold gray sky seemed to wheel as the wind pushed the seemingly endless ranks of blue-green waves toward the west, lifted the two-thousand-ton submersible drilling rig twenty feet into the air, then lowered the twin hulls back into a trough. A welter of spray shot up into the air, was caught by the wind, and whipped away. Though capable of propelling herself from place to place, the *Seadown* was something of a compromise, which meant that she wallowed like a pig.

Chien-Chu, still playing the part of diver-rigger Jim James, peered out through the wheelhouse as Les Foro, a fellow cyborg, conned the *Flyfish* in toward the docking area located between the larger vessel's twin hulls. Given the need to move around beneath the ocean as well as on top of it, the *Seadown* had a clean, streamlined hull.

Having studied the vessel in advance, the industrialist knew that if viewed from above the ship would resemble a capital H, with a saucerlike drill housing located at the center and smooth catamaran-style hulls that flared to either side.

Spray flew up from the *Flyfish*'s bow, splattered across the window, and was attacked by a pair of hardworking wipers. Foro put the wheel over to compensate for the manner in which wave turbulence tried to push the hydrofoil to port, spoke into his headset, and applied more power.

Chien-Chu hung on to a grab bar as the tender surged forward, passed into the relatively calm area between the *Seadown*'s hulls, and entered what the crew referred to as the grab. The industrialist felt the hydrofoil's hull start to rise as a wave lifted both vessels upward, and heard Foro say, "Now!"

There was a gentle *thump* as a pair of computer-operated "arms" cradled the hull—and a momentary sense of vertigo as the machinery lifted the tender up off the surface of the sea. Then the bottom seemed to drop out from under Chien-Chu's feet as the *Seadown* slid into the next trough.

"Fun, huh?' Foro asked, as his big, blunt, plastiflesh fingers flipped a series of switches.

"I wouldn't have missed it for the world," the industrialist lied. "Thanks for the ride."

"No problem," the other cyborg replied. "And that stuff I told you . . . that's between you and me, right?"

Chien-Chu grinned. "What stuff?"

Foro laughed and continued to run through the shutdown procedures. The fact that he had felt it necessary to check spoke volumes. Chien-Chu had taken advantage of the journey down the Jade River and out into the ocean to pump the other cyborg for information. Foro had been cautious, understandably so, but a picture had emerged nonetheless.

According to the cyborg, Boad and his henchmen ran what amounted to a criminal dictatorship aboard the *Seadown*. The crew, all of whom were cyborgs, were forced to pay for lost or broken equipment. Once on board, all incoming and outgoing communications regardless of media were monitored for "inappropriate content," by which the station manager meant any mention of him, his toadies, or their illicit activities. Violations were punished with a three-month "blackout" of all personal communications "privileges." There were darker activities, too—things Foro hinted at but wouldn't elaborate on.

Servos whined as the port lock opened, the *Flyfish* was pulled inside, and deposited on a cradle. Foro hooked a thumb toward the tender's stern. "You might want to grab your stuff and report to the man. That faster you show up, the better Boad will like it. You'll find a ladder out there."

The industrialist thanked the other cyborg, retrieved his duffel bag, and felt his body make the necessary adjustments as he left the warmth of the watertight wheelhouse for the dankness of the marine lock. The external hatch had been sealed by then, but the deck was wet. The entire area, which would serve as something akin to an underwater garage when the *Seadown* was submerged, was long but relatively narrow. There was plenty of space though.

In addition to the *Flyfish*, which, though designed for surface use, could still withstand the same underwater pressures that the *Seadown* could, Chien-Chu saw a variety of six-man, two-man, and one-man undersea sleds racked along the port bulkhead, along with a long line of carefully numbered lockers.

Unsure of where to go, the industrialist intercepted a spider-shaped robot. Its body was made of stainless steel, its legs were equipped with octopus-like suction cups, and a large number "3" had been stenciled onto both sides of the machine's metal torso. Something whirred, and the machine stopped as Chien-Chu stepped in front of it. "I'm looking for Mr. Boad. Directions please."

Consistent with its function Number Three's personal interaction software provided the newcomer with an answer that was direct and to the point. "To reach the platform manager's office you must pass through lock P-1 or P-2, take a lift to deck one, and cross over to hull two. Once on the other side drop to deck two and look for the appropriate sign."

There wasn't much point in thanking a machine, but the industrialist did so anyway. He passed through lock P-2, heard the *thump* of machinery somewhere nearby, and entered one of two lifts. The interior smelled of fresh paint.

A buzzer sounded, the cyborg stepped off the platform and turned to his left. The "bulge," as the industrialist thought of it, consisted of an open space filled with all manner of mysterious machinery. Judging from the vertical structure located at the center of the space, this was the platform from which drills were pushed down through *Seadown*'s hull in order to retrieve core samples from the ocean's floor. Two catwalks, one to either side of the bulge, served to convey foot traffic from one hull to the other.

As Chien-Chu made the crossing he saw three cyborgs, a couple of robots, cables that snaked every which way, racks filled with pipe, welding equipment, workbenches and all manner of other gear. An air wrench screeched, a length of chain rattled through a pulley, and a hammer rang on steel. The cyborg's sensors detected traces of ozone in the air, along with vaporized lubricants, and the tang of seawater.

Once on the other side it was relatively easy to find the lifts, drop one deck down, and look for the correct door. The industrialist noticed that the interior was spotless. Whatever Boad's failings might be, maintenance wasn't one of them.

The cyborg paused in front of a plaque that read: "THOMAS

A. BOAD, PLATFORM MANAGER," and knocked on the door. His plastiflesh knuckles made a dull thumping sound. The hatch was slightly ajar, and the response was nearly instantaneous. "Come."

Chien-Chu stepped over the coaming and entered the platform manager's office. What he saw was impressive indeed. Boad was not only large—he was huge!" So big that the industrialist suspected that the cybernetic body would only barely pass through a hatch.

There was no theoretical upper limit on how large a cybernetic body could potentially be—Chien-Chu knew of some highly specialized "forms" that were larger than the *Seadown* herself—but the size of everyday cyborgs was constrained by cost, the social-cultural environment in which they expected to operate, and by what the industrialist thought of as "the freak factor," meaning that most borgs wanted to look as much like biobods as possible.

Not Boad, however, who not only wanted to *look* impressive, but dominate those around him. The face he had chosen was broad and craggy. He rose from behind the gray metal desk to tower over the industrialist in what could only be interpreted as an attempt to intimidate him. Though not comprised of actual flesh and blood, his dark, almost black eyes seemed to glow with pent-up animosity. A verbal attack stood in for the normal "Welcome aboard."

"Who the hell gave you permission to leave that shipping crate? Foro's report indicates that you were sitting around shooting the shit with the warehouse staff when he arrived. What the hell do you think this is? Some kind of freaking vacation? That crate cost money . . . Three hundred and seventy-three credits, which I will deduct from your pay.

"Now, before you get into any more trouble I suggest that you take your plastic ass down to crew quarters, find your slot, and log on. We have rules on this tub, *important* rules, and now's the time to learn them.

"And remember this . . . There ain't no way off this pus ball except through *me*, so watch what you think, watch what you say, and watch what you do. Otherwise, you could be here till your power runs down and your crew mates decide to cannibalize your body for spare parts. Questions? No? Then get the hell out of here."

It was tempting to end the charade right there, to declare who he was and seize control of the ship. But there was a good deal to learn yet, and given Boad's attitude, he would probably resist. Would others support him? Yes, quite possibly, which was why Chien-Chu backed out of the cabin.

Boad laughed as the *Seadown* rolled, the newbie fell on his ass, and pulled himself up again. A storm was coming—but not in *his* world. The platform manager dismissed the cyborg named Jim James from his mind, opened a heavily encrypted file, and scanned his favorite spreadsheet. Not a *corporate* spreadsheet, but *his* spreadsheet, and the purpose for which he lived. Not sex, since that was largely denied him; not power, since money could buy that, but *wealth*. Great wealth . . . and the sooner the better.

THE FOREIGN CITY OF MYS, ON THE INDEPENDENT PLANT OF LANOR

It was nighttime as Santana made his way past the deeply shadowed garden, through the light that pooled next to the barracks, and along the path that led to the west wall. Most of the staff had left for the night, which meant that except for the ambassador, his family, and their personal staff, the embassy was empty.

Most of the professional staff maintained apartments in the southeast corner of Mys, often referred to as the corporate sector, because most of the off-world offices were located there. The locals lived in Dig Town or farther to the south within Polwa itself.

The sky was clear and the light from LaNor's twin moons glazed the surfaces around him as the legionnaire emerged onto the top of the wall. A sentry was posted there, and her rifle snapped into the vertical position. Her name was Hixon, Alice Hixon, and her white kepi seemed to gleam in the moonlight. Santana returned the salute, said, "As you were," and took a moment to look out toward the west.

Had it not been for the manner in which the moonlight touched the top of their tents, and the hundreds of coal-fed fires that eyed him from the darkness, the officer would never have guessed that an army occupied the night.

The Jade River shimmered a half mile to the south, turning toward the city, prior to diving under the very wall on which Santana stood. "Pretty isn't it?"

Hixon wasn't used to having officers ask her opinion regarding military matters, much less the view. She looked startled. "Sir, yes sir."

"Any contact with the Ramanthians?"

By virtue of a long-standing arrangement, guard duty was generally shared by two and sometimes three off-world military organizations. On that particular night the Legion had been teamed with the Ramanthians . . . an arrangement that Santana viewed with a considerable amount of skepticism. Hixon nodded. "Yes sir. One of their noncoms stopped by about fifteen minutes ago."

"Good. Keep an eye to the north, though; the bugs may have responsibility for the north and west walls, but it'll be *our* ass if something goes wrong."

Hixon grinned. "Sir, yes sir."

Santana nodded and turned toward the south. Now, as he turned his eyes inward to the city of Mys, the officer saw the six-foot-high stone wall that encircled the embassy, the stretch of well-kept park that paralleled the Jade River, the river itself, the maze of ramps, jetties, and docks that lined the south bank, backed by the complicated jumble of roofs, streets, and alleyways that comprised the area known to the off-worlders as Dig Town, "Dig" being short for "indigenous."

Coal-oil-fed lanterns hung at each street corner, rectangles of yellow light indicated places where sweatshops worked through the night, and the occasional snatch of off-world music could be heard as soldiers exited one of the bars.

As Santana crossed over the river and walked parallel to Dig Town, he was struck by the fact that two large buildings were not only smack up against the wall, but their roofs were only ten feet lower than the walkway under his feet. That put the top of the wall well within reach of a short ladder—something he had heard Seeba-Ka complain about.

Now, as the officer approached the point where the west wall met the south wall, he could see the top of Polwa's northernmost wall, the lanterns that marked its corners, and the lights of the city beyond. They were asymmetrical, like diamonds scattered on black fabric, and represented only a fraction of the million-plus souls who lived there. None but a person of noble birth, or a wealthy merchant, could afford to maintain a noka, or night beacon, along with the retainers that normally went with it.

"Evening, sir."

The voice belonged to Private Suresee Fareye, one of the Naa nationals who had fought under Captain Seeba-Ka back on Beta-018, and a crack trooper. Just knowing he was there, prowling the southern wall, made Santana feel better. Given how sensitive the legionnaire's sense of smell was, the officer felt sorry for him. "Evening, Fareye, how's it going?"

The Naa shrugged. "No problems here, sir, but what do you think of *that*?"

The legionnaire handed the officer his electro-binoculars, and Santana used them to probe farther into the night. Data flickered across the bottom of the electronically merged images. Ranges, bearings, and the wind speed on top of the wall all offered themselves only to be ignored. The inner city glowed off toward the right, its boundaries marked by evenly spaced white lanterns, its buildings appearing as ghostly green blobs. Somewhere, safe within one of those blobs, the Dowager Empress Shi Huu slept, plotted, or did whatever royalty did at night.

But beyond that, like a snake winding its way through a maze of obstacles, something else could be seen. Red lanterns, hundreds of them, bobbed, swayed, and jerked as the LaNorians who held them pushed through narrow streets. Now, as Santana stood there, the officer thought he could hear the distant beat of drums, the occasional blare of a trumpet, and something that might have been screams. When he spoke the comment was intended more for himself than the legionnaire who stood next to him. "The Claw."

Fareye nodded. "Sir, yes sir. I think that's who they are all right. And a mean bunch of slimeballs they are . . . Looks like they plan to visit the palace."

"The Imperial troops will stop them," Santana predicted, "but it's interesting nonetheless. Keep your eye on the bastards and let me know if they get past the inner city."

"Sir, yes sir."

Santana returned the Naa's salute, turned to his left, and walked toward the east. What looked like a clutch of LaNorian soldiers, all armed with muskets, stood atop Polwa's northern wall. The gap between the two walls was no more than fifty feet wide. Close enough that the officer might have heard them had the LaNorians spoken a little more loudly. They stood in a group, as if conferring on something, and seemed unaware of his presence.

The juncture where the south wall met the east wall was directly ahead, and Santana squinted into the darkness, hoping to spot one of the Ramanthian sentries. That was when the legionnaire heard a commotion off to his right and turned in time to see one of the LaNorians spring into the air! Except that it *wasn't* a LaNorian, because LaNorians don't have wings, and this individual did. They made a steady *whuf, whuf, whuf* sound as the intruder propelled himself across the fifty-foot gap.

Santana placed a hand on his sidearm as Fareye materialized at his side. The legionnaire brought his assault rifle up to his shoulder and peered into the sight. "I have the bastard, sir. Just say the word."

"Hold your fire, Private," Santana said, as the flier settled onto the top of the wall. "The bastard is one of ours."

The sound of the officer's voice caused the Ramanthian warrior to turn. His wings rustled and disappeared as they folded themselves along the soldier's back.

The sentry recognized Santana as an officer, offered the Ramanthian version of a salute, but made no attempt to justify his actions. Nor was there reason to since there was no arrangement by which enlisted personnel belonging to one off-world detachment were expected take orders from or be responsible to officers other than their own. He was of average height, wore a translator strapped to his chest, and was armed with the Ramanthian equivalent of a submachine gun.

Santana struggled to keep his voice firm but level. "Your name and rank, please."

"Specialist Poth Dusso."

"Thank you, Specialist Dusso . . . Perhaps you would be so good as to explain why you left your post? There's a lot of wall . . . and not very many beings to patrol it."

"Why?" the Ramanthian inquired disrespectfully. "Did someone sneak in?"

"Not that I'm aware of," Santana replied. "But they certainly could have."

The Ramanthian's eyes seemed to glitter in the reflected moonlight. "*Should* something happen tonight, *should* an assassin find his way into Mys, it won't be over *this* section of the wall. I suggest that you look to your own area of responsibility and leave this section of wall to us." That being said, the Ramanthian turned and shuffled away.

"I *still* have the bastard," Fareye said grimly. "Just say the word, and he's toast."

"Thanks," Santana answered wearily, "but I'm in enough trouble already and about to get in more. That last comment had a prophetic quality."

So saying the officer activated the radio clipped to the left side of his pistol belt and spoke into the wire-thin mike that curved out in front of his lips. "This is Red Six to the Red Team . . . Condition four . . . implement *now*. Red Six to Red Five . . . raid the barracks. Double the guards at both entrances to the embassy. Do you read me? Over."

"Red Five to Red Six," Hillrun answered, "I read you . . . and I'm on it. Five out."

Well aware of the fact that the whole thing could be and probably was a waste of time, and that he might very well make a fool of himself, Santana started to run. The officer dashed the length of the south wall, took a right, and ran flat out along the top of the east wall until he saw Hixon, dashed for the stairs, and took them two at a time.

Lights came on in the barracks as Hillrun rousted off duty legionnaires out of their racks, an alarm started to bleat, and a T-2 lumbered toward the rear of the embassy. The lights mounted on its massive head washed across the walkway and bathed a sentry in their harsh white glare. Her name was Fandel, and she looked scared as Santana skidded to a halt. "Everything all right?"

Fandel had a small face, and it looked frightened. "Sir! Yes sir."

"Good. Where's Corporal Wu?"

"Inside, sir. Daw Clo was looking for him, too."

Santana frowned. "Daw Clo? The dig with the wheelbarrow?"

The legionnaire nodded. "Yes sir. He arrived about ten minutes ago. Said he had something for the corporal."

"And you let him in?"

Fandel was worried by then. Her features seemed to constrict themselves into a tight little ball. The truth was that Daw Clo was making the rounds with a tray full of spice-filled dumplings, something he had done many times before, and a practice that many of the noncoms winked at. The private could still feel the warmth of the food in her stomach as she gave her answer. "Yes sir. Daw Clo has a Class Two clearance."

Santana knew that Class Two "chits" as they were called entitled the bearer to move around the main floor of the embassy between the hours of 9:00 A.M. and 6:00 P.M. He also knew that such restrictions were often ignored where trusted members of the staff were concerned. An issue he would pursue in the morning. Meanwhile he decided to enter the embassy, find the LaNorian, and ask him to leave. "Thanks, private. Carry on."

Santana mounted the short flight of stairs, punched his code into the keypad, waited for the telltale *click*, and opened the door. Every third light was on. Their reflections marched the length of the highly polished floor. Santana heard the sound his boots made, resolved to walk more quietly, and wondered why. Was he still a bit spooked? Yes, it seemed that he was. Something that would no doubt please the Ramanthian named Poth Dusso.

A quick check of the first floor turned up nothing. No Corporal Wu, no Daw Clo, nothing. Santana decided to ignore the lift in favor of the stairs and was only halfway up when he saw the rivulet of blood and the body slumped beyond. The crushed kepi and khaki uniform left no doubt as to whom the body belonged. A tray lay on one of the stairs . . . its contents strewn everywhere.

The legionnaire drew his sidearm, checked to ensure that the safety was off, and made his way upward. A quick check was sufficient to confirm that Wu's throat had been slit and that he was dead.

Santana activated his radio and whispered into the mike. Red Six to Red Five . . . Corporal Wu is down halfway up the main stairway inside the embassy. Seal the building, secure the crime scene, and send some low-key backup. I am moving to floor two."

The officer heard two *clicks* as Hillrun used standard patrol procedure to acknowledge the transmission.

Then, confident that Hillrun was on the job, Santana continued up the stairs. Having murdered Wu, chances were that the assassin would waste little time going after his *real* target, Ambassador Soolu Pas Rasha. The ambassador, and members of his immediate family, were asleep on the fourth floor.

Conscious of the fact that the murderer could be lying in wait for him, but even more concerned about what might be about to occur on the fourth floor, Santana threw all caution to the wind and ran up the stairs. Just as the cavalry officer reached the top of the stairs all of the embassy's lights came on, he heard shouts from the bottom of the stairwell and knew reinforcements were on the way.

A large sitting area gave way to a couple of carpeted hall-ways. Thanks to his original orientation tour, Santana knew that the one on the left led back toward the ambassador's bed-room. His boots made a soft thumping noise as he ran down the corridor, rounded the open door, and entered the room. Thanks to the emergency lights which Hillrun had triggered, the would-be assassin stood bathed in a greenish white glare. The legionnaire shouted, "Drop the weapon!" but the hook-shaped blade was already in motion.

Pas Rasha had been awake for a good five seconds by then. His wife, awakened by the lights, started to scream. He saw the assassin, saw the strange hook-shaped blade, but was pow-erless to move. Not without his exoskeleton, which like his wife's, stood motionless in the closet. There was time to think of his children but nothing more.

Razor-sharp steel flashed, a weapon fired, and gore splat-tered the ambassador's bed. There was a *thump* as Daw Clo collapsed across the Pas Rasha's legs, followed by the sound of a human voice. "He's down! Hold your fire!"

All three of the legionnaires who had entered after Santana raised their weapons. The officer provided cover for Dietrich as he moved forward, checked to see if the LaNorian was breathing, and shook his head. "Dead, sir. Nice shooting."

The embassy's physician was summoned to care for the am-bassador's semihysterical wife, the body was moved onto the floor, and the household staff rushed to help Pas Rasha don his exoskeleton. And that's how things were when Seeba-Ka arrived.

The Hudathan surveyed the room, saw the bloodstained bed, Daw Clo's body, and the T-shaped claw-knife. That's when he turned to Santana, saw the weapon in his hand, and scowled. "You shot him?"

Santana came to attention. "Yes sir."

"And you're proud of that?"

"No sir."

"Why not?"

"Because the assassin made it into the embassy and all the way to the fourth floor before being stopped, sir."

"That's right," Seeba-Ka agreed darkly. "See that evidence is collected, take statements from everyone who has a pulse, and report to my office. The major is going to want reports, *lots* of reports, and you're going to write every damned one of them."

THE CITY OF POLWA, ON THE INDEPENDENT PLANET OF LANOR

The sixty-five-year-old Dowager Empress Shi Huu awoke as she always did, on a mattress filled with fragrant mountain moss from her home province of Chi, and in the company of the children she often referred to as dogun or foot warmers.

Both the male and the female had been chosen for the physical beauty, and both would be replaced the moment they turned eight years old. Already wise beyond their years the dogun felt their mistress stir, eased their way out from under the coverlet's warmth, and scampered out into a nearby hall where an older female waited for them.

The Empress, or "gana" (mother) as the dogun were allowed to call her, tended to be in a foul mood when she awoke and it was best to be as far away from her as possible.

Unlike most upper-class females Shi Huu did not allow any of her retainers to enter her suite until certain matters had been attended to. The first step was to crouch over the hand-painted chamber pot, the contents of which would be ceremoniously carried into the Imperial garden, where a Tiz master would cast the bones to determine which tree or shrub would receive "the heavenly harvest."

Then, having relieved herself, the Empress retired to the chamber of beauty, where a window took up most of one wall and threw light onto the marble counter below. It was pink and seemed to glow from within.

Floor-to-ceiling shelves occupied the other walls. They bore hundreds of identical porcelain canisters, each marked with a hand-painted label, and organized by function. Skin conditioners here, wrinkle removers there, and so forth.

The only problem was that in spite of the countless hours spent in the chamber of beauty, and the endless concoctions that the Empress had rubbed, slathered, and in one case baked into her skin, none had the desired effect. Every morning Shi Huu was one day older, one day uglier, and one day closer to death.

The Empress sighed, sat on the hand-carved three-legged "luck" stool, and gazed into the cell-powered, internally lit, 3X Bliss Industries "ladies' mirror and makeup assistant." Just one of the many gifts that the aliens had lavished on her over the last year—and one of the very few that she actually valued.

The underlying structures could still be seen, including the high forehead, the perfectly aligned nostril slits, and the wide thin-lipped mouth. But these features were increasingly obscured by the wrinkled skin, the sagging flesh, and the blotchy "widow" spots that disfigured her once flawless complexion. Skin which the Emperor had once compared to "the first blush of dawn," causing his courtiers to refer to the then young female as the Dawn Concubine, a name which still had currency.

Later, after the Emperor's death, and her ascendancy to the throne, the Dawn Concubine had acquired other less complimentary nicknames some of which she valued as highly as the first.

During the subsequent years, Shi Huu clung to power, surrendering it only once, and then to her son when he achieved his majority. Even then she ruled through him, causing some to refer to him as the Dar Zo, or puppet prince. But those days came to an end as the result of her son's accidental death and her reascension to the throne.

However, enjoyable though political power was, Shi Huu missed those long-ago days when every male who looked upon her wanted her, when princes came to call, and the Emperor himself labored between her legs.

There was hope, however, hope that flowed from promises made by the small furry ambassador. Her name was Fynian Isu Hybatha. She claimed to be something called a Thraki, and, if her claims were true, could restore at least some of Shi Huu's former beauty.

Though far from knowledgeable where the process called nanosculpting was concerned, the Empress knew that the aliens would render her unconscious, scatter tiny computer-controlled machines on her face, and let them remove all of the unsightly wrinkles. Clearly not something the Empress wanted to subject herself to without some assurance that it would work, which was why three homely maidens had been abducted from three separate villages and would soon undergo the process in her place. Then, assuming that all went well, and the alien nanos were able to turn the maidens into beauties, Shi Huu would submit to the process her herself.

In the meantime there was work to do. The Empress washed her face, using water imported from her parents' home in Chi, anointed her face with those balms proven to be most effective, and applied a thick layer of daytime makeup.

Then, feeling somewhat better about herself, Shi Huu rang for her retainers. They arrived in a subservient flood. It took the better part of an hour for them to bathe her body, spritz it with perfume, and wind a dress onto her still trim frame.

In keeping with her station, Shi Huu owned hundreds of different dresses, one for each day of the year, all replete with complicated cultural, historical, and seasonal symbology.

Something of a bore to her, but much loved by the weavers, dressmakers, fitters, jewelers, seasonalists, historians, and fan trimmers who were dependent on the Imperial wardrobe for their livings.

Finally, bound within layers of brightly colored, carefully folded silk, and accompanied by a trio of senior eunuchs, Shi Huu began the long, stately journey from her quarters to the air throne, where the day would officially begin. After an hour spent there, she would be conveyed to the fire throne, the water throne, and the earth throne, each of which was used to communicate with different sets of officials, many of whom had traveled hundreds if not thousands of miles to see her, and waited weeks or even months for the privilege of a ten-minute audience.

Beyond the obvious symbology involved, the purpose of the various throne rooms was to keep that day's supplicants separated from each other and thereby control the extent to which they could interact. A rather useful tactic instituted by the last Emperor's grandfather—and potentially threatened by the introduction of off world telecommunications devices. Just one of the reasons why Shi Huu feared the off-worlders and the impact they could have on her world.

However, before the Empress could reach the air throne and settle into cushioned comfort, it was first necessary to negotiate the maze of hallways, passageways, and corridors for which the inner city was known. Her elevated, jewel-encrusted clogs made a rapping sound as a page led the party through the halls, courtiers bowed, and commoners fortunate enough to witness the procession hurried to prostrate themselves on the cold stone floors.

Some said that the plans for the two-thousand-year-old mostly wooden structure had been handed from heaven, with each room representing an aspect of divinity and each walkway a path to enlightenment.

Others claimed that the complexity stemmed from an effort

to confuse would-be assassins, lead them astray, and provide guards with an opportunity to intercept them.

Still others, Shi Huu among them, believed that the labyrinthine palace was the result of incessant remodeling carried out by generations of royalty, none of whom had much if any respect for the structural decisions made by their predecessors.

Finally, having entered via one of six possible passageways, the Empress and her procession swept into a large chamber that had been decorated to match the throne that sat at its center. A dome provided light from above, clouds had been painted on a pastel blue ceiling, and live field flits sang from inside their golden cages. Even the closely woven throne had been elevated off the floor to resemble a woodsy nest.

The Empress climbed four steps, turned, and took her seat. Her breakfast was ready and waiting. It consisted of a pot of scalding tea, three kas crackers, and six mola berries. A discipline which helped explain why her body remained trim while most females of her age and socioeconomic status had a tendency to gain weight.

Shi Huu took a sip of tea, smacked her lips, and nodded to one of eunuchs. The official day had begun, and in keeping with the symbology attendant on the air throne, the Empress would first hear a series of reports. These varied from day to day but could generally be categorized as having to do with finances, civil matters, or military affairs. Which eunuch would go in which order was generally determined by them, so when Dwi Faa stepped forward, the Empress knew that the first item on the agenda was civil in nature. A rather broad category that covered everything from the policing of street vendors to massive civil unrest. A favorite topic ever since Lak Saa and his fanatics had launched their incessant attacks on the status quo. The eunuch bowed. "Good morning, Your Highness. May I say that your beauty seems to grow with each passing day?"

Shi Huu *knew* Dwi Faa was trying to soften her up, and *knew* that he was lying, but appreciated the effort involved. It would never do to let that show however—which accounted for her reply. "If words were gold, you would be wealthy indeed . . . Now, let's dispense with the flattery and get to work."

The court, some thirty individuals in all, took the opportunity to laugh, but none too loudly lest they offend the eunuch and find themselves banished to one of the more distant provinces.

Dwi Faa was completely unabashed. He bowed in order to acknowledge her order and began his narrative. Though susceptible to flattery, the Empress was no fool, and understood the extent to which negative reports could be shaded to make them more palatable.

During the earliest days of her rule one eunuch in particular had insisted on systematically misrepresenting the extent to which the all-important wheel tax was being ignored until the day came when his head arrived on a platter.

The grisly object was placed on the chair where the minister normally sat, where it remained understandably mute until the meeting was adjourned, and the head was removed. Not a word had been spoken regarding the matter, nor were any required. The lesson was clear: Lie if you wish . . . but be ready to pay.

With that in mind, Dwi Faa launched his report. "It's my duty to inform Your Highness that a most regrettable incident took place during the night. Emboldened by the darkness, and desirous of imposing themselves on the minds of our citizens, some thousand members of the Tro Wa emerged from their hiding places to light lanterns and parade through the streets. During this illegal demonstration they were heard to shout, 'Death to the foreigners!' and two off-worlders were impaled on stakes."

"What kind?" Shi Huu asked, placing a berry between her lips.

"They were hu-mans," the eunuch replied matter-of-factly.

"Serves them right," the Empress said, popping the berry's skin to let the sweet juice flood her mouth. "What were they doing in Polwa to begin with? I gave them an entire city to live in, and now they want more.

Dwi Faa knew the last statement to be false, since the off-worlders had paid an exorbitant sum for the land on which Mys sat, constructed all of the buildings at their own expense, and been taxed to the hilt. But there was no point in saying so, and he didn't. "The off-worlders were ministering to the sick, Highness—as part of what they refer to as a health program."

Shi Huu waved a bejeweled hand. "Meddling, that's what I call it. Continue your report."

"Yes, Highness. Once the impalements were completed the malcontents attempted to march on the inner city but were dissuaded from doing so by members of the Imperial guard. More than eighty members of the Claw were killed, three hundred were arrested, and the rest managed to escape."

Hoo San, the eunuch with responsibility for the military, stood a little taller. The Empress turned in his direction. The Emperor, who had been shrewd in his own way, and unknowingly served as Shi Huu's mentor, had fathered dozens of sayings. One of them fit the situation perfectly: "Praise costs less than gold . . . and is frequently more effective."

The Dawn Concubine nodded. "Thank you, Hoo San, for a job well-done.

The military officer's uncut fans stood straight out from the side of his head. He bowed in mute acknowledgment.

"So," the Empress said thoughtfully, "my old friend flexes his muscles. But why? Because he means to move against me? Or as some sort of diversion?"

"Only the sixteen devils know for sure," Dwi Faa replied vaguely, "but the puzzle has many pieces. I beg your indulgence while I document two more . . .

"First it is my duty to inform you that hill bandits attacked the village of Ka Suu, put your tax collectors to death, and seem determined to stay.

"And second, though equally disturbing, is the fact that your nephew managed to escape from his palace and is presently at large."

Shi Huu considered each item in turn . . . and knew them to be related to each other. Countless efforts had been made to find the hill bandits and put them out of business. Countless efforts had failed. Not only were the criminals dangerous, not to mention expensive, they continued to preach a philosophy of self-governance.

Worse yet was the fact that Mee Mas, the Imperial nephew, took their quasi-democratic rhetoric seriously, and even went so far as to refer to the brigands as patriots. Not openly, of course, but within his circle of intellectual friends, most of whom had never done a day's work in their entire lives.

But if Mee Mas were to hook up with the bandits, and be used by them, her nephew might become more than a mere embarrassment. The Empress felt a steadily rising sense of anger. "His guards, what of them?"

"Under arrest, Your Highness . . . awaiting your pleasure."

"Put the guards to death and force their families to watch. I'll leave the method to you."

"Yes, Highness."

"Redouble your efforts to find my nephew. Kill him if you must—but capture him if you can.

"As for the hill bandits, the Emperor had a saying: 'Never attack an enemy that another will attack for you.' Summon the spindly one, tell him that we need help from his off-world troops, and let them take Ka Suu back from the bandits."

It was a good plan, a *brilliant* plan, and the eunuch offered his deepest bow. "Of course, Highness. It shall be as you desire."

THE FOREIGN CITY OF MYS, ON THE INDEPENDENT PLANET OF LANOR

As befitted her relatively lowly status, Christine Vanderveen's office was on the north side of the embassy, facing the Strathmore Hotel. There was nothing special to look at, but it was a place to focus her eyes while her mind wandered. Big things were afoot, that much was obvious, but only for those in the more senior slots.

The morning staff meeting had been canceled in the wake of the attempt on the ambassador's life, the department heads were meeting to come up with a response to the murders in Polwa, and a roundtable would be held later in the day.

Details were sketchy but it sounded as though two members of the Transcendental Health Corps, both women, had been dragged out of their clinic and murdered by members of the Claw. Vanderveen had met one of them, a big-hearted xeno-physiologist named Jane Munot, and been unable to prevent the tears when she heard news of the physician's death.

Then, as if to prove that the bad things really *do* happen in threes, Frank Busso had called in to notify the ambassador that five members of his flock had been beheaded, and that others were starting to arrive at the mission in hopes that he could protect them.

Vanderveen jumped as the door closed behind her. She turned to discover that Harley Clauson had entered her office. He smiled understandingly. "Upsetting isn't it? Daw Clo, a member of the Claw, it's hard to believe."

"Yes, it is," Vanderveen agreed, her mind going back to the many little favors that the LaNorian had done for her. "It's scary to think that he hated us that much . . . and managed to hide it so well."

"Yes," Clauson said, "It certainly is. Mind if I sit down?"

The question was little more than a formality, and the FSO-2's posterior had already made contact with the chair's cushion before his subordinate could say, "No, of course not."

It wasn't all that warm yet, but little beads of perspiration had still managed to colonize the foreign service officer's fore-head. He used a white handkerchief to dab at them. "Sorry to impose on your morning—but I could use some help. Minister Dwi Faa wants to meet with the ambassador, and I was asked to take part as well. The ambassador plans to lodge a formal protest regarding the murders. It won't change anything, everyone knows that, but the effort must be made. Even though the meeting is scheduled for 9:00 A.M., Dwi Faa likes to keep his visitors waiting, so it could be a long day.

"That being the case, I won't be able to keep an appointment scheduled for ten. All of which is a long, roundabout way of asking if you would be so kind as to attend in my place."

Vanderveen brightened. The meeting couldn't be of much consequence, or the ambassador would have assigned it to himself rather than Clauson, but *anything* was better than writing reports. "Of course . . . I'd be glad to."

"Excellent!" Clauson said gratefully. "The meeting is to take place in the Shawa District just south of the inner city in Polwa. It seems that Madame Las Laa, one of the late Emperor's cousins, would like to make arrangements to import off-world plants to further embellish her garden. She tried to do so but ran into the rules requiring the need for in-depth bioassessments prior to the importation of alien species. A silly thing, really, but you know how it is, we need friends no matter how dotty they may be."

Vanderveen sighed. She was going to attend a meeting with a no doubt imperious and possibly senile old bat. Just her rotten luck. Still, there weren't that many chances to visit Polwa sans escort, and that would constitute an adventure in and of itself.

Clauson, who had a seemingly uncanny ability to read her mind at times, chuckled and shook his head. "No, you won't be venturing forth alone. Major Miraby was kind enough to provide you with an escort."

Vanderveen looked hopeful. "Lieutenant Beckworth perhaps?"

"No," the senior FSO answered easily, "Lieutenant Santana."

"The same Lieutenant Santana who shot Daw Clo?"

"Yes, and I would think you could take comfort from his martial abilities."

Vanderveen frowned thoughtfully. "The lieutenant is something of a loose cannon . . . one that may very well go off. Did you know that?"

Clauson looked genuinely surprised. " 'Loose cannon'? What ever do you mean?"

"Santana was broken to second lieutenant when he refused a direct order from a Ramanthian officer during the Thraki war."

Clauson shrugged. "That's unfortunate, but so what? The Legion must have confidence in his abilities, or they wouldn't have sent him here."

"Would you like to know who that Ramanthian officer was?" Vanderveen asked meaningfully.

"No," Clauson answered slowly, "but I have a feeling that you're going to tell me."

"Damned right I am . . . The officer that Santana refused to obey was none other than Force Leader Hakk Batth, one of Ambassador Regar Batth's two lifemates, and the Ramanthian military attaché on LaNor.

Clauson frowned. "How do you know all this?"

Vanderveen shrugged. "I waited until Miraby went to lunch, sat down in front of his comp, and pulled Santana's P-1 file."

"That was inappropriate, unethical, and possibly illegal."

"Are you going to report me?"

Clauson shook his head. "No, I might lose you if I did, plus your father would pull strings have me sent to Drang. But what I *am* going to do is find an appropriately subtle way to make sure Miraby is more diligent where internal security is concerned—and dump the quarterly activity report in your lap."

"You would have anyway."

Clauson smiled contentedly. "Yes, I probably would."

Knowing that most of the day would be lost to the trip into Polwa, and conscious of the fact that her reports would still have to be written, Vanderveen left for work two hours early.

It had rained during the night. The streets remained damp and a light morning breeze had pushed the worst of Polwa's stench off to the west. There was the sound of a distant trumpet as the Imperial troops started to stir—and a determined *whir* of wings as a flit left the protection of a nearby tree.

Because of the way Mys was laid out, and the fact that Vanderveen's apartment was located in the corporate sector, it was necessary to walk south toward the Transcendental Cathedral, turn west, climb the stairs that led up onto the street that everyone called Embassy Row, but was actually named "Legation Street," face north and cross the Jade River.

It was too early for off-worlders to be up and around, which meant that all of her fellow pedestrians were LaNorians. A fact that wouldn't have troubled the diplomat before but did now.

Many of the locals were on their way to jobs in the shops that lined the southeast side of Embassy Row, the Strathmore Hotel, or the embassies themselves. They tended to nod politely and murmur, "Hoso poro" (good morning), before continuing on their way.

There were others, however, scruffy types who pushed wheelbarrows along the street, or carried huge bundles on their backs. They glowered, sent resentful looks in her direction, and mumbled what might have been insults.

Or, was that her imagination? And how meaningful were appearances anyhow? Daw Clo had dressed as well as someone with his responsibilities could be expected to dress and been unrelentingly polite. That hadn't stopped him from killing Corporal Wu however . . . or from attacking the ambassador as he lay in his bed. Vanderveen wondered how many of those around her would cheerfully slit her throat and walked a little faster.

Once opposite the embassy, and in sight of the legionnaires who flanked both sides of the entrance, Vanderveen discovered that she had been holding her breath. She let it out, crossed both lanes of traffic, and said, "good morning" to the guards.

They knew her, of course, but were still required to check her ID prior to letting her in.

The diplomat entered her access code in the panel next to the door, waited for it to hiss out of the way, and went to work. It seemed like only a few moments later when someone knocked on the door—but a quick glance at the lower-right-hand corner of her comp screen revealed that two full hours had passed.

Vanderveen said, "Come in!" and turned in time to see Corporal Dietrich enter the room. He wore a Class A uniform overlaid by a ceremonial combat harness replete with six ammo pouches, a translator, a radio, and other items of equipment which the FSO couldn't identify.

Like her peers she was familiar with the stubby weapon slung under the noncom's arm however. All foreign service personnel were required to qualify on three basic weapons twice a year. The CA-10 carbine was capable of firing eight hundred rounds per minute and had a muzzle velocity of 2,612 foot-pounds per second. It looked like a wedge with a peg-style grip mounted slightly back of the muzzle, a pistol grip and trigger assembly just to the rear of that, and a thirty-round magazine that protruded from the bottom of the receiver. "That's a lot of weapon for what amounts to a garden party," Vanderveen commented sarcastically.

"I wouldn't know about that," Dietrich replied, eyeing her chest. "The lieutenant sent me to get you."

Given the fact that Vanderveen was attractive and there were more human males on LaNor than human females, the FSO was used to being eyeballed. Both by legionnaires and the virtually identical Jonathan Alan Seebos attached to the Clone embassy. Most of the offenders were a good deal less obvious however. The foreign service officer raised her eyebrows. "If you're finished staring at my breasts, perhaps you would carry a message to the lieutenant . . . Tell him I'll be down in ten minutes."

Dietrich's eyes came up to meet hers. They registered no

sign of embarrassment. "Yes, ma'am. I'll tell him. The cart is out front." So saying, the corporal did a neat about-face and marched out of the office.

Vanderveen shook her head in amusement and walked down the hall. Even the most luxurious of LaNorian toilets was little more than a slit trench fed by a stream of water. It was her ambition to make the journey into Polwa and back without being forced to use one of them.

Fifteen minutes passed before the doors to the embassy opened, and Vanderveen walked out into the morning sunlight. The sight that awaited her caused the FSO's jaw to drop. One of the embassy's enclosed two-wheel carts had been brought around front. Like all such conveyances, the LaNorian carriage included a back step on which either guards or servants could ride, a box-shaped passenger compartment complete with windows, a perch on which the driver could sit, and poles to which a razbul could be harnessed. Except that the draft animal was missing . . . and a Trooper II stood between the traces instead!

Santana came forward to greet Vanderveen, but she spoke first. "What's the meaning of this absurdity? Are you out of your mind?"

The legionnaire stopped where he was. Part of his mind, the male part, couldn't help but notice how pretty the foreign officer was. She had shoulder-length blond hair, strikingly blue eyes, and full red lips, both of which formed a straight line.

The *other* part of Santana, the military part, felt a rising sense of anger. "No, ma'am. By using Corporal Snyder in place of a draft animal we increase our potential firepower by more than 2000 percent and do so without violating Imperial regulations pertaining to the size and composition of off-world groups, parties, and other assemblages traveling within the boundaries of the Imperial city."

It was a clever idea, Vanderveen had to give the officer that, and the words used to justify the plan had been lifted right out of the Imperial decree titled: "Rules and Regulations attendant to movement of off-world beings within the confines of Polwa." Not only that, but Imbulo was correct, and the lieutenant *was* nice to look at.

Still, a cart pulled by an off-world cyborg was bound to attract a lot of attention and might prove provocative. "That's all very nice, Lieutenant," Vanderveen said coolly, "but please allow me to draw your attention to the fact that the purpose of this outing is *diplomatic* rather than military."

Santana took a full step forward, which placed him well within her personal space. Rather than raise his voice he lowered it so only she could hear. "I assume you are aware that two women were murdered in Polwa."

Vanderveen wanted to take a step backward but refused to do so. "Yes, one of them was a friend of mine."

Santana nodded. "I'm sorry to hear that, but the fact remains . . . A crowd materialized out of nowhere, marched through the streets, and pulled your friend out of her clinic. That's when they stripped her naked, lifted her body into the air, and lowered it onto a stake. Based on information obtained from paid informants, it appears that they went to some lengths to ensure that the stake was lodged in her anus rather than her vagina before grabbing her arms and pulling downward. I was on the south wall at the time and could hear her screams from there.

"The purpose of the military escort is to ensure that *you* don't suffer a similar fate. Furthermore, it may interest you to know that Captain Seeba-Ka not only approved these arrangements, but assigned a T-2 to pull the ambassador's cart earlier this morning. Now, if you'll allow me to do my job, I will allow you to do yours. Do we understand each other?"

Never, not in all of her twenty-five years, had anyone ever been allowed to speak to Christine Vanderveen in such a manner, and she fought for control. Her eyes narrowed. "Understood, Lieutenant . . . Now let's see if you can get me to my appointment without killing anyone, which, based on the evaluation in your P-1, appears to be the *only* thing you're good at."

It was a churlish thing to say, and Vanderveen could see the words slam into Santana like bullets fired from a gun. A veil dropped in front of his eyes. The same veil that upperclassmen, many of whom were from families like hers, had seen at the academy. The officer gave a short jerky nod and took a full step backward. "I'll do my best."

With the exception of those who worked in the fields, LaNorian females seldom if ever wore pants. So Vanderveen was dressed in a blouse, a jacket, and a long black skirt. It was slit along both sides in order to ease her movements, and Dietrich watched a long white leg appear then disappear as the FSO entered the cab.

Santana followed the woman into the passenger compartment leaving Dietrich and Fareye to mount the back step while Private Hixon rode in the driver's seat.

Snyder, who had accepted her role as draft cyborg with characteristic good humor, used her graspers to grab the traces, and pulled the cart away from the curb.

Like her peers on LaNor, Snyder was an upgraded variant of the trusty Trooper IIs that had served so valiantly throughout the last three wars.

One arm was equipped with an air-cooled .50 caliber machine gun. The other boasted a fast-recovery laser cannon. Even without the dual missile launchers, which the armorers had removed for the trip into Polwa, the cyborg was still one of the most potent killing machines ever constructed. She could run at speeds up to fifty miles per hour and operate in a wide variety of environments, including the black of night. All of which meant that her presence alone was equivalent to a squad of biobods.

But Snyder was a *person*, a human being in an electromechanical body, something that some officers had a tendency to forget. The fact that Santana not only *liked* cyborgs, but had rescued one under fire, had made the rounds within hours of his arrival. The result was that all of the company's box heads were pulling for the loot even if they had to haul carts around in order to please him.

The metal-clad wheels bumped on the cobblestones as the cart passed over the Jade River on its way toward the city's South Gate. Vanderveen was sitting on the left and caught a glimpse of the imposing Transcendental Cathedral before storefronts intervened to close it off. The edifice seemed too large, too awkward for LaNor, and she wondered why the Confederacy's bureaucracy would prohibit the importation of plants lest they do harm to the native ecosystem but felt no responsibility where ideas were concerned.

Santana cleared his throat. "Here, clip this to your waist-band. It's set to the same frequency that I'm on—and Lance Corporal Bagano is monitoring our transmissions back at the barracks.

"Should something happen to Dietrich, Fareye, Hixon, and me go to Snyder. There are toeholds on the backs of her legs. Climb up and hang on . . . she'll bring you out."

Vanderveen accepted the radio and tucked it away. "You never stop, do you? The soldier-boy thing runs twenty-seven hours a day."

Santana raised an eyebrow. "That's what we have in common. We're very consistent."

Vanderveen frowned, tried to formulate a good retort, and failed. She didn't mean to laugh but did so anyway. "Did you just call me a bitch?"

Santana grinned. "No, ma'am. It's like my father used to say: 'Life is a bitch—girls are a blessing.' "

The laughter was open and honest. Santana discovered that there was something about the sound that made him want to hear more. But the cart had ground to a halt by then, and an Imperial guard appeared at the right-hand window. Short stilts enabled the LaNorian to see inside and he was clearly unhappy. There was a slight, almost imperceptible echo as both translators regurgitated his words. "What is the meaning of the big machine? What permissions do you have?"

Santana was about to try and bullshit his way through the checkpoint when Vanderveen leaned forward. Her voice was calm and soothing. "Is Factor Wah Heh around by any chance? I'd like to speak with him, please."

The guard frowned, seemed to consider the matter, and stumped away. A full five minutes passed, during which all manner of traffic built up behind the cart, and southbound commerce ground to a halt.

Finally, his movements made to the accompaniment of the *reeps, squawks,* and *croaks* produced by LaNorian livestock, not to mention the invective produced by their owners, the FSO spotted the short stocky figure she knew to be Wah Heh coming their way. He wasn't wearing stilts, so Vanderveen passed in front of Santana, opened the door, and let herself out.

The legionnaire was about to follow when he saw the LaNorian official offer an extremely deep bow, which Vanderveen returned in kind. The officer paused as the twosome bowed for a second time, then parted company.

Vanderveen returned to the cab, some sort of signal was given, and the cart jerked forward. "So," Santana said, "who was that? And why did he clear the way?"

"Wah Heh is the Tax Factor assigned to what we regard as the South Gate, but those in Polwa think of us the North Gate.

"I met him at a diplomatic function a couple of months ago, listened to his troubles, and convinced Margo Imbulo to program a handheld calculator with LaNorian numerals. Although his boss isn't aware of it, Wah Heh can complete a full day's work in about half an hour. That leaves him with a lot of time for naps."

Santana raised an eyebrow. "What if he uses the calculator to construct a neutron bomb?"

"Then you can shoot him."

Both of them laughed, the sound leaked through the leather cab, and was audible on the other side. Dietrich looked at

Fareye, and the Naa rolled his eyes. "Officers . . ." the look said. "It must be nice."

From Polwa's northernmost gate, the cyborg-drawn cart made its way south past the Te Sa tenements and onto the so called Great Way, which generations of Emperors had used for parades, ceremonials, and other demonstrations of how important they were.

As befitted such a street it boasted two lanes, a planting strip that ran down the middle, and was fronted by nearly indistinguishable government buildings. They had tray-shaped roofs that functioned to gather rainwater and funnel it down into underground cisterns, deep eaves that served to protect the walkways below, and were trimmed in red.

All of the structures were made out of wood, and in spite of the heavily embossed bronze water reservoirs located at each corner, there were gaps where individual buildings had burned down. Those ministries that happened to be in favor were quickly rebuilt. Those organizations that weren't had little choice but to erect lean-tos and do the best they could among the ruins.

Santana had never been in the city before and decided that in spite of the poverty, the open sewers, and the smoke-polluted air, Polwa had a certain energy, a kind of dusty charm, that made him want to get out and explore.

The cart entered what amounted to a traffic circle and swung to the right. Vanderveen pointed to the heroic sculpture around which all the vehicular traffic was forced to go. "That's the last Emperor . . . Most LaNorians agree that he loved Shi Huu—though it's not clear if the feeling was reciprocal. The inner city is off to our right. If you look hard, you can see a section of wall through the trees."

And so it went until the cart made a turn to the right and entered the Shawa District, where many members of the petty nobility maintained town houses.

Santana had the impression of high walls, low, tray-shaped roofs, and lush vegetation. Alleys provided access to stables and a way for the LaNorian equivalent of tradespeople to deliver food and other necessities to their wealthy clients.

The streets, like the one they were on, were reserved for private carts. Servants stopped to stare as the cyborg jogged by, nobles peered from second-story balconies, and a razbul attempted to bolt.

Then, just as Vanderveen started to worry about the impact their passage might have on the otherwise peaceful neighborhood, the cart slowed and Snyder pulled over to the curb. A gatekeeper appeared out of the shadows, hesitated as if unsure of whether it was safe to approach the off-world machine, and was visibly relieved when Vanderveen opened the door and stepped outside. Santana followed. "Would you like me to come or stay?"

An hour earlier the FSO would have told the officer to stay. Now, for reasons she was quite sure of, she wanted him to come. Vanderveen eyed his sidearm. "Can you leave *that* behind?"

Santana smiled and released the pistol belt. "What? You're afraid I'll shoot the host?"

"Something like that," the diplomat agreed. "It's supposed to be a friendly visit, and a sidearm isn't all that friendly."

Santana kept his radio and translator but placed the weapon inside the cab. Then, having directed a meaningful look at Corporal Dietrich, he followed Vanderveen through the gate.

Hixon, who still qualified as something of a newbie, watched the officer go. "So, Corp, what did the look mean?"

Dietrich smiled. "It meant 'keep a sharp eye out, monitor the radio, and tell Hixon not to lean on the cart. It looks sloppy.' "

Hixon pushed herself away from the vehicle and looked embarrassed. "You're kidding, right?"

Dietrich shook his head. "Nope. I can read the loot's mind. That's why I am a corporal while *you* are a lowly private."

Fareye snickered, Snyder laughed, and the legionnaires did what soldiers have done for thousands of years: They waited.

Vanderveen and her escort followed the gatekeeper through a lush garden, up a short flight of stairs, and onto a broad veranda.

An elderly female rose from her chair and shuffled forward. She wore a peach-colored wind-on dress that matched some of the blossoms in the garden. Fabric swished, and her platform shoes made a clacking sound as she walked. Vanderveen bowed, so Santana followed suit. "Madame Las Laa," the FSO began, "it's an honor to meet you. My name is Christine Vanderveen—and this is Lieutenant Santana. Harley Clauson sends his regrets—but was summoned to a meeting with Minister Dwi Faa. He hopes you will forgive him."

Madam Las Laa bowed in return. She looked frail, but her voice was surprisingly strong. "Welcome to my humble home. It was kind of you to come so far to see me."

Vanderveen bowed again. "The journey was pleasant. Your home is very beautiful."

Madam Las Laa bowed in acknowledgment. "Thank you. Now, if you would be so kind as to step inside, I have a guest who would like to meet with you."

Vanderveen felt her pulse quicken. The meeting with Las Laa was a cover! Someone else wanted to meet with Clauson, someone who couldn't do so out in the open and would now be forced to deal with her. It might be something—or it might be nothing. It was interesting either way. The diplomat delivered her reply. "I would be honored to meet with your guest."

"Excellent," the LaNorian matron replied. "Please follow Duu Tas . . . The lieutenant and I will tour the garden."

The last statement was by way of an order rather than a request. Santana looked at Vanderveen, saw her nod, and extended his arm. "Thank you, Madame Las Laa, I would love to see your garden."

It was gracefully done, and Vanderveen felt a sense of gratitude as she followed the diminutive maid inside the house.

The better part of two hours had passed by the time Vanderveen emerged from the house and joined her hostess out on the veranda.

Santana had been through the entire garden by then, sipped innumerable cups of tea, and was listening to a full inventory of Madame Las Laa's physical ailments when the diplomat finally appeared.

It took another fifteen minutes for the twosome to extricate themselves, enter the cab, and head back toward Mys. "So," Santana said as the cart bumped along, "who *was* the mysterious houseguest anyway?"

"His name is Mee Mas," Vanderveen answered levelly, "and he's the dead Emperor's nephew."

"Sounds interesting," the officer said dutifully. "What did he want?"

"What he wants," Vanderveen said thoughtfully, "is to depose the Empress, take over the planet, and join the Confederacy."

4

Aptitude for war is aptitude for movement.

Napoleon I,
Maxims of War
Standard year 1831

THE FOREIGN CITY OF MYS, ON THE INDEPENDENT PLANET OF LANOR

Like those of the other senior members of the embassy staff, Major Miraby's office was located on the third floor looking out over the riverfront park, the dubious waters of the Jade River, and the native quarter beyond. Rather than the battle-field mementos that many senior officers liked to scatter around their offices, Miraby's was decorated with pictures of him standing with a variety of VIPs.

As Santana, Beckworth, and Seeba-Ka stood waiting for their commanding officer to enter, the lieutenant saw photos of Miraby standing next to General Booly, Miraby conferring with War Commander Doma-Sa, and Miraby laughing at one of President Nankool's jokes. All in his Class A's, all in official settings, and all indicative of a largely bureaucratic career.

There was the sound of footsteps as Miraby entered the office, said, "At ease," and circled his fortresslike bana wood desk. As the major took his seat the other officers did likewise. Consistent with his origins, Seeba-Ka chose one that would put his back to a wall. "So," Miraby said, "how much have you people heard?"

News traveled fast within the confines of the embassy, and all three of the officers believed they had a pretty good idea what was going on, but nobody said so. Miraby, who liked to give briefings, used the back of an index finger to smooth his mustache. "All right then, I'll run it down for you."

"The ambassador was summoned for a visit with Minister Dwi Faa, spent a good two hours waiting for the impudent beggar to show up, and was finally ushered in. The Polwa murders were discussed, as were those at the mission near Nah Ree, and the new atrocities to the southeast.

"Dwi Faa said all the right things, blamed the incidents on the Claw, and promised that the Imperial government would do everything in its power to protect off-world residents.

"However," Miraby continued, his gaze shifting from face to face, "the minister said something else . . . Something that both the ambassador and I find troubling. Dwi Faa indicated that when outsiders arrive, displace workers from their jobs, and attempt to supplant local belief systems with their own they should expect what he referred to as some resentment."

Beckworth started to say something but Miraby raised a well-manicured hand. "I know, impalements and the like extend well beyond any reasonable definition of 'resentment,' but that's what the bugger said.

"Of more importance," the major continued, "at least from a military perspective, was the conversation that followed. It seems that hill bandits invaded the village of Ka Suu, put the local tax collectors to death, and made themselves at home.

"Now, for reasons not entirely clear, the Empress has decided to request off-world military assistance to help liberate the community and restore order."

This particular item had *not* made the rounds, which meant it qualified as news. "It seems damned suspicious to me," Seeba-Ka said cynically. "Here we are, surrounded by thousands of Imperial troops, all drawing pay for doing nothing, and they need help from *us*? That's hard to believe."

"Yeah," Beckworth agreed. "And what happens if we send forces to Ka Suu and the digs attack Mys?"

"I'll thank you not to refer to the LaNorian people as digs," Miraby said primly, "but I understand your concerns. Were it up to me, I would tell the Empress 'no,' but it isn't. The ambassador believes this may be the sort of opportunity we've been hoping for . . . A joint effort that will strengthen our relationship with the Imperial government, foster improved communications, and lay the groundwork for long-lasting agreements.

"More than that, the vast majority of the other ambassadors agree. Accordingly, they have given their approval for a multinational relief force."

The other officers looked at each other in astonishment. There had been some cooperation in the past, guard duty was an example, but nothing like a joint task force.

"And who," the Hudathan inquired, "is slated to lead this force?"

Miraby's eyebrows rose and fell like old-fashioned signal flags. "There were those who hoped that you might lead it— but I put that notion to rest. Should this be part of some elaborate stratagem to weaken our military capability in Mys, your skills will be required *here*. I didn't say that, of course— but such were my thoughts.

"Therefore, I'm pleased to announce that the honor fell to none other than Force Leader Hakk Batth, a relative of the Ramanthian ambassador, and a most capable officer."

Having only recently arrived, and having been focused on the needs of his platoon, Santana had yet to interact with officers from the other embassies. For that reason the news that his old nemesis was on LaNor came as a shock.

The legionnaire was still in the process of trying to assimilate that piece of news when Miraby dropped an even bigger bomb onto the proceedings.

"So," the major said, completely oblivious to the impact his words had on those in front of him, "I put Lieutenant Santana down to lead our troops and ensure that the bandits get the drubbing they so richly deserve."

By that time it was clear that Miraby had never taken time to fully review Santana's P-1, or had skimmed the file so quickly that he had missed the pertinent data and was therefore unaware of the animosity that existed between his subordinate and Hakk Batth.

It was equally clear that the major had either failed to read the report in which Santana suggested that the Ramanthians might have known about the attack on Pas Rasha *prior* to the actual event, or *had* read the report and dismissed the contents out of hand.

Santana started to speak, but Seeba-Ka cut him off. "Thank you for the briefing, sir. If you have no objection I would like to free Lieutenants Santana and Beckworth to prepare their platoons for inspection while I stay and ask a couple of questions."

Miraby looked surprised, but nodded to the junior officers and waited for them to exit. Once out in the hall, and safely out of earshot, Beckworth eyed Santana. "Hey, Tony, the cap is *pissed*. Miraby's gonna get an earful. What's going on anyway?"

Santana sighed. "It's a long way from Beta-018 to LaNor—but not far enough."

NEAR THE VILLAGE OF NAH REE, ON THE INDEPENDENT PLANET OF LANOR

In spite of the fact that the sun had already disappeared over the western horizon, the sky remained blood red as Frank Busso completed his rounds. There was surprisingly little sound, just the occasional murmur of conversation, or the hum of an insect. The air was heavy, as if it too was holding its breath, waiting for whatever darkness would bring.

The Transcendental mission had turned into an entirely different place since Nuu Laa and her family had been murdered.

While some of the converts had remained true to their new-found religion, others had withdrawn, or attempted to, only to learn that the Claw considered them to have been "contaminated."

The net result was that true believers and the "contaminated" alike fled Nah Ree for the mission. The exodus had started the night before and continued throughout the day. Some left everything behind, arriving with little beyond the clothes on their backs, while others brought cartloads of belongings.

Meanwhile back in the village, fingers of black smoke pointed down at their already looted homes where Rog, the god of fire, had been directed to cleanse the land which they and their families had polluted.

Now, camped behind the mission, along the south bank of Gee Nas River, some two hundred families, about eight hundred people in all, were preparing to bed down for the night.

Frank Busso had already supervised the digging of privies downstream of the encampment and put some males to work building communal shelters. They wouldn't be ready for a while, however, which meant his followers would have to make do with tents. There was no two ways about it, the situation was bad, and likely to get worse.

Yet, as Busso circled the camp, the barrel of a hunting rifle resting on his left shoulder, he was continually struck by the bravery of the LaNorian people. Adults bowed politely, youngsters ran hither and yon, and the smoke from their tiny cook fires twisted up into the steadily darkening sky. In spite of all the evidence to the contrary, they believed he could put things right somehow, and that consistent with the church's teachings, the most important thing was that they *reacted* to the calamity. Something most of them were better at than *he* was.

During the last few days the missionary had been scared shitless and still was. More than that, he'd been forced to confront something he had sensed about himself but never been willing to admit. The truth was that while others saw the things he had given up in order to come to LaNor as a sacrifice, he'd been eager to jettison them. His boring job, a half million-credit mortgage, and all the other trappings of a middle-class lifestyle had been like weights hung round his neck.

But now, rather than the paid vacation he'd been counting on, the ministry had turned into a true horror show. Part of him wanted to grab his family, abandon the mission, and make a run for Mys. The only problem was that Bethany believed in the phony him, just like the LaNorians did, and Busso couldn't bring himself to tell any of them the truth. That's why he continued to patrol the grounds, murmur words of encouragement, and play the part that was expected of him. He was down by the river, admiring a newly constructed fish trap, when his daughter Natalie came running up. "Daddy! Daddy! The Claw is coming!"

Busso felt a lead weight fall into the pit of his stomach. He turned to the fish trap's architect—a competent sort named Hwa Nas. "Arm the able-bodied males with sticks . . . Bring them to the front of the mission . . . I'll meet you there."

The LaNorian nodded, rose from a crouch, and turned to go.

"And Hwa Nas . . ."

The LaNorian paused. "Yes?"

"Walk, don't run. We must avoid panic."

The LaNorian nodded for the second time and departed at a fast walk.

Busso turned to his daughter, ordered her to return to the house, and watched her scamper away. Then, confident that he'd done what he could, the human wound his way through the encampment toward the front of the mission. Darkness had fallen by then, and he could hear the rhythmic pulse of the rebel drums.

Then, clearing the front of the dome, Busso saw what looked like a river of fire. They were Claw all right, *hundreds* of them, each armed with a red lantern. The snakelike column twisted, turned, and pooled in front of the tall Transcendental T. The crowd swirled, a body was carried forward, and secured to the bottom of the twenty-five-foot-tall upright. Mark appeared at that point with the other rifle that came as part of the mission kit. The adolescent was scared but determined not to show it. "Hey, Dad, what are they doing?"

"I'm not altogether sure, son," the older Busso answered cautiously. "Go inside . . . I'm counting on you to guard the folks in the dome."

Mark shook his head. "No way, Dad. I'm staying with you. If they make it all the way to the mission, the whole thing is over."

Frank Busso knew his son was correct and felt a moment of pride. The boy had certainly matured during the months on LaNor . . . but would he live long enough to make it off?

Hwa Nas had arrived by then—along with fifty males all armed with poles. Not much as armies go, but better than nothing. Maybe, just maybe, a show of force would slow the Claw down.

Some sort of ceremony began and the drums beat a little bit faster. The lanterns bobbed and swayed as each member of the crowd passed the figure bound to the bottom of the enormous T and dropped something at his or her feet.

Busso had spent six months in the LA Militia back during the Thraki conflict and still remembered how to handle a weapon. The missionary brought the rifle to his shoulder, considered the light-amplification mode, but discovered that the lanterns produced enough illumination to see by. The figure on the pole seemed to leap forward. It was Nit Loo, one of the many LaNorians who had attended a couple of services, and was now "contaminated."

It still wasn't possible to see what the villagers were dropping at the shoemaker's feet, but Busso saw a spark followed by a sudden gout of flames, and knew that the material was flammable. Mark said, "Dad . . ." and Nit Loo started to scream.

The drums beat even faster now as the crowd swirled, a

likeness of the god Rog danced over their heads, and the screams came in short, agonized bursts.

Tears were flowing down Busso's cheeks as he swung the crosshairs over onto Nit Loo's squirming body, applied a long steady pressure, and felt the trigger give. The weapon's butt kicked his shoulder, a 7.62 mm slug drew a straight line between the end of the barrel and Nit Loo's body, and the LaNorian gave a sudden jerk as the projectile took his life. The loud whip-crack sound of the rifle going off followed a fraction of a second later. The crowd moaned and started to back away. Claw agitators drove them forward again.

Emboldened now, and angered by what they had forced him to do, Busso chose a second target. Judging from the manner in which he was exhorting the crowd, this particular LaNorian was a leader, and a rather active one at that. Inspired by the violence, and having given himself over to Rog, the male leaped high into the air, landed in a crouch, growled like an animal, and threw himself left and right.

Busso followed the lantern-lit figure, waited for him to pause, and squeezed the trigger. As luck would have it a second individual stepped in front of the first, staggered as the slug passed through the soft flesh of his throat, and was already falling by the time the now-deformed bullet struck the intended target and blew half his head away.

That was more than the crowd could take. Most had never seen such accurate shooting much less been on receiving end of it. The lanterns scattered like sparks from a fire. Mark raised his weapon but Busso pushed the barrel down. "Save your ammo, son, something tells me we're going to need it."

"I guess you showed them!" Mark said exultantly. "One shot—two hits! That's something to be proud of."

The flames had crawled farther up the Transcendental T by then and spread to its horizontal arms. Busso felt a tremendous sense of sadness. "No, son, it's not something to be proud of. We promised them peace—and we brought them death. I can't think of anything worse than that."

The flames continued to spread, the fire crackled, and the T lit the night.

ABOARD THE CHIEN-CHU ENTERPRISES' SUBMERSIBLE PLATFORM *SEADOWN*, APPROXIMATELY SEVEN HUNDRED MILES DUE EAST OF POLWA, IN THE OCEAN KNOWN AS THE GREAT WET.

When the meteorite arrived hundreds of thousands of years before, it was approximately a mile in diameter and traveling at around twenty-five miles per second.

As the object entered LaNor's atmosphere it became a huge fireball. But that incarnation lasted for little more than a few seconds before the meteorite plunged into the ocean, slammed into the bottom, and exploded with a force equivalent to a magnitude 11 quake.

After the monumental impact, and the destruction it caused, a thirty-foot-high Tsunami raced outward to fling itself up onto every shoreline it could reach.

Enormous amounts of material were blown high into the atmosphere where they formed a thick layer of dust and ash that acted to block the sun. The surface temperature fell almost immediately, killing plant and animal species worldwide.

But then, as the dust started to settle, temperatures began to rise. Because of the high concentration of carbon dioxide and nitrous oxides in the atmosphere, LaNor felt the impact of the greenhouse effect.

Thanks to the materials Chien-Chu had studied en route to LaNor, and reviewed on the *Seadown*, he knew that the impact had been felt for thousands of years, eventually leading to the extinction of some species and the success of others.

Now, more than seven hundred feet below the surface of the Great Wet, the cyborg skimmed over the surface of the debris field that began at the edge of the vast impact crater and stretched for hundreds of miles in every direction. And, while the industrialist was aware that the meteorite had robbed

LaNor of certain assets, he knew that it had gifted the planet with others.

Among them were rare elements such as cerium, lanthanium, and europium, which, along with other members of the lanthanide family, were used to manufacture air cars, industrial ceramics, specialized glass products, high-tech electronics, exotic metals, and advanced medical devices.

The deposits were there all right, passing below his scooter's belly, that much was clear. The only question was whether the concentrations of rare elements were high enough to make a commercial operation feasible. In order to do so it would be necessary to harvest the minerals, process them, and ship the final product off-planet. Assuming the LaNorian government would agree to some sort of licensing arrangement which was far from certain.

All of that would have to wait, however, since Chien-Chu faced other more pressing issues. The first of these had to do with a robot nicknamed "Freddie." The robot had been on a survey run, using his sonar and other sensors to create a highly detailed topographical map, when the machine suffered an on-board malfunction, sent a distress call, and dropped off-line. Nothing had been heard from him since.

Chien Chu, in his role as Jim James, Les Foro, and a cyborg named Cindy Woo had been dispatched to find the machine and rescue him. All three of the borgs were equipped with bodies that could handle pressures down to one thousand feet. They had no need for oxygen beyond that already contained within their "hulls," no need for protection against the cold other than their own internal power sources, and no need for protective outerwear other than the form-fitting black suits designed to protect them against "skin" abrasions.

Some fairly large carnivores called the Great Wet home, so the submersible scooters were armed, as were the cyborgs themselves. Three powerful headlights drilled holes into the stygian darkness as the divers approached the area where Freddie had gone off-line.

There were plenty of undocumented life-forms in the depths, which left the off-worlders free to assign their own unofficial names to the creatures they encountered.

One such animal, a ferocious-looking beast with a large head and a long sinuous body crossed through the tunnels of light, gave a contemptuous flick of its tail, and disappeared into the gloom.

Other less threatening denizens of the deep could be seen out along the margins of the light. They were numerous but less dense than the marine populations found five hundred feet above where the sunlight fed billions of tiny photovores, who fed millions of fish, who fed a smaller number of carnivores, and so forth.

"Okay," Foro said, his voice coming over Chien-Chu's built-in radio, "this is the spot. Bring up the grid, search the section assigned to you, and stay in contact. Holler if you see anything of interest."

Chien-Chu and Wu acknowledged the orders, checked their positions relative to the search grid superimposed over their electronic "vision," and went to work.

The industrialist directed the elongated circle of light toward the ocean's bottom, activated both sidelights, and cruised toward the west. A forest of what looked like white tulips waved at him from below, each seeking to inhale as many of the waterborne microscopic organisms as they could, seemingly unaffected by the passing lights.

Soon after that the texture of the bottom seemed to change, the tulips disappeared, and a field of growth-encrusted tektites, or what Chien-Chu guessed were tektites, came into view. There were thousands of globular shapes, interspersed with what the industrialist thought of as flower gardens, where colonies of reclusive bivalves lived, their bright, ribbonlike tongues stabbing up to snare tiny fish and pull them down below the surface of the sand where they could be digested.

After about ten minutes had passed, the bottom dropped

away, the scooter's lights fell into a vast nothingness, and it became impossible to see.

Chien-Chu fired the scooter's retros, coasted to a stop, and took a moment to check his readouts. The number glowed red: 778 feet. That's how far he was below the surface. "James to Foro . . . Over."

"I read you . . . Go. Over."

"The bottom fell out . . . I plan to follow the cliff down. Over."

"Roger, that. Stay in touch. Out."

Chien-Chu twisted the throttle, pushed the control sticks forward, and allowed the machine to take him down. Little bits of something sparkled in the lights as they swirled up past the cyborg's face. Jagged though it was, ever-inventive life-forms had evolved to live on it, their flat, leaflike organs stretched wide to catch both the nutrients that rained down from above and the tiny bit of light necessary to process them.

And it was then, just as Chien-Chu passed the 875-foot mark, that a weak signal came over his onboard receiver. Freddie was somewhere below!

James to Foro . . . Over."

"Go. Over."

"I've got a signal . . . It's weak but steady. Over."

"Outstanding! How deep? Over."

"I'm at 875. Over."

"Okay . . . proceed to 975 and call in. Wu and I are on the way . . . Over."

Chien-Chu knew that another hundred feet would place him just twenty-five feet shy of his official limit. Close . . . but acceptable. "Roger, that. Over."

The cyborg pushed the scooter into a nose-over and rode it downward. The signal grew louder, but not that much louder, and it was clear that the robot was still some distance farther down by the time that Chien-Chu hit the 975 mark. James to Foro . . . Over."

"Go, James."

"I'm at 975 . . . Still no Freddie . . . Am preparing to ascend. Over."

Suddenly, without a word of introduction, Boad crashed the frequency. Like his body, the cyborg's voice was big and intrusive. "This is Boad . . . Belay that ascent. The official limit on your hull is 1,000 feet, but it was built to handle 1,250, or that's what you claimed when you applied for the job. Now get your ass down there and find that robot. It's on the books for 250,000 credits, and I want it back."

Chien-Chu gave the mental equivalent of a sigh. He had hoped to delay the moment of confrontation for another couple of days. Clearly that wouldn't be possible.

The cyborg brought another radio on-line, formulated a message, and bounced if off the small spaceship that remained in orbit above LaNor. A signal was received on the *Seadown*, programs were altered, and changes rippled through every system on the ship. The entire process took five seconds, which though not very long, was more than sufficient to elicit Boad's anger. "I gave you an order goddamn it, and I want a reply!"

"Okay," Chien-Chu said, directing his scooter up toward the shimmer above, "here's your reply . . . My name is Sergi Chien-Chu, Maylo Chien-Chu's uncle, and I own the *Seadown*. None of my cyborgs will be allowed to make that dive. Not only is the potential recovery not worth the risk, we have other machines for that sort of thing, and I couldn't care less about the money. Oh, and one other thing, *you're fired*."

The response was swift and violent. "Fired? *Fired?* We'll see who's fired! I'm going to rip that box out of your head, run your brains through a blender, and feed the results to the fish!"

There was more of the same, but the comments tapered off after Boad made an attempt to lock the swimmers out, discovered that he no longer had the authority to do so, and flew into a rage. A single blow from the platform manager's fist was sufficient to destroy the comp on his desk, a swipe from one powerful arm leveled a cyborg who happened to be out in the corridor, and a kick from a steel-toed boot shattered the computer-controlled mechanism that provided access to the *Seadown*'s arms locker.

Then, having armed two of his toadies with automatic weapons, Boad made his way down to lock P-1, entered, and waited for his rebellious employee to return. It appeared that Jim James, or whoever the bastard actually was, had some pull. But that didn't mean shit, not on a planet like LaNor, not if you wound up dead.

The problem was that decision to wait in P-1 turned out to be a mistake. Chien-Chu, who was still en route to the Seadown, made use of the newly established data link to access the submersible's security system, "saw" where Boad was hiding, and used an authorization code to secure both of the lock's doors. Later, after the ex-employee tired of his cell, he would be transferred to other quarters.

Together with his two companions, the industrialist made his way to lock P-2, entered, cycled through, and took command of the ship. A battle had been fought . . . and a battle had been won. Now, barring the unexpected, it was time for a nap.

THE FOREIGN CITY OF MYS, ON THE INDEPENDENT PLANET OF LANOR

Given the paucity of things to do on LaNor, the off-worlders had become adept at providing their own entertainment. There were dinners, parties, and even balls, some of which became quite rowdy once the participants had consumed enough stimulants or depressants.

This particular gathering promised to be a little less rambunctious, however, given the fact that the guests of honor were all part of the multinational relief force slated to depart first thing in the morning.

The mostly LaNorian band was already warming up, and Santana could hear the faint strains of music through the open windows as he made his way down the gleaming hall, paused in front of the door marked CAPTAIN DRIK SEEBA-KA, and knocked three times. He heard the Hudathan say, "Enter!" opened the door, and took three steps forward. "Sir! Second Lieutenant Antonio Santana reporting as ordered, sir!"

Seeba-Ka was seated behind his desk. He nodded. "At ease, Lieutenant, take a load off. Would you like a drink? I tested this stuff on another member of your race and he survived."

Santana eyed the large brown jug with the Hudathan markings. There was no telling what sort of poison might lie within but there was only one possible reply. "Sir, yes sir."

Seeba-Ka offered the Hudathan equivalent of a smile, poured three fingers of amber liquid into a dirty glass, and passed it over. Then, having dispensed a full glass for himself, the Hudathan raised it into the air. "Camerone!"

Santana echoed the toast, took a sip of the fiery liquid, and felt it slide down his throat. There was an explosion of warmth when the substance hit bottom and a sense of well-being as the effects spread out through the legionnaire's extremities. Then, inspired by the first toast, Santana offered a second. "Blood!"

The single word, uttered within a military context, served Hudathans as a toast, a war cry, and a statement of solidarity. Seeba-Ka nodded his appreciation, raised his glass, and said "Blood!" The container was empty when he slammed it down.

"So," the Hudathan said as he poured another dollop of liquor into both of the glasses, "let's formulate a battle plan."

"Battle plan? I don't understand."

"I know," Seeba-Ka replied patiently, "that's why you need a plan. First, let's review the strategic situation. For reasons we won't dwell on the command structure decided to create an abomination and call it a multinational relief force.

"Then, based on specious logic, they placed this abomination under the command of a bug, who may or may not be working with the enemy.

"Finally, having screwed everything else up, and not having done their homework to begin with, they chose *you* as executive officer (XO). A rather questionable assignment given the past conflict between you and the aforementioned bug, but a decision that lies well within the bounds of their authority."

Santana started to say something but the Hudathan raised an enormous hand. "Hold your fire, soldier. When the sitrep is over you'll be the first to know.

"Now, where was I? Oh yes, the command structure for your little walk in the woods. Were this just the two of you, a bug and what we Hudathans often refer to as a squat, everything would be fine. The two of you could kill each other, and LaNor would be a better place to live.

"Unfortunately, there are others involved including a squad of cloned squats, a squad of fur balls, and, ancestors help me, a squad of my own legionnaires."

Seeba-Ka stood at that point, placed a pair of gigantic fists on the top of his desk, and leaned forward. "The point is that they deserve outstanding leadership *regardless* of the errors made at the command level, *regardless* of your emotions, and *regardless* of interspecies politics. You will take care of *all* of the soldiers under your command or pay the price . . . Do you read me?"

Santana met the other officer's coal black eyes. "Sir, yes sir."

"Good," Seeba-Ka said, falling back into his high-backed chair. "Now, let's review the ops plan . . . The Landing Zone (LZ), also known as the Strathmore Hotel's ballroom, is located deep within enemy-held territory. Once on the ground you will establish a defensive perimeter and prepare to receive the enemy. Diplomats, soldiers, and yes, human females will attack from all directions. Hold your ground, try not to say anything stupid, and wait for extraction."

Santana grinned at the Hudathan's heavy-handed humor. "Sir! Yes sir!"

Seeba-Ka raised his glass. "Camerone!"

"Camerone!"

Both officers drained their glasses in a single gulp, straightened their ties, and left for the ball.

In spite of the fact that the Strathmore Hotel had been

constructed by a human along the lines of hotels on his native planet, a great deal of thought had gone into the needs and preferences of other species as well.

Vanderveen entered the establishment through a door so enormous that it could accommodate even the largest Hudathan, climbed risers so low that they would be comfortable for even the shortest Thraki, passed under beams so high that a Prithian could perch on them, and was shown into a ballroom that while large also featured nooks and alcoves where small groups could gather and the Hudathan ambassador could press his back against a sturdy wall.

The room featured high vaulted ceilings, three glittering chandeliers, a wooden dance floor, a side platform where the band had already started to play, and a stage on which amateur theatricals, voice recitals, and other entertainments were sometimes held. On this occasion it was empty with the exception of a podium and a mike.

Vanderveen exchanged greetings with Ishimoto-Forty-Six, Ambassador for Clone Hegemony, along with several members of his largely identical support staff before moving on to say hello to Dogon Doko-Sa, who in his role as the Hudathan ambassador was also the ranking military officer on LaNor, since his race made no distinction between the two functions.

Then, as the human diplomat continued to move toward the band, she ran into the diminutive Fynian Isu Hybatha, the Thraki ambassador, and three members of her staff, including Flight Warrior Garla Try Sygor and some of her subordinate officers.

A little farther on Vanderveen paused to warble a carefully practiced greeting to the brightly plumed Prithian diplomat named Sca Sor. He trilled in delight and patted her on the back. He had a yellow beak, and his eyes bulged with emotion. "Very good, my dear! Much better than last time. Before long we will equip you with wings and set you free over Prithia!"

It was his favorite jest where Vanderveen was concerned—and one the Prithian had made use of on two previous occasions. The diplomat laughed, accepted a glass from a passing waiter, and continued on her way. A quick glance was sufficient to establish that Santana was nowhere to be seen. An area of interest she was only barely willing to admit to.

In keeping with the diversity of their audience, the band had been forced to master a broad repertoire of musical traditions many of which required them to make use of synthethizers. Now, as they launched into a Thraki standard, "Flight to Freedom," Harley Clauson could be heard playing the trumpet.

Sweat poured off the FSO's face as he funneled air into the instrument, each note ringing loud and clear. The truth was that while Clauson made a better horn player than a diplomat—he was too regimented in the way he played to succeed as a professional.

Vanderveen waited for the piece to reach its crashing crescendo, led the applause, and saw the pleasure on Clauson's face. Then, having exchanged a few words, the diplomat turned to survey the room for the second time. A cluster of uniforms immediately caught her eye. Some were bright, like the Prithian officer's combination of blue plumage and gold accoutrements, and some were relatively plain, like the four-button olive green jackets that the legionnaires wore, each set off with touches of red. Of even greater interest was one uniform in particular that worn by Lieutenant Tony Santana. Vanderveen allowed herself to drift in his direction.

In spite of the fact that they had fought on opposite sides on Beta-018, and the other officer was a bit pompous, Santana liked Flight Warrior Garla Try Sygor, and had just finished listening to one of her hilarious flying stories, when someone touched his arm.

The legionnaire turned to discover that Major Miraby was standing next to him—along with none other than Force Leader Hakk Batth. Now, having been briefed by Seeba-Ka, Miraby's manner was conciliatory. "Well, I understand that you two know each other, so I won't bother with introductions.

The relief force is fortunate to be led by two such experienced officers. I'm sure you'll make all of us proud."

Santana looked into the Ramanthian's huge compound eyes and saw nothing but hatred. When Hakk Batth spoke the words were deliberately provocative. "Assuming that Lieutenant Santana does what he's told—I'm sure everything will go well."

Blood rushed to Santana's face, his heart beat faster, and he took a deep breath. Then, just as the officer was about to speak, Vanderveen pushed her way in between Miraby and Batth. "Sorry, but this *is* a ball, and Lieutenant Santana owes me a dance. Lieutenant?"

Santana swallowed the words, let the breath out, and managed an answer. The words were stiff and rigid. "Yes, that's right."

Vanderveen literally pulled Santana away from the other officers and guided him toward the dance floor. Other couples, humans mostly, were already on it. The band was playing something slow—for which Santana was extremely grateful. His body remembered the dance lessons received at the academy even if his conscious mind did not. Vanderveen seemed to float into his arms and melt against his body. Her perfume surrounded him like an intoxicating cloud and Santana was struck by how beautiful the diplomat was. "Thank you."

Vanderveen looked up into the soldier's face. "For what?"

"For pulling me out of there before I made a complete ass of myself."

"That's what the diplomatic corps is for," Vanderveen said lightly, "besides, I love to dance, and you're pretty good for a soldier."

"I owe you nonetheless," Santana insisted, "and an officer pays his debts."

"I'm glad to hear that," Vanderveen replied mischievously, "because the opportunity may come as early as tomorrow."

"The relief force is leaving tomorrow."

"I know; I'm going with it."

Santana frowned, missed a step, and recovered. *"Going? Why?"*

"You remember Mee Mas . . ."

"Yes."

"He sent a message. He wants another meeting and asked Ambassador Pas Rasha to send me."

It was an important opportunity for Vanderveen, a chance to break out of Mys and do the kind of work she had always wanted to do, but Santana missed that and focused on the military aspect of things instead. "I don't think you should go . . . It would be dangerous during the best of times and even more so now. Besides, Hakk Batth is unreliable, and capable of damned near anything."

Vanderveen stopped, took a full step backward, and stared up into Santana's face. Her cheeks were flushed with anger. *"Dangerous?* Do you honestly believe that I joined the diplomatic corps because I thought it would be *safe?* And who the hell do you think you are anyway? My *father?* As for Hakk Batth, a board of inquiry decided to demote *you* rather than him, something you would do well to remember."

Santana was still in the process of trying to formulate an answer when the diplomat turned on her heel and walked away. There was a speech after that, not to mention applause, but the evening was over. Santana returned to the barracks, checked to ensure that his legionnaires were prepped, and hit the rack. There were dreams—and all of them were bad.

THE TOWN OF BAL TEE, ON THE INDEPENDENT PLANET OF LANOR

Located as it was at the point where two muddy rivers joined together, the town of Bal Tee had started out as little more than a fishing camp hundreds of years before, evolved into a village, and eventually made the transition to a full-fledged town.

The houses, all of which had been dug into the long sloping

hillside, were made of wood and stood shoulder to shoulder so that one wall could serve two dwellings.

The main thoroughfare was paved with locally fired blue-black bricks, each placed on edge to make the surface thicker, with river sand to fill all the joints. The street started down by the docks, switchbacked up through the town, and ended at the cemetery up on top of the hill.

Now, as hundreds of farmers arrived in Bal Tee for market day, the street delivered them into the level area located halfway up the hill where dozens of stalls had been set up. Brightly colored clothing hung from lines that crisscrossed the street, animals peered out of cleverly woven cages, mouth-watering odors emanated from small braziers, apothecaries crouched within their knee stalls, youngsters chased each other through the crowd, and the Claw set up shop.

The adherents of the Tro Wa were much practiced by then, having put on the same show in many villages prior to Bal Tee, and wasted little time erecting the portable platform on which martial arts demonstrations would take place, the spirit dancers would whirl, and the orators would weave their many tales. Eventually, when the sun finally set, at least ten initiates would be led away to begin their new lives.

Meanwhile, as the crowd continued to filter in from the countryside, three males strode among them. In spite of the fact that they were dressed plainly all of them stuck out. First because of the way they held themselves; second because they bore no burdens; and third because no females walked beside them. One was more noticeable than the rest, however, primarily because of his size. He walked at the center of the group, made occasional use of a staff, and wore long, curved fingernails.

Heads turned, people looked, and most turned away. But a few, those who had met Lak Saa on previous occasions, knew him for who he was: the leader of the Claw. Such individuals brought the tips of their fingers together and nodded. These movements were so subtle as to be barely noticeable to anyone not trained to look for them.

The eunuch saw the gestures of respect, however, took pleasure in the extent to which his support had grown over the last month, and followed an assistant into the town's largest bakery.

The threesome passed through the service area, where customers had queued up to buy freshly baked kas cakes, through the bakery, where hot wall ovens glowed, and through the door beyond. Should Imperial spies be watching the town, as they no doubt were, it would be difficult to keep track of how many individuals entered the shop, how long they stayed, and who they were.

Now, well within the hillside itself, the Tro Wa passed bins filled with various types of grain, waited for an adolescent to pull a section of shelving out of the way, ducked through a low doorway, and entered a hidden sanctuary. The cave had been occupied long before the village had come into existence and the ceiling was black with ancient smoke. A single hole remained open to the sky far above, providing both access for the single shaft of sunlight that splashed the wooden tabletop and the space with ventilation.

The table had been a large cartwheel at one time and still bore the marks of hard service. A single male sat on the far side of it, his face set in rigid lines. The reason for his discomfort was plain to see. The peasant's hands, which were palm down, had been nailed to the tabletop. The heads of the chunky hand-forged spikes could still be seen protruding above the level of his skin. The gray wood was red with his blood.

The individual's name was Nah Hee. He was chief of a village that lay one day's walk to the north. His eyes widened when he saw Lak Saa enter, he tried to stand, but was unable to do so without pulling the nails out through his flesh.

Lak Saa ignored the chieftain, took a seat at the table, and waited for a young female to fetch a pot of tea. Then, once his spirit had been soothed, the eunuch was ready to proceed.

Nah Hee, who was in agony, had little choice but to sit and watch as more than two dozen peasants, shopkeepers, and minor nobility were ushered into the cave, given their instructions, and dismissed. He knew each of them would not only be intimidated by the sight of his predicament, but would describe the sight to others, thereby communicating the fear.

Finally, after hours of such torture, the last visitor was shown out of the cave, and it was Nah Hee's turn to have an audience with Lak Saa. "So," the eunuch said slowly, "you prefer the company of hill bandits to that of the Tro Wa."

"No, Excellency," Nah Hee said desperately, "never!"

Lak Saa thrust one of his razor-sharp six-inch-long fingernails out into the light and examined it for flaws. "Then why," the eunuch asked mildly, "were hill bandits seen to enter your house?"

"They came to *me*," Nah Hee replied, "during the night. There were a dozen maybe more . . . My wife and I had little choice but to let them in."

"So you say," Lak Saa said cynically, "though it's my experience that individuals such as yourself will say almost anything to avoid pain. Tell me—do your hands hurt?"

"Yes, Excellency," Nah Hee answered truthfully, "they hurt a great deal."

"I'm sure that they do," Lak Saa said sympathetically. "Still, what you presently feel is nothing when compared to what you would experience if my assistants were to skin you alive. Now, with that reality in mind, tell me what these hill bandits had to say."

Nah Hee nodded eagerly. "They said that the people of my village should align themselves with the hill tribes rather than the Empress or the Tro Wa. They said a new leader has emerged, a person with a legitimate claim to the throne, who will lead all of us to freedom."

"And did they name this paragon of virtue?" the eunuch inquired softly.

The chieftain shook his head. "No, Excellency, they did not. I asked, but they refused to tell me."

Lak Saa considered what he had heard. The information provided by Nah Hee was consistent with what had been learned elsewhere. The hill bandits were looking for support among the lowland villages. Something they had never attempted before.

As for the mysterious leader, well, that part was easy. After years of talking about high-flown concepts like democracy, it now appeared that Mee Mas was ready to do something about it. The question was whether he was using the bandits or they were using him. "Interesting," Lak Saa said noncommittally, "very interesting. Was there anything else?"

"Yes," Nah Hee said, eager to earn favor. "Every single one of the bandits wore turbans made of Pur Lor green."

In spite of the fact that his face remained impassive Lak Saa felt a rising sense of excitement. The village of Pur Lor was known for many things, including the fine green fabric that came off its looms, the fact that the hill tribes were known to trade there, and the Palace of the Mist. It wasn't large as palaces go, a mere summer residence, one of many the Emperor had constructed. Mee Mas had spent many a youthful summer there and knew the area well.

Was he assuming too much? Possibly, but maybe, just maybe, an important blow could be struck. The eunuch nodded. "You have a keen eye . . . and an honest tongue. Be careful of who you spend time with lest both be plucked from your head."

Lak Saa turned to an assistant. "Release Nah Hee, see to his wounds, and provide him with five loaves of bread for his family."

The eunuch waited until the grateful chieftain had been ushered out of the cave, summoned one of his assistants, and gave the necessary orders. "Send word to the cell near Pur Lor . . . Tell them to watch for the Imperial nephew by both day and night. If he comes, as I believe he will, they are to lay waste to the village and the Palace of the Mist. Mee Mas is to die and every effort must be made to ensure that the hill bandits receive the blame. Am I clear?"

The assistant bowed. "Yes, Eminence."

A runner was dispatched—and death stalked the land.

THE FOREIGN CITY OF MYS, ON THE INDEPENDENT PLANET OF LANOR

Thanks to the fact that the vast majority of the off-world community had partied well into the wee hours, and were therefore still in bed, it was left to the LaNorian street sweepers, many of whom were spies, to see the relief force off.

Aircraft, like the cybernetic fly-forms normally employed by the Legion, could have ferried the troops into position in a matter of hours rather than days, but the use of such technology outside of certain carefully proscribed locations and situations was forbidden by both Confederate regulations and Imperial decree. That meant the troops had little choice but to make the trip using more primitive means.

The column, if such a term could be used to describe the assemblage of loosely grouped animals, clumps of off-world personnel, and the mismatched carts assigned to accompany them had assembled itself in front of the Ramanthian embassy, where it now awaited the order to depart.

The relief force consisted of thirty-nine souls in all. Not a large number—but considered sufficient given the power of their offensive weaponry.

The group was led by three heavily armed Ramanthian warriors in company with a harried-looking representative from the Imperial government, followed by Force Leader Hakk Batth along with six additional warriors, all on reptilian mounts.

Directly behind the Ramanthians were nine Clones, all on foot, two cartloads of Thraki infantry, none of whom would have been able to keep up had they been ordered to walk, the cart assigned to carry Christine Vanderveen, two heavily burdened supply wagons, and Santana's legionnaires.

Not only were they to walk, they had been assigned to walk drag. Batth's orders had been quite specific in that regard and it didn't take much imagination to figure out why. The column included some sixteen razbuls, each of which would generate up to 120 pounds' worth of feces per day. That meant that the Clones, having only ten animals in front of them, could expect to walk through approximately 1,200 pounds of shit during a twelve-hour march, while the legionnaires, back at the very end of the line, would be forced to deal with nearly a ton of manure. An indignity which was far from accidental . . . but one Batth could easily justify.

Military doctrine called for the two officers to be separated should the column be cut in half—not to mention the fact that Santana commanded the single cyborg that Miraby that had agreed to release. Still another decision which could be justified by the need to protect the column's six and the wagons loaded with supplies.

In spite of the fact that Batth had done nothing to rectify the fact that the weapons issued to his troops were incompatible with those possessed by the Thrakies, which were different from those carried by the humans, he *had* taken steps to ensure that all the com gear was compatible, which meant that Santana and his troops heard the order to move out at the same time everyone else did.

In spite of the fact that he could have climbed up onto Snyder's back and ridden the T-2 all day, the platoon leader was determined to walk with his troops. The razbul manure was meant for *him* and the least he could do was deal with the same unpleasantness that they had to.

Santana waited for the last supply cart to jerk into motion, managed to sidestep a large pile of steaming green dung, and began what promised to be a long and unpleasant journey. Thankfully the weather was good and there was no need for the troops to carry more than their weapons, ten spare magazines, and two days' worth of rations. The rest of their gear was loaded on the second supply wagon located directly in front of them. A discipline Santana insisted on.

Two carts farther up the column Vanderveen nearly spilled hot tea on herself as the LaNorian driver slapped his razbul into motion and the cart surged forward. The diplomat swore, took a quick sip of tea to lower the level in her mug, and felt a strange cocktail of emotions. Excitement regarding the opportunity to actually do something, fear lest she commit some sort of error, and a feeling of regret where the nearly nonexistent relationship with Santana was concerned.

Sure, it would have been nice if the legionnaire had been more understanding where *her* feelings were concerned, but she had been equally if not even more insensitive to his situation.

Still, there wasn't much she could do about it, not at the moment anyway, so the FSO settled back into the cushions purchased for the trip, threw her boots up onto the front partition, and resolved to enjoy the journey to whatever extent she could. Vanderveen looked out through the left window, saw the Clone embassy's sterile facade drift by, and knew the column would soon leave the confines of Mys.

Even farther forward, up where the Imperial guide hurled imprecations at the guards, Force Leader Hakk Batth considered the long mostly thankless task ahead. The column would never reach its destination, that much was certain, but he had worries nevertheless.

Thanks to skillful negotiations on the part of his lifemate, Regar Batth, neither the Hudathans nor the Prithians were represented in the column, but the Clones were, and they, plus the legionnaires, could be expected to fight. To save their own skins if nothing else. Something he could hardly prevent them from doing. That's why timing and coordination would be so crucial. *Yes,* the Ramanthian concluded, *even treachery requires a certain amount of skill.* The thought pleased him and something only a fellow Ramanthian would have recognized as a smile flitted across his face.

The gate creaked open, the column crept onto the northern

plain, and Imperial troops parted to let them pass. Harness bells tinkled, carts creaked, and a razbul passed gas. The relief force was on its way.

The first day stretched long and hard as the multinational relief force marched first to the north, and then to the east, each step taking it farther from Mys and the neighboring city of Polwa. As the outlying villages fell behind, and the air started to clear, the road wound its way between tiny lowland farms, carefully maintained woodlots, and scarcely populated pastures.

Their carts, plus thousands of others that contributed to LaNorian commerce, had worn deep ruts in the dirt road. For that reason progress was measured by sighting the workers that Santana thought of as "road men," each being employed by the government, and having responsibility for a three-mile stretch of road.

The essence of the job was to prevent the ruts from going so deep that the average cart would find itself high-centered on the ridge in between, keep the many bridges in good repair, and assist any travelers who might require help. No small task but a crucial one if food was to make its way into Polwa, if manufactured goods were to reach the provinces, and should Imperial troops need to move from one place to another in a short period of time.

Some of the road men were more industrious than others, as could be seen and felt as the column traversed three miles of well-kept road, while others had a tendency to slack off as evidenced by deep ruts and unrepaired storm damage.

There were other ways to mark the journey as well, including the compact-looking fortresses that squatted on the higher hills, walled villages that closed their gates at dusk, isolated farmhouses that lay in ruins, groves of "spirit" trees planted by an emperor long dead, bargelike ferries on which the carts were forced to ride, and all manner of traffic both rich and poor.

But if the off-worlders were looking at the countryside the countryside was also looking at *them*. Entire villages turned out to stare at bugs mounted on razbuls, a group of identical aliens, furries who rode in carts, and, most fantastic of all, the machine that brought up the rear.

Most simply stared, but some of the braver souls shouted Claw-inspired threats, or threw rocks many of which were directed at the T-2. Metal clanged as the missiles struck and bounced off Snyder's armor. A mostly harmless activity so long as the incoming objects were stones rather than grenades.

However, when some of the rocks started to strike flesh rather than metal, Santana waited for Batth to issue orders of some sort, and hearing none, authorized the cyborg to mark the worst offenders with a targeting laser. The villagers pointed at each other as the red dots appeared, screamed, and ran for the safety of their houses.

Still, in spite of the overt hostility expressed by the La-Norian villagers, Santana failed to see any sign that Claw cadres were out and about. He believed that he could *feel* them however, peering at the column from distant clumps of trees, while tracking the off-worlders' progress. Or was that his imagination? There was no way to tell.

The column paused for a brief lunch and was back on the road thirty minutes later. The legionnaire had seen Vanderveen leave the privacy of the cart to stretch her legs but made no attempt to approach her. Now, having had time to reflect on the evening's interchange, Santana realized that what he saw as little more than a threat to his troops the diplomat saw as an opportunity to do what she'd been trained for.

Still, that was the second time she had used his military record as a way to strike back at him, and *once* had been more than enough.

The afternoon passed much as the morning had with one notable exception. The relief force had just topped a rise, and was about to descend into a valley, when they heard the long lonely scream of a steam whistle and turned toward the sound. They saw a pair of shiny north–south tracks and telltale puffs of smoke as the heavily burdened locomotive made its way up a grade and hove into sight. Though a lot more streamlined than its ancient ancestors, and a good deal more efficient, the basic technology was pretty much the same. Something which off-world corporations were forced to accept in return for the right to operate on a Class III world.

The train, which consisted of the locomotive plus twenty cars loaded with newly mined coal, made a distinctive *chuga, chuga, chuga* sound as it passed in front of the relief force, whistled by way of a greeting, and disappeared to the south.

Vanderveen thought about Mee Mas as her cart bumped over the tracks and followed the road up the slope beyond. A whiff of smoke blew in through the window. Assuming that the Imperial nephew was sincere, he envisioned railroads that crisscrossed the country, prosperity for all, and a democratic form of government. Was that realistic? Would it truly be good? The government she was sworn to represent thought that it would be. She hoped they were right.

Eventually, as the sun fell toward the western horizon, and even the razbuls began to tire, Batth finally called a halt. Then, climbing a hill to the ruins of an ancient fortress, the Ramanthian ordered his troops to make camp. The relief force was well short of the point that Batth had optimistically designated as way point one . . . but no one chose to complain.

Santana, who approached the Ramanthian looking for orders, was dismissed with a contemptuous, "Do what you're supposed to do," and left to his own devices.

The legionnaire found the Ramanthian's low-key almost negligent manner to be more than a little surprising especially in light of his experiences on Beta-018 where no detail had been too small for Batth to comment on.

Now, as the relief force placed sensors around the perimeter, sited defensive weaponry, and prepared to settle in for the night, it was as if Batth was simply going through the motions. In fact, it was almost as if the Ramanthian *knew* there was nothing to be concerned about. But that was impossible—or should have been.

But Santana couldn't forget the night when the Ramanthian named Poth Dusso had deserted his post on the south wall, and Corporal Wu had been murdered. That's why he stopped by to have a few words with Platoon Sergeant Quickfoot Hillrun prior to continuing on his rounds.

With no instructions to the contrary, the various NCOs had automatically left their various commands intact, with each group assuming responsibility for one segment of the perimeter. As Santana circled the hill he discovered that while the Clones had positioned command-detonated mines in front of their position, and placed two crew-served automatic weapons behind what remained of a stone wall, the Thrakies were a good deal less prepared.

That didn't come as a total surprise since Santana had fought against the Thrakies on Beta-018 and knew their recent history. Every Thraki on LaNor had been born on a spaceship and spent most of their youth there. So, with the exception of those who had seen combat on the Clone worlds, the Thrakies knew more about the theory of ground combat than they did the reality of it.

Thus, the diminutive aliens had placed their positions so close together that a single grenade could kill half their number, neglected to put any backup ammo next to their firing positions, and seemed oblivious to the way in which their bodies would soon be silhouetted against the bonfire they had built.

They were well intentioned however, and a few words with L-8 Fortho, their senior NCO, were sufficient to put matters right.

Rather than inspect the part of the perimeter for which the Ramanthians had responsibility, and potentially wind up in some sort of confrontation with Batth, Santana instructed Snyder to orient herself in that direction and sweep the entire area with her powerful sensors.

Then, confident that he'd done the best he could, Santana went in search of something to eat. This being the first night out, his legionnaires had prepared the usual "first feast," which consisted of a large kettle of stew into which all manner of things had been tossed. The result was questionable, but still better than the field rations they would subsist on from that point forward.

Vanderveen was invited to join in the meal and nodded to Santana as she took her place on the opposite side of the fire. There were all of the usual stories, toned down out of respect for the diplomat, followed by a heartfelt rendition of "Le Boudin" just as others had sung for hundreds of years before them.

Then, having checked most of the perimeter one last time, Santana brushed his teeth and slipped into his sleeping bag. The officer made one last check to ensure that his radio was not only on, but tuned to the command channel, and almost instantly fell asleep. It felt like little more than two minutes later when a voice whispered next to his ear. "Lieutenant, it's me, Hillrun."

Santana opened his eyes, saw Hillrun silhouetted against one of the planet's two moons, and nodded. "What's up?"

"It's the bugs, sir. We've been keeping an eye on them just like you said."

"And one of our friends went out to meet someone?"

"No sir. A dig belly-crawled up the hill, made contact with the Ramanthians, and passed through the perimeter. He's with Batth right now."

"And our Imperial guide?"

"Sound asleep."

"Interesting," Santana said softly, "*very* interesting. Record what you observed in the patrol diary . . . Add a statement from Snyder. I want this documented."

"Sir, yes sir."

"And Hillrun . . ."

"Sir?"

"Good work."

The Naa grinned, faded into the darkness, and disappeared.

• • •

Outside of the weather, which worsened overnight, the second day was a copy of the first. It began with a cold miserable breakfast, followed by four hours of off-again on-again rain, field rations for lunch, and a long, muddy afternoon.

The terrain had changed by then, becoming a little more rugged as the road followed a river west, and cliffs rose to either side.

Santana was again struck by his commanding officer's failure to send scouts ahead, a role that the razbul-mounted Ramanthians were well equipped to play, and by the general air of sloppiness which had been allowed to pervade the column.

Staff Sergeant Jonathan Alan Seebo-21,112, better known to his troops as "Sergeant Twelve," kept his clone brothers sharp, but, thanks in part to the fact that they were riding in carts, the Thrakies were anything but combat ready as they dozed under tarps, staged mock battles between the small robots that some of them carried, and generally screwed off.

As for the Ramanthians, the only communication Santana had with them was an occasional order to "March faster," and the never-ending mounds of manure their mounts left behind. Manure which the carts mixed into the mud and attempted to spray onto anyone who followed too closely.

Finally, as darkness began to close around the column, Batth called a halt. Santana didn't like the site which though close to the river featured high ground on two sides. The legionnaire offered to place flankers on top of the riverbanks but was refused.

Orders were given, a perimeter was established, and the relief force prepared to bed down for the night. Everyone was tired, especially those who had been forced to walk, and eager to get some shut-eye.

Then, just as Santana was about to eat his lukewarm meal, Batth spoke over his headset. "Lieutenant Santana, please join me in my tent."

The "please" sounded conciliatory but the legionnaire knew better than to take it seriously. He acknowledged the message, swore, and put the meal on a rock. Hillrun, who was crouched on the far side of the small fire, looked up from his food. The rain had matted the surface of his fur but his skin was warm and dry. "Some sort of problem, sir?"

Santana had come to rely on the platoon sergeant and was fairly sure that the feeling was reciprocal. He grinned. "Just the usual one . . . back in twenty. Tell Seavy to check everyone's feet. We walked in and we're sure as hell gonna have to walk out."

Private Ben Seavy was the squad's medic, and the truth was that Hillrun had already told him to check on the team's feet. But the loot was thinking, and thinking the way a good loot should, which meant it was best to go along. Check and double-check. That's how the system worked best. "Sir, yes sir."

Santana rose, considered his muddy uniform, and decided it didn't matter. There was nothing he could do that would make the Ramanthian think better of him.

It was dark by then, but the Thraks had another bonfire going, and the Ramanthians weren't much better. Battery-powered lights hung from branches like ornaments on a tree. If any of the warriors were on guard duty, Santana couldn't see them. Mud sucked at the soles of the officer's boots as he rounded a boulder, cut across a clearing, and arrived in front of Hakk Batth's six-warrior tent.

Judging from footgear lined up outside the rain flap door visitors were expected to remove their boots prior to entering. Santana sat on an ammo box, removed his boots, and tucked them in next to a smaller pair. The human frowned. Sergeant Twelve's? No, they were too small. Then, stepping through the flap, he came to attention. A portable heater hummed in a corner, something burbled on a stove, and a light hung at the tent's center. "Lieutenant Antonio Santana reporting as ordered, sir!"

Batth stood next to a table. Vanderveen sat on a crate. The Imperial stood at her side. All of them turned. It was the

Ramanthian who spoke. The tone was sarcastic. "Nice of you to drop in . . . At ease."

It was bait, but Santana refused to take it. "Sir, yes sir."

Having reasserted his authority, Batth gestured toward the comp. "Take a look at this."

Santana could feel Vanderveen's eyes on him as he took three paces forward and looked down at the screen. The image had been consolidated which meant that the Ramanthian had to be wearing special contact lenses in order to view it. All of the tags had been translated to standard. The legionnaire was careful to keep his face blank but noticed a number of things right away. This particular map was a lot more detailed than the one downloaded to him just prior to departure. And, judging from the tiny date down in the lower right hand corner, it had been updated earlier that day. A flagrant violation of the many restrictions that stemmed from LaNor's Class III status. That suggested that the Ramanthians were hoarding data, making use of illegal satellites to refresh it, and didn't care if he knew. Why?

A cursor blinked over what Santana knew to be their position. It was many miles short of the red delta that marked way point two (WP2). Still another delta, this one marking a location well beyond WP2, designated the crossroads where the off-worlders were scheduled to rendezvous with a detachment of Imperial troops prior to the attack on the village occupied hill bandits. Assuming they were there . . . which seemed doubtful. Batth used a pincer to tap on screen's surface. "Thanks to you, and the rest of your laggards, we're half a day behind schedule."

Santana frowned. "Begging your pardon sir, but the 'laggards' as you call them, have traveled 42 standard miles in 2 days. Not bad for troops on foot."

"Really?" Batth asked, the word practically dripping with venom. "Well, it happens that *my* standards are a good deal higher than yours. It's my opinion that we should have traversed a good 60 miles by now . . ."

"Still," Batth continued, "what's done is done." That being the case we have little choice but to take a short cut which will make up the difference. As you can see the road turns away from the river a few miles west of our present location, loops toward the south, and eventually swings back to resume a westerly path. By driving straight ahead, through *this* area, we can lop an entire day off our journey! A strategy that should appeal to you and your footsore slackers."

Santana stared down at the screen, noted the manner in which the river pooled into a small lake just prior to splitting into dozens of tributaries as it passed through the area marked in green, and knew he was looking at a swamp. That's why the road turned away from the river and looped south prior to turning north and west. The human chose his words with care. "Sir, no sir. Judging from the look of this map there's a swamp up ahead. Not only will it be difficult to push our troops through there, the carts are likely to bog down, and it would be a perfect place to stage an ambush. Besides, the hill bandits must know we're coming by now, so what difference does another day make? Any chance of surprising them was lost the moment we left Mys. If they want to engage us they will. If they don't, they're back in the hills by now. I recommend that we stick to the road."

"Spoken like the coward you are," Batth said caustically. "I hoped you had learned something while serving on Beta-018. Sadly, such is not the case. Your recommendation has been noted, overruled, and will eventually be forwarded to Major Miraby for possible disciplinary action. In the meantime you will prepare your troops for tomorrow's march. Having spent days in relative safety at the end of the column while my warriors led the way the time has come for you and your legionnaires to take the point. One word of disobedience, one sign of cowardice, and I will have you shot. Dismissed."

The Ramanthian's words were so twisted, so unfair, that they rendered Santana speechless. Emotions started to churn, but he forced them back . . . This was battle, a battle of wits, and the key was to remain cool. The whole situation felt like some sort of a setup. Why had Batth chosen to cast everything in such personal terms when there was no apparent reason to do so? How could Batth be so stupid as to take the column into the swamp? And why would he put the legionnaires in the point position after two days of forcing them to walk through piles of shit? Because he *expected* an ambush, that's why . . . and wanted the Legion to take the brunt of it.

Santana opened his mouth to say something, he wasn't sure what, when Vanderveen's eyes locked with his. She raised her right hand. The lamplight reflected off a small vocoder. "If it's any comfort to the lieutenant, I took the liberty of recording this conversation, including his objections to the route."

This was news to the Ramanthian, who turned to stare in her direction. She smiled sweetly. "Should the lieutenant disobey one of your orders, perform an act of blatant cowardice, or kill you in your sleep the recording will support whatever charges are filed against him."

Even though Batth was far from pleased, there was nothing he could do about the diplomat's recording, except take pleasure in the knowledge that she would soon be dead. He nodded, started to speak, but was cut off.

"And one more thing," Vanderveen said, coming to her feet, "I'd like to hear what Dob Zee has to say about this situation. Tell us, Dob Zee . . . which way do *you* think we should go?"

Though equipped with a translator, the LaNorian had found it difficult to track the nuances of the conversation, especially given the fact that the off-worlders seemed to be angry with each other. Though not eager to traipse through a swamp, he did want to end the journey quickly and return to Polwa. "The troops will be waiting for us . . . It is important to be on time."

Batth nodded as if he had known what the LaNorian would say from the very beginning. "You see? Now, I gave you an order, Lieutenant . . . You are dismissed."

Santana came to attention, delivered a salute, and received one in return. It was cold outside, not to mention wet, but he welcomed the night. It was morning that he had reason to fear—and all that could possibly follow.

The early-morning mist shivered as a momentary breeze slid between the tall celery-like trees, caused the carefully banked fire to glow a little redder, and slipped downstream. It was still dark as Platoon Sergeant Hillrun and Corporal Dietrich made their rounds. One by one Privates Taz, Kimura, Pesta, Seavy, Kashtoon, and Horo-Ba were rousted out of their sleeping bags and ordered to attend a team briefing.

There was grumbling, especially given the hour, but that was to be expected. Twenty minutes later the legionnaires were dressed and crouched around the newly invigorated fire drinking hot coffee that Dietrich ladled out of a pot. Snyder, her sensors on max, scanned the surrounding area. She had orders to notify Santana if anyone approached.

The officer was aware of the fact that anything he said might become fodder for court-martial proceedings and chose his words with extreme care. The key was to prepare his troops for what might take place without calling Batth's orders into question.

Santana crouched next to Hillrun and eyed the legionnaires around him. A couple of the troopers had been on guard duty only three hours before and they looked tired. The rest looked alert. All of them waited expectantly. "Here's the scoop," the officer said lightly. "I've got good news and bad news . . . Which do you want first?"

There was a chorus of groans. Pesta, a long, tall legionnaire with a lantern-shaped jaw, answered for all of them. "Sir, we'll take the good news first, if that's all right with you."

Santana grinned. "The good news is that you won't have to wade through half a ton of razbul shit today."

"Uh oh," Taz said pessimistically. "Why do I have a feeling that wading half a ton of shit is about to look real good?"

"Because," Santana answered, "we're taking the point."

"So?" Kashtoon inquired innocently. "What's so bad about that?"

"It happens that we're late," Santana replied carefully, "which is why Force Leader Hakk Batth decided that we should take advantage of a potential shortcut. By following the river west, through a swamp, we should gain one full day."

Something about Santana's posture, and the tone of his voice, combined to trigger Dietrich's suspicions. "No offense, sir, but is that wise? Won't the carts tend to bog down? And what about the possibility of an ambush?"

Santana nodded. "Yes, I think we may have trouble with the carts. Don't be surprised if we end up humping the critical stuff out of there. As for the ambush, well, who knows? But the possibility exists, so I want everyone on their toes. Snyder, you're the key . . . If someone is lying in wait, your sensors should pick up on them. However, assuming they know that, odds are that they'll take a crack at you first. That's why I plan to ride your six."

Servos whined as Snyder shifted her considerable weight from one blocky foot to the other. Her voice had a hard, synthesized sound. "Begging the lieutenant's pardon—but some people will do *anything* to keep their feet dry."

Everyone laughed and Hillrun took notice. He'd been with Top Santana on the day he died. The two humans had a lot in common, starting with a strong physical resemblance and extending to the way they led. Many officers, hell *most* officers, would have ordered the troops into the swamp without a word of explanation.

Others, those who were unsure of themselves, might have babbled on forever. Santana, like his father before him, knew how to walk the thin line between the two. "So," the officer finished, "listen up, keep your eyes peeled, and don't assume anything. The enemy might turn up anywhere. All right, get some chow, pack your gear, and check your weapons. Don't put anything critical on those supply carts. Everyone will carry a full combat load including three days' worth of field rats. That will be all . . . Dismissed."

The legionnaires stood, Santana headed out to have a cautionary conversation with Sergeant Twelve, and Kimura turned to Dietrich. He had a broad forehead and bright wide-set eyes. "So help me out, Corp . . . Is it me? Or was the loot trying to lay something between the lines?"

Dietrich spit into the fire. The saliva sizzled as it hit the flames. "*Trying?* Shit, what does the man have to do? Tattoo the message on your ass? Watch the bugs Kimura—watch the bugs."

Two hours later the column was under way. Dob Zee had the dubious honor of leading the way. Snyder came next, with Santana riding her back. The rest of legionnaires followed with Hillrun last.

The Clones came next, their spacing intact, ready to dive off either side of the trail should the need arise.

In spite of Santana's best efforts to warn the Thrakies without saying anything that could be construed as mutinous, they continued to hunker down in their wagons, with many going so far as to take surreptitious naps.

Vanderveen, still confined to her cart, fumed as the two-wheeled vehicle rattled along behind the Thrakies. Santana might be a bit of a xenophobe where Ramanthians were concerned, and more than a little self-centered, but he knew his military stuff. The diplomat was sure of that. So sure that she had even gone so far as to divide her luggage into two categories, the things she needed to survive and the things she could live without. That's why she sat with a day pack strapped to her back and her feet on a long, narrow fiberglass case. If the time came, no *when* the time came, Vanderveen would be ready.

Farther back, behind the side-to-side lurch of the supply wagons, Hakk Batth glanced as the device strapped to his left tool arm. Less than one standard hour. That was how long he would have to wait for the farce to end.

It was right about then that the road took a sharp turn toward the south, the column headed into the swamp, and Santana spotted the freshly cut poles. There was one to either side of the muddy trail. Each bore a skull so white that it appeared that the flesh had been boiled off. Both of them were human.

5

Religions, especially those which find the means to bridge cultures, can bind disparate races together, or pry them apart.

Mowa Sith Horobothna
Turr academic
Standard year 2227

ABOARD THE SPACE STATION *ORB I*, IN ORBIT OVER THE PLANET LONG JUMP, THE CONFEDERACY OF SENTIENT BEINGS

Thanks to its position at the very edge of the Rim, Long Jump made an excellent place to refuel, cut business deals, and have some fun. All things spacers need to do. Though half the size of space station *Halo*, which had been destroyed by the robotic Sheen many months before—*Orb I* was still quite large.

As Legion General Bill Booly followed the corridor that circled the outer edge of the wheel-shaped space station, he found himself rubbing shoulders with all manner of fellow beings, including brightly feathered Prithians, hulking Hudathans, work-worn androids, exoskeleton-clad Dwellers, cybernetic humans, and more.

Rather than his uniform, the legionnaire wore beat-up black leathers and could have been taken for a spacer, a prospector, or a smuggler. No one had recognized him, not as far as he could tell, which made for a good start.

Ships were announced, beings were paged, and audio ads

were projected into Booly's ears. "Hey, big boy," one of them began, "are you ready to party? Try Tina's on E Deck."

There was visual input, too, like the Soro Systems' "zip" ads that circled the electroactive walls, ambulatory holos like the whiskey canister strolling along to his left, and the animated deck decals that were hard to read with so many bodies in the way.

A Transcendental missionary lurched out of the crowd, her begging terminal extended in both hands, and Booly circled to the left.

A briefly glimpsed decal promised that a bank of lift tubes waited up ahead. The crowd flowed like a river, and the officer allowed a side current to carry him off to the right. His suite was located on C Deck, so the legionnaire followed a pair of Thraki merchants onto a "down" platform, and marveled at the way in which the Confederacy's onetime enemies had managed to integrate themselves into the very structure they had once attempted to destroy.

The platform coasted to a stop. Booly stepped off and entered a checkpoint where his retinas were compared to those of Lonny Fargo, a well-established smuggler with a fat bank account and a reputation for flash.

The files were identical, the man named Fargo was admitted to the "rez" deck, and directed to his suite. If felt good to escape the circuslike atmosphere of the public areas and slide into the expensive but extremely comfortable ambience maintained on D Deck.

After a relatively short walk the officer arrived in front of Suite 1010, where he peered into a reader and heard a tone followed by a loud *click*.

Booly opened the hatch-style door, felt cool air push past his face, and stepped into the semidarkened room. The lights failed to come on the way they should have, but there could be any number of reasons for that. The soldier was about to call for additional illumination when a voice called from the adjoining bedroom. "Lonny? Is that you?"

The voice was familiar, *very* familiar, and Booly grinned. "Yes, dear, how's my snugums?"

There was the sound of girlish laughter as the legionnaire half walked, half stumbled through the suite, leaving a trail of clothes behind him. Then, spotting the bed in the half-lit murk, Booly crawled up toward a mountain of white pillows. A pair of warm arms reached up to pull him down, two long slender legs wrapped themselves around his hips, and the unforgettable scent of Maylo Chien-Chu's perfume rose to fill his nostrils.

Much to Booly's enjoyment, he discovered that his wife was not only naked—but as hungry for him as he was for her. Moments later she pulled him in, took command of his body, and closed her eyes.

Then, with an intensity born of their long separation, the pace of their lovemaking increased until Maylo dug her fingernails into Booly's back, and the pleasure carried them away.

Finally, their limbs still entwined, Maylo kissed her husband's shoulder. " 'Snugums?' Where did *that* come from?"

"Hey," Booly replied jokingly, "that's the way smugglers talk to their girlfriends."

"You really need to get out a little bit more," Maylo said, "but not till I'm done with you . . . come here."

What with more lovemaking, a meal ordered from room service, and the need to catch up on each other's activities, many hours passed before the two of them were ready to tackle the mission that had brought them together on *Orb I*: Find both the *Ibutho* and the *Guerro* so that the navy could either capture the ships or blow them away. A task made more difficult in the wake of the assault on Syndicate Base 012. Always secretive, the mutineers would be even more so now that they knew the Confederacy was gunning for them, *and* the ships on which their power was based.

"So," Booly said, pulling on what he thought of as his Lonny clothes, "how's your uncle?"

Maylo, who normally wore very little makeup, painted her

mouth a little bit larger. The idea was to look like the sort of woman that a smuggler like Lonny would hang out with. "Uncle Sergi is fine as far as I know . . . He's on a Class III planet called LaNor. The company purchased some subsea mineral rights there, and he went to check things out. He loves that sort of thing even though it drives Aunt Nola nuts."

Booly had been so busy during his on-again off-again romance with Maylo that even though they were married, he had a tendency to forget that she was the president of a star-spanning corporation and a millionaire. Or was she a billionaire? He wasn't quite sure . . . But that's why she could not only afford to meet her husband on the Rim, but loan him the very thing he needed most, a beat-up spaceship.

The officer walked across the room, placed his hands on his wife's shoulders, and started to massage them. "A Class III planet? I should be surprised, but I'm not. Your uncle is the most amazing man I've ever met."

"He's pretty special," Maylo agreed, "but *you* give better back rubs. No wonder I married you—this is better than sex."

"*Better?*" Booly demanded. "So much for my male ego . . . I'll never make love again."

"I could turn you into a liar," Maylo replied, "but the process would smear my makeup. How do I look?"

Booly looked at his wife's face in the mirror. Even the extremely heavy makeup couldn't conceal her beauty. She had black hair, large almond-shaped eyes, and high cheekbones. It was a wonderful face, his favorite face, and the one that haunted his dreams. "You look like a high-class whore."

"You say the sweetest things! Now, let's get out of here before I throw you on the bed again."

Twenty minutes later the couple was down on F Deck looking out through an armored viewport. The ship beyond had been old before either one of them had been born. She looked like what she was, a clapped-out intersystem freighter that had long ago been displaced by larger, faster ships and relegated to the Rim where she was destined to live out her remaining days running supplies to isolated colonies, or ferrying less legitimate cargoes for the likes of Lonny Fargo. "So," Maylo said proudly, "there she is . . . The newly christened *Solar Princess*. What do you think?"

"She's kind of old to be a princess," Booly said dryly, "but otherwise perfect. Assuming the baling wire holds . . . and the rust keeps her together."

"Oh, she'll hang together all right," Maylo said confidently. "I made sure of that. Looks can be deceiving. She has reconditioned drives, more armament than any ship of her size should, and a reasonably clean cabin for use by the owner and his high-class whore."

Booly frowned. "You aren't coming. What about the company?"

Maylo looked into her husband's eyes. "Oh, yes I am. Even CEOs get to go on vacation. You're stuck with me. Besides, no Maylo, no ship."

Booly felt the trap close around him. He had assumed, incorrectly as it turned out, that his wife's responsibilities would force a return to Earth. Now here she was, insisting that she be allowed to come, in spite of the fact that the mission could be extremely dangerous.

The legionnaire knew he could say "no," and obtain a ship from the government, but his refusal to let her take the same risks that he did would make her angry. Which, he had to admit, was the same way *he* would feel were their positions reversed. Booly swallowed the words he wanted to say in favor of those he *should* say. "Okay, *if* you agree to wear less makeup."

Maylo knew her husband extremely well and could guess at the thoughts that ran through his mind. She grinned. "That was hard, wasn't it?"

Booly laughed. "Damned hard."

Maylo kissed him on the cheek. "The good news is that I'm worth it. Come on . . . I'll give you a tour of your ship. The owner's cabin is especially nice. I think you'll like it."

The tour lasted the better part of four hours, most of which was spent in the owner's cabin. It was small, plain, and badly in need of some fresh paint. But Maylo was correct. Booly *did* like it . . . and for reasons that had nothing to do with the decor.

THE PLANET JERICHO, THE CONFEDERACY OF SENTIENT BEINGS

The shuttle chased its own delta-shaped shadow as it flitted over the triple-canopy jungle below. Unlike so many of the planets brutalized during the course of two wars, Jericho had been spared the use of nuclear weapons and was already well on the way to rehabilitating itself. A process which the Ramanthian ambassador thoroughly approved of in light of the fact that Jericho was one of three planets his race had so recently received as reparations for the destruction inflicted by the barbarous ridge heads.

All of which was rather fortuitous given the fact that Orno's race would have been forced to *seize* some of the very same worlds had the Hudathans not been so considerate as to cleanse the planets of sentient life, lose two ensuing wars, and forfeit all rights to them.

Even now the Ramanthian diplomat could look down and see the ruins of a bombed-out city that was already partially concealed by the encroaching jungle. Later, say two hundred local years in the future, the surface of Jericho would resemble that of Hive. An orderly place where the descendants of the tercentennial birthing would grow crops on the surface, hunt within carefully maintained game preserves, and live in vast subterranean cities.

And not just on Jericho, but on two similar worlds, each of which would dominate its own planetary system and provide much needed protection for Hive, which, like a jewel at the very center of a perfectly conceived brooch, would be surrounded by lesser though still impressive gems.

Yes, Orno thought as he watched a series of glittering lakes slide under one of the shuttle's stubby wings, *luck played a role in certain aspects of the design, but the overall creation was the product of my imagination, my vision, and my skills at negotiation. Do others understand and appreciate that? No, probably not, but it makes no difference. I know—and that knowledge will sustain me even as I enter the great darkness.*

There was an announcement, the shuttle began to descend, and Orno forced himself to focus on the task at pincer. Just as the Hudathans had unintentionally assisted the Ramanthians in the past Orno hoped to trick them once again

Excellent though his skills at negotiation had proven to be the diplomat had been unable to convince the Confederacy's Senate to simply grant his race a significant portion of the now-deactivated Sheen fleet.

In fact, judging from the pace of the most recent discussions, the robotic ships were likely to remain in orbit around Arballa's sun until the next ice age wrapped Hive in a frigid embrace. But not if Orno could help it. His race needed ships, a lot of ships, to colonize planets like the one below. Now, having promised the Queen that he would steal the necessary vessels the diplomat would have to do so. More than that Orno hoped to convince the Hudathans to help him, and assuming things went well, to assume more than their share of the blame.

That was the plan anyway, but success would depend on the newest member of their ruling triad, a conservative named Horo Hasa-Ba. If the intelligence reports were correct the newcomer had dedicated himself to the full restoration of Hudathan autonomy.

A goal opposed by the formidable Doma-Sa, who, along with the cyborg named Chien-Chu, had engineered the current arrangement in which the Hudathans had surrendered their right to a deep-space navy in return for membership in the Confederacy.

Assuming the reports regarding Hasa-Ba were correct, and he *did* want to restore Hudatha to full independence, then the opportunity to seize a significant part of the Sheen fleet would be attractive indeed.

And, making the arrangement that much sweeter was the fact that a victory for Hasa-Ba would amount to a defeat for Doma-Sa, the very individual who had killed the War Orno in single combat. Death would be better of course, much better, but not even that lay outside the realm of possibility.

Satisfied that his plan made sense, and confident of his powers of persuasion, the Ramanthian allowed himself to relax.

Meanwhile, on the surface below, the vast temple of the Lords sat dozing in the sun. The ruins were enormous. *So* huge that studies carried out by human archeologists before the Hudathan wars covered less than 1 percent of the surface structure, never mind what might lie below.

A scar, lighter than the surrounding rock, showed where a missile had struck many years before, a bomb crater marked the center of a dark flower. The petals consisted of burned-out vehicles and hand-dug graves. The rest of the temple remained as it had been for thousands of years.

Inside the west end of the long rectangular structure, not far from the squat boxy shape of a Hudathan assault boat, Horo Hasa-Ba stood with folded arms. Huge figures, each physiologically different, stared down at him. The Hudathan stared back. *Who were these beings* he wondered? *And why were members of such apparently disparate races all seated together? Were they leaders of a star-spanning religion? Or, and this seemed to make more sense, had the gigantic figures been members of a political alliance similar to the Confederacy?*

Yes, Hasa-Ba said to himself, *that would make sense.* The real question, however, was not who the figures were—but who had put them out of business? Monuments if any should be constructed to honor those having the intelligence, the strength, and the determination to impose their will on others. Not losers such as those who brooded in the niches around him.

The Hudathan heard a thin, insectlike whine as the Ramanthian shuttle circled the ruins, followed by the scream of the ship's twin engines, an echoing roar as the ship swooped in through the hall's east entrance. The incoming vessel fired its retros and started to slow.

Hasa-Ba had suggested that they meet under cover, where they were less likely to be observed, but regretted the comment as the shuttle came straight at him.

Still, to move would be to show weakness, something the Hudathan was determined not to do. He remained where he was, eyes fixed on the blunt bow, until forward motion stopped, and the vessel settled onto its skids.

Hasa-Ba felt a wave of heat wash over him, waited for the engines to spool down, and made for the port side. Servos whined, a ramp extruded itself from the ship's hull, and the Ramanthian appeared. Though not especially fond of *any* alien race, the Hudathan thought that the bugs were especially ugly, and was careful to keep his face empty of all expression.

All of the intelligence reports agreed . . . The Ramanthians, and *this* Ramanthian in particular, were very dangerous indeed. In fact there was more than sufficient evidence to indicate that the bugs had aided if not actually taken part in the plot to destabilize the Confederacy by meddling with Earth's government. Later, when *that* plot failed, the bugs formed a secret alliance with the Thrakies, hoping to benefit from the ensuing chaos. All of which served to emphasize that while Ifana-Ka and Doma-Sa had been correct to cut a deal with the Confederacy, they were wrong to honor it. So long as the Hudathan people lacked their own deep-space navy they would remain vulnerable to beings like the Ramanthians.

So, assuming that the bugs were greedy enough, not to mention stupid enough, to help his race acquire thousands of ships, the Hudathan would cooperate with them.

Then, after the other members of the triad had been brought under control or removed, Hasa-Ba would treat the Ramanthians like the insects they were. He would stomp them, scrape the mess off his boots, and move on. The thought evoked the equivalent of a smile as the Hudathan moved forward to greet his coconspirator.

The ensuing conversation lasted for the better part of four local hours, and a pervasive gloom had settled into the great hall by the time the two politicians boarded their ships, and roared out into the night.

Then, once the invaders had left, the temple fell silent. The Lords, as if considering what they had heard, stared into the darkness.

6

> Nine-tenths of tactics are certain, and taught in books: but the irrational tenth is like the kingfisher flashing across the pool and that is the test of generals. It can only be ensured by instinct, sharpened by thought practising the stroke so often that at the crisis it is as natural as a reflex.
>
> T. E. Lawrence
> The Science of Guerrilla Warfare
> Standard year circa 1925

EAST OF KA SUU, ON THE INDEPENDENT PLANET OF LANOR

As the Trooper II passed between the two grinning skulls and the poles that supported them, Santana felt the swamp wrap him in a dank embrace.

Mist rose wraithlike from the soft mushy ground as the first rays of the sun found their way down through holes in canopy of leaves that served as the swamp's living roof.

It had been months since Santana had ridden a T-2, but he was a cavalry officer, and the requisite skills soon came back. The key was to relax, lean against the harness, and use his knees as shock absorbers. Then, with his hands free to hold the assault weapon, and his headset jacked into the patch panel located just behind the cyborg's neck, he could shoot, move, and communicate. The three tasks that ground pounders, even mounted ones, are paid to do.

The platoon leader flicked a switch that took him off the allied radio net and allowed him to communicate with the T-2 via intercom. A necessity if he didn't want Hakk Batth to hear. "Snyder?"

"Sir, yes sir."

"Run your sensors up to max, sort for anything with a heat signature larger than a LaNorian child, and electromechanical activity of any sort. If somebody so much as sets their watch, I want to know about it."

The cyborg was already on it but knew the officer was just doing his job. "Sir, yes sir."

"And monitor Force Leader Hakk Batth's radio transmissions as well. If our leader sends or receives a message to or from someone outside of the column, I want to be the second person to hear about it. Watch the volume of radio traffic between Batth and his troops as well . . . If they start to get chatty, let me know."

Snyder felt a chill run down her nonexistent spine. Not only did the loot expect some sort of ambush—he clearly believed that the Ramanthians might be in on it!

Disastrous if true, but what if it wasn't? Santana had taken a fall from first loot to second. Everyone knew that—and everyone knew why. The platoon leader had gone head-to-head with Batth back on Beta-018 and come in second. That being the case one had to wonder . . . Were Santana's concerns justified? Or the result of a heavy-duty grudge?

They were tough questions, but the cyborg's duty was clear. Listen up, pay attention, and follow orders. That's how the system worked, and that's what she would do. The reply was the only one that a corporal could give. "Sir, yes sir."

The trail disappeared under six inches of brown liquid. Water splashed as Snyder's enormous podlike feet rose and fell. There was a sudden flurry of activity as something long and sinuous hurried out of the way.

Snyder felt the mud give under her considerable weight, then suck at the bottom of her steel "boots" when she tried to

pick them up. The cyborg figured the razbuls would do fine—
but wasn't so sure about the carts. The swamp was a strange
place for a person who still thought of herself as a city girl to
end up. But, like most of the Legion's borgs, Snyder had been
given very little choice.

The jury had taken less than fifteen minutes to find her
guilty of vehicular homicide while under the influence of alcohol, and the artificial intelligence known as JMS 12.2 had
sentenced her to death. The better part of a year passed while
her case was appealed, confirmed, and referred back to JMS
12.2. That's when the offer was made.

Snyder was going to die the same way that her twelve-year-
old victim had. Nobody could prevent that. She would be tied
in place, struck by a ground car traveling at 72 mph, and
thrown approximately fifty feet through the air. Just like the
little girl she had hit. That was her sentence—and that's what
would happen.

What followed was up to her. Once Snyder was pronounced
dead the authorities could leave her there, wherever "there"
was, or bring her back. Not as a human, since her physical
body would be little more than a jumble of flesh and bone by
then, but as a brain-in-a-box. An onboard control system for
one of the Legion's most potent weapons.

That was how Snyder wound up as a quad on Beta-018, and
later as a T-2, once her commanding officer approved a transfer.
Not because she didn't like the larger bodies—but because of
the responsibility involved. Quads are required to carry troops
into battle, troops that die if their borg makes a mistake, a risk
Snyder wasn't willing to take. She had already taken one innocent life and would never do so again.

The cyborg's thoughts were interrupted as one of her onboard receivers registered a brief transmission. It lasted only
one second, but came in over a seldom-used frequency and was
heavily encrypted. Snyder knew that a whole lot of information
can be packed into a very short burst and hurried to make her

report. "I intercepted a radio transmission, sir. A one-second burst."

Santana felt his heart beat just a little bit faster. "Encoded?"

"Yes sir."

"Keep monitoring. Let me know if someone replies."

The second burst came so quickly it was as if Santana knew what would happen. "Outgoing, sir. One second long."

"Roger that," the officer replied grimly. "Sign and counter-sign. Now listen carefully . . . The ambush is up ahead. We have no choice but to trip it. Once we do I want you to lay down suppressive fire, retreat along our line of march, and stop when I give the order.

"Between our people and the Clones we should be able to put up a pretty good fight. If the Thraks join in, then so much the better. But remember this . . . We may take fire from the *rear*. If we do I want you to take the bastards out."

Snyder didn't have to ask who the "bastards" were—the answer was obvious: the Ramanthians. It seemed hard to be-lieve, *very* hard to believe, but the loot had been correct where the radio transmissions were concerned. That meant anything was possible. "Sir, yes sir."

Now, as the swamp closed in around them, Santana began to sweat. He was afraid, a rather natural reaction given the circumstances, but not just for himself. He feared for the sol-diers, *all* of the soldiers, and for Vanderveen, who had an amaz-ing capacity to make him feel protective, defensive, and angry all at the same time.

All of them were counting on him to one extent or another and the knowledge was heavy on his shoulders. The waiting was agony but there was very little that Santana could do ex-cept endure it.

The trail came up out of the water, passed over a relatively dry hillock, and descended again. The cavalry officer scanned the soft ground for any sign of prints, saw some animal tracks, but nothing large enough to represent a threat.

Enormous stalks of what looked a lot like celery, each

topped with frothy green foliage, rose to both sides. Smaller plants, many of which of were equipped with large light-gathering leaves, grew in symbiotic clusters. Vines, some of which could sense movement, writhed like snakes.

As the air warmed more and more insects appeared. Some seemed respectful of the bug repellent that Santana wore, but others were less impressed, and quickly developed an appetite for human flesh.

The officer slapped them at first, each contact leaving a small smear of blood, but was soon forced to give up. Every bit of attention directed at the insects was that much less for the rest of his environment—a rather dangerous place that could harbor something a lot more threatening than some hungry bugs. Santana forced himself to ignore the pinpricklike bites to his face, neck, and arms and focus on his surroundings.

Snyder, who was oblivious to such mundane concerns, paused on a low rise. The cyborg switched from video to infrared and back again. The path, such as it was, vanished from time to time only to resurface, and zigzag its way across a sizable pond. Then, having completed that particular part of its journey, the trail mounted a hillock and disappeared from sight.

An unseen animal made a V-shaped ripple as it swam just below the surface off to the right. That suggested the water was a good deal deeper than anything encountered so far. Clusters of large lily-pad-like plants floated here and there, each leaf being two or three feet across and serving as landing platforms for at least one species of insect. The waterborne vegetation contributed to a rather peaceful-looking picture.

The only problem was that while the leaves acted to shield them, at least fifteen sources of heat lurked beneath the pads, as if hoping to evade detection.

The cyborg whispered into the intercom. "I've got them, Lieutenant—or at least I think I do. They're hiding under those lily-pad things."

Not wishing to give anything away the officer looked right

then left. Santana hadn't noticed anything before, but now, in the wake of the cyborg's comments, some of the leaves *did* look suspicious. The only problem was the fact that the heat signatures could be indicative of a Claw ambush—or members of a native life-form that liked to lurk just below the surface. The officer muttered into his boom mike. "How are they arranged? Randomly? Or in some sort of formation?"

Snyder switched back to infrared. "In a line, sir, all on the left."

Santana took the cyborg's meaning. It seemed unlikely that naturally occurring heat sources would arrange themselves in a line—and even more unlikely that all of them would choose to dwell in the water off to the left. The legionnaire swallowed. "Good work, Snyder. Is your recorder running?"

The question was unexpected. Which answer did Santana want? Yes? Or no? Snyder settled for the truth. "Yes sir. Standing orders, sir."

"Good," Santana replied. "Stand by . . ."

The rest of the legionnaires had arrived by then and Santana used hand signals to deploy them to the right and left. Then, switching to the command frequency, the legionnaire made his report. "One Five to One Six . . . Over."

The reply came so quickly it seemed as though Batth had been waiting for the transmission. "This is Six . . . go."

"We have fifteen, repeat one-five, potentially hostile heat signatures on our left flank. Request permission to conduct a reconnaissance by fire. Over."

" 'Potentially hostile?' " Batth demanded scathingly. "Let me know when you encounter actual resistance. Unnecessary gunfire will only serve to let the hostiles know that we're coming. Permission denied. Over."

Santana discovered that he'd been holding his breath. Here it was—the decision he'd been dreading. If he followed orders the ambushers, assuming that's what they were, would wait until the column was stretched out in front of them, rise up out of the water, and open fire. Then, assuming that the digs closed the trap the way *he* would, additional attackers would appear at the top of the next rise and fire down at them. Casualties would be heavy—extremely heavy. Even given the somewhat primitive firearms the Claw were said to have.

If, on the other hand, he ordered Snyder to fire on what appeared to be a row of ambushers, and turned out to be wrong, his career would be over. He would be court-martialled for disobeying a direct order, and, given his history with Batth, the outcome was a foregone conclusion.

All of that passed through Santana's mind in a flash—but it was something his father had said that helped make up his mind. He could even see Top's weather-beaten face as he spoke. "Do what's right, son. Take care of your troops, and let the rest sort itself out. That's all any leader can do."

Santana brought his assault weapon up, allowed it to rest on Snyder's shoulder, and peered through the open sight. One pad in particular seemed a lot higher than it should be. The officer took a breath, held it, and squeezed the trigger.

The weapon made a flat cracking sound as the slug slammed into its target, a geyser of blood shot up into the air, and all hell broke loose.

Batth had already started to scream at the platoon leader as fourteen members of the Claw stood up and opened fire. However, rather than being equipped with the primitive single-shot weapons that Santana had been told to expect, these individuals were armed with fully automatic Ramanthian-made Negar III assault rifles. The weapons roared as the LaNorian rebels opened up and the legionnaires returned fire.

Santana heard slugs spang off the T-2's armor as Snyder swung into action. Her arm-mounted .50 caliber machine gun started to chug, and casings arced through the air as the ambushers started to die. Hillrun and other members of the squad had already accounted for three, and Snyder nailed two more as an even worse threat emerged.

Santana spotted the movement over the cyborg's right shoulder and yelled into his radio. "Snyder! Two o'clock!"

Snyder detected both the motion *and* the heat even as Santana spoke. The cyborg turned, raised her right arm, and fired the energy cannon. A fountain of mud flew up into the air, but the dig with the rocket launcher remained unharmed. The spirits had protected him just as the Tro Wa said they would. He screamed in exultation.

Snyder knew it would take 2.5 seconds for the energy cannon to recycle and brought the .50 up to cover the target. The dig fired at the same moment Santana did.

The LaNorian was already dead by the time the rocket detected a second source of heat, chose the hotter of the two, and roared over the T-2's head.

The Thrakies sitting in cart one never knew what hit them. One moment they huddled around the portable stove, trying to stay warm, and the next they were dead. There was a primary explosion as the rocket hit, quickly followed by a secondary, as some ammo went up. Four bodies soared into the air, seemed to pause there, and fell one after another.

The Thraks were still in the process of falling as Vanderveen grabbed the case under her boots, opened the door, and bailed out. It wasn't a moment too soon as a hail of bullets ripped through the cab and killed the LaNorian driver.

The diplomat turned, realized that the projectiles were coming from the *rear*, and caught a glimpse of a Ramanthian firing from the back of a razbul. He spotted the human and spurred his sluggish mount forward.

Vanderveen used a word that would have appalled her mother, turned, and ran toward the front of the column. The razbul that had been pulling her cart had been hit. It flailed about, screeched pitifully, and rolled its eyes. The diplomat passed the animal, spotted the second cartload of Thrakies, and hurried to join them.

The surviving Thrakies had exited their conveyance by then, but L-8 Fortho had been killed, and they weren't sure what to do. Vanderveen skidded to a stop. Her radio was on, and her voice went out over the team's freq. "We're taking fire from the rear! Get down, load your weapons, and prepare to fire."

With no one else to direct them, the Thrakies took the orders seriously. Unfortunately, they were still in the process of deciding whether it was absolutely necessary to lie down in the mud when the Ramanthian rounded Vanderveen's bullet riddled cart and raised his assault rifle.

The empty fiberglass case lay at the diplomat's feet. She raised the custom-made Sycor Scout, brought weapon's butt up to her shoulder, and squinted through the sight. Vanderveen's father had given the scope-mounted .300 magnum hunting rifle to his daughter on her twelfth birthday and subsequently taught her how to use it.

The Ramanthian was directly ahead by that time firing from the waist. The diplomat heard something whip past her right ear, parked the crosshairs on the center of the trooper's chest, and applied a slow gentle pressure to the trigger. The butt kicked her shoulder as the slug hit the Ramanthian dead center, blew him back out of the saddle, and dumped his body into the well churned mud.

Unaware of the fact that its rider was dead, and badly frightened, the razbul continued to charge. A Thraki fired, but the bullets went wide. Vanderveen knew that *if* she missed, *if* the animal got past them, it would pile into what remained of the column with potentially disastrous results.

The diplomat worked the bolt on her weapon, tried to ignore the fact that a couple of tons' worth of reptilian flesh was thundering her way, and aimed for the beast's head. The first slug hit the oncoming behemoth right between the eyes. The second, which was by way of an insurance policy, struck its mottled chest.

The razbul stumbled, nosed into the mud, and started to skid. A small tidal wave of mud arrived before the reptilian snout stopped just short of Vanderveen's size seven and a half boots.

Meanwhile, up toward the front of the column, Platoon Sergeant Hillrun saw the LaNorian with the launcher fall, heard a *whoosh* as the rocket passed over Snyder's head, and felt the subsequent explosion. A couple of legionnaires turned to look thereby incurring the NCO's wrath. "Where the hell do you think you are? At the company picnic? Kill the bastards in the water!"

But the order came too late for Private Kashtoon who staggered as a hail of hardball ammo hammered his body armor and worked its way up toward his face. A puree of blood and bits of spinal column sprayed the ground behind him as the Ramanthian bullets severed the legionnaire's neck and his head hit the ground.

Revenge came quickly as the other legionnaires, backed by a full squad of Clones, opened fire on the remaining Claw. Bullets churned the water around the LaNorians, as the now-disciplined fire found them and tore their bodies apart.

Santana, Vanderveen's voice still ringing in his ears, ordered Snyder to turn. "We're taking fire from the rear!" That's the message she had inadvertently sent and there was little doubt as to the source of the attack.

The T-2 lumbered by a dead razbul, the remains of the first cart, and four fire-blackened bodies. Moments later the cyborg passed the second cart, which was still intact, and arrived in front of the third, which had been riddled by bullets. There was the flat whip-crack sound of a rifle shot as Vanderveen put the wounded razbul out of its misery and lowered her rifle. Four Thrakies, still reluctant to go facedown in the mud, stood in a semicircle behind her.

Snyder came to a halt, Santana jumped down, and the diplomat turned. She was angry and it showed. "You were right, Tony . . . The Ramanthians attacked us from the rear."

The platoon leader looked from the first razbul to a second and the dead trooper beyond. "*You* did all that?"

"I didn't think I had a choice," Vanderveen said defensively.

"No," Santana agreed soberly, "I guess you didn't. Good work . . . Thanks for covering our six. Where did the rest of the bugs go?"

"I don't know," Vanderveen replied. "They seem to have disappeared."

The officer looked up at Snyder. "How 'bout it, Corporal? Anything on your sensors?"

The cyborg shook her huge head. "No, sir. They're not only gone . . . they're *long* gone."

Santana nodded. "Odds are that they think we're dead. Let's do what we can to keep it that way." He turned to one of the Thrakies. "Go back up the column . . . Find Sergeant Twelve and Platoon Sergeant Hillrun. Tell them I want every radio in the outfit turned off until further notice. Go."

The Thraki delivered a sloppy salute and turned to go. Santana reached out to stop him. "Hey, soldier . . ."

"Sir?"

"Turn *your* radio off as well."

The Thraki looked embarrassed. "Sir, yes sir. Sorry, sir."

Santana shook his head and looked off toward the east. Vanderveen followed his gaze. "What are you thinking?"

"It took us a little more than three days to get here . . . but that was pushing it. Four should take us back."

Vanderveen frowned. "*Four?* What are you talking about? We need to push on."

Santana looked at the diplomat in surprise. "You must be joking! Thanks to desertions and casualties our force has been cut by a third. The bandit thing was loony to begin with . . . it's even crazier now."

"I couldn't care less about the bandits," the diplomat replied stubbornly. "It's the meeting with Mee Mas that's important. He's waiting in the village of Pur Lor, which happens to be a lot closer than Ka Suu."

"So you can advance your career."

Santana regretted the words the moment they exited his mouth but knew that it was too late to pull them back.

Vanderveen looked hurt then angry. "Listen, Lieutenant, your were right about Hakk Batth, I'll give you that . . . But what you don't know about the political situation on this planet could fill a large empty space like the one between your ears.

"The Empress is a self-concerned tyrant, but the head of the Claw, an ex-minister named Lak Saa, is even worse. Mee Mas is the *only* individual who might lead his people somewhere good. But he needs help in order to do that, a *lot* of help, and that's where we come in. Now, if you can't understand the importance of that, or just don't give a damn, then head for Mys. *I* plan to continue."

Santana sighed. What was it about Vanderveen anyway? He *liked* the diplomat, even admired her, but always made her angry. Not only that—but the diplomat had a talent for putting him into tight spots. His orders didn't cover the situation at hand—and the treacherous Hak Batth had absconded with the only radio capable of reaching Mys. That meant the officer couldn't bump the question upstairs even if he'd been willing to break radio silence to do so, and would have to make the decision himself.

Santana could *force* Vanderveen to return to Mys, with who knew what sort of official reaction, or go along with her request with equally unclear repercussions.

But when it finally came down to it, the decision pretty much made itself. Right or wrong, there was no way that the soldier could let Vanderveen traipse all over the countryside by herself and still face himself in the mirror. He looked her in the eye, "You are a real pain in the ass."

"So are you."

"I'll probably regret this."

"You probably will."

"Have you seen any sign of Dob Zee? It appears that Batth took our guide with him, and my map isn't as detailed as his was."

The diplomat shrugged. "Batth never took me seriously . . . Maybe that's why he left me waiting in his tent while he went out to take the Ramanthian equivalent of a leak. His map was on the table. It took less than one minute to hand-scan it."

Santana shook his head in wonder. "I should have known."

"Yes," Vanderveen said smugly, "you should have."

It took the better part of four hours to bury the dead, reassemble what remained of the convoy, and retrace their steps. It wasn't long before they came across Dob Zee's body. The LaNorian had been tied to a tree and shot. A single casing lay on the ground. It was Ramanthian.

The off-worlders provided the Imperial guide with the best burial they could manage, left the swamp, and turned to the south. The plan was to bypass the swamp, head toward the village of Ka Suu, but stop in a place called Pur Lor, where Vanderveen and Mee Mas were scheduled to meet.

Santana rode Snyder, and together they took the point. The Clones were next, followed by three carts and a group of dejected Thrakies. They had been ordered to march two miles, ride for one, and march again. The platoon leader's way of getting them into shape without killing the diminutive soldiers in the process.

Sergeant Hillrun, along with the surviving legionnaires, walked drag. Not for the reasons Batth had put them there, but because Santana wanted to ensure that their six was covered, and that both halves of the column would have the capacity to fight were it to be cut in two. The troopers still had to cope with steaming piles of what they called razshit, but there was less of it, and that made them feel better.

Farther out, beyond the effective range of Snyder's sensors, eyes tracked the column's progress. A message was written, a messenger ran, and the hunt began.

NEAR THE VILLAGE OF NAH REE, ON THE INDEPENDENT PLANET OF LANOR

The attack, when it came, was completely unexpected. Ever since what Frank and Bethany Busso still thought of as "the night of fire," both they and the burgeoning group of 1,504

LaNorians now camped on the mission grounds had worked day and night to prepare themselves for another similar attack.

They didn't have much, but the one thing they *did* have was people power, and every bit of it had been put to good use. A deep semicircular trench had been dug from a point upstream, around the prefab mission complex, and back to the river.

That was no small accomplishment, but Hwa Nas, the LaNorian Frank had placed in charge of the project, went the extra mile. It was he who directed the convert workforce to not only pile the newly excavated soil on the inside edge of the moat, thereby creating still another barrier for the Claw to overcome, but to place well-sharpened stakes at the bottom of the ditch in hopes that potential attackers would jump into the water and impale themselves.

Other preparations had been made as well, including the creation of a steadily growing arsenal of clubs, spears, and even some crudely made bows.

As things turned out, however, none of their efforts were sufficient to protect the missionaries from an act of sabotage.

With so many people packed together into close quarters, disease was rampant—and the Bussos had transformed their home into a combination hospital and day-care center. And it was there, on an otherwise unremarkable day, that Bethany entered the living room just in time to witness what appeared to be an act of mindless destruction.

The LaNorian's name was Baa Hef, a large brute, with the instincts of a bully. The hammer, a hand sledge appropriated from Frank's workshop, made a horrible thudding sound as it rose and fell.

Trudy, the Busso's AI, raised her voice in protest. "Stop! This unit has sustained damage! Stop! This unit . . ."

But it was too late. Baa Hef continued to hammer the console, it shattered, and the sledge smashed through the electronics concealed within.

Bethany screamed, ran forward, and threw herself onto Baa

Hef's back. Some volunteer nurses heard and came to the missionary's assistance. They wrestled the attacker to the ground, managed to bind his limbs, and summoned Frank. The AI was damaged, but maybe, just maybe, the missionary could put Trudy right.

But Frank Busso *couldn't* put Trudy right, not without a whole lot of parts he didn't have, and the implications were enormous. No Trudy meant no radio, and no radio meant no link with the embassy in Mys, and no link with Mys meant that the chances of receiving help anytime soon were slim to none. Especially if Ambassador Pas Rasha believed that the Bussos were dead, which he probably would.

It didn't take a genius to realize that the situation in Nah Kee was untenable and that the only hope for Frank's family and the LaNorians under their care was a military escort strong enough to help them reach the city of Mys.

And, thanks to a long series of radio conversations, Pas Rasha had agreed even going so far as to promise help the moment that allied troops returned from their mission to Ka Suu. The missionary had objected, going to some pains to point out that if Pas Rasha waited too long there wouldn't be anyone to evacuate, but the diplomat, with support from Major Miraby continued to hold his ground. Desperate though the Bussos' plight might be there was the embassy to think of, not to mention other off-worlders scattered across the countryside, and the Confederacy had limited resources.

Now, with all communications having been severed, it seemed likely that the mission and its needs would fall to the bottom of the embassy's priority list.

But, before the Bussos could address that problem, there was the matter of Baa Hef to cope with. The LaNorian had been hog-tied and hauled outside where Hwa Nas had taken charge.

Having examined what remained of Trudy, Frank Busso emerged from the mission to find Hwa Nas standing over the prisoner club in hand. He was furious and his eyes flashed with pent-up anger. "Baa Hef murdered Trudy—now he must die."

Although AIs had some rights under Confederacy law, they were regarded as property unless specifically freed from servitude, which meant they lacked the rights that "naturals" took for granted.

Thus, Frank wasn't sure whether Trudy had been murdered or simply destroyed. The first was a capital offense and the second wasn't. Not that Confederacy law meant anything on a planet like LaNor.

First, however there was the matter of intent. Was Baa Hef simply mad? Or had he been acting on behalf of the Claw? The answer would make a considerable difference.

Frank used his facility with the LaNorian language to question the prisoner in his own tongue. The results were questionable at best. Baa Hef babbled incoherently about what he referred to as the table devil, and seemed to believe that he had done something heroic by killing the spirit called Trudy.

But were the words genuine? Or little more than thin cover for an act of intentional sabotage?

There was no way to know for sure, and the Bussos couldn't stomach the idea of what would amount to a lynching, so they took what Frank thought of as the middle course. Baa Hef and his family of five, were banished from the mission.

Interestingly enough, the newly ejected convert showed no signs of distress regarding what would be a death sentence for anyone the Claw considered to be "contaminated," collected his meager belongings, and herded his family across the hand-sawn planks that served to bridge the moat. Then, with not so much as a backward glance, the peasant took the road toward Nah Ree.

Hwa Nas, who like many others took exception to the decision, spit into the moat. The spittle sent ripples out through the nearly stagnant water and seemed to serve as a signal. The sky grew darker, thunder rumbled off to the west, and the air was heavy with moisture. The rainy season was about to begin.

•   •   •

It had been raining for the better part of a day when Frank Busso and Hwa Nas sat down with a youth named Yao Che.

Rather than meet in one of the newly established longhouses, where ears were always ready to listen and tongues were always ready to wag, the get-together took place in a remote corner of the compound under the protection of a gray tarp. The makeshift roof shivered as a breeze hit, causing hundreds of raindrops to slide down off its edges and splatter onto the pebbly ground. A tiny driftwood fire provided what little warmth there was. Frank Busso sat on a handmade three-legged stool and held his hands toward the uncertain flames. The LaNorians squatted the way their ancestors had for thousands of years. "So," the human said, "you're sure you want to attempt this?"

Yao Che gave a single nod. "Yes, I am sure."

The missionary felt a lump form in his throat and was barely able to swallow it. "All right then, your hat, is it ready?"

Yao Che touched the cone-shaped felt hat that rested on his head. Such caps were standard attire among adult males and this one had been selected with care. Not too old, and not too new, it looked like thousands of others.

But it *wasn't* like thousands of others, not since Yao Che's mother had split the hat open, inserted a carefully waterproofed letter between the lining and the felt, and sewn it back up again. If the convert could get the letter to Mys, and if he could make contact with Ambassador Pas Rasha, the missive could save hundreds of lives. The youth met the human's eyes. "Yes, the hat is ready."

"And your cover story?" Hwa Nas demanded. "What about that?"

Yao Che put his hand on a small red earthenware pot. The lid had been sealed into place with heavy layers of wax in order to protect the contents from the elements. "The remains of my mother's mother reside in this funeral pot. As oldest son it is both my duty and privilege to convey gana's ashes to the city of Mys where they will be blessed and interred with those of my grandfather."

"Exactly," Hwa Nas agreed, knowing that such trips were a common occurrence and would provide the youngster with a believable reason for traveling cross-country during troubled times.

More than that however was the fact that a *second* letter, identical to the first, had been secreted at the bottom of the ash-filled pot. That way, should one container be lost, there was a chance that the other would make it through.

"Here's some money for your journey," Frank said, handing the youngster a rope heavy with metal coins. "I suggest that you sort through these, find those having the most value, and secrete them in various places on your body.

"If the rope is stolen, let it go. Your mission is to reach Mys, not defend a string of coins. Is there anything else we can do for you?"

Yao Che shook his head.

"Okay," Frank said, "it's time to pray."

The threesome knelt around the fire, called on God to watch over Yao Che, and visualized his safe arrival in Mys.

Then, after a quick good-bye to his mother, Yao Che was gone.

Frightened, but excited as well, Yao Che guided the small raft downriver. Both Frank and Hwa Nas had stressed how important it was to escape the local area without being detected. The youth and the rest of his family were very well known in and around the village of Nah Ree, which meant that were he to be intercepted, members of the local Claw contingent would see through his story in an instant. They *knew* his mother's mother was alive—and would put the youngster to death.

That's why Yao Che lay facedown on the tightly bundled reeds, used his feet to manipulate a makeshift rudder, and aimed his vessel for the center of the channel. There was flotsam out there, plenty of it, and the raft would blend in. The fact that Hwa Nas had laid some branches over his back would help as well.

The main current caught the fragile craft, spun it in a full circle, and propelled it forward. Water surged over the bow, flowed toward the stern, and soaked the front of the youth's clothes.

Yao Che didn't care, though—not so long as he was on his way. Because, truth be told, the youngster had an appetite for adventure and this was the first opportunity to come his way. He checked to ensure that his hat was secure—and that the pot was tied to his wrist. The river took care of the rest.

Ironically enough the peasant assigned to watch that particular section of the river on that particular day was none other than the hammer-wielding Baa Hef.

However, because the sentry had decided to supplement the stipend of bread provided by the Claw, his attention was divided. In fact, at the moment when the raft shot past, Baa Hef was standing in the shallows with his back to the river. The fishing net was empty—but the message was on its way.

THE FOREIGN CITY OF MYS, ON THE INDEPENDENT PLANET OF LANOR

In spite of the rain that had fallen during the night, the new day dawned bright and clear, something which normally put Ambassador Pas Rasha in a good mood. But today was an exception and for a very good reason.

It had been only yesterday that Force Leader Hakk Batth had radioed in to inform his superiors of the terrible news. It seemed that against his better judgment the Ramanthian had allowed Lieutenant Santana to lead the column along what was supposed to be a shortcut but subsequently turned into a death trap. Most of the expeditionary force had been killed while Batth, along with most of his Ramanthian troops, were barely able to escape. In spite of the terse formality of the report it was clear that Batth was distraught and, contrary to all common sense, blamed himself for the debacle.

Now, as the ambassador sat with his back to his desk, and stared south toward Polwa, his spirits were at the lowest ebb since Corporal Wu's murder. Here, as the result of a single blow, he had lost Christine Vanderveen, a promising young diplomat of whom he was genuinely fond, Lieutenant Antonio Santana, who though somewhat impetuous, had saved Pas Rasha's life, and at least thirty other souls, none of whom deserved to die in a LaNorian swamp. Later that afternoon the diplomat would be forced to sit down and write a report to his superiors, not to mention to each next of kin, informing them of the fate that had befallen their loved ones.

Meanwhile, as if to add to the sense of gloom, there were reports of terrible atrocities out in the countryside. Two railroad workers had been killed in their beds, their throats slit from ear to ear, and a Prithian trading post had been burned to the ground.

Adding to the misery was the fact that in spite of repeated attempts to contact the Busso family, there had been no response, and it was feared that the Transcendental mission had been destroyed.

Worse yet were reports that Imperial soldiers had done nothing to protect off-worlders—and in some cases appeared to be giving aid to the Tro Wa. Still another indication of the manner in which Empress Shi Huu was attempting to play both sides against the middle. The diplomat's thoughts were was interrupted as a tone sounded and his assistant spoke over the intercom. "Citizen Chien-Chu is here to see you . . . Shall I send him in?"

Pas Rasha glanced at his comp, confirmed that the appointment was there, and realized that he had forgotten about it. A business type if he wasn't mistaken . . . after some kind of mineral rights. A boring but welcome distraction. The ambassador touched a button. "Send him in."

Chien-Chu was seated in the outer office. A pleasant room equipped with a variety of furniture, which in spite of the need to cater to a wild assortment of different physiologies, still managed to look congruent somehow. Perhaps it was the fact that all the pieces were made of the same dark wood and upholstered with matching fabric.

LaNorian landscapes decorated the walls, and the cyborg had just zoomed in on a rather impressive sunset, when the spindly-looking Dweller spoke. "The ambassador will see you now."

Chien-Chu rose, nodded to Pas Rasha's assistant, and entered the diplomat's office. There was more matching furniture, a display case filled with local pottery, and shelves loaded with memorabilia, including pictures, plaques, and framed notes.

Servos whined as Pas Rasha's exoskeleton helped the Dweller come to his feet. The diplomat, eternally sensitive to cultures other than his own, extended a fragile-looking hand. Careful to exert a minimum amount of pressure on the ambassador's bones, Chien-Chu shook it. "Good morning Ambassador—it's good to see you again."

Pas Rasha looked surprised, "We've met before? My apologies . . . I can't say that I remember your face."

"And for good reason," Chien-Chu replied. "My face was a good deal different back then. There we are . . . right over there."

The diplomat followed the cyborg's finger to one of the many photos that decorated his shelves. The picture showed a much younger version of himself standing shoulder to shoulder with a corpulent human, and not just any human, but *Sergi Chien-Chu,* the then president of the Confederacy. The name alone should have triggered his memory but had somehow failed to do so. "That was taken just before my biobody gave out," Chien-Chu said conversationally. "I've occupied any number of cybernetic vehicles since then."

Pas Rasha was astounded. Sergi Chien-Chu, *the* Sergi Chien-Chu, assuming the cyborg was who he claimed to be, was on LaNor! "I am honored for a second time," the Dweller said sincerely. "But these are troubled times . . . would you be offended if I asked for some form of identification?"

"Not at all," the industrialist replied easily. "If you would be so kind as to bring up the embassy's security template, and enter the following sequence of numbers, you should receive some sort of clearance."

Both individuals sat down. Chien-Chu in one of the two guest chairs that fronted the ambassador's desk—and Pas Rasha in a special frame designed to accommodate the exoskeleton that he wore.

The cyborg recited a long sequence of numbers, the diplomat punched them into his terminal, and a likeness of President Nankool materialized over Pas Rasha's desk. The Chief Executive Officer was human and looked a little puffy. "Regardless of what sort of body he may have on at the moment, and what sort of mischief he may up to, the individual before you is probably Sergi Chien-Chu. He is a past president of the Confederacy, a Reserve Navy admiral, and the owner of Chien-Chu Enterprises. He has a Nova class clearance—and runs occasional errands for me. Please be nice to him."

The holo turned to mist and Pas Rasha laughed. "I can't say that I've ever seen or heard an endorsement better than that one! Welcome to LaNor, Mr. President . . . What can I do for you?

The cyborg grinned. "Knock off the 'Mr. President' stuff for starters. Friends call me Sergi."

"All right, Sergi," the diplomat conceded, "what brings you to LaNor? One of those 'errands' the president alluded to?"

Chien-Chu shook his head. "No, I'm not working for the government, although there could be some crossover. One of my company's subsidiaries was fortunate enough to obtain the permissions required to explore certain sections of the ocean floor. An activity which the Imperial government considered to be a waste of time but was still happy to charge us 2 million credits for."

Pas Rasha could guess where the conversation was headed,

and diplomat that he was, began to consider the implications. "And?"

"And we found what we were looking for," the industrialist continued. "Hundreds of thousands of years ago a meteorite hit what the LaNorians call the Great Wet.

"The impact caused an incredible amount of damage and had a profound effect on all of the planet's ecosystems.

"However, viewed from the perspective of the present, the meteorite did the LaNorians a tremendous favor. All sorts of debris were scattered over the ocean floor, including commercially viable quantities of rare elements including europium, lanthanum, and cerium.

"So," Chien-Chu finished, "the so-what of all this is that should the people of LaNor license a company like mine to exploit these natural resources, and if they were to take a reasonable percentage of the profits, they would have a vast sum of money."

Servos whined as Pas Rasha leaned backward in his chair. He was reminded of the wheel tax—and the manner in which it acted to suppress technological development. Perhaps, if another source of revenue were available, the tax could be dropped. "Would there be enough money to lift this world out of the steam age?"

The cyborg nodded. "That and more . . . Assuming they had a government that acted in their best interest."

"And your company's interest?"

"In return for the capital investment necessary to harvest these minerals, my company deserves a reasonable profit," Chien-Chu responded easily.

"Not something you could be assured of at the present time."

"Exactly. LaNor requires a stable and enlightened government."

"I couldn't agree more," the diplomat said fervently. "But the political situation continues to deteriorate. The Empress wants to maintain the status quo, the Claw seem bent on some sort of semireligious dictatorship, and the one hope we had for something better, a noble named Mee Mas, is running for his life. A member of my staff, a woman named Christine Vanderveen, was on her way to meet with him when she and most of her party were killed in an ambush."

"Not *Charlie* Vanderveen's daughter," the cyborg inquired. "He'll be devastated."

"Yes, I'm afraid so," Pas Rasha replied. "And we lost some other good people as well."

Both individuals were silent for a moment. Chien-Chu was first to speak. "So, perhaps it would be best to keep this information to ourselves for now. Until we see how things turn out."

"Yes," the Dweller agreed, "although it's damned near impossible to keep a secret around here. There are spies lurking behind every door. And don't forget the fact that I represent *all* of the Confederacy's members—including those who compete with Chien-Chu Enterprises."

"Understood," the cyborg replied. "That's why I didn't choose to burden you with the exact location of our find."

"And I'm glad you didn't," Pas Rasha said cheerfully, "I have enough problems already."

"Yes," Chien-Chu said dryly, "you certainly do."

The two of them parted company after that, and a robot, no larger than the dot over an "i," scurried away. It had a report to send . . . and very little time in which to send it. The ambassador's office was scheduled for debugging in less than fifteen minutes. Still, that was an eternity in bug years, and the robot had plenty of time in which to make its escape.

EAST OF KA SUU, ON THE INDEPENDENT PLANET OF LANOR

Once free of the wetlands what remained of the allied column was able to make much better time. There were clouds, some of which appeared threatening, but hurried off toward the west. That's when the sun appeared and bathed the land in a soft gold light.

The road continued south for about five standard miles prior to turning west again, and skirting the edge of the swamp. Softly rounded hills lay ahead, none of them very tall, or large in circumference. The road, which had clearly been built for the convenience of farmers rather than soldiers, wound its way between them.

Santana, who had a taste for history, not to mention an excellent vantage point from high on Snyder's back, was fascinated by the fact that some sections of the ancient thoroughfare were actually paved. That, plus the remains of what could have been watchtowers, and the ruins that decorated each hilltop suggested a well-ordered kingdom.

This notion was reinforced by the gradual appearance of what the legionnaire thought of as hillside vineyards, although it was certain that the now-ancient vines had been planted to produce something other than grapes.

Peasants, pruning knives in hand, paused to shade their eyes and stare at the alien convoy. Most had never seen anything like the T-2 before—and simply stared. Others, braver souls perhaps, would occasionally wave.

Santana waved back, but continued to be conscious of the fact that the farmers who *appeared* to be friendly might belong to the Claw. And, regardless of whether the peasants were members of the Tro Wa or not, there were plenty of signs that the column was being tracked.

On more than one occasion Santana and Snyder had seen flashes of light from distant hilltops, as if the sun had been reflected off the surface of a highly polished weapon, or a carefully polished lens.

There were also times when the cyborg spotted what could have been LaNorian heat signatures crouched within thick clumps of vegetation, "seen" suspicious movements beyond the range of Santana's unaided eyes, and "heard" two extremely brief radio transmissions.

The Ramanthians had provided the Claw with modern weapons—examples of which had been placed on cart number two. Had the bugs given the Tro Wa some short-range transceivers as well? Yes, the cavalry officer suspected that they had. Were the two groups still in communication with each other? Maybe, although he hoped they weren't, and believed the odds were slim.

So, convinced that the column was under surveillance, and concerned lest the enemy attack during the night, Santana wanted to find a very special place to camp.

With that in mind, Hillrun, the best scout at the officer's disposal, had been forced to inspect three different hilltops before finding one that matched the platoon leader's requirements. The effort involved a lot of cross-country running, which was why Private Kimura and a Seebo nicknamed "Fiver," stood soaked with sweat as Hillrun, still apparently fresh, made his report. "I think we found what you're looking for, sir. A hill with a path to the top . . . and a deep ravine on the far side."

Santana eyed the countryside from Snyder's back. He saw five gently rounded hills. "Which one?"

Hillrun was far too experienced to point and potentially provide observers with information regarding the column's intentions. "The one at three o'clock sir, with the lone tree on top."

Santana looked to the right, spotted the hill in question, and nodded. "Good work, Sergeant. I want to reach the summit well before sunset. Let's give the bastards an eyeful before the sun starts to set."

Hillrun said, "Sir, yes sir," and turned to the now-exhausted troopers. "Come on, let's get moving, what do you think this is? A frigging tea party?"

Santana grinned. He doubted that the Naa had ever taken part in a tea party, or ever would, but had acquired the phrase from another NCO. It worked nonetheless. The scouts returned

to their places, the carts jerked forward, and the road meandered toward the hill with the tree.

Vanderveen, who had chosen to walk rather than ride one
of the remaining carts, hurried forward. She carried the rifle
openly now, cradled across the crook of her left arm, ready for
action.

Santana saw the diplomat coming, unplugged his headset,
and dropped to the ground. Snyder continued to plod west-
ward.

"So," Vanderveen said, as the two of them came together,
"what's up?"

"We're under surveillance," the officer replied, falling into
step beside her. "There's no way to be absolutely sure—but I
would be willing to wager a month's pay that the Claw will
attack during the night."

"And you have a plan."

It might have been sarcastic but Santana saw that it wasn't.
Whatever else the diplomat might think or feel about him she
had faith in his military expertise. "Yes, I do. Here's an over-
view . . . tell me what you think."

The officer spoke, the diplomat listened, and eyes continued
to watch.

As the sun sank in the west, and darkness crept in to claim
the land, a fire appeared at the very top of Lone Tree Hill. A
large fire, which having been fed by the off-worlders, was visible for miles around. The blaze blinked whenever bodies
passed in front of it, and shivered when a breeze caressed the
hill, but was otherwise steady like a beacon in the night.

The aliens are stupid, Noc Paa thought, very *stupid, a failing
for which they are about to pay.*

A cobbler by day, and one of the Tro Wa's enforcers by
night, Noc Paa had been tracking the aliens since their departure from the swamp. Now, hidden among the ruins on the
top of a neighboring hill, the LaNorian and his band of cutthroats had little to do but eat the cold kas balls stored in their

commodious pockets, gossip in low tones, and consider the task ahead.

Noc Paa had known that the foreign devils would spend the night on a hilltop—the only question was which one. The answer became clear the moment that the mechanical giant followed the path up toward the top of Lone Tree Hill. The razbuls, the carts they pulled, and all manner of strange-looking troops followed.

Then, once a camp had been established and weapons placed around the top of the hill, the LaNorian drivers had been sent down to lowlands below, each leading an enormous razbul, with bedrolls on their backs.

All of which made sense since the animals consumed a great deal of food each day and could forage along the edge of the nearby swamp during the night. Then, when the sun rose, the drivers would bring their animals up to the hilltop again. Except that they wouldn't be able to do so, not without their heads, which would have been removed from their shoulders by that time!

But that was a minor detail, a chore to be handled *after* most of the aliens had been slaughtered, while a couple of them roasted over the coals of their own fire.

There were dangers, however, since foolish though they were, the off-worlders had managed to escape the ambush in the swamp. More than that they had killed all of their attackers—the leader of which had been none other than Noc Paa's younger brother.

That's why the Claw would wait until all but the sentries were asleep, slit their throats, and drown the rest like water rising from the bottom of a well.

Noc Paa found the thought comforting, and continued to relish it as he popped a kas ball into his mouth, and darkness claimed Lone Tree Hill.

It was pitch-black at the top of Lone Tree Hill, but thanks to the standard-issue night-vision visors and goggles worn by the off-world soldiers, they had no difficulty seeing each other or the intense green glow generated by the fire. While pretending to set up camp they had actually been preparing to leave.

The razbul drivers had been sent down to feed their animals, and then, as soon as darkness fell, to leave the area before the Claw could come after them.

Meanwhile the carts had been unloaded, the contents sorted, and those items deemed most critical distributed to the troops. Santana believed there were only three categories of items worth carrying under the present circumstances and those were ammo, food, and medical gear. Everything else, including tents, extra clothing, and Batth's folding furniture would be left behind.

Corporal Dietrich, with help from Private Horo-Ba, had been able to rig an oversize pack frame, which Snyder wore on her back. They didn't put any ammo on the frame, since the T-2 was what Dietrich referred to as "a bullet magnet," but it was an excellent way to transport most of the food supply, thereby lightening each trooper's load, and making them more mobile.

Now, before the Claw could move in from wherever they were hiding, Santana wanted to get what he thought of as his platoon down off the hill. Radios were off and orders were delivered via whispers. The T-2 glowed a ghostly green. "Snyder, you first. Cover us once you reach the bottom."

"Sergeant Twelve . . . Your men go next. Find positions around Snyder and cover our withdrawal."

The ravine was climbable, they knew that, because Private Pesta had scouted the route shortly after the group's arrival. The ravine had started as a fissure, grown wider as daily fluctuations in temperature caused chunks of rock to break off, and been further deepened by torrential rains.

Debris, much of which was quite loose, formed a gigantic staircase that the soldier used to reach the bottom. That's where he found the ruins of an old stone building, a spring filled with freshwater, and lots of animal tracks. Then, with four newly filled canteens slung across his back, Pesta made his return to the summit.

Still, even though a bio bod could make the climb didn't mean that a T-2 could, and Snyder was forced to move with great care. Marvelous though it was, her body had never been designed for climbing. It was difficult to find places to put her feet—each one of which was the size of a standard concrete block. Not only that but her hands, really more like graspers, were practically useless for rock climbing.

Slowly, testing each foothold prior to putting her weight on it, the cyborg made her way down through the boulder-strewn ravine.

Snyder could "see," however, since the surrounding rocks glowed green where some of the sun's energy had been stored, and that helped the legionnaire to navigate.

Servos whined, pebbles rattled as they fell away, and the cyborg's systems began to overheat as they strained to cope with the unexpected load.

Then, some fifteen feet from the bottom, a piece of seemingly solid rock sheared in two, the T-2 lost her balance, and fell over backward. There was a moment of free fall followed by a loud crash as Snyder hit the ground. The pack frame splintered, and most of the food packs were irretrievably smashed, but they helped pad her fall. A quick check revealed that all of the cyborg's systems were in the green.

Noc Paa, who was halfway down the adjoining hill by then, heard the clatter and urged his subordinates on. "The devils are up to something! We must move faster! Follow me." Quickly, like rain in a storm, the Claw flowed downhill.

Santana swore as Snyder hit. The Clones had departed by then, but that left the Thrakies, Vanderveen, and his legionnaires.

One of the Thraks, a female named Narvony, seemed a little brighter than the rest. So Santana had promoted her to L-1, a rank roughly equivalent to lance corporal, and put in charge of her three surviving comrades. The officer touched the noncom's shoulder. "Take them down, Corporal, quickly now, before the enemy can react to the noise."

Narvony nodded, whispered an order to her troops, and led the other Thrakies down into the ravine. Now, in a situation where their relatively small stature was an advantage rather than a hindrance, the Thrakies could excel.

Santana watched the green blobs diminish in size as the Thraks seemed to flow down hill never making a sound.

Satisfied that the Thrakies were clear, Santana turned to Vanderveen and signaled the diplomat forward. She nodded, backed into the ravine, and was gone.

"All right," Santana said, turning to Hillrun, "send the rest."

The Naa whispered some orders, watched his legionnaires drop into the ravine, and turned back again. "They're gone, sir."

"You counted them?"

"Yes sir."

"Excellent. Let's circle the fire, give the bastards something to look at, and get the hell out of here." Hillrun stood, the officer followed, and they walked around the fire.

Noc Paa spotted the movement, smiled grimly, and waved his force forward. "Victory awaits! Now my friends, now!"

The Claw were halfway up the side of Lone Tree Hill by the time Santana and Hillrun started down.

Vanderveen watched from the bottom of the ravine. The second green blob, the last one to leave the hill, would almost certainly belong to Santana. The diplomat knew that. What she didn't know was why his safety was so important to her. Was it because she needed the officer in order to complete her mission? Or was it something more? A possibility she was hesitant to admit—even to herself?

The question went unanswered as the legionnaires jumped to the ground and hurried into the center of a circle comprised of green blobs. "All right," Santana whispered, "let's get out of here. Stay alert, patrol order, move."

The off-worlders had traveled less than a quarter mile when the Claw infiltrated the empty weapons pits, swept across the top of Lone Tree Hill, and discovered that the aliens had withdrawn.

Noc Paa swore bitterly, and was about to issue new orders, when a subordinate spoke. "Look! The fools left one of their weapons behind!"

Noc Paa was still in the process of forming the word "no," when the underling grabbed for the weapon, jerked a piece of monofilament line, and triggered a detonator.

The booby trap, which consisted of thousands of rocks packed in and around a core that consisted of Ramanthian ammo plus five pounds of plastic explosive, roared as it went off. There was a flash, followed by a 360-degree hail of rock, some of which landed half a mile away.

None of the off-worlders turned to look since to do so would compromise their carefully maintained night vision. But a LaNorian shepherd saw the explosion from five standard miles away and told of a blast that lit the top of the hill, swept the Lone Tree aside as if it were no more than a blade of grass, and caused a sound like thunder.

In fact, so devastating was the explosion that with the exception of a few stray body parts, there was no trace of Noc Paa or his party of thirty-eight assassins when locals arrived on the scene shortly after sunrise.

Santana, well aware of the fact that more pursuers would soon join the hunt, pushed the column through the night. The moons rose, cast a wan light on the road ahead, and lit the way.

THE CITY OF POLWA, ON THE INDEPENDENT PLANET OF LANOR

The Imperial palace had no central heat—which meant it was cold during the fall and winter. A fact that had everything to do with why the Empress Shi Huu tended to spend a disproportionate amount of time on the fire throne during those seasons.

But it was summer now, which explained why none of the three stoves were lit and had potted plants sitting on them.

The walls were painted gold, a mural depicting the mountains of fire circled the room chest high, and more than five hundred candles burned in all manner of holders, niches, and sconces in order to provide light in the windowless space.

The center of the room, where Shi Huu's retainers, advisors, and servants were forced to stand was warm, *very* warm, almost like the sixteenth and final chamber of hell. Especially if one was dressed in three or four layers of complicated court attire.

That's why Shi Huu's elaborate blue-gray "rain dress," which symbolized the third day of the rainy season, was made of the lightest possible silk. A stratagem which allowed the Dawn Concubine to rest comfortably while her court sweltered in the heat.

Aware of their discomfort, but not especially interested in it, Shi Huu continued to push ahead. The Empress had already dealt with no less than five urgent messages from Ambassador Pas Rasha by the simple expedient of ignoring them, sentenced a provincial governor to death for skimming her tax revenues, and approved preliminary plans for the spring flower festival. She raised a carefully manicured hand. Jewels gleamed with reflected light. "What's next?"

In addition to his responsibilities where civil matters were concerned, the eunuch named Dwi Faa also served as Shi Huu's de facto master of ceremonies, master at arms, and executive assistant. He consulted a hand-lettered scroll. "At this point Your Highness is scheduled to review a science experiment . . . followed by a number of private meetings."

The Empress brightened. The "science experiment" referred to the use of what the Thrakies called "nano" on the three homely maidens. Had the nano improved their appearance? She could hardly wait to see

Then, following the session with the maidens, Shi Huu

would take part in individual meetings with twenty or thirty private informants. With the exception of the surgically mute bodyguards who stood to each side of the throne, no one would be present during those consultations, not even senior advisors like Minister Dwi Faa.

That created an atmosphere in which Shi Huu's spies felt free to report on *anyone*, regardless of rank, which was critical to her efforts to remain in power. Still another lesson learned from the Emperor.

Shi Huu inclined her head. "Thank you, please clear the court."

Those courtiers slated to leave prior to the scientific review, which included everyone but Dwi Faa, bowed and began the all-important process of backing out of the throne room without bumping into each other.

The most junior members of the court went first, followed by those of middle rank, and culminating with individuals such as Hoo San the eunuch in charge of military affairs.

It was a bittersweet moment since the courtiers were eager to escape the heat, but were well aware of the so-called experiment, and eager to learn the results.

It wasn't to be, however, so the throne room was cleared, the Thraki ambassador was ushered in and reintroduced. Then, having received the go-ahead from Dwi Faa, Fynian Isu Hybatha put a gray metal box on the floor, and launched into her presentation.

The Empress gave an involuntary start as three semitransparent maidens appeared out of thin air. All were naked, and while blessed with shapely bodies, were extremely homely. Conscious of the delicacy of her task, not to mention the potential payoff should the initiative go well, the Thraki chose her words with care. She had five minutes . . . and hoped to make the most of them. "Here is a depiction of the maidens *before* nanosculpting . . . and here are the same maidens afterward."

A door opened on cue, the maidens glided into the room

and bowed to the Empress. Then, having paid their respects, the young females took their places next to their respective likenesses. Silk whispered as it fell to the floor.

Shi Huu stared in speechless wonderment. The maidens had been transformed! Each face was unique yet absolutely beautiful. The Empress knew it, and even more importantly *they* knew it, as could be seen in the way that they held themselves.

Fascinated, but not absolutely convinced, Shi Huu rose from her throne. Dwi Faa made as if to assist the Empress but the Dawn Concubine waved him off.

Shi Huu approached the first maiden, examined her holographic likeness, located a birthmark high on the female's left thigh, and checked to see if the flesh-and-blood version bore the same flaw. She did.

Then, conscious of the manner in which off-worlders could construct realistic-looking mechanical bodies the Empress ran her hands over the entire surface of the second maiden's body, even going so far as to probe her genitals. An indignity which her subject suffered in silence. There was no doubt about it . . . Everything about the way the youth looked, felt, and even smelled was as it should be.

Now, moving to the last maiden, the Empress subjected her to a series of questions regarding the more experiential aspects of the beautification process. How did she feel? Did it hurt? And what did she think of the results?

The maiden was extremely happy, as she should be, and said as much.

All three of the experimental subjects were ushered out of the throne room after that, leaving Shi Huu with the Thraki ambassador, her minister of civil affairs, and two bodyguards. Satisfied that the results were genuine the Empress returned to her throne. "So," she said, addressing Hybatha directly, "they are as you said they would be. Each will be given to one of my most trustworthy nobles in recognition of services rendered. More than that I myself will undergo treatment beginning tomorrow.

"Now, assuming that all goes well, how can I express my appreciation?"

The Thraki ambassador was far too vigilant to miss the qualification inherent in Shi Huu's words but experienced a sense of triumph nevertheless. This was the moment she'd been waiting for and Hybatha was quick to seize it.

"Your Highness is very kind . . . It has come to my attention that an off-world company called Chien-Chu Enterprises has located some valuable mineral deposits on the floor of the ocean. If the Thraki people were granted exclusive rights to this important resource we could harvest the minerals on your behalf and split the profits with your government."

Dwi Faa decided to intervene. "It should be noted that Chien-Chu Enterprises paid for the right to explore under the Great Wet with the understanding that their company would receive preferential treatment if the effort was successful."

Shi Huu cocked her head. "Interesting . . . So you want me to take this opportunity away from Chien-Chu Enterprises and give it to you?"

When it came to opportunities of this magnitude Fynian Isu Hybatha was absolutely shameless. She nodded. "Yes, Highness, that is my hope."

Now, certain that she was dealing with a personality as ruthless as her own, the Empress locked eyes with the Thraki diplomat. "How much money would the government realize?"

"That's hard to say until we obtain more information regarding the extent of the deposits, bring in the appropriate equipment, and start production.

"However, *if* things go well, and market conditions remain relatively stable, I estimate the agreement would be worth at least half a billion credits over the first five years."

Shi-Huu assumed the off-worlder had started intentionally low—and made a mental note to insist on a percentage rather than a flat fee. Still, even the low figure would produce more revenue than the wheel tax would in the same period of time. Would Chien-Chu Enterprises offer better terms? Perhaps, but her instincts told the Empress that the difference wouldn't be all that large, plus the fact that Isu Hybatha could offer something Shi Huu wanted very much: a brand-new face.

"The minerals are yours," the Dawn Concubine said firmly, "conditional on the successful completion of the revitalization process.

"Dwi Faa will work with you to create the necessary documents. I will sign them when I look into the mirror and see the past."

Hybatha wanted to turn somersaults but managed a bow instead. "Thank you, Majesty, the Thraki people are most grateful."

THE VILLAGE OF PUR LOR, ON THE INDEPENDENT PLANET OF LANOR

The village of Pur Lor was made of wood. Homes and businesses, many of which shared the same buildings, burst into flame as Bak Aba and her so-called red lanterns jogged through the streets.

In addition to the red lanterns, which symbolized fire, the females carried the real thing held high in their right hands. The torches trailed tails of fire as they danced this way and that, made contact with thatched roofs, flew through windows, and were tossed into piles of straw.

Bak Aba saw her gana's home ahead but didn't hesitate. Even though she should have known better at her age the old fool still mumbled about democracy and was known to provide kas to the hill bandits.

The others watched as Bak Aba fired her grandmother's house, took strength from her example, and started to chant. *"Capa ta dum pas, Mee Mas, Capa ta dum pas, Mee Mas, Capa ta dum pas."* (Come out and play, Mee Mas, Come out and play, Mee Mas, come out and play.)

The words made reference to the summers when Mee Mas and other youngsters of noble birth had been sent up into the foothills to escape Polwa's simmering heat.

Though they stayed at the Palace of the Mist, the youngsters entered the village on an almost daily basis. Most of the locals remembered the Imperial nephew as a pleasant young male who, in spite of the fact that he was spoiled, was forever doing good deeds, pestering the villagers with questions, and fighting imaginary battles.

And that, as Bak Aba knew, was the very reason why it was so important to find the noble and kill him. The Empress and Lak Saa might be at odds—but both leaders feared the same thing: a leader, *any* leader, who favored the concept of "democracy." A hellish system that would almost certainly lead to chaos and destruction.

There were screams as villagers struggled to escape their burning homes, and the red lanterns felt additional heat wash across their backs as the two-story hundred-year-old Pur Lor dye factory exploded into flames and more than a hundred nar rats dashed out into the street.

"To the palace!" Bak Aba shouted, "To the palace!" and the lanterns obeyed. "Come out and play, Mee Mas," they chanted. "Come out and play."

Mee Mas was asleep when the attack on Pur Lor began, lost in a complex dream, when Faa Cha touched his shoulder. "You must get up, little one—the lanterns are on the way."

Mee Mas opened his eyes, realized it was dark, and frowned. "Have you lost your mind, Faa Cha? What are you doing? Let me sleep."

"Not unless you want to sleep forever," the elderly retainer replied firmly. "The Claw set fire to the village and they're on the way here. Come, while there is still time to preserve both your life *and* your dreams."

It was then that Mee Mas heard the distant shouts, rolled out of bed, and rushed to the nearest window. He could see the red glow over the trees behind the palace and knew that Faa Cha spoke the truth. "I must go to them, Faa Cha, and order them to stop."

"Don't be foolish little one," the retainer admonished.

"There is only one person they will listen to and he carries his genitals in a jar. But remember this night, fight for that which is right, and live your dreams."

So saying Faa Cha pulled the princeling out of his room, down a long hall, and out into the central courtyard. Her husband, a male named Sii Sas, stood waiting at the well. A pile of materials lay heaped at his feet. He bowed respectfully. "Good evening, your lordship. Please slip your arms through the holes."

The oldster bent, lifted a strange-looking contraption off the ground, and offered it to Mee Mas. The prince eyed the handmade rope vest, saw that it was connected to some rather hefty stones, and realized that the old couple meant to hide him in the well. "No, I won't do it."

"Ah, but you must," Sii Sas said gently, "because you have work to do. You will die one day, as all of us must, but not today."

"But I'll drown," Mee Mas said plaintively.

"No," Faa Cha said as she guided his arms through the loops, "not with *this* in your mouth."

Sii Sas grinned a toothless smile and shoved a tube into the prince's mouth. It had been made from a length of Razbul intestine and twine had been wrapped around one end to form a crude mouthpiece.

Mee Mas saw that the other end was married to a length of hollow tasa tuber which Faa Cha held so that it was pointed at the sky. Was it long enough to reach the bottom of the well? The prince hoped so.

Mee Mas could hear the lanterns calling his name by then and knew that the Claw was close. Faa Cha and her husband guided their young charge up onto the top of a box—and from there to the edge of the circular well. Moonlight gave the scene a ghostly quality—like a scene from one of the prince's dreams.

"Remember," Faa Cha whispered into his ear, "you must remain at the bottom of the well until the sun appears directly overhead. The Claw will have looted the palace by then, consumed a vast quantity of Empress Shi Huu's wine, and gone home to sleep it off. Good-bye, my child, and remember your dreams."

Mee Mas was about to reply, about to tell the couple that he loved them, when Sii Sas gave a mighty push. The prince fell, hit the surface of the water, and felt the rocks pull him down. Finally, after what seemed like an eternity, Mee Mas felt his feet hit bottom. A quick check was sufficient to confirm that the breathing apparatus worked and that he wasn't going to drown. Not at the moment anyway. Far above, viewed through the shimmery surface, the prince saw one of the planet's two moons gleaming above.

Meanwhile, high above, there were additional splashes as Sii Sas dumped a load of carefully selected debris into the water. Wood scraps for the most part, which would bob around the surface, and help conceal the end of the tuber.

Then, being too old to run, Faa Cha and her mate retired to the small temple by the waterfall from which the summer residence had taken its name. That's where they were when the Palace of the Mist went up in flames and the Claw found them.

7

A journey, a *true* journey, is measured not by ground covered, sights seen, or deeds done but by changes to the landscape within.

Nok Daa
LaNor philosopher
Standard year 1958

THE VILLAGE OF PUR LOR, THE INDEPENDENT PLANET OF LANOR

Roughly half the village of Pur Lor had survived, but that was more a matter of luck than any mercy shown by the Claw. The older structures, all of which were located toward the southern end of town, had perished, but those which lay north of the palace had survived, primarily because both the red lanterns, and the male Claw who flooded in to support them, were distracted by the opportunity to loot the Imperial residence. There were guards, twelve in all, but they fled.

The first thing Santana saw was the smoke, rising to stain an otherwise blue sky, and warning of trouble ahead. He was exhausted, as were his troops, but loath to bivouac out in the open. They needed walls, something that would be relatively easy to defend, which was where the palace came in.

That's what the legionnaire hoped for anyway, but those hopes started to fade as the column approached the outskirts of Pur Lor, and the full extent of the carnage could be seen. Bodies, their throats slit ear to ear, were scattered in the streets.

Many lay near empty water buckets, as if some villagers had run outside to fight the fire, only to be ambushed by members of the Claw.

Homes, most of which had been reduced to little more than a stone foundation, an oven-fireplace, and a heap of still-smoldering timbers, lined both sides of the street.

Livestock, those animals that survived, ambled, strutted, and hopped through the ruins. An elderly razbul stood and chewed contentedly as the grim-faced off-worlders, weapons at the ready, followed the narrow twisting street north through the village.

Just one shot, one rock thrown from behind a crumbling wall, and Santana planned to let Snyder hose the place down. A distant aspect of the platoon leader's mind knew there might be other, more sophisticated ways to handle the situation, but he couldn't muster the energy required to think of them. It had been more than a planetary rotation since he had last slept, and it was all the officer could do to take the next step, scan left, scan right, and keep his finger on the trigger.

Vanderveen stumbled, caught herself, and tried to clear her mind. The Claw had attacked the village, the dead bodies were mute testimony to that, but what about Mee Mas? Was he dead as well? There was no way to know.

The diplomat spotted an old crone. Perhaps her brain had been addled by the violence, or she was simply senile, but whatever the reason she was busy sweeping a passageway as if the houses to either side were still there.

Vanderveen veered off in that direction. The diplomat tried to look friendly but suspected that the effort was wasted. Especially given the fact that she was not only an alien, but a tired, dirty alien, who was armed with a rifle. "Excuse me . . . "We're looking for the Palace of the Mist . . . Could you tell me where it is?

The oldster met the alien's eyes and pointed to the northeast. "Look for the stone guardhouse and the stairs beyond."

Vanderveen gestured to her surroundings. "The Claw did this?"

The LaNorian looked down to her broom, then up again. Tears made tracks down through the dust on her wrinkled cheeks. "No, *we* did this."

The words were so clear, so unexpected, that all the diplomat could do was nod in agreement, thank the oldster, and race to catch up with Santana. He listened to her report, said "Thanks," and pointed up the street. "That looks like the guardhouse . . . ahead on the right."

The structure in question was small, round, and surmounted by a conical roof. To Santana's eye it was more like a ceremonial kiosk than a serious barrier suggesting that the *real* defenses if any lay somewhere beyond. A quick peek was sufficient to ascertain that whatever guards had been posted there had been taken prisoner, killed, or fled. The legionnaire would have placed his money on the third of the three possibilities.

Santana posted two Seebos on the guard station, ordered them to keep a sharp lookout for anything that looked like enemy activity, and led the rest of his ragtag band down a long flight of stone stairs.

Lush foliage grew to either side, ancient stone gods peered out from their carefully maintained niches, and the first flight of stairs ended in front of a large fountain. It was made of black stone. Water spewed from the mouth of a mythical beast, splashed into a large stone bowl, and drained away. Benches offered a place to rest and over arching tree branches provided shelter from the sun above.

Santana wanted to pause and splash cold water on his face but resisted the temptation to do so. If he took a break, everyone else would want to do likewise, and it was important to secure the palace and establish some sort of defensive perimeter before his troops took time to rest.

The second flight of stairs carried the off-worlders down through more formal gardens to the point where a twelve-foot-tall defensive wall cut across their path. It had been pierced with a sturdy-looking black iron work gate which hung on pintle-style hinges. The barrier appeared to be undamaged which added further support to Santana's theory regarding the Imperial guards. They had almost certainly abandoned their posts, or worse yet, allowed the Claw to enter.

Santana stepped through the opening his weapon at the ready. The walls of the palace had been constructed of stone and therefore continued to stand. But the structural beams, framing, and roof supports had been made of wood and were vulnerable to fire. At some point during the night the upper portion of the residence had collapsed into the lower, creating a jumble of half-charred timbers, fallen masonry, and red roofing tiles. Smoke continued to trickle up through the debris, suggesting that the fire continued to burn deep within the ruins.

There was no way to pass through the palace so Santana followed the debris-strewn courtyard to the north and found a way around it. Snyder walked followed to the rear, her servos whining, little bits of masonry exploding beneath her massive feet.

The officer saw a red lantern, crushed where the mob had trampled it, a richly carved sideboard that had been carried out of the palace but abandoned owing to its weight, colorful dinnerware that had been smashed to pieces, and an antique screen that had been slashed with a sword.

To his left, and off to the north, the cavalry officer could hear a waterfall and feel the fine, almost invisible, mist it produced. A balm in the summer, and one reason why stone benches lined that edge of the property.

Then, having descended still another short flight of stairs, the officer entered the front courtyard. It faced the east, so the Emperor could watch the sunrise, and the entire width was protected by a vine-covered arbor. And there, dangling like badly abused dolls, hung two elderly LaNorians. The ropes creaked as the bodies twisted in the breeze.

Santana turned to wave Vanderveen forward. She saw the bodies and winced. "The male . . . Is that Mee Mas?"

The diplomat shook her head. "No, the prince is a good deal younger."

Santana nodded and gestured to Dietrich. "Corporal . . . Get some help and cut those bodies down."

The noncom nodded, shouted for Private Taz, and went to work.

Santana activated his radio. "One Five this is One Six . . . We'll bivouac here. Sweep the grounds to make sure the area is secure. If you find anyone bring them to me. FSO Vanderveen is looking for a dig named Mee Mas . . . and I would love to get some intelligence. Put out sensors, put some sentries on the wall and force people to drink plenty of water. Work with Sergeant Twelve and L-1 Narvony to set up three shifts all integrated. We're going to need every trooper we have to make it out of here and that means working together.

"I'll take the first shift, you take the second, and Twelve will command the third. Let's rest Snyder right off the top. Any questions? Over."

Hillrun waved from the far side of the courtyard. He sounded tired but alert. "One Five to One Six . . . Roger that . . . no questions. Over."

"One Six to One Four . . . questions? Over."

"This is Four . . . "No, sir. Over."

"One Three . . . You, okay? Over."

"Yes sir," Narvony replied. "Over."

"Okay, then," Santana said, "Execute."

Vanderveen felt a terrible sense of hopelessness as she surveyed the destruction that surrounded her. Had Mee Mas been killed? Taken prisoner? There was no way to know.

One thing was clear however . . . Mee Mas had disappeared and any chance that the LaNorian people might have had for something resembling democracy had vanished with him.

Wearily, hoping for a drink of water, Vanderveen ambled over to the well and bent over to look inside. Seen from below her face was little more than a shadow. But what Mee Mas could see, and what he'd been praying for, was the unmistakable glow of the sun! It glowed like a beacon of hope.

The prince was cold . . . So cold that it was difficult to move and the possibility of death offered a welcome respite. Mee Mas made use of his tongue to push the tube out of his mouth, shrugged his way out of the makeshift vest, and allowed himself to float up toward the surface.

Vanderveen had a canteen in her hand and was reaching downward when Mee Mas exploded up through the surface of the water. The diplomat reeled backward, Santana sprinted toward the well, and Mee Mas spluttered. The prince had been found.

WEST OF THE IMPERIAL CITY OF POLWA, ON THE INDEPENDENT PLANET OF LANOR

Once clear of the area around his home village of Nah Ree, the youth named Yao Che managed to ground his increasingly waterlogged raft on a sandbar, where it turned end for end, dumped him into the shallows, and took off for parts unknown.

The accident didn't make much difference however since Yao Che was already soaked to the skin. A quick check was sufficient to confirm that his conical hat, which had a very important letter sewn into the lining, and the carefully sealed earthenware pot, which contained a *second* letter, were both intact.

Thus reassured the youngster eyed the channel that separated him from the shore and the flat-bottomed boats pulled up beyond. It was evening, right around dinner time, and there wasn't a soul in sight. Fisherfolk suggested a village, a village implied a road, and nearly all of the major roads led to Polwa, the very place the youngster was determined to go.

In spite of the speed with which the Gee Nas River whipped through the side channel the water appeared to be only knee deep. That meant Yao Che could cross it on foot, assuming he managed to remain standing. Failure to do so could be disastrous since a fall could carry him downstream, out into the main stream, and to his death.

However, like any youngster who had grown up near a river, Yao Che knew a thing or two about how to deal with such situations. First the courier removed the clothing below his waist in order to reduce the pressure of the water against his legs. Then, shivering in the cold, the youngster made the garments into a pack which he secured to his back.

Satisfied that the bundle was secure the teenager walked over to a pile of driftwood, selected a tuber that was approximately one arm's length longer than he was, and tested the pole to ensure that it wouldn't break.

Now, as ready as he ever would be, Yao Che entered the current. His sandals, which he still wore, helped provide a stable footing. The stick, which he placed upstream, acted to break the current's force.

Then, having chosen a destination slightly downstream of the boats, the youngster eased his way out into the channel. There were some bad spots, like a hole that threatened to suck him in, but the courier managed to keep his feet.

Finally, right about the time that the lower part of his legs had grown numb from the cold, the bottom came up, the current lost most of its force, and Yao Che made his way up a steeply shelving beach. A rock ledge ran parallel to the channel and the fisher folk had made use of it to chronicle high- and low-water marks for more than a hundred rainy seasons. Valuable information for people who make their livings from the river.

Yao Che stuck the pole into the soft soil above the ledge in case someone else might be able to use it, removed the bundle of clothes from his back, and put them on. They were wet but helped cut the breeze.

Then, eager to find a warm fire, some hearty food, and a place to sleep, Yao Che sought the nearby village. Like most such settlements he knew it would be located a good mile or two from the river, safe from all but the most determined of floods, and far enough from the water to give river pirates reason to pause.

An hour later the youngster was seated at the end of a long table packed cheek to jowl with fellow travelers. Most had finished their dinners by then and held vast mugs of beer. There was very little to do but play a game of stones, argue over inconsequential matters, and pepper Yao Che with questions.

The teenager expected nothing less and allowed his elders to draw his story out of him as he worked his way down through a bowl filled with kas, vegetables, and chunks of tasty fish. There were grunts of sympathy regarding his gana's death, stories regarding similar journeys they had made as youngsters, and plenty of well-intended advice.

Then, warmed by the food, not to mention the inn's fuggy embrace, it was time to go upstairs, wrap himself in the cleanest blanket he could find, and curl up in a corner of the long dormitory-style guest room. It was noisy, what with the tavern located directly below him, but the youth fell asleep within minutes.

Yao Che awoke nine hours later to discover that he had been robbed. The coin rope, which was still clenched in his hand, had been severed to either side of his fist leaving him with nothing beyond a short length of cord.

The courier's first reaction was one of shame, that he could have been victimized so easily, but he had taken Frank Busso's advice and hidden those coins having the greatest value here and there throughout his clothing. That, plus the knowledge that he had paid for his lodging in advance, made the youngster feel better.

Still, Yao Che had a role to play, that of country bumpkin on his way to the city, and the theft demanded appropriate histrionics. Thus the youngster uttered a loud wail, proclaimed his loss, and had little choice but to endure the callous comments offered by fellow guests, the disingenuous expressions of sympathy voiced by the establishment's proprietor, and his staff's poorly concealed snickers.

The innkeeper *did* offer the youngster a complimentary breakfast, however, along with six kas balls for the road and some sage advice. "There's some mighty rough characters out there so watch your step . . . One mistake and you could lose more than a rope with some coins on it."

The courier bowed respectfully, thanked the elder for his counsel, and was soon on the road. The next couple of days passed reasonably smoothly, as the youngster used his native wit, charm, and carefully hoarded money to hitch rides on Polwa-bound carts, walk in the company of organized groups, and pass the evenings at inns very much like the first.

It was on the third day that the opportunity, if that's what it could properly be called, came as Yao Che rounded a bend, and ran into a large contingent of Claw. All of them were male, wore identical red bandanas, and carried a wild assortment of weapons. They, like thousands of others, were like iron filings drawn to a magnet. The city of Mys was the place where the foreign devils lived, where they feasted on LaNorian babies, and where the blood would be let.

The group, some forty individuals in all, had paused to take a break. While doing so they had established an informal road-block, which they used to vet fellow travelers, extract what they referred to as voluntary donations, and flirt with any fe-males who happened along.

The moment that Yao Che appeared, a big lout named Ply Pog ambled over and blocked the youngster's passage. "So," the Claw remarked rhetorically, "what have we here? An Imperial courier with an urgent message for Empress Shi Huu?"

The question came so close to the truth that Yao Che felt his heart skip a beat. The other members of the Tro Wa laughed. The teenager felt relieved. Rather than accuse him of what amounted to a crime the ugly-looking brute with the missing ear fan was making fun of him!

Much practiced in the role of dutiful grandson the teenager summoned an expression of surprised consternation and bowed respectfully. "No, Excellency. My name is Yao Che—and my family sent me to Polwa with my gana's ashes . . . Perhaps you could tell me if I'm on the correct road?"

" 'Excellency?' " one of the ruffians demanded. "Excellent at what? Drinking beer?"

The jest drew gales of laughter from the jokester's cronies and Ply Pog frowned. "Give me the pot . . . maybe it contains ashes and maybe it doesn't."

The youth felt frightened, *very* frightened, and for very good reason. Others had stopped him, had forced him to tell his story, but no one had attempted to look inside the pot. Most LaNorians were too superstitious for that, but it seemed that this individual was the exception, or just hell-bent on looking tough for his companions.

Yao Che had no choice but to put the best possible face on the matter, surrender the earthenware vessel, and hope for the best.

Ply Pog accepted the pot, appeared to weigh it with his work-callused hands, and tugged on the lid. The wax was still in place however, which meant that the warrior had to cut through the seal with the hook-shaped metal claw that he wore on the middle finger of his right hand. There was a tiny release of air as pressures were equalized and the lid came free.

The youngster held his breath as the older male peered inside and stirred the ash with one of his blunt fingertips. "Sorry, lad," Ply Pog said, returning the vessel to its owner, "but these are troubled times. Why just yesterday we stopped a farmer with a cartload of razbul manure. One my friends used a spear to check the load and what do you think he found?"

Yao Che shook his head. "I have no idea . . . What?"

"A devil!" the Claw said triumphantly. "Hiding inside a pile of shit! Can you beat that?"

"No," the teenager replied, "I can't. What did you do with the foreigner?"

"Well," Ply Pog replied, "we tied both the farmer and his devil to long poles and roasted them over the fire. They screamed for hours."

Yao Che thought of his friend Natalie Busso, imagined her bound to a spit, and felt a lump form in his throat. He was barely able to swallow it. "And a good thing, too."

"Exactly," Ply Pog replied. "Now, what was it that you wanted to know?"

"Is this the road to Polwa?"

"Why, yes it is," the warrior answered jovially, "and that's where we're headed. Why don't you come along? We'll deliver your gana's ashes, drink some big-city beer, and kill every devil in Mys . . . What do you say?"

There was only one thing that the youngster could say, which was how Yao Che became a member of the Tro Wa Reds and subsequently entered the Imperial city of Polwa.

THE FOREIGN CITY OF MYS, ON THE INDEPENDENT PLANET OF LANOR

The restaurant in the Strathmore Hotel provided a neutral setting in which *all* beings could meet so long as they didn't mind everyone in the off-world community being aware of it. And Fynian Isu Hybatha didn't mind at all—especially if on-lookers discovered that she had not only bested Chien-Chu Enterprises, but Chien-Chu himself, the very individual who was most responsible for the manner in which her people had been defeated during the recent war.

That's why the Thraki ambassador was already seated at the linen-covered table when the cyborg entered the room and looked around. It was lunchtime, and at least two dozen sets of eyes followed Chien-Chu as he walked over to the diplomat's table and took his place in front of a place setting he had no reason to use.

The Thraki's "form," a tiny robot that was more pet than functionary, did a headstand next to Hybatha's elbow. She formulated a human-style smile and extended her hand. The industrialist shook it. "Good afternoon, Ambassador . . . and happy Flight Day."

The diplomat, who was seated in what amounted to a fancy high chair, was taken aback. With the exception of a few scholars very few humans had troubled themselves to study her people's history.

Flight Day, the day on which her entire race had taken flight from the murderous Sheen, was the equivalent of a national holiday. The fact that the industrialist *knew* that, or had taken the trouble to conduct some research prior to meeting with her, served to remind the diplomat that Chien-Chu was a formidable opponent indeed. She manufactured a second smile. "Thank you. That's the problem with postings like this one . . . we don't even get the day off!"

"Yes," Chien-Chu agreed dryly, "and you've been *very* busy indeed."

There were any number of things that the Thraki didn't like about humans—and the direct manner in which they often chose to communicate was one of them. Her form did a cartwheel across the surface of the table, nicked a bud vase, and threatened to turn it over. The diplomat managed to catch the container before it could fall. "So, you heard?"

"Yes," Chien-Chu acknowledged. "I did. My source tells me that you offered to make the Empress look young again in return for rights to the subsea minerals that my company spent millions to find and evaluate. An effective strategy—but not a very ethical one."

A LaNorian waiter approached but Hybatha waved him off. Her eyes narrowed and her ears went back against her skull. "Spare me the moralistic nonsense Citizen Chien-Chu . . . Representatives from your company paid the LaNorian government only a fraction of what the exploration rights were worth."

"That's not true," Chien-Chu replied calmly. "We paid fair market value, especially in light of the fact that government officials refused to read the tutorial materials we prepared for them, and believed that the entire effort was a complete waste of time."

There was silence for a moment as both individuals eyed the other. Hybatha spoke first. "Look, I understand how you feel, but let's be pragmatic . . . Rather than fight over the find we could cooperate. My government has the mineral rights . . . and you know where the deposits are. Yes, we could import the necessary equipment, and find the minerals ourselves but why go to that expense? Especially if we can come up with a suitable agreement."

Chien-Chu raised an eyebrow. "Terms?"

"Three percent of whatever we negotiate with the government."

"No."

Hybatha, who had expected Chien-Chu to be a good deal more pragmatic, was genuinely surprised. " 'No'? Why not?"

"There are three reasons," Chien-Chu replied evenly. "First, I don't like you. Second, the arrangement wouldn't be ethical. Third, it's my opinion that Empress Shi Huu will no longer be in power thirty days from now, which will leave you out in the cold. Good day." And with that the industrialist got up and left.

The form, still intent on entertaining its owner, did a double backflip. Hybatha, her eyes on Chien-Chu's back, failed to notice.

WEST OF THE FOREIGN CITY OF MYS, ON THE INDEPENDENT PLANET OF LANOR

As front after front rolled in from the west the rainy season began in earnest.

There were downpours that flattened crops, roiled the surface of fishponds, and led to flooding.

There were on-again off-again showers, here one moment and gone the next.

And there were "mist storms," when the water seemed to

mix with the atmosphere, and hang suspended in the air.

That meant everyone was wet twenty-seven hours a day. They woke up wet, marched wet, and went to sleep wet. In fact, the only thing that prevented the entire group from succumbing to hypothermia was the fact that the air was relatively warm.

Still, it was a miserable, muddy-looking procession that snaked its way from one small hamlet to the next, eternally aware that death dogged their steps.

Nearly three days had passed since Mee Mas had surfaced in the well—and a lot had happened since then. Though eager to leave Pur Lor before the Claw could mount an attack of some sort, Santana was well aware of how tired the troops were, and the need to rest them. Accordingly, he forced himself to stay until everyone had the benefit of at least one uninterrupted sleep cycle.

The prince, who was overjoyed to see his rescuers, quickly proved himself to be both an asset and a liability. An asset in that he had an intimate knowledge of the surrounding countryside—and a liability because he was incredibly spoiled. The latest manifestation of which came as the column slogged down an especially muddy section of road. Snyder was on point. Santana came next, followed by the Seebos, the Thraks, Vanderveen, the prince, Sergeant Hillrun, and the rest of the legionnaires.

Santana was so engrossed in the simple process of placing one mud-caked boot in front of the other that he wasn't even aware of Mee Mas until the LaNorian cleared his throat. The officer turned to see what looked like a bedraggled legionnaire. Rather than his usual finery Mee Mas was decked out in a camouflage rain poncho, a pair of Private Taz's trousers, and a sturdy set of sandals. Though far being an expert on the nuances of LaNorian facial expressions, the platoon leader could see that the noble was pissed. His voice had an imperious quality. "I am wet."

"I can see that."

"I wish to be dry."

"We all do."

"You will stop at the next village."

"No, I won't."

Mee Mas, who was not accustomed to hearing the word "no," looked surprised. "But you must! I am a prince."

"That's all well and good," Santana replied patiently, "but *I* am a lieutenant, and right here, right now, I outrank your ass. Now, get back to where you're supposed to be, and shut the hell up."

Sergeant Twelve snickered and Mee Mas stood in stupefied silence until Vanderveen caught up with him. At least *she* was friendly—and the prince fell into step next to her. "So," the diplomat said, "how did it go?"

"Not very well," Mee Mas admitted. "He told me to return here 'and shut the hell up.' "

"You can't say I didn't warn you," Vanderveen commented mildly.

"Can he do that?" the prince inquired. "Can he tell individuals of higher rank to 'shut up'?"

"Perhaps he *shouldn't*," the diplomat said philosophically, "but he can. That's because he cares more about the safety of the people under his command than currying favor with his superiors. If we were to stay in the next village the locals might betray us, we'd be forced to fight on their ground, and there would be a lot of collateral damage. That means dead civilians."

Mee Mas looked thoughtful. "He told you this?"

"No," Vanderveen replied, "not directly, but I'm learning how he thinks."

"And this is a good way to think?"

"Yes, it is. For a soldier at any rate."

The two of them were silent for a moment. Mee Mas looked at his feet and wondered if he could ever get them clean. "If I am to lead my people, I must learn to be a soldier."

"Yes," Vanderveen agreed, looking up the line to where the

massive T-2 led the way, and the solitary figure who marched behind. "There are times when they *do* come in handy."

It was early the next morning when Santana held a council of war. Sergeant Hillrun was there, as was Sergeant Twelve, L-1 Narvony, Vanderveen, and Mee Mas. Breakfast was over, a fine mist hung in the air, and they clutched mugs filled with hot tea. The fire, which was fueled by moisture-impervious heat tabs rather than wood, glowed rather than burned.

"So," Santana said, using his combat knife to make marks in the mud, "here's the situation. We're less than a day's march from Mys. That's the good news. The *bad* news is that we're being followed. Sergeant Hillrun, tell us what you saw."

The Naa, who came from a planet where the average surface conditions made LaNor's rainy season look mild by comparison, was muddy but otherwise unperturbed. "Sir, yes sir. Corporal Dietrich and I went for a little walk two hours before dawn. As all of you know some three or four individuals have tailing us ever since we left Pur Lor. Now, judging from the number of fires we saw, it appears that approximately two dozen digs, I mean LaNorians, have joined the chase."

Santana let the words sink in for a moment. He used his knife as a pointer. "So, thanks to the intelligence gathered by Sergeant Hillrun and Corporal Dietrich, we know the enemy is right about *here*. We're *here* . . . and Mys is *there*. The sudden arrival of additional warriors would seem to signal the possibility of an imminent attack.

"The question is this, do we go for it, and try to reach Mys *before* the Claw can catch up with us, or do we lay some sort of ambush?"

Mee Mas observed the proceedings with a considerable amount of interest. Here, much to his amazement, was a seemingly strong leader who, unlike all the generals of the youth's acquaintance, not only shared information with his subordinates, but even went so far as to solicit their opinions. Was that good or bad? Weak or strong? The prince waited to see.

"Well," Sergeant Twelve put in, "*I* favor an ambush. Remember all the Imperial troops we passed as we left Mys? They sure as hell didn't look very friendly. Who knows where things stand now? What if the folks to the rear are the hammer—and the Imperials are the anvil?"

It was good thinking—and Santana nodded accordingly. "Thanks, Sergeant. Hillrun? What do you think?"

"I'm with Twelve," the Naa replied. "Let's get 'em off our tails so we have a clear line of retreat if we run into trouble."

"I-1 Narvony? Any opinions?"

The Thraki didn't relish the idea of an unnecessary fight and looked doubtful. "I don't know, sir. What if we lay an ambush and they flank us? Even if we win all it would take is a few causalities to slow us down. That would give the Claw the opportunity to summon *more* warriors and attack again."

In spite of the fact that Santana was somewhat suspicious of the Thraki's true motives, everything she said made sense and would have to be taken into account. "Those are excellent points, Narvony. Well said. How 'bout the civilians among us? Any suggestions?"

"What about a compromise?" Vanderveen inquired. "You provide Mee Mas with an armed escort, send them toward Mys, and *we* stage the ambush."

Santana noted the "we" and understood the diplomat's reasoning. She wanted to protect the prince. The officer didn't want to divide his force however, and was about to say so, when the Mee Mas broke in. "No! If *you* fight, then *I* fight. Please provide me with a weapon."

There was a long drawn-out silence as Santana looked from person to person. His eyes came to rest on Vanderveen. The diplomat raised both of her carefully plucked eyebrows and gave an elaborate shrug. Somehow, in spite of the mud smeared across one cheek, she still managed to look beautiful.

"All right," the platoon leader said, "you heard the prince. Give him a rifle."

•   •   •

The Tro Wa "blues" were strung out in a long line, well separated in case of an ambush, and armed with cheap semiautomatic weapons purchased from human gunrunners. Unlike the farmers, weavers, and metalsmiths who followed him, Orl Kno actually had some military experience. Hard-won experience gained while serving under General Has Doo in the bandit-ridden western provinces. But that was back in the days when the Emperor was alive—and Shi Huu had been his consort.

Now, with more than sixty birthdays behind him, Orl Kno should have been sitting by the fire, warming his bones.

But the Claw were active in his village, *very* active, and each family was expected to do its part. That's why Orl Kno had volunteered, so his son wouldn't have to, and could remain with his young family.

Had he been asked the old soldier would have described himself as apolitical, not caring which despot ruled from Polwa so long as they didn't raise taxes too high, and stayed out of his village.

However, having been forced to take up arms on behalf of the Tro Wa, Orl Kno was determined not only to carry out the mission he'd been given, but to bring as many of his poorly trained peasants home as he could.

That's why the oldster never ceased to harp on the basics. Things like the importance of military discipline, the need to keep weapons scrupulously clean, and the difference between rhetoric and reality.

Claw leadership persisted in preaching all sorts of nonsense, including the notion that truly devout followers of the way were impervious to bullets, that the most fervent red lanterns could fly, and that the off-worlders were cowards.

So, thanks to Orl Kno's experience and levelheaded leadership, his detachment of "blues" were better organized and trained than most such groups were.

Their primary mission was simple: overtake the enemy and kill them.

There was a *secondary* mission, however, one which reeked

of politics and made the LaNorian extremely nervous. By some miraculous means, his superiors didn't say how, Orl Kno was supposed to inspect the party of off-world beings to determine if a prince named Mee Mas was among them, and then, absurd though the notion was, take the princeling alive. All based on orders handed down by some idiot named Lak Saa.

But orders are orders, and there was bound to be at least one informant in the group, which meant that Orl Kno had to at least *pretend* to follow orders. That's why he had dispatched a young rather athletic youngster to pass the devil beings during the hours of darkness, examine them as they passed by, and report via one of the two cheap handheld radios that had been issued to the team.

Now, as the old soldier slogged up a hill, a voice sounded in his pocket. "Orl Kno? Are you there?"

The oldster frowned as he fumbled the unfamiliar device out of his pocket, located the "talk" button, and pressed it down. "Of course I'm here . . . Where else would I be? Sitting on Shi Huu's throne?"

The youngster, an apprentice named Pok Tay was used to the oldster's somewhat cranky ways and knew the question was rhetorical. "I found a hole in the embankment, made it larger, and climbed inside. Then, using some brush, I covered the opening. The devils walked right by me! I could have reached out to touch them."

Orl Kno doubted that but was impressed nonetheless. "Good work, lad, what did you see?"

"The machine passed first, followed by the off-worlders, and a single LaNorian."

"A LaNorian? You're sure?"

"Yes," the youngster replied confidently. "He wore devil clothes, but he was a LaNorian all right, and armed with a weapon."

"Good," Orl Kno said, "stay where you are . . . The rest of us will arrive shortly."

Though not capable of running as he once had—Orl Kno

could jog, and he proceeded to do so. He moved over to the edge of the road, where the ground was firmer, and waved his troops forward.

The blues caught up with Pok Tay fifteen minutes later, picked up speed, and topped the rise just in time to see two figures vanish over the summit of the next hill.

Orl Kno shouted, "Forward! Kill everyone but the La-Norian! Then he led his troops down the reverse slope to the bridge below. A river broke white over water-smoothed stones, hurried to duck under the span, and rushed toward the sea.

Once across, and on the other side, the oldster planned to send his fastest warriors left and right in attempt to flank the off-worlders. Then, having brought the main part of his force straight up the middle, Orl Kno hoped to engage the aliens and hold them in place long enough for the rest of his troops to close from the sides.

It was a *good* plan, a *sensible* plan, and had the enemy force been comprised of LaNorians it probably would have worked.

But the T-2, not to mention its many capabilities, was outside the realm of Orl Kno's experience, which meant he had no way to know that Snyder had been well aware of Pok Tay's presence next to the road, had intentionally bypassed the youngster, *and* monitored their subsequent radio transmissions.

And so it was that the blues charged down the hill, thundered over the wooden bridge, and split into three groups.

Meanwhile, directly behind them, Snyder emerged from under the bridge and opened fire. Her .50 caliber slugs blew big muddy divots out of the ground, consumed one group of flankers, and pounded them to mush.

An energy bolt struck Pok Tay in the small of the back and blew him in half.

That's when more than a dozen off-worlders appeared on the crest of the hill and opened fire on the Claw below.

Orl Kno fired his rifle on the chance that a miracle would occur and one of his bullets would hit something. The oldster remembered the bench that sat outside his front door, the warmth of the summer sun, and the contentment of old age. That's when something slammed into his chest and knocked him off his feet. Orl Kno fell—but never hit the ground. There was the smell of recently turned earth, the gurgle of water from the pump, and the sound of his mate's voice. Dinner was ready—and it was time to go in.

Santana yelled, "Cease fire!" and heard two more shots as muscles reacted to messages already en route from the brain.

Then, with others at his side, the cavalry officer made his way down the slope to where the bodies of the butchers, bakers, and farmers lay tumbled about.

Mee Mas, his bloodstream still full of naturally produced stimulants, gazed in wonder. "Congratulations, Lieutenant . . . You won a glorious victory."

Santana looked down at an elderly male, arms outspread, eyes staring at the sky. His voice was gruff. "There is no glory *here*, my lord, none at all."

THE IMPERIAL CITY OF POLWA, ON THE INDEPENDENT PLANET OF LANOR

The interior of the hodo (warehouse) was a long rectangular space normally used to dry pica leaves—but empty until the end of the rainy season when the spring caravans would arrive from the west. Rain pounded on the boards above, and water dripped, trickled, and poured through the myriad holes, cracks and gaps that penetrated the roof the building. The smell of the spice mixed with that of damp clothing and wet earth to form a thick odor that clung to the back of Dee Waa's throat and caused him to swallow.

The interior of the hodo was filled with members of the Claw. They lined both walls three ranks deep. Those to the rear stood, those in the middle sat on wooden benches, and those in front squatted on their heels.

A line of vertical posts ran down the center of the warehouse each supporting not only the roof but two fish oil lamps. The soft yellow glow served to illuminate the arena's center all but surrendering the margins to darkness.

At first there was no noise other than that made by the rain and the insistent beat of a single drum. Then hinges squealed, a door banged open, and clothing rustled as Dee Waa and those around him turned to look. A rectangle of gray light had appeared. It seemed to flicker as a file of fifteen prisoners were ushered into the room. Their clothing was soaked and plastered to their skins.

The prisoners were a mixed lot, including what appeared to be two members of the petty nobility, a scattering of portly merchants, and plenty of sturdy peasants. Something Dee Waa assumed was not only intentional but replete with meaning: No one was so high as to escape the hand of justice—and no one was so insignificant as to slip through the net.

There was something that united the prisoners however— and that was the common denominator of fear. No one had told them their fate but no one had to. There were many crimes that one could commit, but one sentence, and that was death.

Guards positioned the condemned at equal intervals along the length of the hodo. Then, much to Dee Waa's surprise, each of the prisoners was issued a weapon. Some received swords, others were given spears, and one confused-looking merchant found himself clutching a rusty battle-ax.

Some seemed comforted by the gifts, even going so far as to try a few experimental swings with their swords, but most simply stood with their eyes on the ground.

Then, as the tempo of the drum increased slightly, the door opened again. A solitary figure stood silhouetted against the gray light. He took a moment to look around, stepped forward, and was bathed in the soft yellow light. The newcomer was larger than the average LaNorian male, and with the exception of a white turban and matching loin cloth wore no clothes whatsoever. He bore no weapons other than the long reinforced fingernails on each hand. A thick layer of fat covered his smoothly rounded torso and jiggled when he moved.

It was a strange, almost comical sight, but nobody laughed, least of all the prisoners, because they knew who he was. This was the noble named Lak Saa, the ex-minister who referred to himself as the gudar (advisor), and the eunuch who carried his privates in a jar.

Dee Waa held his breath as the Tro Wa master closed on the first prisoner and paused. Such was the strength of his voice that every person in the warehouse could hear without difficulty. "Look upon those brought before you and know them for the spies, traitors, and devil lovers that they are. All of them have been sentenced to death, all of them deserve to die, yet all of them have been given the opportunity to live. All they have to do is kill me."

There was a murmur of protest to which Lak Saa raised his hand. "Thank you. I treasure your loyalty, and take strength from it, but hear me well. Should I be killed you are hereby commanded to set *all* the surviving prisoners free. That is my wish . . . Do I have your word that you will obey?"

There was a roar of acknowledgment as Dee Waa and all the rest of them strove to shout the roof down. But even as he took part in the demonstration of support, the schoolteacher was busy analyzing the situation. Were the prisoners listening? *Truly* listening? Because if they were, the eunuch's words not only provided each one of them with a reason to fight, *but to attack as a group.*

But that would require a leader, someone with the courage to step forward, and the clarity to formulate a plan under the worst of conditions. Did such a person exist? Or would each prisoner fight singly? Assuming they fought at all.

Lak Saa bowed to both sides of the room, took a moment to leave the material world behind, and entered the shadowy realm that lay between mind and spirit. The eunuch's feet flowed like water, his hands floated through the air, and his body rotated through the three positions of truth: seeking, finding, and enlightenment.

The first prisoner had been presented with a sword, and

while it was true that he had used one before, there was a marked difference between the sort of butchery he and his fellow "greens" practiced on unarmed Transcendental converts and the kind of combat demanded of him now. The prisoner raised the sword high over his head, waited for what he judged to be the correct moment, and brought the weapon down.

Lak Saa glided, spun, and was two paces away when the blade fell through empty air.

Prisoner number one lived long enough to realize that he had missed, that the blood spilling down the front of his tunic belonged to him, and that death smelled like spice.

There was a roar of approval as the first prisoner was executed and Dee Waa absorbed the meaning of the lesson. Here, right before their very eyes, Lak Saa had demonstrated the power of right thinking, the primacy of spirit over mind, and the manner in which skill can triumph over technology. A sword represents power, yet it, like the weapons manufactured by the aliens, was nothing when confronted with the knowledge of a Tro Wa master. There was much to learn—and much to teach.

The second prisoner, a merchant convicted of spying on behalf of Shi Huu, was armed with a spear. He eyed the eunuch, thrust the spear into the ground, and stood with folded arms.

Lak Saa performed a forward somersault, rose in front of his victim, and used his right hand to honor the sky.

The merchant jerked as the eunuch's razor-sharp claw ripped through both his clothes and abdomen alike. There was a gurgling sound as prisoner number two's bowels fell down around his knees, and his eyes went blank.

The crowd roared and the body was still falling as the gudar walked what other Tro Wa practitioners knew to be "the six stepping-stones," before reaching the next appointment with death.

Except that prisoner number three was a natural leader, who backed by all twelve of his surviving comrades, looked formidable indeed. He roared an order, and charged Lak Saa, even as the others circled to the sides.

The eunuch was a leaf, propelled by the wind, skittering along a forest path. He touched a tree, then another, and still *another* knowing that each would fall.

Then, spinning as leaves do, he released four additional souls from their bodies even as spears slid along the surface of his skin, swords hacked at his legs, and a battle-ax nicked his throat.

Now, with only six opponents left, the Tro Wa master accepted a sword from a dying hand, appropriated another from the ground, and caused both to dance. The blades glittered like sunlight on the surface of a lake as the eunuch attacked the spaces where the remaining prisoners would have little choice but to appear. One by one they went there, throwing themselves under the bloody blades, falling as metal bit into bone.

Then, with only one prisoner left, Lak Saa did a strange thing. Rather than take the farmer's head off, as Dee Waa had assumed that he would, the Tro Wa master dropped both weapons onto the floor.

The prisoner had soiled himself by that time, and made no attempt to escape as Lak Saa approached to place a single finger on the peasant's chest. Then, speaking with an authority that penetrated every corner of the room, the eunuch uttered a single word: "Die."

The farmer's eyes rolled back in his head, his heart stopped, and he died. The onlookers stood, stomped their feet, and shouted Lak Saa's name.

Dee Waa, ever the student, knew what would happen next. Every person present would go forth and not only *tell* the story, but *elaborate* on it, until a new legend was born. A legend in which Lak Saa ordered a hundred traitors to die and they hurried to obey him.

And it was that moment when the teacher, not to mention all those around him, knew he had chosen the correct side.

Nothing could stand in the way of the Claw . . . and victory was as sure as the dawn of a new day.

THE FOREIGN CITY OF MYS, ON THE INDEPENDENT PLANET OF LANOR

The room was just large enough to contain a gigantic bed, an oversize dresser, and an enormous easy chair. Rain splattered on the only window. With the exception of the metal-framed mirror that hung above the dresser the walls were bare. A monastic space but one that more than met the needs of its current occupant.

It was late afternoon and Legion Captain Drik Seeba-Ka was in a foul mood. *Not* because of the rain, which was nothing by the standards of his native planet, but because the damnable Dracs had seen fit to throw a party, which meant he would have to go.

It was difficult to gauge which was worse, the tight, stifling embrace of the dress uniform now laid out on the surface of his bed, or the absurd small talk that diplomats loved to engage in.

Even more unpleasant, from Seeba-Ka's perspective at least, was the purpose of the gala, which in the words of the written invitation was ". . . to celebrate Force Leader Hakk Batth's safe return and hear of his many adventures."

This, for an officer who the Hudathan believed should probably be under investigation for incompetence, but had been received as a hero.

The officer's thoughts were interrupted by three sharp raps on the door. He turned toward the sound. "Enter!"

The door swung open, and First Sergeant Neversmile stuck his head in. "Sorry to bother your, sir, but I have good news. *Very* good news."

"That seems hard to believe," Seeba-Ka said, buckling his belt, "but I'll take it . . . What's up?"

"Bagano picked up a radio message, sir. It was from Snyder . . . She says there was some sort of ambush, and Batth took off with the only long-range set. It seems that Santana, Hillrun, Dietrich, Taz, Kimura, Pesta, Seavy, and Horo-Ba are all alive and their way in.

"Kashtoon was KIA (killed in action) along with half the Thraks plus some of the digs, but the Clones made it, along with FSO Vanderveen and some prince or other. The whole lot of them should hit the North Gate in an hour or so."

Like most Hudathans, Seeba-Ka wasn't known for demonstrations of emotion so when the officer slammed his ham-sized fist down on the dresser, and said, "Yes!" Neversmile knew the company commander was happy.

"So, I should tell the ambassador?"

Seeba-Ka's mind began to race. "No," he said thoughtfully. "Nobody talks to Pas Rasha until I have a chance to debrief Santana. In the meantime I want you to find Lieutenant Beck worth. Give her the good news and tell her I want a couple of T-2s along with her entire platoon out in front of the North Gate. I'll meet her there . . . And another thing, tell Beckworth to take the back way out, rather than march down Embassy Row."

The NCO nodded. "Sir, yes sir. And Major Miraby? What shall I tell him?"

Seeba-Ka turned to the mirror mounted over the dresser. "Tell him everything you know, *if* you can find him, which might be difficult what with the party and all."

The *real* meaning was clear, and the Naa grinned. "Sir, yes sir."

The door closed and the Hudathan crossed to his bed. The sword, which had been in his clan for hundreds of years, lay gleaming on the Legion-issue olive drab blanket. Its name translated to "Death Giver," and it hadn't seen action for a long time.

Metal sang as the soldier pulled the blade out of its scabbard and allowed the light to ripple along its carefully honed edge. The clans still existed, in name at least, but not for long. Soon, within a hundred years, the Hudathan population would be as homogenized as the humans were.

But *one* clan would live on, a clan forged in the heat of battle, and to which a warrior could be true. That's why Seeba-Ka had paid an armorer to inscribe new words on old steel. *Legio Patria Nostra.* "The Legion Is Our Country."

Santana had mounted Snyder's back in order to get a better view. Finally, as afternoon gave way to evening, the rain dwindled to nothing. Not the mud however, which continued to slow the column's progress, and made the march miserable.

Of more concern, to Santana's mind at any rate, was the scene that greeted him as the T-2 topped the last rise and provided the officer with a sweeping view of the plain on which Polwa, and eventually Mys had been built. There were campfires, thousands of them, and they glittered like rubies.

The fires closest to the city walls, where the Imperials were camped, had been laid out in precise rows. Farther away, and outnumbering the Imperial fires at least three to one, the officer could see a random scattering of civilian encampments. The road, which appeared as a ribbon of black, wound its way between the fires to terminate at the North Gate.

Above, beyond the thick walls, Santana could make out the glow that emanated from Mys and Polwa beyond. What was going on in within he wondered? Had conditions deteriorated? Or stayed about the same?

The question foremost on his mind however was how many of the fires in front of him belonged to the Claw? How good were the Tro Wa's communications? And did the locals have orders to attack his column regardless of cost? If so, the troops under his command were outnumbered thousands to one, and no matter how hard they fought the column would never make it to the gate.

Still, assuming that the forces in front of him were the anvil, and those eliminated in the recent ambush had been the hammer, then it was possible that the locals didn't know that the column existed.

But there were other concerns as well . . . Batth had been back for days by then, or so the cavalry officer assumed, which meant that the authorities had only one version of what had taken place in the swamp, the Ramanthian version, which was certain to be full of lies.

Would Seeba-Ka and Miraby believe *his* version of events? Especially given the history between Batth and himself? There was plenty of room for doubt.

But that would have to wait. First, Santana had to cross the plain successfully and enter Mys. The officer ordered his column to "Close it up," pulled the intercom jack out of Snyder's neck, and jumped to the ground. His boots sank a good four inches into the mud and it took considerable effort to pull them out. Vanderveen appeared at his elbow and it seemed natural to fall into step with her. Mee Mas, disguised to look like a legionnaire, was to the rear with Hillrun.

"So," the diplomat said, "this should be interesting."

"That's one word for it," Santana agreed soberly.

"You're worried about Batth, aren't you?"

"I'd be lying if I said I wasn't."

Vanderveen looked into Santana's eyes. "I was there . . . I'll tell them what happened."

Santana nodded. "Thanks, I appreciate that, I really do. However, even if I'm able to prove that Batth was derelict in performing his duties, the bastard could *still* nail me for disobeying a direct order back in the swamp. Even a bad order. That's how the military works."

Vanderveen was about to offer her opinion on how the military functioned when a pair of flares soared upward, made an audible popping sound, and started to drift downward. An eerie blue-green glow lit the landscape. Anyone who hadn't been paying attention suddenly was and all eyes turned in the direction of the road. The good news was that Santana could see his surroundings—and the bad news was that his surroundings could see him.

A radio transmission followed the flares. Santana recognized the voice as belonging to Lieutenant Mary Beckworth. "Red Six to Blue Six . . . over."

Santana made note of the need to adjust call signs. "This is Blue Six . . . go. Over."

"Welcome home Blue Six . . . You have a reception party at twelve o'clock. If we see so much as a kid with a pocketknife we have orders to fire. Stay on the road so we know where you are . . . and don't put any ordnance near the gate."

"Roger that," Santana said gratefully. "We're on our way, over."

Two additional flares popped high in the air, were caught by the easterly breeze, and blown toward the distant ocean.

Now, fully aware that a party of off-worlders was among them, the civilians, and that included a significant number of the Claw, were drawn to both sides of the road. They stood three and five bodies deep, weapons clutched in their hands, walling the column in.

Vanderveen heard a distinct *click* as Santana released the safety on his CA-10 carbine. The diplomat took her rifle off safety as well and prepared to defend herself.

Meanwhile, a youth named Yao Che stood next to the Claw known as Ply Pog and watched the first aliens plod by. Having spent time with the Bussos, and been allowed to watch hundreds of videos prior to Trudy's untimely death, the youngster had seen all sorts of amazing technology. So, while interesting, the sight of the enormous T-2 didn't have the mesmerizing effect on Yao Che that it did on many of those around him.

What happened next was more the result of impulse than a well-conceived strategy. He was relatively small, but so were one group of aliens, and that suggested a plan. Stepping forward, then sliding along the front rank of onlookers, his mouth open in what he hoped was an expression of wonderment, Yao Che waited for the next set of flares to go off. It seemed to take forever as he stepped on someone's toes, staggered as they cuffed the side of his head, and felt his hat fall off! The same hat he had worked so long to protect.

Yao Che's first impulse was to go after the missing cap then run to catch up. But better sense prevailed as the youth realized that the hat as well as the message hidden inside it had probably been trampled into the mud by then, and once engaged in trying to find it he would never be able to catch the aliens.

The youngster clutched the earthenware pot to his chest, continued to edge along the front of the crowd, and waited for the next set of flares. He and his companions had attempted to enter Polwa the day before and been denied. It seemed that the Empress had grown concerned about the number of Tro Wa who had entered the Imperial city of late and started to turn them away. A factor that made Yao Che's task that much more difficult.

Then, just when the LaNorian messenger had decided that there wouldn't be any more flares, they went off. Nearly everyone looked upward, was momentarily blinded by the glare, and forced to stare at spots for a moment or two. No one, nor even the Thrakies themselves, noticed that their number had grown by one.

Yao Che marched head down and kept his eyes on the alien in front of him. The gate, the one that would admit him to the foreign city of Mys, loomed ahead. It looked green under the flares and torches could be seen to either side.

Meanwhile, Captain Drik Seeba-Ka, resplendent in his dress uniform and armed with handgun and sword, approached the North Gate. Though still at their respective posts, the La-Norian guards had effectively been neutralized by the sudden appearance of six legionnaires, all of whom claimed they were there to "help."

The ranking Imperial was still in the process of explaining that he didn't need any help, and demanding some sort of credentials, when Snyder whirred past him. The LaNorian tried to rally his troops, to block what he saw as unauthorized access, when someone tripped him. The Imperial swore, fell in a pile of raz shit, and felt a combat boot land on his chest. First Sergeant Neversmile grinned. "Ooops! Sorry about that; don't move. I'll call a medic."

The Imperial was explaining that he didn't *need* a herbalist, and wanted to get up, when the senior NCO saw Sergeant Hillrun pass through the gate and removed his foot from the LaNorian's torso. Seconds later the Naa were slapping each other on the back, the Imperial was scraping shit off his uniform, and the second platoon was backing its way into the city. Whatever spell had held the crowd at bay seemed to expire as the last of the legionnaires withdrew, the doors slammed shut, and the enormous crossbar fell into its brackets.

Then, like an animal denied its prey, a roar of protest was heard. A hail of rocks rattled against the doors, a volley of shots were fired, and fire arrows streaked over the top of the walls. One struck a cluster of shacks located west of the gate and set a roof on fire. The occupants yelled at each other and ran to throw buckets of water on the blaze.

Meanwhile, Seeba-Ka joined Santana as the column took a right, then a left, and paused behind the Thrak embassy. The Thraki troops wanted to be released and said so. Seeba-Ka opposed that, for the next hour at least, and ordered them to remain where they were. No one noticed as one of their number faded into the shadows and vanished from sight.

"All right," the Hudathan said, pulling Santana to one side, "tell me what happened out there, and be careful what you say. One lie, one attempt to bullshit me, and I will have your ass for breakfast."

Though well aware of the fact that he would have to go through what promised to be a rather painful debriefing process, and fill out dozens of reports, the cavalry officer was surprised by Seeba-Ka's urgent manner.

Still, he had spent countless hours thinking about all that had taken place, and discovered that he was able to deliver a fairly cogent verbal report. Seeba-Ka listened intently, nodding from time to time, and interjecting questions.

When Santana came to the evening prior to the ambush, and his recommendation that the column avoid the swamp, a new voice chimed in. "You might be interested to know that I taped that conversation—listen to this. Both officers turned to discover that Vanderveen had joined them. She smiled sweetly and triggered the vocorder.

Seeba-Ka listened to the relevant part of the conversation and nodded. "Thank you, FSO Vanderveen, please continue to safeguard that recording . . . we're going to need it. What happened next?"

Santana's throat felt dry. He swallowed in attempt to lubricate it. Then, careful to stick to the facts, the cavalry officer recounted how the column had entered the swamp, how he requested permission to fire, and how his request was denied.

Then, knowing that he might well be sealing his fate, Santana told Seeba-Ka how he had intentionally disobeyed Batth's order, triggered the ambush, and pulled back only to discover that the Ramanthians were firing on the column from the rear.

It was dark, but the lights were on within the Thraki embassy, and the glow lit the left side of the Hudathan's face. It was so grim as to appear skeletal. He turned to Vanderveen. "Did you see the Ramanthians fire toward the column?"

"I certainly did," the diplomat said calmly. "One of them tried to kill me."

"Really?" Seeba-Ka asked, "What happened?"

"She shot him," Santana put in succinctly. "One bullet—right through the chest."

"How very economical," the Hudathan said dryly. "If only our legionnaires were equally parsimonious. You would testify to that?"

"Of course," Vanderveen assured him. "With pleasure."

"The Claw were armed with Ramanthian-made Negar III assault rifles," Santana put in. "We brought one of them back."

"Good," Seeba-Ka said. "Keep that weapon secured. All right, what happened next?"

It took ten minutes to provide the company commander with the highlights of the march to Pur Lor, the way Prince Mee Mas had surfaced in the well, and the trip back. The Hudathan listened intently as Santana explained his decision to set up an ambush and the outcome.

Then, satisfied that he had a pretty good understanding of what had taken place, Seeba-Ka eyed the junior officer's soiled uniform. "You look like hell—but that could work to our benefit . . . Now listen carefully, strange as it may seem, I'm about to take you to a party. Not just *any* party, but a party that the Dracs are throwing for Batth, to celebrate his safe return. Never mind the fact that if the bastard were telling the truth, he lost 75 percent of his command. Anyway, I think it might be very interesting to have you show up right about now, especially in light of the fact that the scumbag filed a report claiming that his troops buried you in the swamp."

Santana's eyes grew wider. "Sir, you've got to be joking."

"Have you ever heard me tell a joke?"

"No sir."

"Nor are you likely to. Let's go."

"I'm coming, too," Vanderveen put in cheerfully, "I wouldn't miss this for the world."

"That's up to you, ma'am," Seeba-Ka replied grimly, "but it won't be much of a party."

The Drac embassy was on the other side of Legation street from the Strathmore Hotel. In contrast to the structures erected by other off-worlders, most of which were intentionally imposing, the building the Dracs had sequestered themselves within consisted of a featureless concrete box having four doors and no windows.

The public areas of the embassy's interior were equally stark. Screens depicting clouds of swirling gas hung on some of the walls, while others were entirely bare. Furniture, all of which was made of bare metal, crouched here and there.

There were private areas, of course, rooms pumped full of the gas mix that the Dracs physiology required them to breathe, but none of the other off-worlders had ever been invited to enter those, and would have required space armor to survive.

An attempt had been made to decorate the room in which diplomatic functions were held. However, given the fact that the Dracs were color-blind, and saw everything in shades of gray, the streamers, table decorations, and other items had been chosen without regard to whether the colors were complementary.

The fact that the Drac diplomats wore dull black pressure suits and made gurgling noises as they breathed did nothing to lighten the atmosphere.

Still, everyone present was used to such realities, and did a masterful job of ignoring both the decor and the manner in which their hosts were forced to dress. Once everyone had been given a chance to sip, slurp, or siphon the stimulant or depressant of their choice the festivities could begin.

In spite of the fact that most of those present thought it was inappropriate to celebrate the survival of one group while so many others had perished, it seemed such gatherings were common among the Dracs, who saw them as memorials to both the living and the dead. Pas Rasha had been unwilling to attend, but rather than offend the Drac Axis, sent FSO-2 Harley Clauson to represent him.

It was warm inside the Drac embassy, *too* warm, and Clauson used a cocktail napkin to dab the beads of perspiration on his forehead as the Drac ambassador mounted the platform at the far end of the room. His name was Fas Doonar, and he was a close personal friend to both Ambassador Regar Batth, and his military corollary, Force Leader Hakk Batth. The microphone served to amplify both his voice *and* the gurgling noises that his respirator made.

"Good evening. Thank you for joining us. I have been in the diplomatic corps long enough to realize that there are those among you who consider a gathering like this one to be distasteful if not outright inappropriate. For the Drac such celebrations serve a positive function, however, reaffirming the value of life, and bringing those who survive together.

"Like you, we were saddened to learn that the relief column had been ambushed, and in spite of the valiant defense put up by the Thrakies, Clones, and Ramanthians, nearly wiped out."

Clauson, who like everyone in the diplomatic community was well aware of the claims Batth had made regarding Lieutenant Santana's persistent incompetence, couldn't help but notice the fact that no mention had been made of the legionnaires *or* Christine Vanderveen, for whom he felt responsible. The entire Mee Mas thing had been highly speculative at best—and in retrospect the FSO knew he should have opposed it. Now he would have to write a letter to her father, something which would not only be unpleasant, but also not especially good for his career.

"However," Doonar continued, "in spite of our grief we can still take a moment to celebrate the accomplishments of the brave officer who fought off the Claw, brought his troops back through hostile territory, and survived to join us tonight. I give you Force Leader Hakk Batth."

There was light applause as Hakk Batth backed out of his chair and made his way up to the platform. Like the other military officers present that evening, the Ramanthian wore his dress uniform complete with a red pillbox hat, gold epaulettes, two rows of medals, a pleated kilt, and a chromed sidearm. His sword hung Ramanthian-style down his back. The Ramanthian nodded to the Drac diplomat and launched into some prepared text. Meaningless drivel for the most part, extolling the accomplishments of those who died in the ambush, while subtly polishing his own reputation.

Clauson, who found the whole thing to be depressing, had just grabbed two pastries off a passing tray and was about to shove them into his mouth, when a door slammed open and Captain Drik Seeba-Ka invaded the room.

Major Miraby, who had been wondering where Seeba-Ka was, watched in amazement as his subordinate marched up the aisle, mounted the platform, and commandeered the microphone. Batth said something by way of an objection but the Hudathan was louder. "Good evening, gentle beings . . . It may interest you to know that while some of our brave soldiers were killed in action—many of them survived. Please welcome Lieutenant Santana, FSO Vanderveen, Prince Mee Mas, and the troops who accompanied them."

Santana heard his cue, pushed the door open, and made for the stage. Vanderveen followed. But that wasn't all. . . . Even as the military officer and the diplomat walked toward the front of the room, a T-2 bent nearly double in order to pass through the door, Sergeant Twelve entered with Seebos in tow, L-1 Narvony led her bedraggled troops into the hall, while Sergeant Hillrun and six legionnaires brought up the rear.

The sight of the soldiers brought forth exclamations of amazement, many shouts of joy, and all manner of confused conversation. "Now," Seeba-Ka continued, "take a good look at the beings that Force Leader Hakk Batth assured you were dead and know the actual truth. . . . For reasons I can only speculate on, Batth cut some sort of deal with the Claw, led the column into an ambush, and ordered Ramanthian troops to fire on the allied force as well.

"Then, certain that all the potential witnesses were dead, he returned to Mys. Under the circumstances, Lieutenant Santana had little choice but to assume command. Though unable to complete the original mission, the lieutenant *was* able to assist FSO Vanderveen in locating Prince Mee Mas and successfully brought what remained of the column back through enemy-held territory."

Even allowing for differences in culture and physiology there was no mistaking the look of stunned amazement on Force Leader Hakk Batth's face. His eyes bulged, his parrotlike beak opened and closed, and his tool arms jerked spasmodically.

It should have been impossible, but Santana had not only managed to escape death at the hands of the Tro Wa, but made it back to Mys. All of which meant that Batth had not only failed, but shamed his mates in the process, for which there could be no forgiveness.

The Ramanthian used both arms to reach back over his head, grasp the sword's twin hilts, and pull the weapon out of its scabbard. Santana would die first, followed by the Hudathan and the human diplomat.

But Seeba-Ka had anticipated the move, more than that *hoped* for such a move, and *Death Giver* had already started to sing even as the Ramanthian reached back over his head.

Santana had just started to reach for his sidearm as metal flashed under the overhead lights, Hudathan steel connected with Ramanthian chitin, and Batth's head flew off. Blood fountained into the air, one of the Prithians uttered the human equivalent of a scream, and the Ramanthian's torso toppled forward into the crowd.

Guests scattered, furniture was overturned, and one of the Thraki diplomats fainted.

Seeba-Ka, sword still in hand, left the platform.

Regar Batth, the Ramanthian ambassador, knelt next to what remained of his mate.

Clauson, both pastries still uneaten, turned to Miraby. "Well, Major, I don't know about you, but I'd say *this* party was anything but boring. My compliments to Captain Seeba-Ka on his swordsmanship. Now, if you'll excuse me, it's time to say hello to FSO Vanderveen . . . I'll see you in the morning."

The party was over—but it was one that none were likely to forget.

8

The ideal officer in any army knows his business. He is firm and
just . . . An officer is not supposed to sleep until his men are bed-
ded down. He is not supposed to eat until he has arranged for his
men to eat. He's like a prizefighter's manager. If he keeps his
fighter in shape the fighter will make him successful. I respect those
combat officers who feel this responsibility so strongly that many
of them are killed fulfilling it. .

Bill Mauldin
Up Front
Standard year 1945

THE FOREIGN CITY OF MYS, ON THE INDEPENDENT PLANET OF LANOR

Major Homer Miraby's office looked much like those used by
other senior officers except that none of the photos, plaques
and other memorabilia that decorated the room had anything
to do with combat. In spite of repeated requests for a line
command Miraby had progressed from lieutenant to major
without having seen action, and not having had the opportunity to prove himself in battle, would rise no further.

It wasn't fair really, since it had been his skill at interarmy
politics, administrative matters, and procurement that caused
superiors to put him behind a long succession of desks, but
that's how it was. Unlike some of his peers, whose ambitions
had been frustrated by wounds suffered in battle, the appli-

cation of ill-considered strategies, or the vagaries of high-level military politics, Miraby's career suffered because he was good at tasks that, while important to the Legion, were not considered to be sufficiently warrior-like.

And so it was that Captain Drik Seeba-Ka and Lieutenant Antonio Santana found themselves standing at parade rest in the center of a room hung with photos of Miraby standing with all manner of other REMFs (rear echelon motherfuckers), politicians of various stripes, and corporate bigwigs.

The better part of twenty minutes had passed since they had been ushered into the office, and the major had yet to arrive. The officers suspected it was Miraby's way of preparing the ground, of putting them in their place, and there was nothing they could do but wait. Both had spent most of the night writing reports. Santana for Seeba-Ka, Seeba-Ka for Miraby, and knowing how the pecking order worked, Miraby for Ambassador Pas Rasha.

Now, nearly dead on his feet, Santana discovered that he had momentarily fallen asleep when the door slammed and jarred him awake. Both officers came to attention.

Miraby, his freshly shaved head gleaming in the light, his mustache nicely combed, and his uniform starched to perfection strode to the other side of the room, took his place behind a barricade-like desk, and speared them with his eyes.

"Would you like to know where I've been? I'll tell you where I've been . . . I was with Ambassador Pas Rasha—trying to figure out how to deal with the political fallout attendant to last evening's execution."

Seeba-Ka started to speak but Miraby held up a hand. "Don't try to bullshit me, Captain . . . I read the reports. You met with Santana prior to the party, came to certain conclusions, and passed sentence.

"Having done so, you created a deliberately provocative situation, made what can only be described as incendiary statements, and engineered the response you hoped for.

"Predictably enough the Ramanthian ambassador is pissed,

seriously pissed, and looking for a way to get even. He plans to forward a protest to Senator Orno, who will raise the matter in the Senate, thereby generating all sorts of complicated hell.

"Now, as for *you*," Miraby said, his right index finger pointing at Santana's chest, "let me be very clear . . . There is no room in the Legion for officers who refuse to obey orders. Fortunately for you, and for Captain Seeba-Ka as well, FSO Vanderveen did an exemplary job of documenting what took place out in the field, and the radio transmissions downloaded from Snyder's onboard computer serve to support her records.

"In fact, you might want to buy her a drink, because if I were to believe the reports that *she* wrote, I'd get the impression that you are competent, which I happen to know you aren't.

"Thanks to FSO Vanderveen's efforts, not to mention the ambassador's, there's at least some chance that the two of you will be able to avoid court-martial.

"Now," Miraby said, circling his desk to stand right in front of them, "hear me good. Copies of all the relevant documentation have been forwarded to the Ramanthian embassy. That means Ambassador Batth knows what we know. Based on preliminary communications I think the Ramanthians will deny that they cut some sort of deal with the Claw, write what happened during the ambush off to the 'fog of war,' and position Batth's withdrawal as an honest mistake. *We*, and that includes the two of you, will accept that version of events so the bugs can save face. Force Leader Batth is dead . . . and so is this incident. Understood?"

The officers answered in unison. "Sir! Yes, sir!"

"Good, then get the hell out of my office."

Both officers saluted, did an about-face, and left the room.

Once in the hall, with the door closed, Seeba-Ka paused to flick an imaginary piece of lint off his arm. "That went well, don't you think?."

Santana frowned. "No offense, sir, but you must be joking. The Ramanthians cut some sort of deal with the Claw, and our own diplomats are participating in the cover-up."

Seeba-Ka's face twitched in what might have been the Hudathan equivalent of a smile. "First, I never tell jokes. Second, Batth is dead. And third, whatever the bugs were trying to accomplish has been disrupted. Regardless of what Miraby says, that's what *I* call a good day's work."

Then, his arms swinging as if on parade, the Hudathan marched down the hall.

It had been a busy morning, a *very* busy morning, what with the aftermath of the party to deal with but Clauson made time to have lunch with Vanderveen, and the two of them were sharing an umbrella on their way to the embassy when a LaNorian dashed out of a passageway to accost them. He was filthy and held some sort of pot clutched in his arms. He spoke clear nearly unaccented standard. "Sir! Ma'am! My name is Yao Che. A human named Frank Busso sent me. I must see the ambassador."

There had been no radio communications with the Bussos for some time and they were generally believed to be dead. Still, how would a street beggar learn to speak standard? And know who the Bussos were?

The diplomats paused. Raindrops fell from the edge of the umbrella. Clauson raised an eyebrow. "*Frank* Busso? Describe him."

"He's tall," Yao Che replied, "taller than you are, and not so fat. He has hair on his head, a big nose, and smiles a lot."

Vanderveen managed to suppress a smile at the less than tactful comparison. "That sounds like Busso all right . . . what's the message?"

"Yes," Clauson said reaching for some LaNorian coins. "You tell *us* . . . and we'll tell *him*."

"*No,*" Yao Che replied stubbornly, "the message is for the ambassador. I must deliver it to him."

"Okay," Vanderveen said soothingly. "We'll take you to see the ambassador. The guards will have to search you . . . and inspect that pot."

"They mustn't open the pot," the youth replied anxiously. "It contains my gana's ashes—and they might spill."

"No problem," Clauson assured him. "The guards have machines that can look inside the pot without removing the lid. Assuming you don't have a bomb concealed inside everything will be fine."

Somewhat reassured, but still concerned lest the letter show up on the off-world machines, Yao Che allowed himself to be herded up to the embassy's front entrance where a legionnaire patted him down. Subsequent to that the youth was ushered through a metal framework and out into the embassy proper. His sandals left muddy marks on the floor. No one said anything or made an attempt to stop him.

Thus reassured Yao Che followed Clauson into a small room, gave an involuntary yelp as it started to move, and deduced that he had entered some sort of machine.

Then, following a wait while Clauson went in to brief the ambassador, the female human led the courier into a large richly furnished office. The being who rose to greet him was of a species Yao Che had seen on the Bussos' vids but never met in person. His body looked as if it consisted of sticks covered with pale almost translucent skin and machinery whirred when the off-worlder moved. He had a nice voice, though—and spoke LaNorian without the aid of an electronic translator.

"Welcome . . . FSOs Clauson and Vanderveen tell me that you brought a message all the way from the village of Nah Ree."

"That is true," Yao Che responded solemnly. "Frank Busso's message is hidden inside *this*."

The earthenware pot made a thud as it landed on Pas Rasha's desk. Yao Che had resealed the vessel with a new layer of wax. The Dweller used a ceremonial dagger to pry it open. He eyed the contents. "What have we here?"

"I told people they were my gana's ashes," the youth replied, "but Frank got them out of the mission's fireplace."

"Clever," the diplomat said, probing the ashes with one of his long slender fingers, "*very* clever."

"There was another letter," the youngster said helpfully, "hidden in my hat. But I lost that while sneaking into the city."

"You did well," Pas Rasha observed as he dragged a waterproofed envelope out of the ashes and shook it off. "Citizen Busso will be proud."

It took less than two minutes to read the tersely written report—and the subsequent plea for help. When Pas Rasha looked up he found that Yao Che's eyes were waiting to greet him. "So, you will send help, yes?"

The diplomat knew it would take hours if not days to decide what if anything the embassy could do to help. He produced what he hoped the LaNorian youth would interpret as a friendly smile. "I'd like to say 'yes,' but I don't know if I can. You saw what it's like beyond the walls . . . We may be fighting for our lives within a day or two. Tell me something—how long did your journey take?"

Yao Che was intelligent, just one of the reasons why Frank Busso had chosen him, and immediately understood the true nature of the question. What the diplomat really wanted to know was whether the missionaries and their converts could hold out long enough for help to reach them. Consequently, Yao Che did the only thing he could do—he lied.

"I made excellent time, Excellency—the entire trip lasted only three days."

"That's remarkable," Pas Rasha said more to himself than Yao Che. "Please allow me to thank you for what you did. It was extremely brave. Perhaps you would be willing to join my mate and myself for last meal? We would love to hear of your adventures.

"In the meantime FSO Clauson will take you to my assistant. She will make arrangements for a bath, some new clothes, and a bed. How does that sound?"

Yao Che bowed respectfully. "Thank you, Excellency. I would be most grateful."

"You're most welcome," the ambassador replied. "I'll see you tonight."

Pas Rasha waited for Clauson and his young charge to exit the room before speaking to Vanderveen. "First the party, then Mee Mas, now this . . . Is there any end to it?"

"Trouble comes in threes," Vanderveen said confidently. "The next news you hear is likely to be good."

"I hope so," Pas Rasha answered politely, but knew she would be wrong.

It was afternoon, halfway between lunch and dinner, which meant that the Strathmore's restaurant was nearly empty. Chien-Chu had claimed one of the four linen-covered tables that faced the street. Raindrops spattered against the fifteen-foot-tall window, and the cyborg turned to watch as a human dashed across the street, a pair of upper-class LaNorians strolled under a leather parasol, and a beggar stood with her hand extended. Not the sort of day to venture out unless forced to do so . . . but all the streets were becoming more crowded as off-worlders and prosperous locals crowded into the city of Mys. The industrialist toyed with the drink he had no intention of consuming, heard voices as someone arrived, and turned to look.

Like most of his kind, Captain Jonathan Alan Seebo-1,324 was right on time. He entered, allowed one of the staff to take his rain cloak, exchanged words with the maitre d', and looked in Chien-Chu's direction.

Then, having chosen the shortest possible route across what seemed like acres of burgundy carpet, the officer made his way over. All the Seebos had the same black hair and the same dark eyes but their were differences. Age for one thing, since the Hegemony decanted thousands every year, sending them to military prep schools at the age of four. Seebo-1,324 appeared to be in his late twenties.

Of more importance were the differences inside their heads, because even though the military clones looked identical, each had experienced life differently, which meant that he had his own distinct personality. There were inherited tendencies, however, which helped shape their personas, and made them good at war. The Seebo paused in front of the industrialist's table. "Citizen Chien-Chu?"

The cyborg nodded and gestured toward the seat on the other side of the table. "Captain Seebo . . . please take a seat."

The Clone sat down. His high-collared uniform was gray, with black buttons and trim to match. Now, from a distance of a few feet away, Chien-Chu could see the slightly faded bar code that had been printed onto the soldier's forehead, the wrinkles around his eyes, and the scar that crossed his left cheek. The Thraki war? Yes, quite possibly.

A waiter hurried over, the officer ordered a drink and met the cyborg's gaze. "So, what would a billionaire, reserve admiral, and ex-president of the Confederacy want with a ground pounder such as myself?"

The industrialist smiled. "You pulled my file."

Seebo-1,324 shrugged. "It seemed advisable. Ambassador Ishimoto-46 wondered why you would want to meet with the Clone military attaché rather than a diplomat. I wondered the same thing."

Chien-Chu rotated his glass. "The answer is simple . . . I need some military advice."

The Clone's drink arrived. He thanked the waiter, and took a tentative sip. "Military advice? Why would an admiral need military advice?"

"Because I didn't exactly work my way up through the ranks, because I know very little about the tactical details of ground combat, and because I don't want to make any mistakes."

"Still," the Seebo objected mildly, "you could call on Major Miraby for that sort of thing . . . Why me?"

Chien-Chu gestured toward the rain-splattered window.

"You're familiar with the situation out there . . . what's going to happen?"

"The digs are going to attack. It's just a matter of time."

"Exactly," the industrialist agreed. "And if they do, *we*, by which I mean the entire off-world community, will be forced to band together to fight them off.

"I don't know for sure, but it's my guess that most if not all of our diplomats are stalling, hoping the whole thing will blow over. When it doesn't, and they finally send for reinforcements, it's going to take weeks if not a month for them to arrive.

"Counting diplomats, their staffs, military contingents, missionaries, and businesspeople like me, I figure there are something like two thousand off-world beings on LaNor, most of whom are in Mys. Have you been to the Transcendental Cathedral lately? It's packed with LaNorian converts, and more arrive every day. Or take a stroll through the native quarter . . . the place is bursting at the seams.

"We're going to need food, water, and medical supplies, not to mention any munitions we can lay our hands on plus the materials required to construct barricades."

The Clone nodded. "I agree, but the question remains, why me? What did Miraby have to say?"

The cybernetic body had disadvantages, plenty of them, but advantages as well. One was the ability to exercise greater control over facial expressions. Chien-Chu kept his face blank. "I shared my concerns with Major Miraby and offered to help mobilize the corporate sector by of making all possible preparations."

"And?"

"And Miraby turned me down. He feels that any effort to accumulate supplies, or strengthen our defenses, could be interpreted as being warlike and therefore provocative."

Seebo laughed. "That sounds like the major all right . . . Did you try Captain Seeba-Ka? I'm not overly fond of Huda-thans but this one has a level head on him."

The industrialist nodded. "He wanted to help but couldn't take action without permission from Miraby."

"Okay," the Clone replied, "I need to check with Ambassador Ishimoto, but let's say he approves. What then?"

Chien-Chu reached under the table, found the roll of paper, and placed it on the table. "This is a map of Mys . . . I would like you to study it. Assuming we aren't able to hold the entire city—what can we hold? Where we would we fall back to? And where, should it come to that, will the community make its final stand?

"Once you lay out a plan, and with support from Ambassador Ishimoto, I will be able to work with other members of the private sector to position supplies where they are least likely to be captured, and build barricades where they will do the most good."

Captain Seebo looked at Chien-Chu with a new level of respect. "Not bad for an admiral . . . Would you mind if I consult with Seeba-Ka? I think he'll go along if I approach the matter sideways. Truth is that a great deal of the load will fall to the Legion if the shit hits the fan."

The cyborg nodded. "I would be most grateful."

The Clone raised his half-empty glass. "To victory . . . or something damned close."

Chien-Chu raised his drink as well, knew the alcohol would never hit what remained of his circulatory system, but drained the glass anyway. Maybe the toast would bring some luck . . . and they were certainly going to need it.

The embassy's dining room had been redecorated by the former ambassador's husband, who, in spite of a weakness for hunting scenes had a fairly good eye. The walls were covered with La-Norian tapestries. Each rectangle provided a slice of pastoral life, which when viewed with those around it, combined to provide the viewer with a sense of how many Naa lived. There was a family harvesting kas, a boatman pulling his craft up through some rapids, a village perched on a hill and three more.

Two imported chandeliers hung over the long, linen-covered bana wood table. It was set for eight. Ambassador Pas Rasha sat at one end of the table, his back to the tall window that looked out onto Legation Street. His mate, a graceful-looking creature named Mytho Lys sat at the other end, in front of a mirror in an ornate frame.

Arrayed along the right side of the table were the richly dressed Prince Mee Mas, who sat next to the ambassador, Yao Che, who looked uncomfortable in a brand-new set of clothes, and Christine Vanderveen, who looked absolutely radiant. To Santana at any rate, who had been seated directly across from the diplomat, and found it difficult not to stare.

Vanderveen wore her hair piled high on the back of her head—pinned there by a clasp that cost more than a lieutenant made in a year. Her blue eyes were the same color as the earrings that dangled from her earlobes and the large gemstone that hung at the center of her V-shaped neckline. The dress was made of blue velvet and clung to her slim figure as if it had been sprayed on. Their eyes met and she winked at him as if to say "Isn't this amusing?"

But it *wasn't* amusing, not to Santana, because the entire scene served to underscore the social gulf that existed between them.

Her father was a well-known diplomat, not to mention multimillionaire, while Santana's father had been a noncommissioned officer, and left his son with a few thousand credits, a couple of beat-up footlockers filled with service memorabilia, and a lot of sage advice, one item of which seemed to apply to the situation at hand: "Be careful what you ask for son, you might just get it. What then?"

It was a good question but one which went unanswered as a servo whined, and Pas Rasha raised his glass. Harley Clauson, who sat to Santana's right, and Major Homer Miraby, who occupied the chair next to him, turned attentively. "This seems like the perfect moment for a human-style toast," the Dweller said, "and we certainly have some guests well worth toasting.

To Prince Mee Mas, and his vision for the future . . . To Yao Che, our valiant messenger . . . To Christine Vanderveen, our intrepid diplomat . . . And to Lieutenant Santana, an officer who demonstrates moral as well as physical courage . . . May each of you lead long, prosperous, and extremely boring lives!"

Everyone except Yao Che laughed, raised their glasses, and took a sip of well-chilled kas wine. The youth raised his glass two seconds late, resolved to a keep a close eye on Mee Mas from that point forward, and do whatever *he* did.

Appetizers were served after the toast, and Pas Rasha did a masterful job of guiding the conversation in such a way that the social niceties were observed, and his guests were entertained at the same time.

It didn't take much prompting to get Mee Mas to go first. However, in place of the long egotistical diatribe that Pas Rasha half expected to hear, the prince chose a self-deprecating story about the journey from Polwa to the Palace of the Mist. It seemed his retainers had hidden the young noble in a wagon driven by a grizzled teamster, who, not being privy to his passenger's true identity, spent the entire trip telling scandalous stories about the royal family.

By the time the main course rolled around it was Yao Che's turn. Though still somewhat intimidated by the company he was keeping the youth was a little looser by then and regaled Pas Rasha and his guests with the full story of how the Claw had emerged to seize the village of Nah Ree, the repeated attacks on the Transcendental mission, the manner in which hundreds of converts had taken shelter there, and the Busso family's efforts to protect them.

Finally, after the youngster's description of his cross-country journey, the ambassador made use of a napkin to dab at his mouth. "You are a remarkable youngster and a credit to your family as well as your village.

"I know you are concerned regarding the safety of those you left behind . . . and have an announcement to make. After consultations with FSO Clauson, and Major Miraby, I authorized them to send a platoon of legionnaires to Nah Ree in an attempt to bring everyone out.

"This is a dangerous enterprise made all the more risky by the fact that the situation in and around Polwa continues to deteriorate and is likely to spill over into Mys. I pray that won't occur, but if it does, we will need every soldier we have.

"There may be a window however, a short period of time during which a well-armed group of legionnaires can slip out, complete their mission, and make their way back before things come to a head."

Yao Che bowed his head. "Thank you, Excellency, my people will never forget."

Pas Rasha eyed the young LaNorian. "You are very welcome. Our force will require someone to show them the way . . . I hate to ask, especially in light of the hardships you have already suffered, but would you be willing to serve as a guide?"

Yao Che inclined his head yet again. "I would be honored."

Vanderveen, who had not only followed the interchange with considerable interest, but knew the question Santana was aching to ask, did it for him. "May I inquire as to which officer will lead the rescue attempt?"

Pas Rasha looked at Miraby, saw the officer nod, and turned back again. "Yes, you may. Based on his considerable combat experience, not to mention the recent stroll through the LaNorian countryside, both the major and I agree that Lieutenant Santana would be ideal for the job. May I extend my congratulations, Lieutenant? Along with my condolences?"

Santana felt a host of conflicting emotions but still managed a smile. "I appreciate your condolences, sir, but must say that I look forward to avoiding the dangers that you and the rest of the diplomatic staff confront every day. I was fortunate to escape last night's party with my head still on my shoulders."

Everyone laughed, especially Clauson, whose face was cherry red from the effects of both the heat and the wine.

But Vanderveen saw, or believed she saw, doubt in the officer's eyes. She could imagine the questions that were on his mind. Was he considered to be an embarrassment? An officer whom Miraby could get along without? Was that why the command been given to him rather than someone else?

A quick check of Clauson's flushed countenance and Miraby's carefully neutral expression seemed to confirm her suspicions. There was nothing she could do about it however, except try to meet Santana's eyes, only to see them slip away. Why? Because he was embarrassed? Or for some other reason?

Suddenly, something about the awkward manner in which he sat there, like a hawk among doves, told Vanderveen something she should have known all along. The very situations in which she felt the most comfortable were those that he hated the most. More than that, seeing Santana here, in her milieu rather than *his*, served to remind the diplomat of certain social realities. Barriers that Vanderveen tried to ignore but knew were real.

For the briefest of moments the FSO tried to imagine dinner at her parents' house on Earth, with Santana at her side, and her father seated where Pas Rasha was. Would he see the soldier as a fitting companion for his daughter? The same daughter he had groomed to succeed him, and who he jokingly referred to as Madame President?

No, she feared not, and knowing that raised still another question: What did *she* want? And if Santana was the answer, would he make it back from Nah Ree? An ice-cold fist seemed to grip her stomach and Vanderveen left her dessert half-eaten.

The meal came to an end not long thereafter, and Vanderveen had just accepted her coat from a LaNorian servant, when Clauson appeared at her elbow. Like her the senior FSO lived in the corporate sector. "May I see you home?"

Vanderveen smiled. Her reply was loud enough for Santana to hear. "Thank you, Harley, but the Legion offered to provide me with an escort."

The diplomat looked at Santana, then back again. "Really? The Legion never offered *me* an escort."

Santana took Vanderveen's coat and held it for her. "I'll

speak to Major Miraby . . . I think he's available." All three of them laughed.

Five minutes later, Vanderveen and Santana passed between the legionnaires who guarded the main entrance, hoisted a single umbrella, and headed south along Legation Street. The rain was little more than a fine mist, the acrid odor of coal smoke hung in the air, and there was the occasional *pop, pop, pop* of small-arms fire as members of the Claw fired from beyond the walls. Harassing fire for the most part, although a Hudathan trooper had been wounded the day before, and a LaNorian street sweeper had been killed by a spent round. It was no longer safe to stand in one place on top of the city wall, enter Polwa in anything less than squad strength, or venture beyond the gate without a major show of force.

"So," Vanderveen said, slipping her arm through his, "I hope you don't mind."

"No," Santana replied honestly, "I was working up the courage to ask."

"That's strange . . . I don't remember any lack of courage on the trip to Pur Lor."

"That's because *you* scare me more than the Claw does."

They had arrived at the point where Legation street passed over the Jade River by that time—and Vanderveen paused to look out over the dark oily water to the native quarter beyond. The mist turned the lights into a smear of color. "You frighten me as well."

Santana put an arm around her waist. "In what way?"

"In *every* way. You scare me because you see things differently than I do, because you make me feel things I haven't felt before, and because it's too early."

"Too early?"

"Yes. Absurd as it may sound, I planned the way my life would go when I was ten years old. School, followed by the diplomatic corps, followed by elected office, followed by a family. That's the plan."

"And you figured he'd be there? Waiting for you?"

"Yes," Vanderveen said emphatically. "It's stupid, but I did."

Santana grinned. "So this is inconvenient."

Vanderveen looked up at him. "Yes, damned inconvenient."

Santana said, "I'm sorry," and kissed her on the lips. They were soft yet insistent. He pulled her close and her hands rose to touch the back of his neck.

The moment might have lasted forever but a cart rattled past and brought the kiss to an end. Vanderveen shivered and Santana took her arm. "Come on . . . let's get you home. Which way is it?"

Vanderveen led Santana across Legation Street to a poorly lit flight of stairs. A LaNorian maid bobbed her head as she emerged out of the darkness and hurried off to clean one of the embassies.

The couple followed the stairs down to the point where they met the northwest corner of what had come to be called Church Square. Portable lights had been set up to illuminate the front of the Transcendental Cathedral. Hundreds of LaNorians were hard at work building a wall made of metal cargo modules. Sparks flew as two of them were welded into place. A specially equipped cyborg lifted one of the containers and carried it across the plaza.

Santana frowned. "What's going on?"

"They're building a defensive wall," Vanderveen explained. "To stop the Claw if they enter the city."

"Under whose direction?"

"The overall plan was put together by Captain Seebo in response to a suggestion from an old friend of my father's. His name is Sergi Chien-Chu."

"The ex-president?"

"Among other things, yes."

"Was Miraby consulted?"

"Yes, although both he and Pas Rasha felt the project was premature."

"What would they have us do? Wait until the bastards enter the city?"

Vanderveen shrugged. "Something like that, yes."

The soldier shook his head in disgust, wondered what he would find on his return from Nah Ree, and feared the worst.

They turned away from the square and walked down a dimly lit street. Some of the residents had darkened their windows, especially on the second and third floors, to lessen the likelihood that someone would shoot at them. Others seemed less concerned, and not only left their lights on, but their shades up. Strains of off-world music could be heard, interspersed with the slamming of doors, and the rattle of trash cans. It all seemed so peaceful compared with what the legionnaire knew lay beyond the city walls.

The diplomat seemed to sense the direction of this thoughts. "So, what do you think of the mission they dumped on you?"

Santana shrugged. "It sounds like the right thing to do . . . and that's what they pay me for."

"That's it? That's all you feel?"

"No," Santana admitted, "I have other feelings, but none of them make any difference. What is, *is*."

They paused in front of a three-story apartment building. It faced north and was a long way from the wall, so most of the lights were on. Vanderveen raised a perfect eyebrow. "That's kind of fatalistic isn't it?"

"Maybe," Santana conceded, "but I'm not sure that life can be laid out like a day planner. Some things simply happen."

"Like us?"

"Yes, maybe."

"And what would 'us' be like?"

"Like it is now," Santana replied. "Like finding a part of yourself."

"And then?"

Santana thought about his parents, about the way his father

loved his mother, and knew the answer. "And then you grab on and never let go."

"I don't know if I'm ready for that," Vanderveen said cautiously.

"Because it's scheduled for later on?"

"Partly," the diplomat admitted, "but for other reasons as well. The kind of commitment you're talking about takes a tremendous leap of faith."

Santana nodded soberly. "That's true."

"You could come up," Vanderveen ventured, "and spend the night."

Santana shook his head. "No, I'd like that, but it wouldn't be right."

Vanderveen searched his face. "Isn't something better than nothing?"

There was silence for a moment. Santana cupped her face in his hands. They were big and rough. "Sometimes . . . but not always. There are certain times, certain situations, in which nothing less than everything will do."

That being said, the soldier kissed her lips, took a full step backwards, and delivered his best salute. Then he turned and walked away. Had Santana turned to look, had the light been just so, he might have seen the tears. The rain drifted around her and there was little Vanderveen could do but watch the darkness swallow him up.

The ground floor of the Confederacy's barracks housed a maintenance facility, a workout room, and the only access to the building's subsurface arsenal. It was light outside, but it may as well have been dark since Santana had ordered Sergeant Hillrun to spray paint the windows, place the facility off-limits to anyone who wasn't involved in the project, and post guards wearing civilian attire.

Now, as saws screeched, sparks flew, and a wrench rattled, Santana forced himself to ignore the partially disassembled wagons, the parts that lay hither and yon, and the activities related to them. The armorers had been working on the T-2s all night, and it was time to inspect their work.

Sergeant Carlos Zook had been on what amounted to light duty within the embassy compound while Corporal Norly Snyder had been out traipsing across the Claw-infested countryside. That being the case Santana started with her. The techs, all red-eyed with fatigue, stood at parade rest. They knew that any platoon leader worth his or her salt would want to check their work prior to going out on patrol. Especially a long-distance patrol with no air cover, no resupply, and iffy communications.

Since most legionnaires wore tattoos, cyborgs were permitted to have personal artwork, so long as it met certain standardized criteria. Like many of her comrades, Snyder had the First REC's insignia emblazoned on her left arm, and the words "In memory of Missy," inscribed on her right. No one knew who Missy was, only that it wasn't a good idea to ask, and that the mere mention of the name was sufficient to make the T-2 both angry and sad.

Each Trooper II had inspection plates located at various points on their mechanical anatomy. In order to thumb the highest ones open it was necessary for Santana to stand on a mechanic's footstool. Power, 96 percent. Coolant, 98 percent. Ammo, 100 percent. Life support, 100 percent. Electronic countermeasures, 88 percent, Communications, 100 percent, and so forth, until all ten of the readouts had been checked and matched to the printout that the officer held in hand.

"So," Snyder growled, "is the lieutenant going for a walk?"

"Not only is the lieutenant going for a walk," Santana confirmed, "but he wouldn't think of going without you."

The sound the T-2 produced was similar to that made by a broken garbage disposal but the officer knew it to be laughter. "Sir, yes sir."

Then, with Snyder accounted for, it was time to look at Zook. Santana had just completed the sergeant's inspection, and thumbprinted the maintenance log, when Captain Drik Seeba-Ka entered the west end of the bay.

Someone shouted, "Ten-shun!" over the sounds of construction, and the legionnaires were still in the process of popping to attention when the Hudathan said, "As you were," stepped over a power cable, and wove his way between the wagon carcasses.

A lot had changed between the two officers by then. None of it had been voiced because there was no need to do so. Each had proven himself to the other and the result was a feeling of trust. A rare bond given the gulf between their two cultures. Santana met the company commander out toward the center of the room. Salute met salute. "Captain Seeba-Ka."

"Lieutenant Santana."

"Is there something I can do for you, sir?"

"Yes," the other officer replied with just the hint of a Hudathan-style grin, "you can explain why the windows are blacked out, why Corporal Dietrich seems to be sunning himself with a handgun concealed beneath his towel, and why my state-of-the-art maintenance facility had been transformed into a primitive carpentry shop."

"Sir, yes sir. The windows are blacked out to ensure that LaNorian spies can't see inside, Dietrich and some other troopers have been detailed to keep everyone away, and the carpentry is a bit more complicated."

"I'm sure it is," Seeba-Ka said indulgently. "Please enlighten me."

"Well," Santana answered tentatively, "I learned some lessons during the march to Pur Lor. One of the first things I learned was that word travels fast out there, even without radios, which it now appears that at least some of the Claw have. Success will depend in large part on our ability to reach Nah Ree quickly, round everyone up, and get them out before the enemy can mass their troops to stop us.

"In light of that I want to get my entire platoon well beyond the outskirts of Polwa and Mys without anyone being the wiser.

"In order to do so I ordered Hillrun to buy six four-wheeled freight wagons and the razbuls required to pull them. The animals are being held elsewhere under Yao Che's supervision."

Seeba-Ka looked at the construction work with new eyes. Now, having heard at least some of Santana's plan, the Hudathan realized that the LaNorian wagons were being rebuilt from the ground up.

The frameworks that held them together had been reinforced with lengths of steel, wood casings were being fitted around off-world wheels, and U-shaped cradles had been fastened to each wagon bed. The more senior officer shook his head in wonder. "You plan to smuggle the T-2s out in the wagons!"

Santana nodded. "Yes sir, and the troops, too, not to mention their gear. I figure if we put some LaNorian drivers up front and load some realistic cargo on top, we should be able to pull it off."

"Clever," Seeba-Ka said admiringly, "very clever. But why so many wagons? You have two T-2s yet I count *four* cradles . . . Don't even think about stripping the unit of additional cyborgs. Miraby wouldn't approve, nor would I."

"Sir, no sir. The other two cradles are for two RAVs (Robotic All-terrain Vehicles.) I submitted the req about 0330 in the morning."

Seeba-Ka hadn't checked his messages as yet but knew the request would be there. "And you assumed I would approve?"

"Sir, no sir. I *hoped* you would approve and used my initiative to get started in case you did."

The reply had a rehearsed quality, but Seeba-Ka expected nothing less. Santana had a plan—and that was good. "So, assuming I approve the requisition, how do you plan to use them?"

"Well," Santana replied, "the second lesson I learned on the trip to Pur Lor was how vulnerable a small number of troops would be without any mechanical leverage. Sure, we can throw a lot of slugs at the enemy, but there's a limit to how many we can carry. That goes for food and medical equipment as well. The simple fact is that without Snyder's armament, sensors, and strength all of us would be dead.

"So, while the RAVs aren't the same thing as sentient T-2s, they can carry a lot of supplies, casualties should we have some, and provide limited fire support. No small thing when we might have to face hundreds or even thousands of enemy troops."

Seeba-Ka eyed the RAVs which stood against the south wall. They weren't sentient, the way T-2s were, but the vehicles did have fairly sophisticated onboard computers, which handled navigation, med support, and fire control.

Each unit consisted of two eight-foot sections joined together by a pleated accordion-style joint located at the center of its long ovoid-shaped body.

Four articulated legs enabled the robots to negotiate even the toughest terrain. Two cargo bays, one forward and one aft, could accommodate up to four thousand pounds of supplies plus two causalities. And though not designed for offensive purposes each RAV was equipped with two turret-style forward-facing machine guns plus a multipurpose grenade launcher. Properly deployed, and properly dug in, each robot could be used to defend one sector of the platoon's perimeter. Each RAV wore a fanciful monster face complete with vicious snarl, white fangs, and red eyes.

The robots had not been very useful within Mys, but would provide Santana's platoon with some much-needed support. Seeba-Ka nodded. "Request approved. I see a problem though . . . Freight never leaves from Mys because there aren't any factories or warehouses here. The Claw will stop your wagons ten minutes after they roll through the North Gate."

"Yes, sir," Santana acknowledged dutifully, "except that I don't plan to leave via the North Gate. With FSO Vanderveen's help I hope to pass through the *South* Gate, enter the city of Polwa, and leave through the western wall."

The Hudathan looked at his subordinate with a renewed

sense of respect. "No offense to your maternal parent, Lieutenant, but you are one crazy sonofabitch."

Santana remembered the party, the way the Hudathan's sword had sliced through Ramanthian flesh, and grinned. "Sir, yes sir, but look who's talking."

There was silence for a moment . . . followed by what sounded like a series of hacking coughs. Seeba-Ka was amused.

THE CITY OF POLWA, ON THE INDEPENDENT PLANET OF LANOR

For the first time in may years the Dowager Empress Shi Huu had something to look forward to—the partial restoration of her youth! The prospect of that caused her to wake half an hour early, beat the dogun out of bed, and trigger a full-blown domestic crises.

For year piled upon year the Dawn Concubine had been a creature of regular habits. So much so that the Tiz master in charge of distributing the "heavenly harvest" to the plants that graced the Imperial gardens could predict the quantity of feces Shi Huu would produce on each day of the week. Knowledge he had used to win any number of bets.

As a result none of Shi Huu's retainers were ready for an early awakening, and the servants assigned to clean the leaves on the plants directly outside the Imperial bedchambers were treated to the sounds of loud recriminations, the slap of paddles on flesh, and wails of pain as everyone from the senior maid to the lowliest fan trimmer paid for their lack of attentiveness with units of carefully measured pain. Then, with discipline restored, the procession could begin.

First came the heralds, shouting for everyone to get out of the way, soon followed by a brace of Shi Huu's bodyguards, the eunuch Dwi Faa, maids bearing that day's finery, and two male servants bearing a small chest filled with cosmetics. Not because the Empress expected the nanosculpting to fail, but because even in the full flower of youth it had been necessary to enhance nature's gifts that they might be appreciated more fully.

Now, as the Imperial convoy swept through the maze of hallways, eyes peered out through holes, gaps, and cracks. This was the day when Shi Huu would receive her new face and everyone wanted to see what it would look like.

There was nothing to see however, not yet at any rate, because even though the vast majority of the biosculpting activity had already been carried out many days before, the microscopic surgeons had been tidying up ever since, all hidden by a feature-hugging mask.

Idealized features had been painted onto the mask, so the Empress could present some sort of face to the court, but no one knew what lay beyond. Beauty? Or not beauty? Since "ugly" was an adjective which could not possibly be used in conjunction with Shi Huu even in the privacy of one's mind.

Even now the executioners had been stationed not ten paces from the room where the off-worlders waited and the mask would be removed.

Did the Thrakies understand the danger they were in? No, probably not, but such were the risks that *all* courtiers took.

Though not aware of the fact that his life was on the line the Thraki medicologist whom Ambassador Hybatha had prevailed upon to accept the case was nervous nonetheless. His name was Togunda, and in spite of the fact that the science of nano-based biosculpting was widely employed by all of the more advanced races that success was based on years of experience and millions of clinical trials.

LaNorians were similar to other races, but different as well, and that meant things could go wrong. Not terribly wrong, as in *dead* wrong, but wrong nevertheless. What if the Empress didn't like her face? What if the suboceanic mineral rights went to the humans? What if he were sent to look after the crew on a Class IV nav station somewhere beyond the Rim?

But the medico's thoughts were interrupted as cymbals crashed, the Imperial entourage swept into the room, and the moment of truth was at hand. "Quickly," Ambassador Hybatha whispered, "you must take charge."

Thus prompted the Thraki propelled himself out into the middle of the specially equipped room, bowed, and gestured in the direction of a power-assisted chair. "Good morning, Highness, please be seated."

Normally it was Shi Huu's prerogative to speak first but the Empress was so excited that she allowed the gaffe to pass unpunished rather than delay the unveiling for even a few seconds.

Moving with a speed that belied her sixty five years Shi Huu turned, backed into the chair's well-padded embrace, and heard machinery whine as it adjusted to her slender body. Assuming the surgery went well, and there was no need to kill the Thrakies, she would demand *four* such chairs one for each throne room.

"Excellent," Togunda said, moving to the Dowager's side and mounting the footstool placed there for his convenience. "Now, close your eyes. I will spray a solvent onto the surface of the mask. It will dissolve into what will feel like cold cream. Then, once the residue is wiped away, the results will be clear. Do you have any questions?"

"*Yes,*" Shi Huu responded impatiently. "When will you shut up and get on with it?"

Togunda's ears went back against his skull. He glanced at Hybatha, saw the look in her eyes, and managed to swallow his pride.

The cylinder felt heavy and cold. The Thraki shook it three times to ensure that the contents were well mixed, aimed the nozzle as Shi Huu's face, and fingered the release. Cool white foam squirted onto the face mask.

The medicologist handed the container to an assistant and took up two spatula shaped instruments which he used to smear the solvent over the entire surface. Then, satisfied that the foam was evenly distributed, he put the tools down.

"Well?" Shi Huu demanded. "Is it ready yet?"

"No, Highness," Togunda replied, "the mask is still in the process of dissolving. Please be patient."

The last was a definite breach of etiquette and Ambassador
Hybatha heard a loud sucking sound as all thirty of the
Imperial retainers took deep breaths and waited for the blood
to fly.

But Shi Huu wanted the new face very badly and, though
aware of the insult, was loath to do anything that might compromise the surgery's outcome. For that reason she managed
to contain her ire and remained silent as the seconds continued
to tick away.

Finally, once the foam had lost its loft and started to liquefy,
the wait was over. Togunda's assistant moved in to wipe the
solvent away, Shi Huu's Bliss Industries makeup mirror was
rolled into position, and the moment of truth was at hand.

Shi Huu waited for the last of the foam to be removed, heard
the alien say, "You can open your eyes," and hurried to do so.
Her vision was blurry at first, but the room soon snapped into
focus. The Empress looked into the mirror and her heart leaped
for joy.

The image that floated before her was like a window into
the past. The wrinkled skin, sagging flesh, and widow spots
had vanished! Now, seemingly impervious to the passage of
time, the Empress found herself face-to-face with the long-lost
Dawn Concubine. There was not only the high forehead, the
perfectly aligned nostril slits, and the fashionably thin lips,
but the blemish-free skin, the blush of youth, and the firm
perfectly shaped chin. Only her eyes remained the same. They
were dark, like bits of coal, and glowed as if lit from within.
They looked every bit Shi Huu's true age or even older.

There were cries of joy and astonishment as Shi Huu turned
to Hybatha. Each of her retainers stared unabashedly at the
Empress's face, sought to memorize that particular moment in
time, and looked forward to sharing their impressions with
those less fortunate. "It is as you said it would be. Dwi Faa
will finalize the agreement made earlier. You may go."

Though not used to being dismissed in such a perfunctory
manner Hybatha had what she had come for and was eager to

escape. She bowed, Togunda did likewise, and the Thrakies withdrew.

Conscious of the fact that hundreds if not thousands of her subjects were waiting for news regarding the surgery, and eager to let them see what her revitalized face looked like, Shi Huu ordered the room to be cleared of all but her personal attendants, applied her makeup, allowed herself to be bound in red silk, slipped into a pair of thick-soled clogs, and was soon on her way to the water throne.

Having already heard about the positive outcome, and no longer afraid of how the Empress might react, hundreds of servants, advisors, cooks, carpenters, gardeners, grooms, and all manner of other retainers emerged from their various nooks and crannies to line the hallways, bow deeply, and honor what had already become known as "the new face."

Shi Huu remembered the days *before* she became a concubine, when villagers turned out to stare at her, and felt a renewed sense of power.

The water throne rested on a circular island at the center of a tiled pool and could be accessed by either of two slightly arched footbridges. White, gold, and black fish swam all around it and served to symbolize all the creatures that lived in the Great Wet. The throne itself was carved to resemble a seashell and was supported by four fanciful sea serpents.

Once the Empress was seated her court had little choice but to gather around the perimeter of the pond and gaze inward. As usual it was Dwi Faa who spoke first. He did so as if greeting her for the first time that day. "Good morning, Your Highness. May I say that it has been my privilege to witness *two* dawns during the same day?"

It was a graceful allusion both to the full restoration of Shi Huu's beauty—*and* to the Emperor's pet name for her. The Empress was touched by the minister's words but frowned nonetheless. "No, you may not. I suspect that more sleep and less wine would go a long way toward resolving your double vision."

The court tittered but the eunuch knew his mistress well and took the *true* response from the look in her eyes. "Yes, Highness," the minister said, "it shall be as you say."

"Good . . . What troublesome news do you have for me today?"

Regardless of what she might pretend Dwi Faa knew the Empress to be in a good mood and gave thanks for that fact. "The worst sort I'm afraid, Highness . . . In spite of the army's best efforts to find and apprehend the prince it appears that Mee Mas was able to slip out of Polwa and rendezvous with the hu-mans. They smuggled him into Mys where he now resides, within the Confederacy's embassy."

If true, this was bad news, *extremely* bad news, and Shi Huu sought to ascertain how reliable it was. She frowned. "By what means do we know this?"

"We have a spy within the embassy," Dwi Faa replied, "a new one. She saw the prince with her own eyes."

"And how reliable is this spy?"

"*Very* reliable, Highness. We have her one-year-old son in custody."

"Excellent," Shi Huu replied approvingly. "See that she has the opportunity to visit her son. Make sure that the bond remains strong. We will have need of her in the future."

"Yes, Highness."

"As for the prince, and the off-worlders who chose to befriend him, what do we know of their starships? How many circle above?"

"None, Highness, not at the moment. The next ship, a freighter, is scheduled to arrive in four weeks' time."

"Good. And their message things? What of those?"

Dwi Faa knew that the "things" the Empress referred to were what the off-worlders referred to as message torpedoes. Miniature spaceships that could travel through space and take messages to distant stars. "We aren't entirely sure, Highness . . . Although our intelligence operatives suspect that each embassy has at least two or three such devices circling our planet."

"So," Shi Huu said thoughtfully, "once word is sent, how long before the off-world armies would arrive?"

"At least a month," Dwi Faa answered, "but probably more."

"That should be more than sufficient time," the Empress replied. "Send the following message to Ambassador Pas Rasha: 'You have one day in which to hand over Prince Mee Mas, plus any other LaNorians who may have entered the foreign sector, or the entire city of Mys will be put to the sword.'"

Though pleased Dwi Faa was careful not to show it. The prince was a threat, not only to the Shi Huu's power, but to *his*, since there would be no place for him in a government run by Mee Mas.

Of even more concern, given the fact that the prince had a relatively small following, was the off-world community itself, which by its very presence continued to poison LaNorian culture.

Now, after months of dithering, the Empress had finally made her decision, and it was a good one. If the aliens acquiesced to Shi Huu's demand, then fine. If they defied her, which he secretly hoped that they would, the Empress would have no choice but to eradicate them. More foreigners would come, but negotiations would start afresh, and more-advantageous deals could be struck. Certain aliens, the Ramanthians and Huda-thans came to mind, would receive favorable treatment in recognition of the strong relationships they had forged with the Imperial government. The tax revenues received from the Ramanthian factories, plus the income that would be derived from allowing the Thrakies to harvest minerals from the ocean floor were far too important to lose.

Yes, Lak Saa would have to be dealt with, but that would come later. For this particular moment in time the Imperial government would enter into what amounted to a tacit alliance with the Tro Wa, using the secret society like a shield, thereby sheltering itself from off-world retribution. In fact, if things went extremely well, it might be possible to blame *everything* on the Claw. He bowed deeply. "Of course, Highness. I shall dispatch the letter within the hour."

"See that you do," Shi-Huu said briskly. "Now, what other nonsense must I deal with?"

THE FOREIGN CITY OF MYS, ON THE INDEPENDENT PLANET OF LANOR

It was just before dawn, that time of day when most citizens were still asleep, the criminal element had returned to their various lairs, and only street sweepers plied their trades. It wasn't raining, but it had been, and the air was relatively clean.

The top of the wall separating Mys from Polwa served as the roof to Factor Wah Heh's rather opulent office—and the South Gate lay directly below his well-shod feet. That made it possible for the customs official to walk to the north side of his office, open the shutters, and look down on the foreign city of Mys, or reverse direction, open *those* shutters, and peer into the Imperial city of Polwa.

Not that he normally spent much time looking in either direction since it was more pleasant to sit at his desk, nap on his daybed, or nip out for a bite to eat.

The fact that he had time for such niceties was largely due to the extra hours granted him by the magic calculator which the hu-man named Vanderveen had so kindly given him.

Now, with that individual pacing his office like a caged animal, the LaNorian had little choice but to grant the favor she asked or risk having his secret revealed.

The off-worlder had called upon to "expedite" six wagon-loads of steel track. The alien was perfectly willing to pay the considerable fees involved, along with the "handling charge" routinely tacked on by Wah Heh and his subordinates, and that should have made the customs official happy. It didn't.

Steel track implied railroads, the Tro Wa *hated* railroads, and their spies were everywhere. The Factor thought his staff was free of informers but there was no way to be sure. Would the Claw view his involvement with the shipment as support for the foreigners? Yes, he feared that they would, and didn't want to die while holding his own entrails in his hands.

That's why Wah Heh was happy when Vanderveen said, "Here they come," and rushed to the north window in order to take a look.

It was dark outside, but the streetlights still burned, and the wagons were momentarily visible as the rolled through the cones of warm yellow light. They were large vehicles, reinforced in order to handle the steel trucks, and covered with well-secured leather tarps. Each wagon required a team of two razbuls, and Wah Heh could hear the animals complain as the LaNorian drivers urged the reptiles forward with, long supple whips.

The customs inspectors, all of whom had been forewarned, not to mention bribed, hurried to open the gigantic gate as the first wagon drew near.

Vanderveen could feel the vibration through the soles of her boots as the door hit its stops and the convoy passed under the arch. The diplomat waited for the first wagons to disappear, turned, and crossed to the other side. The *first* vehicle, the one that contained Santana and half his troops had entered Polwa by then, and was headed toward the point where it would turn right onto the east–west thoroughfare that led out through the Imperial city's West Gate.

Watching the wagon, knowing he was in it, made Vanderveen hurt inside. She wanted Santana to stay, or failing that, to take her with him but knew it couldn't be. He had his job, and she had hers, and neither left much room for anything else.

Still, there was something special about Santana, about the honesty in his eyes and the clarity of his vision. What was it he had said? That there were times when nothing less than *everything* would do? No one had ever said anything like that to her before—and the words had taken root in her heart. Now, as she looked down on the last wagon to pass under the arch, Vanderveen felt her vision blur, and wondered if she would see him again.

There were potholes in the road, lots of them, and the legionnaires suffered through an unending series of spine-jarring jolts as the wagon's wheels dipped into one after another. The entire vehicle rocked from side to side, the frame creaked from the stress, and something groaned. Santana prayed the conveyance would hold up under the strain and gave thanks for each foot of forward progress.

The first wagon, the one in which Santana rode, contained roughly half of the sixteen bio bods he'd been permitted to bring along.

The second wagon carried Corporal Norly Snyder, the third carried the first RAV, the fourth carried Sergeant Carlos Zook, the fifth carried the second RAV, and the sixth carried Sergeant Hillrun plus six legionnaires and their gear.

The rest of Santana's platoon, some fifteen legionnaires in all, had been left in Mys to help secure the embassy.

It was dark under the leather tarp but Santana had authorized one glow stick in the first and last wagons in case the convoy ran into trouble and his troops were forced to bail out via the trapdoors cut into the floors.

Seconds would count in that eventuality and the platoon leader had decided that the ability to exit the vehicle cleanly outweighed the risk that someone would spot the faint green glow that served to illuminate the wagon's interior.

The first squad included Sergeant Bonnie Cvanivich, Corporal "Dice" Dietrich, Lance Corporal Carolyn "Bags" Bagano, Private Nick Kimura, Private Lars Hadley, Private "Doc" Seavy, Private Rockclimb Warmfeel, and Private Bok Horo-Ba, who, given his size, occupied enough space to accommodate two humans.

Dietrich appeared to be napping but the rest of the squad was clearly awake. Cvanivich met the officer's eyes and gave him a thumbs-up. She knew what Santana didn't, that Seeba-Ka's entire company would have volunteered for the current mission had they been allowed to do so. The loot had a rep for having a cool head, a low tolerance for bullshit, and a fierce loyalty toward his troops. That's about as good as it got and she felt lucky to be in his platoon.

Meanwhile, seated on the hard wooden bench-style seat at the front of the wagon, and dressed in a way that made him appear years older, Yao Che applied the long slender whip to the razbul on the right, called the beast names that would have shocked his mother, and urged the reptile to greater speed. That particular animal was male, had mottled green scales, and what could only be described as a bad attitude. It uttered a long *reep* of protest, released a quantity of gas, and expelled a basketload of steaming manure. The wheels rolled through the disgusting mess, mixed it with the water in the next puddle, and sprayed the goo along both sides of the vehicle.

It was lighter by then which meant that Yao Che had little difficulty spotting the four-lane thoroughfare that led west toward what was sometimes referred to as the merchant's gate because of the great caravans that passed through it during the spring, summer, and early fall. In spite of the street's considerable width all manner of parked carts, piles of rubbish, and construction materials had been deposited on the two outside lanes rendering them impassable.

Every sixth or seventh building had been burned, either as the result of an errant spark, a carelessly placed candle, or, and such places were easy to spot, arson on the part of the Claw. They were marked with the letters "TW," for "Tro Wa," and served as a warning for any who might stand against them.

In fact, so powerless, or so sympathetic were the municipal authorities, that Yao Che's wagon passed beneath a banner that spanned the width of the street and gave warning to all: "He who collaborates will die, as will his family, and all of those they hold dear."

It was a bone-chilling reminder of not only the risks he was taking—but the reason for taking them. Yao Che had been impressed by Mee Mas and come to believe that something better was possible.

Now, as the long slender fingers of smoke reached up toward the sky, lights appeared in windows, and some of the shopkeepers opened their doors, the city began to wake. Conscious of how important it was to exit Polwa as early as possible Yao Che flicked his whip yet again and glanced back over his shoulder.

The other drivers, all of whom believed they were hauling lengths of steel track, "knew" that the Claw was unlikely to approve of such a load and was hot on his trail. Like Yao Che they wanted to escape the city and the Tro Wa as early in the day as possible and seek shelter in the foothills.

Satisfied that his peers were on the job the LaNorian turned his attention forward and noticed the way the neighborhood had started to change. Two-and three-story buildings, many of which had shops at street level, were giving way to the nearly featureless hodos in which incoming and outgoing goods were stored. This was the western warehouse district, a sure sign that the gate lay not too far ahead and reason to make his heart beat a little bit faster.

Thanks to the efforts of FSO Vanderveen the first gate had opened like a flower to the sun but this one promised to be more difficult. Though equipped with carefully forged documents, and the heaviest loop of coins the youth had ever been forced to lift, customs officials were notoriously fickle. Strict one moment, and lax the next, it was nearly impossible to predict what he might encounter.

One thing was for certain, however, and that was that he would have to deal with whatever problems presented themselves, since there was no one else to call upon. A fact which made him feel both proud and frightened as the same time.

The gate appeared in the distance, Yao Che produced what he hoped was a look of bored indifference, and snapped the whip. The wagon lurched forward.

It was early, *very* early, and although four customs inspectors were supposed to be on duty, three of them were asleep in the guardhouse, leaving only one of their number to handle the thin trickle of morning traffic. His name was Jas Jee and he was bored. The wagons, six of them no less, looked like a welcome diversion.

Jas Jee used his stilts to step over an open sewer, stumped across the pavers, and approached the first wagon. Yao Che pulled on the reins, uttered a long shrill whistle, and stepped on the foot brake. The razbuls came to a stop, blew air out through their noses, and looked around.

"Morning," Jas Jee said levelly, "what are you carrying?"

"Metal," Yao Che replied, spitting onto the road by way of demonstrating his disgust. "And it's damned heavy . . . Could take all day to reach the first inn."

"Metal, eh?" Jas Jee said suspiciously. "For what?"

Yao Che looked left and right as if to make sure that no one could hear. "Rails, for one of the railroads, or that's what the devils believe. Me? I've got other ideas . . . but that's neither here nor there. Here's the paperwork—and coins to cover the fees."

Jas Jee's eyes widened. The Tro Wa *hated* the railroads, everyone knew that, which meant the load could be harmful to his health. "You've got other ideas? Like what?"

Yao Che looked left and right yet again, leaned forward, and lowered his voice. Behind him, below the surface of the tarp, Santana strained to hear. But the voices were muffled and he couldn't distinguish the words. "You never heard it from me—but it's my guess that the rails will never reach their destination. You know the hook-shaped knives the Tro Wa use on their enemies? Well, someone could melt the rails down, and use the resulting metal to make *thousands* of hooks! Enough that people like you and I could have one. Wouldn't that be wonderful?"

Jas Jee blinked. What was the driver saying? That *he* was a member of the Claw? That the load would be hijacked? That the other drivers were in cahoots with him? Maybe, and maybe not. Whatever the case the mere possibility that he was dealing with the Tro Wa was sufficient to suggest a certain level of circumspection.

The customs official swallowed hard, glanced at the papers, and handed all of them back. "Yes, well, your paperwork appears to be in order, and you are free to go."

Yao Che looked surprised. "Really? Shouldn't you count the coins?"

"No," Jas Jee replied handing the heavily laden rope up to the driver, "there's no fee for taking steel out of the city prior to the ninth hour of the day. Please move along . . . the morning rush is about to begin."

Yao Che inclined his head in a gesture of respect, slapped the razbuls with both reins, and felt the wagon jerk ahead. Imperial guards, about a dozen of them, leaned on their rifles and watched the convoy pass. Their comrades, the ones still camped around the city of Mys, had risen by then. The driver could hear the occasional blare of a trumpet, see the wink of their carefully aligned campfires, and smell the odor of freshly brewed tea.

Farther out, beyond the last rank of Imperial soldiers, the Tro Wa were camped. Most were still asleep, but a few were up, cooking their morning kas. Was his old friend Ply Pog among them? Probably, and he hoped the rascal would stay there.

The wagons passed over a defensive ditch, through a cordon of ratty-looking Imperials, and onto the great western road.

Santana peeked out from under the rear edge of the tarp, watched the cities of Polwa and Mys grow smaller, and heaved a gigantic sigh of relief. The stratagem had worked—they would soon enter the foothills and make their way toward Nah Ree. After that it would be a relatively simple matter to round up fifteen hundred refugees, march them across country, and sneak them into Mys.

The absurdity of the notion caused Santana to laugh. The legionnaires looked at each other and shrugged. The loot was an officer, officers were crazy, and this officer was crazier than most. So what the hell? Wheels creaked, chains rattled, and the wagon rolled west.

9

Though much has been said regarding the mutiny, and war which followed, a good deal less commentary has been devoted to the fate of those who participated in the rebellion. Having been forced to flee, thousands of mutineers made their way to the very edge of the Confederacy, where after a period of criminal activity, many made permanent homes and thereby pushed what is commonly referred to as the Rim farther out into the blackness of space.

Dr. Lightburn Deepthink
The Third War
Standard year 2633

ABOARD THE *SOLAR PRINCESS*, OFF RIM WORLD CR-9013

In spite of the fact that Rim World CR-9013 was nameless insofar as the official records were concerned, the drifters, smugglers, mercenaries, criminals, prospectors, and eccentrics who frequented the world called it "Nexus," a word that means "link," and described the role that it played in their hard-scrabble lives.

Nexus was a place where one could sell things, buy things, get drunk, get laid, and head out again. All without being hassled by the law.

That made the planet a natural port of call for the mutineers who had seized the Confederacy warships *Ibutho* and *Guerro*, and now used them to raid commerce out along the Rim.

Now, as the *Solar Princess* dropped into orbit around CR-

9013, Legion General Bill Booly and his wife, Maylo Chien-Chu, stood in the aft portion of the freighter's small control room and looked down on the planet below. The polar caps were white, as were the areas swathed in clouds, but the rest of the world was tan. Though gifted with lots of rivers and lakes Nexus had no bodies of water large enough to qualify as oceans.

Though not possessed of rare minerals, CR-9013 was an attractive planet in many important ways. It had a breathable atmosphere, something approximating Earth-normal gravity, and broad temperate zones above and below the equator.

There was no sentient race to cope with, the indigenous flora and fauna were manageable, and preliminary surveys had identified the presence of substantial mineral deposits. For these reasons, Nexus might well have attracted millions of would-be settlers except for one thing: The planet was not only on the Rim, but slightly *beyond* the Rim, which kept shipping costs prohibitively high.

That, plus the fact that there were other equally attractive planets closer in toward the Confederacy's core, meant that CR-9013 was likely to remain much as it was for another hundred years or so: a haven for outlaws, eccentrics, and a variety of religious cults that had established settlements in the wilderness that the locals referred to as the Great Wander.

Nexus had none of the formalities connected with making planetfall common to more civilized worlds which meant that anyone who wanted to visit simply dropped into orbit, took up whatever position they deemed prudent, and stayed as long as they liked.

As a result of this laissez-faire attitude newcomers were forced to protect themselves from hundreds of tons' worth of debris that previous visitors had dumped and left to circle the planet. The freighter's defensive screens flared as small pieces of trash hit and were deflected. In order to protect the *Princess* from larger items, like loose cooling fins, cargo modules, and wrecked shuttles, the vessel's NAVCOMP stood ready to hit them with repulsor beams, or should that fail, open fire on them before they could make contact with the ship's hull.

The vessel's captain, an ex–naval officer named Henry Mort, shook his head in disgust. "It's a disgrace, that's what it is, and something should be done. Some of this stuff is large enough to do real damage."

"They're also large enough to contain a boarding party," Booly replied thoughtfully. "After all, why buy what we have to sell if they can steal it?"

Mort, who in keeping with his role as master of a tramp freighter had been prevailed upon to allow his beard to grow, looked worried. The possibility that someone might attempt to board the ship hadn't occurred to him. He looked at Maylo and she nodded. "My husband is correct . . . The entire crew should remain on the highest state of alert until we break orbit."

"Yes, ma'am," Mort said obediently. "We'll keep a sharp eye out."

Maylo glanced at Booly and could tell that he took scant comfort from the master's words. Though a master of naval technology, procedure, and tradition Mort was outside of his comfort zone, and it showed. Perhaps she should have agreed to a military crew, but it was too late for that now. The ex–naval officer would have to do.

"Well," Booly said, "it's time to land, let the locals know we have spares for sale, and see what happens. If luck is with us the Syndicate will hear about our cargo, buy the spares, and lead us to the *Ibutho* and the *Guerro*."

Her husband made it sound simple, like a walk in the park, but Maylo knew the mission was likely to be a good deal more complicated than that. If the Syndicate had been paranoid *before* the attack on Base 012—they would be even more so now. Outside of their freedom the mutineers had nothing left to lose. Suddenly, for the first time since the adventure had begun, Maylo was afraid.

ON THE SURFACE OF RIM WORLD CR-9013

It required the better part of eight standard hours to check in with the heavily cloaked naval vessel that lurked well outside of the planet's gravity well, launch one of the freighter's two shuttles, and make the long bumpy ride down through the Rim world's atmosphere.

Maylo, who was dressed to fit the image of what she thought Lonny Fargo's mistress would look like, was at the controls as the flat black delta-shaped shuttle approached the settlement of Four Points from the east.

Booly had the impression of a broad, swiftly flowing river, a defensive wall, a tightly packed hodgepodge of one-, two-, and three-story buildings, another wall, what looked like a shantytown, and a maze of well-cut trails that wound in and out between what he thought of as "circle trees."

Each evergreen-like tree featured a central trunk, many of which appeared to be twenty or thirty feet tall, surrounded by a circle of thick vegetation. Some of the circular structures were intact, but many appeared to have been damaged, as if something heavy had ripped them open. Light green foliage had started to fill many of the gaps, as if the trees sought to reinforce their defensive screens.

Maylo put the shuttle into a wide left-hand turn. There, on the opposite side of the river from Four Points, what passed for a spaceport could be seen. A defensive wall had been built around that as well. All manner of shuttles, lighters, and small freighters sat, crouched, and in one case lay within. Scorched metal showed where fire had consumed most of its port wing, causing the ship to slump onto its side. There was no sign of a control tower—and none of the messages one would expect from an automated landing system. "Shall I put her down? Or go around again?"

"Go around again," Booly instructed, "as slowly as you can. Let's take another look."

The second circuit enabled the officer to get another look

at the settlement's layout. The first thing he noticed was that the defensive walls were made of what appeared to be steel-reinforced duracrete, and judging from their thickness, were extremely strong. A walkway circled the top of the wall and was accessed by both ladders and stairs.

The second feature that Booly noted was that the walls formed a diamond, with one point directed to the east and the other pointed toward the west. Not an impossible shape for a fort, but minus some of the advantages that a six-pointed star, or a well-laid-out rectangle could offer. A fact which could be attributed to poor planning—or might say something about whatever the locals wanted to keep out.

The third item of interest was that with the exception of the shantytown, and what looked like an extensive junkyard, both of which were located at the western end of the town—everything else lay within the protective walls.

Interestingly enough, there were no antiaircraft emplacements or missile launchers aimed at the sky. That suggested that whatever it was the townspeople feared couldn't fly.

The river glittered as it pushed its way west toward one of the enormous lakes that dotted the planet's surface. The shuttle passed over the tributary for the second time, lost altitude, and came in for a landing.

Maylo took advantage of the runwaylike strip that bisected the spaceport, dropped the shuttle's flaps, fired the repellors, and killed the main drive. Then, with her hands dancing across the controls, the executive turned the spacecraft on its axis, brought the bow up, and *backed* into a vacant slot.

It was virtuoso performance, and Booly, who had never learned to pilot anything more complicated than an air car, clapped his hands in appreciation. "Nicely done! If the CEO thing starts to fade—we can put you to work as a shuttle pilot."

Maylo made a face. "I already have a backup job, remember Lonny dear?"

Booly eyed his wife's scanty two-piece outfit and raised an

eyebrow. "It's hard to forget. Are you sure you need to dress like that?"

"Like what?" Maylo inquired innocently. "The metropolis of Four Points awaits . . . Let's go."

Booly strapped a sidearm to his right thigh, stuck a second weapon down the back of his pants, and donned a short leather jacket. The black duffel bag contained their toiletries, two changes of clothes, and some extra ammo. More than enough to see them through a short stay. The officer carried the duffel in his left hand, which left the right one free. An old habit that had served him well over the years.

Maylo used a remote to activate all of the shuttle's defensive systems, clipped the device to her belt, and threw a cape over her shoulders. It hung almost to the ground and served both to conceal *and* reveal her long slim legs.

They left through the lock, used the self-extruding ramp to reach the ground, and took deep lungfuls of unrecycled air. It tasted fresh and clean.

Metal pinged as it cooled, a power tool rattled nearby, and a slightly out-of-tune engine roared as a disreputable-looking ground effect vehicle rounded a squat-looking freighter, threw a curtain of dust out to the starboard side, and accelerated up the runway. It had been red once, but that was a long time ago, and the paint had faded to a rosy pink.

As the floater came closer Booly was able to make out the word TAXI stenciled across the vehicle's rounded bow and removed his hand from the low-slung sidearm as the volume of noise dropped and the car coasted to a stop.

The man who jumped out appeared to be middle-aged. He had short white hair, goggles that had been pushed up onto his head, and a two-day growth of beard. His clothing consisted of a much-washed orange ship suit with the name "Denny" embroidered over the left breast pocket, a worn leather belt, and a pair of military-style combat boots that hadn't been shined in a long time. When he smiled two rows of yellow teeth appeared. "Hi! My name's Jack, except most of my customers call me Jacko, which is fine so long as they pay what they owe! I saw you circle the town and thought you might need a lift."

Booly raised an eyebrow. "Nice to meet you Jacko, my name is Fargo, Lonny Fargo, and this is Star . . . What happened to Denny?"

"Who the hell knows?" the taxi driver replied, his eyes roaming Maylo's body. "I bought this ship suit in Shantytown. It was reasonably new then—but that was a couple of years ago. So, how 'bout it? You plan to ride or walk?"

"That depends," Booly replied cautiously. "How much is the fare?"

"One hundred credits," Jacko responded, "and a bargain at that."

"A bargain? I doubt that."

"Never been here before, have you?" the taxi driver asked knowingly. "You ain't seen noth n' yet! Most everything we have got here the hard way. Wait till you pay ten Cs for a cup of coffee! Makes a ride look cheap by comparison."

Fargo was supposed to be a high roller, the kind of person who would never walk if he could ride, so Booly nodded. "One hundred Cs it is."

Jacko ushered Maylo into the backseat, left Booly to fend for himself, and circled the floater to take his position behind the controls. The engine coughed, produced a puff of dark gray smoke, and caught. Lift fans sucked air in under the hovercraft's skirt, the body of the vehicle rose off the ground, and the rear-facing propeller started to spin.

Booly held on as the taxi turned and felt the air press against his face as Jacko guided the floater down the strip, waved to some colorfully plumed Prithians, and turned onto a well-graveled road. It led to a rusty steel bridge and the settlement beyond. There was traffic, quite a bit of it, most of which seemed to be headed into town. It was necessary for Booly to lean forward in order to be heard over the roar of the taxi's engine. "What are the walls for?"

"They're to keep the humps out," Jacko replied, half-turning to let the words float back over his shoulder. "Hold on . . . I'll show you what I mean."

The floater slowed and came to a stop in the middle of the much-abused bridge. The decking was made of wood and in need of maintenance. A woman on a homemade four-wheeled all-terrain vehicle rattled past. She wore a helmet, a jumpsuit, and had a baby strapped to her back. There were other residents as well, including a man on an old-fashioned bicycle, a work-worn robot hitched to a heavily laden cart, and two men dressed in robes. They walked with heads down as if preoccupied by prayer.

Jacko parked the hovercraft in such a way that it blocked the right lane, took no notice of the difficulties that caused, and gestured for his passengers to disembark. "Take a look at that!"

Booly stepped up to the rail and followed the man's index finger out toward a jumble of rocks, and the wild tangle of sun-bleached bones beyond. Many were huge, and there must have been tons of them, judging from the size of the pile.

"They're what we call humps," Jacko said, " 'cause of the big humps on their shoulders. They live in huge herds out east of here. Once a year, on what we call Hump Day, the bastards stampede toward the west and the winter grass that grows there. You can see where they ran into the boulders, piled up, and died. "The first folks to land here didn't know about the humps—and paid the price. Those fortunate enough to survive built the walls."

"Why not just move the town?" Maylo asked pragmatically. "Wouldn't that have been easier?"

"Yes, ma'am," Jacko replied, "except for one thing . . . Right after the firsties landed they pushed a thermal tap down through the center of town. That's where our power comes from . . . and they didn't have the wherewithal to sink another. The walls were built, the humps were forced to go around them, and here we are. Gotta build some new ones, though 'cause it's gettin' kinda crowded. That's why you're gonna have to pay a five-hundred-credit wall tax as we pass through the south gate.

"That's the bad news . . . The *good* news is that the humps are on the way! They started running about three days ago and should pass through here sometime tomorrow. You're in for a treat you are . . .'cause the whole town is gonna celebrate."

Booly looked at Maylo. She made a face. It was difficult to imagine how the celebration would help them find the people they were looking for. Still, there wasn't much the couple could do about it, so they returned to the taxi. It started with a roar, another puff of smoke, and completed the journey over the bridge.

Someone had mounted a huge hump skull over the gate and the creature's empty eye sockets stared down at the newcomers while a bored-looking woman accepted the city's wall tax. Judging from the bar code on her forehead the tax collector was a Clone. Maylo wondered what quirk of fate or free will had brought the woman to Nexus. There was no way to know.

Jacko deposited his passengers in front of the town's only hotel. It appeared to be fairly large, but was packed with Hump Day revelers most of whom were drunk. The desk clerk knew of a resident however, an ex-spacer, who occasionally let out his guest room, and wrote the address on a scrap of paper.

The firsties had laid the settlement out on a simple grid pattern. That made it relatively easy to find the intersection of Ninth and Carson and identify the silolike structure that stood between a duracrete box and a fanciful-looking house constructed from native wood.

The tower appeared to be about sixty feet tall, and if Booly was correct, had once served as a spacegoing tank. Now, with various fins and other items welded to its sides, the dwelling looked like an early rocket ship poised for takeoff. The words MAIN LOCK had been stenciled onto the slightly curved door. Maylo rang the bell.

An old-fashioned droid answered. Its smooth humanoid face

was devoid of all expression. "Yes? How can I be of assistance?"

"We were told that the owner might be willing to rent us a room," Booly replied. "Is that true?"

The robot looked from one human to the other as if sizing them up. "Yes, we have a cabin for rent. The cost is one thousand credits per night. The first night is payable in advance."

Booly was still in the process of running a mental inventory of the cash on hand when his wife presented the android with two crisp five-hundred-credit notes. "We'll take it."

The robot accepted the payment, stepped back out of the way, and allowed the humans to enter. There was no sign of the home's owner, not directly anyway, although the bulkheads were covered with stats that showed a handsome man with dark wavy hair standing in front of various ships, watching cargo being loaded into holds and shaking hands with nameless dignitaries.

A small lift tube had been installed to serve the dwelling's upper reaches, and there was plenty of time to pursue Walker's press clippings, commendations, and diplomas as the platform jerked its way upward.

Then, once the elevator came to a halt, the couple were shown into what amounted to a nicely maintained guest room. The suite had a spacegoing feel, as if it had been lifted out of a small liner, and occupied all of one floor. It had its own bathroom, a couple of chairs, and what looked like a comfortable bed. The robot provided the guests with the front door code, showed them where the towels were stored, and left them alone.

"So," Maylo said, dropping onto the bed. "How 'bout some sight-seeing?"

The room could be bugged, both of them knew that, which meant they would have to maintain their roles even while in the room alone. Besides, if the place *was* bugged, that could work to their advantage. The whole idea was to get the word out and it didn't matter how. Booly shook his head. "What's to see? Besides, we've got work to do . . . We need to find some customers. Those spares aren't making any money sitting in the hold."

"Spares, smares," Maylo said petulantly, "you work all the time."

"And *you* enjoy the money," Booly replied. "So, let's freshen up and make the rounds. There's a whole lot of people in town, and that could work to our advantage."

It was early evening by the time the twosome hit the streets. The settlement was even more crowded by then, as people from miles around continued to flow in through the gates.

Four Point's bars seemed like a logical place to begin so they went from establishment to establishment, striking up conversations, talking up the spares they had for sale, and suffering the backslapping, loud laughter, and public drunkenness that was an integral part of the Hump Day celebration.

Most of the revelers were too inebriated to talk business, but a few expressed interest until they learned that the spares were for huge cruiser-class vessels, and waved the couple off. It seemed that the market, such as it was, centered around smaller intersystem freighters, shuttles, and lighters.

Finally, having already visited six of Four Point's seven bars, the couple forced themselves to enter the last establishment on the list. It was called the Black Hole, and in keeping with the name, the interior was extremely dark. Both the ceiling and the walls had been painted flat black, the lighting was intentionally dim, and the air was thick with smoke.

Booly noticed that the Hole was a whole lot less crowded than the other establishments they'd been in. Because of the depressing decor? A reputation for poor service? Or, because the place was downright dangerous? Yes, the officer concluded as he scanned the rough-looking clientele, the last answer seemed the most likely.

Maylo had attracted a certain amount of attention in the saloons they had already visited, but it had been limited to some good-natured whistles, catcalls, and horny stares. But now, as the couple crossed the filthy floor and took seats at an empty table, there was almost complete silence as dozens of eyeballs stripped her clothes off. For the first time that evening Maylo felt frightened.

Booly felt the difference as well, wished they hadn't entered, but knew a sudden retreat could trigger the very kind of incident he hoped to avoid. Slowly, using the darkness for cover, the officer eased the backup gun out of his waistband and tucked the weapon under his left thigh. The same side his wife was seated on.

Then, once they were settled, most of the eyes left them to caress the frail-looking stripper who had climbed up onto a disk-shaped platform, where she proceeded to remove what few clothes she had on. Almost everyone present had seen her charms on previous occasions, but they clapped anyway. "Take it off, baby! Shake that thing! Show me what you got!"

But one pair of smoldering eyes remained where they were, glued to Maylo and the man she was with. They belonged to a man named Jurvis, Coster Jurvis, and he had two things on his mind: humiliate the man and thereby enhance his already substantial reputation—and take possession of the woman. Jurvis came to his feet and started across the room. Music pounded, the stripper removed her top, and audience shouted their approval.

Booly watched the man approach. He stood well over six feet tall, was broad through the shoulders and narrow at the waist. The local wore what looked like a blaster in a cross-draw holster—and a knife on his right hip. He had a single eyebrow, perpetually hooded eyes, and hair that crawled down off his cheeks and onto his neck.

The man grabbed a chair, turned it around so the back was forward, and took a seat. That meant that the back of the chair not only blocked Booly's view of the blaster but would allow the local to move up and back without anything getting in the way. "Hi, my name is Jurvis—and who are you?"

Booly removed the hideout gun from beneath his thigh. "My name is Fargo . . . This is Star."

Jurvis nodded agreeably. "Glad to make your acquaintance . . . especially yours, Ms. Star. It's hard to tell, what with that cape and all, but I'm guessing that you have a very nice body. Why don't you get up on the platform and show the boys what you got? We could pass the hat and split the money. Your boyfriend won't mind . . . will you, Mr. Fargo? You've seen the goods—why not let someone else enjoy them for once?"

Booly dropped his right hand down along his side. Not *on* his weapon but close. Jurvis had anticipated such a move, and with the chair to provide cover, pulled the blaster from its holster.

"I suggest that you stand up and walk away," Booly responded softly. "There are nicer places to die."

Jurvis laughed. It sounded unnaturally loud. That's when Maylo realized that the music had disappeared and that all conversation had stopped. The confrontation *was* the entertainment—and nobody wanted to miss it. "Me?" the local said, his voice pitched so everyone could hear. "Walk away? I don't think so . . . The woman belongs to me now. *You're* the one who needs to leave. Unless you'd like to see her strip . . . in which case feel free to stay."

Two men had left the bar to take up positions next to Jurvis. They wore weapons and looked like they knew how to use them.

"Okay," Booly said calmly, "have it your way. Make your move."

Jurvis was surprised. He had used the ploy before and most men left. This one was either stupid, or extremely confident, and the question was which? Not that he had much choice since the whole bar was watching there was only one thing he could do.

The problem was the solid seat back. He could blast a hole in it, but a second bolt would be required to take Fargo down, and the fraction of a second required to accomplish that might be critical. That meant the odds would be better if Jurvis came up off the chair, fired the blaster as cleared the top, and fired again. He sent the necessary message to his leg muscles and started to rise.

Maylo had been waiting for Jurvis to move. From the moment her husband had pushed the backup weapon into her hand she had known what he wanted her to do. The safety was off as the handgun cleared the table, barked twice, and threw Jurvis back onto the floor. His blaster went off, burned a hole through the ceiling, and fell from his lifeless hand.

The other men, their weapons half-drawn, found themselves looking down the bore of Booly's semiautomatic service pistol. It looked like the entrance to a railway tunnel and neither one of them moved.

"That's enough, wouldn't you say?" Booly asked conversationally. "I suggest that you boys two-finger those weapons, drop them on the bar, and retire to the opposite side of the room." Both men did as they were told—but they didn't like it.

Maylo stood first and used her weapon to cover the patrons at the bar. Booly rose second, was careful to stay out of his wife's line of fire, and kept an eye on the rest of the room.

Then, side by side, they backed out of the saloon. Once clear they turned and ran. Booly dodged around the first corner he came to. Fifty or sixty revelers had spilled out of another establishment and onto the street. The couple dived into the crowd, pushed their way through, and turned to look. There was no sign of pursuit. "Nice work," Booly said approvingly. "The bastard kept his eyes on my right hand. He never saw it coming."

Maylo nodded, tried to come up with an appropriate remark, and threw up instead.

Booly waited for the heaves to stop, wrapped an arm around his wife's shoulders, and took her home. Then, after a couple of hot showers, they went to bed.

High above them, sitting within the transparent dome which topped his rocketlike home, Captain John Walker sat and stared at the stars. They were a long way off—and he missed them very much.

Booly was the first to rise the following morning. He had just stepped out of the shower, toweled himself dry, and reentered the room when he noticed the envelope on the floor. It had been shoved under the door and bore an embossed "W."

The officer picked up the envelope, took one look at the name that had been printed across the surface of the white paper, and felt something heavy fall into his stomach. Rather than being addressed to Lonny Fargo, as it should have been, the envelope was made out to "General Bill Booly."

Booly ripped the flap open, withdrew the note, and read the text:

> Dear General,
> It would be an honor if you and Ms. Chien-Chu would join
> me for breakfast. Take the lift to the top.
> Sincerely,
> Captain John Walker, Ret.

Somehow, some way, their host had not only seen through the carefully constructed identities but done so in very short order.

Booly woke his wife and waited until she had showered before showing her the note. Maylo's almond-shaped eyes widened as she read both the name on the envelope and the note within. "Damn! What are we going to do?"

Booly shrugged. "There doesn't seem to be much we can do except get dressed and join Captain Walker for breakfast."

Twenty minutes later the couple stepped into the small capsule, touched the button labeled "6," and felt the car jerk into motion. Like many of the mechanical systems on Nexus the lift tube was a one-of-a-kind solution engineered by a local resident. It took a while for the platform to reach the top. When it finally did, and the door opened, Booly and Maylo stepped out into a bright sun-splashed room. A single glance was sufficient to see that the transparent dome afforded an excellent view of Four Points, the river, and the valley through which it flowed.

"Good morning," a smooth-sounding voice said. "I'm glad you could join me."

Booly turned to discover that an android, the *same* android they had met the day before, had emerged from a small galley-style kitchen. It took a moment to absorb the robot's words. The officer frowned. "Captain Walker?"

"Yes," Walker said. "I no longer occupy the body my mother gave me and choose to make do with this one instead. Arturo served me for many years, but parts became scarce, and I was forced to take him off-line. Moving into his body seemed like a fitting way to honor his memory."

Booly accepted the cyborg's cool metal hand, shook it, and stood to one side as Walker moved to greet Maylo. The notion of honoring a machine, much as if it had been a person struck the officer as odd, but so what? Everything about Walker was strange.

"Please," the ex-spacer said, gesturing toward a well-set table, "have a seat. My caloric requirements are rather modest these days . . . but there was a time when I enjoyed a good hearty breakfast. The food is in the warmer . . . I'll bring it out."

The cyborg disappeared behind the freestanding partition that screened the galley leaving the couple to exchange looks and wonder what would happen next.

True to his word Walker took two plates out of the warmer, removed a couple of items from a small reefer, and placed everything on a tray. "Here you go," the ex-spacer remarked placing the food on a circular table. "Bon appétit."

Booly took one look at the locally produced eggs, bacon, and toast, realized he hadn't had a real Earth-style breakfast in a long time, and proceeded to dig in.

Though still in the process of recovering from the violence

of the night before Maylo forced herself to take a few bites.

Walker, who seemed to derive satisfaction from watching his guests eat, took advantage of the interlude to tell a series of stories about meals eaten on distant planets. Most were quite amusing and time passed quickly.

Fifteen minutes later, after the last bit of egg had been wiped off Booly's plate and coffee had been served, there was a moment of silence. Booly chose to break it. "The breakfast was excellent . . . thank you. Now, let's get down to business. You know our true identities. How?"

The challenge was apparent but Walker was unmoved. "When I was forced to retire certain parties approached me and offered a part-time job. I agreed to keep my ear to the ground, submit regular reports, and assist with special projects."

Booly eyed the cyborg over his coffee cup. "You work for Intelligence."

Walker shrugged. "Something like that . . . although I can't reveal the details."

"No offense, but why should we believe you?" Maylo inquired.

"Because I know who you are and why you're here," the cyborg answered simply.

"That's just great," Booly said cynically, "except for one thing. Military Intelligence reports to a general who reports to me . . . and when we put this mission together your name never came up."

"That's because I don't work for Military Intelligence," Walker answered evenly.

"I'll bet he works for the Confederacy's Department of Intelligence (CONINT)," Maylo said thoughtfully, "which reports to the president himself."

Booly knew that the Confederacy's various intelligence-gathering groups had a tendency to feud with each other, which meant that Maylo could be right. "Is that correct? You report to CONINT?"

"Sorry," Walker replied stolidly, "I'm not in a position to

either confirm or deny your wife's theory. The main thing is that I know you're trying to locate two extremely important items—and I think I can help."

"All right," Booly said reluctantly, "let's say we believe you . . . What would you suggest?"

"The Syndicate has hundreds of suppliers," the cyborg replied evenly. "I can't prove it but I believe that one of our locals, a woman named Prosser, is one of them."

"And where," Maylo inquired, "would this Prosser person be found?"

"Carly Prosser maintains what amounts to a junkyard adjacent to Shantytown. But the junk is little more than a cover. The real business has to do with other items that move in and out of her hands."

"Okay, we'll check it out," Booly agreed. "But keep this in mind . . . Before we call on Ms. Prosser, we're going to upload a message to our ship, telling the crew that we are about to pursue a lead supplied by *you*. If we disappear, or wind up dead, some very unpleasant people will come to call on you. Understood?"

Walker's face was incapable of displaying emotion but the annoyance was clear to hear in his voice. "I'll bear that in mind. Don't forget that today is Hump Day. When the siren sounds you will have fifteen minutes to get inside the walls. After that they stay locked until the stampede has passed. And one more thing . . . The gentleman you killed last night has friends all of whom are on the lookout for you."

Booly raised his eyebrows, and the cyborg nodded. "That's right, I make it my business to know what's going on around here. These folks are bad news, so I suggest that conclude your business with Prosser as quickly as possible, and get the hell out of here."

Booly nodded. "Thanks for the advice. We'll do the best we can."

Later, safely ensconced in their room, the twosome sent a radio message via the shuttle's com gear, confirmed receipt, and did what they could to change their appearance.

Maylo dressed down, trading the flashy-looking clothes she had been wearing for a pair of plain blue overalls, a utility belt, and a pair of sturdy boots. A lot less makeup, a billed cap, and some carefully applied grime served to complete the disguise.

Booly went in a slightly different direction by trading his jacket for a hump-hide vest, passing the backup weapon to Maylo, and sticking the sidearm down the back of his pants.

Then, walking thirty paces apart, the couple headed for the north gate. Four Points was packed with rowdy visitors. There weren't very many places to go but that didn't prevent them from patrolling streets, swilling beer, and shouting at each other. Maylo knew the crowd would make it difficult for their enemies to see them, but the reverse was true as well, a fact that made her nervous.

The north gate was open, but most people were entering the settlement rather than leaving it, and Booly was stopped. The gatekeeper had an unkempt beard, a huge belly, and a world-class case of halitosis. "Hold it right there, stranger . . . Where you headed?"

"Shantytown."

The local raised both of his bushy eyebrows. "Shantytown? Are you sure? Most of the folks from down that way are inside the walls by now. You never know which way the humps will turn—and last year they took Shantytown apart."

"Thanks," Booly replied. "I'm running an errand that's all . . . I'll be back in thirty minutes or so."

The gatekeeper shrugged. "It's your skin, pal. If you're still out there when siren goes off, run like hell. The doors close fifteen minutes later—and there ain't nobody that's gonna open them up."

Booly nodded, thanked the man for his counsel, and stepped out through the portal. A well-packed trail led to the left and the officer followed it away from the gate. Bones, thousands of them, marked both sides of the path. Some lay on the surface, gradually wearing away under the assault of wind, rain and snow, but many remained at least partially buried in the red-dish soil.

Booly paused, saw Maylo, and waited for her to catch up. Someone either dropped or threw a bottle off the wall fifteen feet to the west. It shattered and glass flew in every direction. The couple looked up to find that the top of the wall was lined with drunks. Everyone wanted to watch the humps and space was at a premium. A woman waved and Maylo waved back.

Meanwhile, having been alerted by the gatekeeper, a man named Canty watched the couple through binoculars. The peo-ple around him had them as well so no one thought it strange. Though not exactly friends with Jurvis—he couldn't think of anyone who was—Canty had backed the bully the night be-fore. A consistently good thing to do in the past.

Now, only halfway through the following day, people who had witnessed the encounter had taken to calling him "half-draw Canty" because of the speed with which the man called Fargo had frozen him in place.

The answer, the only one that would shut them up, was to put both of the off-worlders in the ground. A task that worried him at first but not anymore. Canty grinned, murmured some words into a handheld radio, and signaled for one of the street vendors to bring him a beer. It tasted cool and crisp.

Booly and Maylo walked along the edge of the depression left by the previous year's stampede and followed it to the left as the wall narrowed to a point. The hump run continued straight through Shantytown and out onto the plain beyond.

The place was pretty much deserted, and for good reason, since the humps could be expected to make short work of the wood shacks, shipping crates, and tarp-clad lean-tos that the residents had left behind. Trash, including bits of paper, scraps of plastic, and pieces of clothing lay thick on the ground.

Booly wound his way through the maze of temporary struc-tures until he saw the salvage yard Walker had spoken of. It was normally protected by a nine-foot-tall razor-wire fence, but that was to deter people rather than animals, and most of it was down. Three rolls of wire lay against one of the settlement's walls—and two exoskeleton-clad men were busy removing the last section of fencing from a row of sturdy-looking metal poles.

A black woman, her hair shot with gray, stood and watched them. She wore a pleated vest, a wide leather belt, culottes and a pair of steel-tipped boots. The megaphone in her hand suggested that she was ready to give instructions, and it was Booly's guess that this was the woman they were looking for.

Booly looked at Maylo, she nodded, and they advanced together. Prosser couldn't possibly have heard their footsteps, not over the noise being made by the exoskeletons, but she turned anyway. She had high cheekbones, large green eyes, and a generous mouth. It smiled. "Citizen Fargo, I believe? And Citizen Star? I wondered when you'd show up."

Booly was surprised but knew he shouldn't be. They had been shopping their wares all over town after all so it wasn't surprising that someone like Prosser would have heard about it. He smiled. "You're very well informed. Yes, as you probably know by now, we have some cruiser-class spares for sale."

There was a shout. Prosser looked up toward the top of the wall and waved at someone she knew. "Come with me . . . The humps aren't due for an hour yet. Let's have a cup of tea. Some of the folks on the wall can read lips."

The twosome followed the junk dealer down an aisle formed by stacks of salvaged ductwork and into a metal shipping container. It was outfitted as an office although most of the contents had been packed into trunks. A kettle simmered on a two-burner stove. The dealer gestured toward a pair of ragged-looking chairs. They had graced the dining salon of a small liner once and still bore the company's crest. "Have a seat . . . I'll be right with you."

Five minutes later Booly found himself having a sociable cup of tea with what he would later learn was one of the Syndicate's most important suppliers.

"So," Prosser said gently, her eyes flicking from one face to the other, "what exactly do we have? There are a lot of parts in a cruiser most of which are relatively easy to find or fabricate. Some of them are stacked right outside the door. My interest, if any, lies in the 5 percent that are a little more difficult to find."

Booly nodded. "I know what you mean. This is the good stuff . . . I'm talking four accumulator coils, three jump actuators, six transfer modules, two shift locks, one screen matrix, and a nav interface. All like new."

Prosser raised both eyebrows and took a sip of tea. "I'm impressed. Where did you get all this stuff?"

The officer cocked his head. "Where do *you* keep your money?"

Prosser laughed. "Point taken. The source doesn't matter. Are the components available for inspection?"

Booly nodded. "Whenever you like."

"And, assuming I had a buyer, could you deliver the shipment on my behalf? I have a freighter—but it's at least four weeks out."

The soldier felt his pulse race. Would he deliver them? Hell yes, he would deliver them! Along with a ship packed with Naa commandos! It wouldn't do to appear too eager however so Booly narrowed his eyes. "Maybe, if the price is right."

Prosser raised her cup by way of a salute. "Don't worry, it will be."

The siren sounded a fraction of a second later. Prosser stood. "There's the signal—it's time to get out of here."

Booly and Maylo stepped outside. The dealer turned her stove off, emptied the cups into a bucket, and placed her tea set into a well-padded box. With that accomplished it was a simple matter to pull the steel doors closed, latch them in place, and walk away.

There was no sign of the exoskeleton-clad workmen as the threesome made their way back toward the north gate. Booly assumed they had finished their work and reentered the city.

There was no need to run since there wasn't far to go but

Prosser set a brisk pace nevertheless. The people who lined the top of the wall yelled everything from obscenities to words of encouragement as the party followed the bone walk up to the gate.

Canty, still perched above, watched with a rising sense of anticipation.

Prosser frowned when she saw that the gate was closed, pounded on one of the double doors, and yelled the gate-keeper's name. "Hurley? Where the hell are you? Open the door!"

But there was no response as Booly felt the ground tremble beneath his boots, looked toward the east, and say the rising cloud of dust. The humps were on the way.

"Hurley!" Prosser shouted. "We have five minutes yet! Open the door!"

But there was still no response. Onlookers looked at each other, wondered what to do, but were reluctant to take action. That's when Canty appeared directly over the gate. He had to shout in order to make himself heard. "So, how does it feel, Fargo? Knowing you're going to die?"

"I don't know," Booly yelled back. "You tell me!"

Booly recognized the man's face as belonging to one of the men he had faced the night before. It didn't take a genius to figure out that the man had somehow arranged for the gate to remain closed.

It was a difficult shot, one the officer didn't think he'd make, but he had to try. The big semiauto came up, jumped in his hand, and a hole appeared at the center of Canty's forehead. He was still in the process of falling back into the crowd when Maylo grabbed her husband's arm. "The junkyard! Run!"

Prosser had little choice but to follow as the other two began to run. She heard people yelling, felt the ground continue to shake, and knew there wasn't much time.

That's when the dealer tripped over a half-buried hipbone, landed flat on her face, and knew it was over. Her ankle hurt, *really* hurt, and she wouldn't be able to run.

But the other two came back, lifted the dealer up, and half carried her toward the junkyard. "The cargo module!" Maylo shouted. "That's our only chance!"

Booly nodded, used his right hand to get a grip on Prosser's belt, and used that to help keep her upright.

The crowd cheered as the threesome rounded the point where the north and south walls met, made bets as to who if anyone would survive, and fought for the best view. Higher up, watching the action from the room at the very top of his silolike home, Walker shook his head in dismay. The situation didn't look good.

Thousands of hoofbeats combined to generate a loud rumble. Booly looked back over his shoulder and saw the oncoming horde. Each hump was about two-thirds the size of an Earth elephant—or a little larger than one of the dooths on his home planet of Algeron. They had huge, lumpy heads, four tusks each, and enormous shoulders. Suddenly they were close, *too* close, and the officer turned his head forward again.

Maylo spotted the steel cargo module, yelled, "We can make it!" and redoubled her efforts. Together the threesome covered the last thirty feet, stumbled inside, and turned around.

"The doors!" Prosser shouted. "Close the doors!"

Metal squealed as the other two hurried to obey the dealer's command. There was no inside latch so Maylo grabbed a length of rope, and was in the process of wrapping it around the vertical lock rods, when the avalanche of flesh and bone struck.

The humps hit the salvage first. Some were crushed to death, others suffered long gashes from sharp pieces of metal, and some were impaled on steel rods.

But the herd couldn't stop, *wouldn't* stop, not for another day yet. Dead bodies became ramps, the onslaught continued, and metal groaned as it was pushed aside.

The tidal wave hit the cargo module shortly thereafter. The metal box shook from the force of the impact, the entire container was pushed ten feet to the west, and the humans were thrown to the floor. That's when the rope broke, the doors flew open, and Maylo saw a torrent of brown bodies surge past. Dust swirled, the ground shook as if seized by a tremor, and the animals made loud squalling sounds.

One of the beasts turned, and seemed poised to force an entry, when Booly fired two shots over its head. The noise, which was amplified by the metal walls, had the desired effect. The hump turned and was swept away.

For one brief moment Prosser thought they were safe, that the humps would simply pass on by, but she was wrong. Outside, beyond what they could see, a hump tripped and went down. That seemingly inconsequential event was sufficient to turn the animals behind causing them to strike the module's side.

Maylo felt the floor tilt under her feet, struggled to keep her footing, and saw Prosser's furniture start to slide. Shelving crashed to the floor, the angle became steeper as more animals were forced in under the container, and the executive lost her footing.

That was when the container flipped all the way over, was hit once again, and pushed along the surface of the ground.

The humans were thrown about, Prosser cried out in pain as her already injured leg struck the edge of the overturned desk, and she was dumped onto what had been a wall. Trunks of carefully packed office materials thumped to either side.

Finally, just as Booly decided that the torture would never end, the last of the humps swept by. It took the better part of ten minutes for the last of the herd to clear the area, for the dust to settle, and for the survivors to emerge from hiding.

A cheer went up as they appeared, a rescue party came out to assist them, and a Nexus-style investigation was launched. The honorary mayor went looking for the gatekeeper, couldn't find him, and soon gave up. Booly was ordered to pay for Canty's burial—and the case was closed.

Better yet, they had a buyer, the right buyer, and the deal was nearly done. All they had to do was show Prosser the goods, come to terms, and go wherever she said. The rest would be easy. That's what Booly told himself anyway—but knew it wasn't true.

PLANET ARBALLA, THE CONFEDERACY OF SENTIENT BEINGS

Once known as the *Reliable*, the *Friendship* still looked like a battleship, in spite of her new role. Her hull was five miles long and covered by a complex tracery of heat exchangers, tractor beam projectors, com pods, and weapons blisters.

Just as impressive as the vessel herself was the purpose to which she had been dedicated. Having won the first Hudathan war, but unable to decide where the capital of the newly formed Confederacy should be located, the Senate agreed to an idea put forward by President Sergi Chien-Chu: The Confederacy would use a spaceship as its capital, a different race would host the vessel each year, and no one would be slighted. A noble concept and one that had worked so far.

Arballa's sun played across the vessel's port side as the Ramanthian shuttle received permission to land, locked on to a traffic control beacon, and began its final approach.

Senator Alway Orno had been through the process hundreds of times before but this visit would be different. Sadly, since the Ramanthian diplomat loved his job, and had actually enjoyed much of the time spent aboard the *Friendship*, this would be one of his last visits. Because unfortunate though it was for the thousands of beings who would be killed—the battleship's days were numbered.

Not because Orno hated those on board, but because he loved his race, and they needed ships. *Thousands* of ships like the Sheen vessels that co-orbited Arballa's sun in company with the planet itself. Ships which would be used to transport billions of newly hatched nymphs to the worlds being prepared to receive them.

For weeks, no *months*, the diplomat had agonized over how to steal the mothballed vessels. No easy task given all of the navy ships assigned to guard not only them, but *Friendship* herself, which was only a four-hour shuttle ride away.

The problem appeared insurmountable at first, and he had despaired of solving it, until the answer came in a dream. At some point during one of his frequent sand baths the Ramanthian drifted off to sleep. The dream began innocently enough, with Orno drifting godlike through space, looking down on Arballa. That's when the diplomat saw the *Friendship*, knew something horrible was about to happen, and saw the battleship explode.

Orno felt dozens of tiny pinpricks as smaller vessels raced in from all directions, passed through the surface of his nebula-like body, and rushed to help.

And that was the moment when the Ramanthian not only awoke, but understood the solution to his dilemma and could lay the necessary plans.

Bit by bit, part by part, the components for a powerful bomb would be smuggled onto the *Friendship*. There was only so much one could cram into one of the standardized diplomatic pouches, so the process would take some time.

Then, when all of the necessary parts were in place, the device would be assembled and moved to the center of the ship. Later, on a day of Orno's choosing, a signal would be sent and the bomb would explode. Damage would be done, *tremendous* damage, but not so much as to obliterate the ship.

No, the whole point was to create a disaster of such magnitude that at least some of the beings on board could be rescued thereby drawing most if not all of the navy ships in toward Arballa.

That's when Ramanthian vessels would attack whatever ships remained with the Sheen fleet, specially trained Hudathan commandos would board the ships chosen to be hijacked, specially designed interfaces would be installed, coordinates would be entered, and thousands of ships would vanish into hyperspace. All within a matter of one standard hour.

Momentary darkness swallowed the shuttle as it entered the

Friendship's vast launch bay. Later, when Orno's luggage was unloaded, three diplomatic pouches would come off with it. The saddlebag-like suitcases would be scanned but the pouches were inviolate. It was the humans who had insisted on that particular tradition—and Orno couldn't resist the Ramanthian equivalent of a smile.

PLANET HUDATHA, THE CONFEDERACY OF SENTIENT BEINGS

It was so dark that if it hadn't been for a scattering of lights, the castle would have been invisible against the surrounding mountains. The keep was built of stone, the only material that could withstand Hudatha's unpredictable weather and still remain standing for the better part of a thousand years.

Like most such fortresses, it had been constructed high on a crag, forcing any who wished to take it to fight their way up steep slopes, through narrow defiles, and along a path that followed the edge of a cliff before reaching the *true* obstacle, which consisted of a fifty-unit-wide air moat spanned by a wooden drawbridge. The Ka clan had lost battles over the last nine-hundred-plus years but never the castle itself.

But the defenses that had once been sufficient to stop entire armies were nothing against an enemy who arrived by air— and carried credentials so lofty that those who guarded the keep had little choice but to let them enter.

The fact that the leader of the threesome, the recently elected Triad Horo Hasa-Ba and his retainers arrived unarmed served to further allay any fears that the Ka security forces might have had and the visitors were allowed to enter the keep.

Triad Ikor Ifana-Ka, old warrior that he was, awoke from a troubled sleep. Something was wrong but what? A Ramanthian war drone had shot him more than fifty years earlier. His leg hurt but there was nothing unusual about that. The medics wanted to take the limb off but he had refused. Now he wished that they had. The pain had grown worse with age. The medications helped but the discomfort continued.

Still, he was used to that, and felt sure that something else had served to waken him. Danger of some sort. But that was absurd. All the Hudathan needed to do was open his eyes and look around the dimly lit bedchamber to see that with the exception of the old battle flags that draped the walls, the enormous slab of wood that served as his desk, and a leather easy chair the room was empty.

That was when the intercom sounded and the castle's majordomo spoke. Hudathan culture was such that there was no need to announce himself, apologize for the intrusion, or use extraneous words. "You have visitors, sir."

Ifana-Ka wasn't expecting visitors and didn't want any. He sat up in bed. "Who are they?"

"Triad Hasa-Ba and two retainers, sir."

The old warrior blinked. Such a visit, especially an *unannounced* visit, was highly unusual. Whatever had brought Hasa-Ba out in the middle of the night must be very important indeed. But important to whom? And in what regard? "Make them comfortable. Tell them I will receive them shortly."

The triad lifted a handset, dictated a message, and entered the time he wanted it to be sent. A waste of time most likely but so what? A person of his advanced years was entitled to be a bit eccentric.

With that out of the way, Ifana-Ka rang the majordomo, gave permission for the visitors to enter his bedchamber, and felt for the handgun he kept under his pillow. Not because he had particular reason to fear Hasa-Ba, but because he was Hudathan, and naturally suspicious of *everyone*. That was why *he* had survived when so many hadn't. The weapon was where it should be. He moved it down under the covers.

Hasa-Ba's cape swirled and his boots made a rhythmic thumping sound as he and two of his warriors made their way down the ancient hallway, nodded to the sentries who stood guard outside the old warrior's room, and were permitted to enter. The door closed with a heavy thud.

"So," Ifana-Ka said, "what brings the newest member of the

triad out in the middle of the night? Something important I trust?"

"Yes," Hasa-Ba replied stolidly. "Something very important."

"Well?" Ifana-Ka demanded irritably, "Out with it."

Hasa-Ba approached the foot of the old warrior's bed. Ifana-Ka looked weak, too weak to rule, yet there he lay. An impediment to progress, to the new order, to the glory of the future.

Still, the oldster had served his people with courage, and deserved an opportunity to die peacefully. Hasa-Ba went straight to the point. "I came to accept your resignation."

"How considerate of you," Ifana-Ka said sarcastically. "Why would I tender it?"

"The people want change," the younger Hudathan replied simply, "and I plan to give it to them. Even as we speak efforts are under way to take the ships we need, reconstitute the Hudathan navy, and restore full autonomy to our race."

"Efforts?" Ifana-Ka asked. "What efforts?" His mind raced. This was far worse than anything he had imagined. Slowly, bit by bit, he slipped one hand under the blanket.

"The vessel known as the *Friendship* will be destroyed," Hasa-Ba replied flatly. The navy will rush to help. That's when our forces will strike. Thousands of ships are there for the taking. Many will be ours."

"And the rest?"

"The Ramanthians need ships just as we do. They will receive the balance of the alien fleet."

"And then?"

"And then we will regroup, reorganize, and prepare to defend ourselves."

"That's right," Ifana-Ka said bitterly, his fingers wrapping themselves around the gun butt. "We will be attacked, and attacked, and attacked. We lost two such wars in the past. What makes you believe that we can win this one?"

"Outside of ourselves, the Ramanthians, and the Thrakies the Humans are the only race that has a credible military force.

The bugs will be on our side, and the fur balls will remain neutral, which leaves the humans on their own. There's no way to know what the Hegemony will do, but given the strength of our revitalized navy, we can defeat them if necessary."

Ifana-Ka sighed. Even if the plan was successful it would divert much-needed attention away from the need to escape their increasingly hostile solar system, kill off millions of Hudathan citizens, and take the race back to the days of barbarism. He could have said that, *should* have said that, but knew it would be a waste of time. "Does Doma-Sa know about your plans?"

"No," the other member of the triad replied, "but he will soon."

"You plan to request his resignation as well?"

"No, I plan to kill him."

"I see," Ifana-Ka replied calmly. "Well, based on what I've heard, it appears as though you'd better kill me as well."

The handgun came up, caught on the bedclothes, and was smothered as both of Hasa-Ba's troopers threw themselves onto the bed.

Ifana-Ka cursed his own weakness, tried to call out, but gagged on a wad of cloth. That's when the old soldier saw the injector in Hasa-Ba's hand and knew how he would die: A powerful drug would stop his heart, the other triad would call for help, and it would be over.

Then, having assassinated Doma-Sa, the remaining member of the triad would be free to install two of his vassals into the recently vacated positions, and rule the Hudathan race. A time-tested strategy.

Ifana-Ka felt the injector bite his arm, struggled to free himself, and finally managed to do so. Suddenly, and for reasons the warrior wasn't quite sure of, his leg felt fine.

10

WEST OF THE FOREIGN CITY OF MYS, ON THE INDEPENDENT PLANET OF LA NOR

Since it had rained most of the previous day, and well into the night, Santana was pleased to feel the sun on his back as he and the other eighteen members of the first platoon continued to slog their way toward the west. From his position high on Snyder's back, the lieutenant could see gently rolling hills, patches of cultivated land, and a distant plume of smoke. A farmhouse? Or something more sinister? There was no way to be certain.

Santana turned to look back over his shoulder. The first squad under Sergeant Cvanivich was following along behind the T-2, well separated in case of an attack, and paralleling both sides of the road in order to avoid the worst of the mud. Yao Che, who had taken a liking to Cvanivich, tagged along behind.

The RAVs came next, both robots burdened with thousands of pounds' worth of gear, ammo, and food. They walked with a strange mincing gait, as if reluctant to place their pods in mud and resentful of the effort required to free them.

The second squad, under the watchful eye of Sergeant Via, followed the RAVs with Zook walking drag. It was a nasty job, walking backward half the time, but critical to ensure that the column's six stayed clean.

Platoon Sergeant Hillrun was mounted on the second T-2's back, saw Santana turn to look, and raised a hand by way of a greeting. The platoon leader responded in kind before turning back toward the front.

Later, in about thirty minutes or so, one of the legionnaires would be invited to ride drag, Hillrun would rotate to Snyder, and Santana would walk. Both squad leaders, and both corporals, would take turns on the lead cyborg's back as well. Gradually, over time, the rest of the troops would have an opportunity to ride on Zook.

The point was to keep fresh eyeballs up front, provide the noncoms with the experience of riding point, and give everyone an occasional breather.

Though not especially thrilled about a mission deep into what Corporal Dietrich insisted on referring to as "dig country," the cavalry officer did enjoy being out on his own, and was pleased with the way things had gone so far.

Once free of Polwa the wagon train had made its way into the foothills, turned off onto what appeared to a little-used track, and pulled up behind the crown of a low-lying hill. That was when Yao Che dismounted, called the other drivers together, paid *two* day's wages rather than one, and sent the LaNorian teamsters packing.

This was a critical juncture, and one which Santana had been worried about since there was always the possibility of treachery, especially given the fact that the drivers no doubt assumed that Yao Che was alone.

Yes, it would have been relatively easy to kill the LaNorians, but the platoon leader wanted to avoid bloodshed if at all possible.

However, thanks to the cover story, and the fact that the drivers were afraid of what might happen to them if the Claw discovered that they were transporting steel rails, the locals were eager to leave.

Yao Che watched until the teamsters were out of sight, waited for another five minutes just to make sure, and rapped on the side of wagon one. "Lieutenant Santana! You can come out now! The drivers are gone."

The platoon leader dropped through the floor-mounted escape hatch, scrambled out from under the wagon, and stood to look around. It was raining and he raised a hand to shield his eyes. The rise served to shelter the convoy from the main road but they were vulnerable nonetheless. All it would take was for a group of Tro Wa to come along, grow curious about the deeply cut wagon tracks, and decide to follow them around the side of the hill. He got on the radio.

"This is Bravo Six to Bravo Five . . . Use Bravo Two Six and her squad to establish a defensive perimeter. Once they become available you can place both T-2s as you see fit.

"Bravo Three Six, I want you and your squad to open wagons two and four, followed by three and five. Once that's accomplished, run the diagnostics on the RAVs to make sure that they're good to go. Over."

There was a series of "Rogers," as the troops set about their various tasks. Santana spotted Yao Che and waved him over. "You did a nice job. That took guts. Thank you."

The LaNorian made a mental note of the colloquial expression and was quick to add it to the growing store of other sayings already harvested from the legionnaires. His ear fans fluttered with both pleasure and embarrassment as he looked down at his muddy feet. "You are most welcome, Excellency."

Santana shook his head. "Forget the 'Excellency' stuff. 'Lieutenant' will do just fine. Now, here's what I want you to do . . . Go to Sergeant Hillrun, tell him you need two escorts, and get them to help you unharness the razbuls. Herd the bastards about a quarter of a mile south of here, find something they like to eat, and turn them loose. Understand?"

Yao Che had no idea how far a "quarter of a mile" was but figured his escorts would know. He answered the way he heard the legionnaires do. "Sir! Yes, sir!"

Santana grinned and slapped the youngster on the back. "Good. Once that's done you get your butt back here fast as you can. We need to pack up and put some miles between ourselves and these wagons before the sun goes down."

The LaNorian nodded and scampered away. One hour later the razbuls had been released, the RAVs had been checked, and the team was ready to move.

Santana would have preferred to burn the heavily modified wagons rather than leave them for the wrong sort of people to find, but knew the resulting smoke could attract trouble. So he left the vehicles where they were, cut across country, and hit the main road three miles to the west.

Now, well into the next day, the platoon leader had other things to worry about. There was traffic on the road, plenty of traffic, like heavily laden carts approaching from the west. They were rickety affairs, outfitted with enormous wooden wheels, and drawn by animals so old their skins had faded white. The LaNorians who accompanied the vehicles, two or three families by the look of them, were so dumbfounded by the sight of the enormous T-2, the aliens who followed behind, and the carnivorous-looking robots that they stared in openmouthed amazement as the column of off-worlders marched past.

The farmers were typical of the passersby the soldiers had encountered thus far and because of that Santana knew they would not only tell the next people they encountered about the aliens, but the youngest of them would tell children yet to be born.

So, assuming the Claw didn't know about the column already, they soon would. It would be easy for them to send runners, assemble some sort of ambush, and spring it as the legionnaires passed by. Yes, Snyder might well be able to detect the trap before they entered it, but any sort of contact could result in casualties.

Besides, the mission was to rescue missionaries, not engage in unnecessary firefights. Consequently, Santana used the next rotation as an opportunity to hit the ground, drift back to where Yao Che was walking, and engage the youngster in conversation. "How are you doing?"

The youngster smiled. "Just fine, Lieutenant."

"Good. Listen, I could use some advice . . . If we continue to march along this road there's a good chance that we will walk into some sort of trap. Is there another route we could take? Something off the beaten track?"

Yao Che considered the question for a moment. There were routes, lots of them, but none so direct as the road they were on. But the off-worlder knew that . . .

Careful to be as factual as possible the youngster made his reply. "Sir, yes sir. There are other thoroughfares, paths mostly, which the locals use to bring their produce into the villages. We could make use of these routes but it would be easy to get lost."

It was an honest answer to an honest question, and Santana considered his options. The back routes would reduce the likelihood of an ambush, but suck up a certain amount of time even if they *didn't* get lost which they easily could. Still, when faced with what appeared to be a fifty-fifty trade-off, his father had counseled him to "go with your gut."

"All right," the cavalry officer replied, "I'm promoting you to scout. Can you run? Good, because Warmfeel and Fareye could run the ass off a wheel. I'm going to send the three of you up ahead. Listen to their advice, do what they say, but make up you own mind as to which turnoff we should take. Once you have it tell them and they'll let me know. Got it?"

Yao Che nodded enthusiastically. "Sir! Yes, sir."

Santana made use of his radio to pass the word to the scouts, watched the three of them veer off the road, and knew the youngster was in very good hands. Not only were the Naa experts at fieldcraft, they could smell a campfire from a mile away, sense warmth through the soles of their feet, and move around in weather that would appall anyone except a Hudathan.

The better part of an hour had passed before the column topped a rise, the scouts materialized next to the road, and fell in next to Santana to make their report. "I think we found the right spot, sir," Warmfeel began. "It's about a mile ahead."

"That's right," Fareye agreed enthusiastically. "The road gets real muddy and passes through a small stream before it starts up the next slope. All we have to do is make a right turn *into* the stream, follow it for half a mile or so, and exit to the west. It's rocky there, but not too steep for the RAVs, and we won't leave any tracks."

Santana was quick to see the plan's virtues. Only the closest of observers would be likely to notice the difference between the impressions made in the downhill muck and those in the uphill muck. The stream made a perfect off-ramp. "Good work—that sounds perfect. So, Yao Che, what do you think? Will the plan work?"

Thrilled to be asked, and eager to add his opinion to the report, the youngster nodded. "Yes, I think it will. I have never been in the area north of the main highway before but I know that Su Ruu lies northwest of here. There should be plenty of cart trails in the vicinity of the village. After a day's march we could jog southwest and head for Nah Ree."

"Excellent," Santana replied, "let's do it. Warmfeel, Fareye, pass the word to the NCOs and take the point. Once we hit that stream you're in charge. I want a nice clean departure from the road."

The scouts said, "Yes, sir," almost in unison, and jogged away.

Time passed, a party of tired-looking LaNorian merchants trudged past, their animals loaded with packs, but outside of the offerings left at the occasional roadside altar, there was little else to be seen.

The departure, when it eventually came, was almost anticlimactic as Snyder made her way down a muddy slope, saw the scouts, and sidestepped into the stream. After that it was an easy matter to turn, splash toward the north, and await further instructions. The column followed.

An hour later, the rest of the legionnaires left the stream, and followed the Naa up a rocky slope. Once on top, Santana climbed up on Snyder's back and made use of the extra height to chart a course to the northwest. They marched through a field of something similar to wheat, passed a recently burned-out hut, and hit one of the tracks that Yao Che had predicted would be there.

Then, turning to the left, they followed the trail in a generally northwesterly direction. It felt good to be off the main road, but the countryside seemed unnaturally quiet, as though something evil was afoot, and even the normally loquacious flits knew about it. Still, the way was clear, that's what Snyder said, and the cavalry officer believed her.

The next couple of miles were comparatively easy. There were soft spots, places where the mud had been churned up in the fairly recent past, but nothing like the unending muck found on the main road.

The question was who had disturbed the mud and why? They were mounted, a trail of razbul shit left little doubt as to that, and Yao Che estimated that as many as eight animals had passed that way. However, little more could be gleaned than that.

Then, as the hill country gave way to a plain, they came to an intersection. A place where their path crossed another. Of more importance however was the recently disturbed soil that marked the center of the crossroads and the tasa tubers that stuck up out of the dirt.

Santana signaled a halt, ordered Hillrun to post flankers,

and authorized a break. Zook stood guard while Snyder took the opportunity to stand down.

Like soldiers everywhere those who weren't on security duty were quick to get off the trail, rest against the light packs they wore, or line up to see "Doc" Seavy. There were plenty of blisters and it wasn't long before the medic was in business.

Those who didn't require medical attention checked their weapons, lit fuel tabs in order to brew a cup of tea, or simply sat and talked. One, a private named Dilley, scribbled on the surface of his PDA. Nobody knew what he was writing but there were plenty of theories.

Santana called for Yao Che, led the youth to the intersection, and pointed at the mound. "What the hell is that?"

The LaNorian stopped dead in his tracks. His eyes grew larger, his ear fans went back, and his hands started to tremble. He jammed them into the sleeves of his jacket. "I've never seen one Excellency, only heard about them, but that's what the Tro Wa thugs call a flower garden. Religious converts, or others suspected of trafficking with off-worlders, are forced to dig a large hole. Once the pit is large enough, they are instructed to stand on their heads. Those who are unable to do so are roped to poles driven into the ground. Once they are in place tubers are inserted into their nostrils and the soil is replaced."

Santana's eyebrows shot straight up. "They're buried alive?"

Yao Che remembered that he wasn't supposed to say "Excellency," and said, "Yes, sir," instead.

"You mean there are people down there right now? Breathing through those tubes?"

The youth nodded. "Yes, if they're still alive."

Santana yelled down the road. "Sergeant Hillrun! I need six troopers with shovels! On the double!"

The only implements available were the collapsible trenching shovels the legionnaires carried but they were up to the job. Dirt flew as the legionnaires hurried to dig the LaNorians out.

Santana tried to imagine what it would feel like to be buried alive and shuddered at the thought. It was hard to believe that anyone could be so cruel, but the officer had studied the history of war, and knew that *his* race had done worse.

Private Hadley shouted, "We have one! She's alive!" and there was a flurry of activity as a small soil-encrusted body was lifted up and out of the hole. It turned out to be that of a female, a youngster about Yao Che's age, and she *was* alive, though the rest of the "flowers" hadn't been so lucky. Her name was Pwi Qui, and her father, mother, and younger brother had all been suffocated.

One by one their bodies were removed from the pit, cleaned up, and laid on the path. Pwi Qui wailed, the sound of her grief requiring no translation, as Yao Che sought to comfort her.

The youngster wanted to remain with the bodies, to somehow find the means to cremate them, so the souls of her family could go free. That was impossible of course, since a fire would make smoke, and there was no doubt as to what would happen if the Claw were to return.

Santana was about to order the corpses buried, and have Pwi Qui strapped to one of the RAVs, when Snyder offered a possible alternative. "I could use my energy cannon on the bodies, sir, if that would help."

The officer took the idea to Yao Che, who explained it to Pwi Qui, who reluctantly nodded.

And so it was that Yao Che was transformed from scout to native priest, a role for which he had never been trained, but did the best he could.

Snyder used short highly focused bursts of energy to cremate the bodies, quickly reducing flesh, muscle, and bone to a light scattering of ash, which the wind blew toward the east.

Then, hanging on Yao Che's arm, Pwi· Qui was forced to leave the place where she had grown up behind and walk toward the setting sun. It was blood red and fell off the edge of the world.

THE FOREIGN CITY OF MYS, ON THE INDEPENDENT PLANET OF LANOR

It was a little after two in the morning but the Strathmore Hotel was ablaze with lights. The ballroom, which was packed with all manner of off-worlders, looked as though a bomb had been detonated at its very center. All manner of exotic furniture was turned this way and that. Long tables, still laden with the picked-over remains of the meal served hours earlier, waited to be cleared. Napkins, scraps of paper, and bits of cast-off clothing littered, the normally immaculate floor while a Clone slept in a corner.

Meanwhile, the architects of this destruction, the beings whose job it was to represent their various governments on LaNor, sat and bickered over the same questions they had debated for the better part of two days, namely, should they accede to Empress Shi Huu's demand and hand Prince Mee Mas over to the Imperial government, or should they refuse and deal with the potential consequences?

Ambassador Pas Rasha stood at the front of the room and looked out over his squabbling peers. He was tired and angry. His fellow diplomats had dithered their way down to the first deadline, appealed for more time, and received one twenty-seven-hour extension. Now that too was in danger of expiring and the group was no closer to consensus.

Basically there were two camps: The Ramanthians and the Thrakies wanted to hand Mee Mas over . . . while nearly everyone else felt the Confederacy should protect him. The Drac, in the person of Ambassador Fas Doonar, saw no reason to take any position whatsoever and had already returned to his embassy.

Now, with dawn fast approaching, the Dweller had run out of patience. His exoskeleton whined as he walked over to Captain Seebo and held out his hand. "Your sidearm please."

Seebo looked at Ambassador Ishimoto-Forty-Six who shrugged. "Let him have it. Maybe he'll put me out of my misery."

The Clone drew his weapon, handed it to the diplomat butt first, and pointed at the latch. "That's the safety . . . let me know if you need more ammo."

But Pas Rasha was in no mood for jokes. He took the weapon, turned, and raised it over his head. There were three loud reports. The slugs passed through the ceiling, missed a guest by a foot and a half, and lodged somewhere above. Every being in the ballroom looked at the front of the room and there was a moment of silence. Pas Rasha, the gun still in his hand, allowed his eyes to roam the room. He had been talking for hours, and his voice was hoarse.

"The discussion is over . . . Every diplomat in this room reports to a government which is part of the Confederacy. *I* represent the Confederacy, and while interested in your opinions, am under no obligation to honor specific recommendations. Objections, and I'm sure there will be plenty, can be filed through normal channels.

"In the meantime Prince Mee Mas, along with any other LaNorians desirous of our dubious protection, will remain here in Mys.

"Now, in keeping with the provisions of Senate Resolution 179274128.62, I hereby activate the joint defense pact to which all of your governments agreed, and name Major Homer Miraby to command what will now be known as the Joint Defense Force or JDF. Please order your respective military attachés to report to Major Miraby for orders. That will be all."

There was a long and profound moment of silence. It ended when Sergi Chien-Chu pushed his chair back, came to his feet, and started to applaud. Others did likewise, and the gesture of support continued until even the Ramanthians and the Thrakies were forced to join in.

A waiter carried a tray of dishes into the hotel's kitchen, dropped his apron onto the floor, and dashed out the back. The off-worlders had refused Shi Huu's demand—and Minister Dwi Faa would want to know.

THE VILLAGE OF NAH REE, ON THE INDEPENDENT PLANET OF LANOR

When the sun finally rose, and struggled to push its pale sickly light down through a new layer of clouds, the latest horror was revealed.

The Claw had attacked during the night. It started the way it always did with the *thump, thump, thump* of the drums. Then came the red lanterns, hundreds of them, bobbing and twisting through the night.

That was the moment that Frank Busso, his wife and two children had come to dread the most, the pause before the next assault, when there was nothing to do but wait, and listen to the drums.

Then, just when they, plus the more than one thousand souls in their care had begun to hope that the Tro Wa *wouldn't* attack, they always did. Sheets of fire arrows fell like red rain. Hundreds had landed on the mission, which though constructed of flame-resistant materials, and having survived a dozen previous attacks, finally succumbed as one of the burning shafts found its way inside and landed on a pile of moss dressings.

The initial onslaught was surprisingly ineffective against the hundreds of LaNorians crouched behind the water-filled ditch. Most of the arrows hit the surface of the damp soggy ground, sizzled as they dived into the moat, or thudded into the large densely woven mats behind which most of the females and their offspring had taken temporary shelter.

However, once the mission started to burn, and Busso was forced to lead a rescue party in to get the patients, he and companions were exposed to a second flight of arrows.

It was no accident that *these* shafts bore poisoned tips. That meant anyone who suffered so much as a scratch was soon transformed from one of the rescuers into a casualty. Nor were those farther back spared. Many of the juveniles died, but most of the adults didn't, thereby placing an even greater burden on the remaining defenders. The poison caused cramps and vomiting, which soon led to severe dehydration unless efforts were made to boil river water, and force it down.

All of which meant that scores of converts fell as they rushed through the hail of falling wood to invade the makeshift hospital, pull their relatives, friends and fellow converts out of the dome, and carry the invalids back to where the mats could offer some protection. All in the dark, with a light rain falling from the sky, and mud underfoot.

That was when the *second* attack began. Having prepared the way with a storm of arrows the Claw launched another in the long series of brutal assaults to which the Transcendentalists had become accustomed over the last few weeks.

The Tro Wa came as they always did, under covering fire provided by a wild assortment of muskets, trade rifles, and a couple of Negar III rifles obtained from the Ramanthians.

Frank Busso, Hwa Nas, and the rest of the males still able to fight had little choice but to grab their makeshift weapons and assemble behind the berm that lined the northern edge of the moat. The Claw had attempted to throw portable bridges across the gap two days earlier and been thrown back when the defenders set the Tro Wa spans alight with homemade fuel bombs that Busso had cobbled together using locally brewed alcohol and odds and ends scrounged from Bethany's laundry room.

More than thirty Claw had died in the moat on that particular night and many continued to rot there. The stench of their decomposing bodies added to the already noxious miasma created by the open-pit latrines, the smell of vomit, and the muck excavated from the moat.

But the Claw learned from its mistakes and this attack was different. Leadership had performed the rituals necessary to render their followers invulnerable to bullets, blades, and arrows, formed their troops into four columns and driven them forward.

The drums beat out an insistent rhythm, the Tro Wa started

to chant, and there was the *pop, pop, pop* of small-arms fire as Claw snipers went to work.

Busso, who had learned the importance of being able to see during previous engagements, yelled, "Lights!" and was rewarded by the glare of battery-powered spots which threw a gruesome green glare over the area beyond the moat.

The missionary knew he wouldn't have that advantage for long. The reactor had gone off-line the moment that Trudy was assassinated—and the never-ending overcast made it next to impossible to pull a full charge out of the six solar panels that the mission had. But that problem would come later and this was now.

The Tro Wa entered the wash of light at a jog and went straight for the moat. Each column was spaced out in order to divide the defenders into smaller groups.

Busso led one contingent of converts while Hwa Nas and two of his most trusted lieutenants took the other three. Given the fact that the columns were only two bodies wide there were only two individuals to aim at. Busso shot both, saw them fall, and watched the column march right over their bodies. Within seconds the third rank was at the edge of the moat, their bodies falling into the ditch, as the fourth rank attempted to move forward. They looked like peasants, *scared* peasants, rather than the half-mad fanatics the missionary expected to see.

That was when the off-worlder understood the true genius of the latest strategy. The purpose behind the columns was to fill the moat with bodies so that those in the rear, the *real* warriors, could march across!

And there wasn't a damned thing he could do about it except encourage his troops to drop arrows and spears into the *center* of the oncoming phalanx in an effort to kill as many of the hard-core Claw as he could.

"Aim for the center of each column!" Busso shouted to his lieutenants. "That's where the meanest bastards are hiding!"

Orders were given, and the archers, many of whom were female, directed a hail of arrows up into the sky. The fell in nice tight groupings, hitting many of the Tro Wa faithful, cutting the columns in half.

Many of the shafts the defenders launched had been fired into the compound by the Claw, gathered into bundles by daring youngsters, and dumped at the archers' feet.

But the archers became targets for Claw snipers some of whom were quite good. Busso, who made it a practice to keep moving, if only from side to side, saw one of his archers stagger and fall back into the mud as a rifle bullet struck her chest.

A youngster, who couldn't have been more than twelve, grabbed her mother's fallen bow, fitted an arrow to the string, and fired. The shaft took one of the Tro Wa in the throat. He was tugging at it even as he slipped and fell.

That was the moment when Busso heard his wife yell, "They're on the river!" and knew that the *third* and quite possibly final attack had begun. Having engaged the religious community from the front, and managed to weaken it, the Claw hoped to drive a dagger into its back.

The possibility of a downstream waterborne assault had been there all the time which was why lookouts had been posted upstream and defenses erected along the river's edge. Busso wanted to go there, to be with his wife, but knew he couldn't. The frontal attack had stalled, but it wouldn't take much to get it going again, and he was needed to be where he was.

Bethany stood at the river's edge, gave thanks for the lights that illuminated the water with their glare, and waited for the first boat to appear. There was a plan, a *good* plan, but timing was everything. Two teams of LaNorian males watched anxiously, waiting for the signal that would send them backing in opposite directions, their hands clenched around two-inch-thick cables.

Then, like the ghosts that were said to ride the waves at night, the first of three heavily laden fishing boats entered the light. The Tro Wa stationed in the bow stood, shouted something unintelligible at the Transcendentalists, and gave an involuntary jerk as Mark Busso put a bullet through his head.

There was a splash as the body tumbled into the river followed by the sound of Bethany Busso's voice as she said, "Readddy . . ." and the LaNorians pulled the slack out of their respective ropes.

The second boat entered what Bethany thought of as "the killing zone," quickly followed by the third, and she took a deep breath. "Pull!"

Both teams of LaNorians backed in opposite directions, the cables made a zinging sound as they passed through well-secured pulleys, and the carefully weighted net came up off the bottom of the river. It jerked tight, seemed to shake itself as the current pushed past, and made a formidable barrier.

The first fishing boat hit almost immediately, the second crashed into the first, and the third wobbled as those with paddles struggled to arrest its forward progress. Voices shouted and water foamed white as the last vessel made a stand against the current and began to win. That was when Natalie Busso, along with thirty archers of about the same age, hollered "Fire!"

Such were the distances that the arrows went nearly straight up and disappeared into darkness before falling like a lethal rain. At least half of them dived into the river, popped to the surface, and were swept away. The rest hit those who were in the water, those struggling to free their boats from the net, and those in boat three.

Two of their paddlers fell; the open-hulled craft slid broadside to the current, and was pushed into the wreckage below.

A second volley of arrows whispered into the air and fell into the thrashing mess that had been caught in the net. Natalie felt sick as she heard the subsequent screams but knew what she had to do.

A *third* flight of arrows flew up out of the light, descended on the survivors below, and found their marks. There was very little noise this time, just a lot fewer heads, and a net full of bodies.

The Claw pulled out after that, and faded back toward the village of Nah Ree, where they would lick their wounds and prepare for the next attack.

But as the morning light caressed the body-strewn battlefield Busso wasn't sure there would be a "next attack" for him and his family. The Tro Wa would break through soon—if not that night then the next—and the final slaughter would ensue. Not just killing, but the worst sort of torture that the mind could imagine, and it would last for days.

But Busso's family would be spared that. The missionary had three rifle bullets set aside for them—all zippered into his breast pocket. He would shoot Natalie first, Mark second, and Bethany last. Then, true to the promise that he had made to them, Frank Busso would die with his flock.

That's what the missionary was thinking about when the mist on the far side of the corpse-strewn field seemed to shiver, then parted to reveal something he had given up all hope of seeing: a hulking T-2 with a small figure perched on its back. "Frank!" Yao Che called, "It's me!" and waved his arm. "I told you I would come back and I did!"

There was more to see, *much* more, but the tears got in the way. Busso's prayers, the ones said every morning for weeks on end, had finally been answered.

THE FOREIGN CITY OF MYS, ON THE INDEPENDENT PLANET OF LANOR

Rather than begin as Pas Rasha fancied that it might with a desperate battle, the first day of the siege was characterized by chaos and confusion.

Having had only four hours sleep since the dramatic conclusion to the meeting at the Strathmore Hotel the diplomat was tired and crabby as he took the lift down to his office, waited for the door to open, and came to face-to-face with just a few of the beings in line to see him. A sort of communal wail went up as the Dweller stepped out and plowed his way toward his office.

Voices called the diplomat's name, hands plucked at his clothes, and a legionnaire shouted for order. There were missionaries, business beings, LaNorian nobles, staff from various embassies, and at least one robot, all hoping for an audience with the person in charge of Mys. The line started just outside his reception area, ran down the hall, and spilled onto the stairs.

Pas Rasha waved, shouted assurances, and hurried into the relative tranquillity of his office. Servos whined as his assistant brought the usual cup of tea plus a stack of messages. "You're rather popular this morning, sir."

"Too damned popular," the ambassador responded grouchily. "How come I'm the only one doing any work around here? Send for Harley Clauson, Christine Vanderveen, Marcy Barnes, Yvegeniy Kreshenkov, Dr. Hogarth, and Willard Tran. Once I'm done with them it'll be Major Miraby's turn."

Cerly Nor Nama nodded and turned to go.

"And Cerly . . ."

The other Dweller paused. "Yes?"

"Call the kitchen . . . let's offer the people in the hall some tea. Maybe that will take the edge off."

Nor Nama smiled. "Yes, sir."

The staff members arrived fifteen minutes later. Not a lot of time, but enough for Pas Rasha to pour himself a second cup of tea and scribble some notes on a scratch pad. He waited for them to get settled, ordered Nor Nama to hold his calls, and immediately got down to business. "All right, I'm sure all of you have questions, but please put them on hold for the moment. You saw the insanity in the hall . . . I'm sure it's worse out in the streets. We need to impose some order and do it fast. The details, and there be plenty, can wait till later.

"Harley, you will act as liaison between me and the other ambassadors. Your job is to facilitate communication, foster cooperation, and listen to all the bitching. I won't have time.

"Christine, you saw the people on the stairs. The moment this meeting is over I want you to interview each one of them.

Find out who they are, what they want, and assign a priority to each. Those who can be taken care of by one of our subject matter experts should be routed to them. Those who truly need to see me will receive appointments in priority order. Once that task is completed check on the prince. Make sure that he's safe and reasonably comfortable.

"Marcy, in your capacity as our agriculturist I'm placing you in charge of the city's food supply. Round up some help from your peers in the other embassies, inventory what we have, and place all of it under guard.

"Once that has been accomplished figure out some sort of communal kitchen, a multispecies menu, and a rationing system that's fair to everyone. That includes the LaNorians as well.

"Then, as soon as you can manage it, take a second look at storage. Is the food located where we can protect it? Or should it be moved to a safer location? Major Miraby or one of his officers can help you with that."

Barnes was writing furiously. She didn't look up but nodded once.

"Yvegeniy, given your expertise where science and technology are concerned, you seem best qualified to accept responsibility for the city's power and water supplies. As with Marcy I recommend that you call on your peers in other embassies for additional support.

"Willard, see what you can do to solicit help from the business community. Find Sergi Chien-Chu. I'm embarrassed to say that he came to get my support for defensive measures and was turned away. Please convey my apologies and see what if anything he can do.

"And Willard, I want you to establish some sort of constabulary to control hoarding, prevent predatory pricing and the possible emergence of a black market. Understood?"

It was a big order—but Tran met the ambassador's eyes. "Yes, sir."

"Good. Dr. Hogarth, I need a hospital, and I need one fast.

We're likely to see a lot of casualties during the days ahead. Work with Major Miraby to chose the best site, recruit medical personnel from all of the embassies, and work with Marcy to stockpile all the medical supplies you can find. Once that's accomplished see what you can do to manufacture more."

Hogarth, a mild-mannered woman with red hair, chubby cheeks, and an ample bosom eyed the diplomat over the mutable 10X med specs that she wore nearly all the time. "Is that all?" she inquired sarcastically. "Or would you like me to transform water into wine as well?"

"Nope," the diplomat replied serenely, "that's Marcy's job. All I need from you is a hospital. We'll meet here at 6:00 P.M. each day for the duration of the crisis. Have your preliminary plans ready for the first get-together. Now, do you have any questions? The kind that only I can answer?"

The staffers, all of whom had been pleasantly surprised by the manner in which the sometimes vague diplomat had stepped up to the administrative challenge exchanged glances. It was Clauson who spoke. "Yes," the FSO answered, "I have a question, the same one that people will ask us. Have we sent for help? And if so, when will it arrive?"

Pas Rasha nodded. "Quite right . . . Here's the answer: Every message torp we had was programmed with the same message and dispatched last night. It will take them at least three weeks to reach the *Friendship*, and assuming that the government acts expeditiously, at least the same amount of time for a relief force to make its way here.

"But that's the *optimistic* estimate. A more realistic scenario, one that takes the political process into account, would allow for at least two weeks of senatorial posturing before some sort of response is finally authorized. So I suggest you tell people eight weeks . . . and use ten for planning purposes. Especially where food, water, and medical supplies are concerned."

Vanderveen considered the diplomat's words. Ten weeks. It was a long time. Could the off-worlders really hold Mys for that long? And what about Santana? Assuming he was alive, and managed to make it back, how would the legionnaire enter the city?

Somewhere, out beyond the walls, a muzzle-loading cannon was fired. The projectile, an iron ball that weighed nearly twenty pounds, fell into the Jade River. Water geysered up into the air, a flock of flits took off from the adjacent park, and passersby turned to look. The first shot had been fired.

NEAR THE VILLAGE OF NAH REE, ON THE INDEPENDENT PLANET OF LANOR

A defensive perimeter had been thrown around the compound and both T-2s stood guard as brush crackled, sparks flew, and smoke billowed up into the lead gray sky. The converts had set fire to the first of two funeral pyres. One for their relatives and friends—the other for members of the Tro Wa.

It had been raining on and off for a long time and dry fuel was hard to come by. A farmer attempted to light the second pyre but it failed to catch. Busso sloshed what remained of his locally distilled alcohol onto the bodies, gave the liquid time to trickle down into the fuel below, and gave a nod. Hwa Nas tossed a torch onto the pile and there was a loud *Whump!* as the accelerant took off.

Santana felt the wave of heat wash over his body and managed to resist the temptation to hold his hands out toward the warmth of the fire.

The LaNorians began to chant as the souls of their loved ones were released into the spirit world. The officer heard the crunch of gravel and turned to find Busso at his side. There was something about the tall lanky missionary that the legionnaire liked. A calm no-nonsense professionalism that stood in marked contrast to the righteous verse-spouting ideologue he had imagined. "So, Lieutenant, what now?"

Though innocent enough the words had the effect of shifting responsibility for everything that happened next to the soldier. Appropriate given the circumstances—but sobering nonetheless. "We need to get out of here," Santana answered, "and the sooner the better."

"I don't know," Busso replied doubtfully, moving sideways as the breeze shifted and smoke from the first pyre hit his face. "Twenty-seven members of my congregation have wounds so serious it will be impossible for them to walk."

Santana ran the various possibilities through his mind. Based on the information that Busso had provided earlier he knew that 958 LaNorians had survived the repeated attacks. That meant there were more than enough potential stretcher-bearers should he decide to return the way he had come.

But how in the world would two squads of legionnaires manage to protect such a long, presumably slow, column? The Claw would attack at will, and even with the extra firepower available from the T-2s, many if not all of the refugees would die. No, an overland journey was to be avoided if at all possible, but what other option was there?

Movement caught Santana's eye as the current pulled a piece of driftwood down the middle of the river and past his position. Suddenly he had an answer, or the possibility of one, depending on what lay downstream.

"Come on," Santana said, "let's take a look at my map. Maybe Hwa Nas can help as well. The First REC is a cavalry outfit . . . and maybe we can ride."

THE IMPERIAL CITY OF POLWA, ON THE INDEPENDENT PLANET OF LANOR

If pedestrians on the street were curious regarding the identity of the tall individual in the white robes, or the short hunched figure who was completely swathed in black, they gave no sign of it, for these were troubled times, and there were many ways to die. So the citizens of Polwa looked right through the strange twosome and the thugs who accompanied them as if they weren't there.

As for the four-unit-long cylinder that one of them carried, well, that was none of their business either, and best forgotten.

Though carried on the Ramanthian rolls as a lowly "specialist," the soldier named Poth Dusso was a member of Military Intelligence and often outranked the officer to whom he seemed to report. Now, in the wake of Force Leader Hakk Batth's untimely death, responsibility for the sub rosa relationship with the Tro Wa had fallen to him. That included not only the "security" arrangements that made it possible for the Ramanthian factories to run unimpeded, but for the ongoing military advice and support which served to fuel continuing cooperation, something Ambassador Regar Batth considered to be even more important now that Mys was under siege.

A domesticated bush bird squawked and dashed from one tiny apartment to another as Lak Saa turned, climbed a second flight of litter-strewn stairs, and emerged on a flat roof. Not just *any* roof, but a special roof which because of its proximity to the southeast corner of Mys, and the shuttles that routinely took off and landed there, made it the perfect platform from which to launch a heat-seeking missile.

One look at the newcomers was sufficient to send a dozen residents fleeing to the stairway and down into their various abodes. Lak Saa, apparently unaware of their fear, took a long slow look around.

Though less than pleased by the LaNorian's insistence that the Ramanthians *prove* the efficacy of the weapons they were about to deliver, Dusso couldn't help but admire the eunuch's savvy. Claims were one thing . . . deeds were another.

In spite of the fact that the roof was visible from the top of the wall that acted to separate Mys from Polwa a maze of crisscrossing clotheslines, cages filled with highly excitable flits, and thickly planted "tub gardens" provided plenty of cover.

It was a simple matter to open the cylindrical case, remove the surface-to-air missile (SAM), and prepare the weapon for use.

In spite of the close relationship the Ramanthians had maintained with the Drac Axis over the last few years it was one of *their* shuttles that was slated for destruction. Partly because of the manner in which Ambassador Fas Doonar had allowed Force Leader Hakk Batth to be killed within the Drac embassy, partly because of a lack of support during the last few weeks, but mostly because the gassers were the only off-worlders with a ship in orbit. Not counting a yacht that is, which belonged to one of the humans, and was small enough to enter the atmosphere.

But would the Dracs flee? Yes, Dusso's sources said that they would, and soon, too. Unlike some of the other embassies, which maintained pads of their own, the gassers relied on the public facilities adjacent to the Transcendental Cathedral in what most people referred to as the corporate sector. That's why the Ramanthian felt confident that the Dracs would take off right in front of him.

The one thing the agent couldn't be certain of was *when* the gassers would lift . . . which meant that he and his companions would have to sit and wait. A necessity which the agent decided to take advantage of by pumping the rebel leader for information. Lak Saa smelled of urine but the Ramanthian managed to ignore it.

"So," Dusso began, "it looks as though the Imperial government and the Tro Wu are allies, for the moment at least."

A breeze caused the surrounding laundry to flap and Lak Saa gazed out over the surrounding rooftops. His eyes were bleak. "The Empress hopes to destroy you, blame the destruction on *me*, and negotiate new agreements with your successors. Does that sound like an alliance?"

"No," the Ramanthian was forced to admit, "it doesn't. There are some common objectives, however, like maintaining traditional values, ridding the planet of off-world influence, and neutralizing Prince Mee Mas."

Lak Saa lowered himself onto a crate and used one of the long curved claws to scratch the center of his back. "Yes, that much can be said, although there will always be a place for *true* allies, such as yourselves."

Dusso didn't believe it, not for a moment, but pretended that he did. "Thank you, Excellency, the ambassador will be gladdened to hear it."

The conversation might have continued had it not been for the communicator that vibrated on the Ramanthian's utility harness. He touched a button. There were plenty of electronic ears and it would pay to be brief. "Yes?"

The voice belonged to a Ramanthian trooper stationed on the east wall. "They're boarding the shuttle."

"Affirmative," the agent replied. "Out."

"They're coming," Lak Saa said, as if he too were able to see them.

"Yes," Dusso answered, reaching for the SAM. "Any moment now."

"Can you control where the aircraft will crash?"

The Ramanthian stood, settled the weapon onto his right shoulder, and peered into the fractal sight. The Tro Wa's launchers would be equipped with sighting devices appropriate to them—but the agent saw no reason why he should have to deal with alien optics. "Maybe," he allowed, "to some extent. *If* the shuttle doesn't explode in midair—and *if* the pilot doesn't interfere. Why? Do you want it to crash in Mys?"

"No," Lak Saa replied evenly. "I want it to crash in Polwa."

"In Polwa?" the Ramanthian echoed. "That seems strange."

"Only to *you*," the LaNorian replied coldly. "Do as I say."

"Yes, Excellency," Dusso said obediently, as a shuttle rose from the other side of the wall, and drew fire from every conceivable direction. "It shall be as you say."

The pilot of the shuttle, a Drac named Bof Hofor, swore as all manner of musket balls, rifle bullets and arrows rattled against the aircraft's hull armor. He turned the ship toward Polwa on the theory that he would take less fire from an area occupied by civilians, pushed the throttles toward the instrument panel, and felt the shuttle respond.

The in-system drives didn't need a lot of run-up time, but they did require some, and he planned to enter a steep climb at just about the point where he would clear the south wall. Ambassador Doonar, who was seated aft of the pilot, was screaming by then. Spittle flew as he shouted useless orders.

Hofor ignored the diplomat, watched Mys fall away, and felt the gee forces push him back into his seat. That's when the audible went off, a warning light came on, and the aviator knew the truth: Someone, there was no way to know who, had fired a missile at him. *No,* he told himself, *that's impossible! It must be a malfunction of some . . .*

Dusso waited until the shuttle had passed overhead and engaged its in-system drives before squeezing the firing bulb. The SAM shoved the Ramanthian backward, as the engine ignited and the missile flew off its launcher. The infrared homing head looked for heat, found it, and locked on.

Lak Saa watched in morbid fascination as the missile accelerated toward the delta-shaped aircraft, looped in behind it, and flew up one of exhaust channels. The subsequent explosion blew the fuselage into a hundred pieces two of which were large enough to track with the naked eye. One fell into a tenement, collapsing the roof, and plunging down through dozens of squats. The other tumbled end over end, landed in the middle of a densely crowded market, and erupted in flame. Secondary explosions, three in all, killed more than a hundred LaNorians.

Dusso lowered the launcher as Lak Saa nodded his approval. " 'Foreign devils attacked the peace-loving people of LaNor.' That's what the flyers say . . . They were printed last night. Those who didn't have a reason to care about the conflict have one now."

It was cynical, very cynical, and sure to work. That's when Dusso thought of something the should have considered earlier . . . What if Lak Saa's efforts to mobilize the populations were so successful that they rose up and rolled over *all* the off-worlders Ramanthians included? But it was too late for such considerations as a column of smoke rose into the sky, fire spread from one flimsy booth to the next, and people continued to die.

NEAR THE VILLAGE OF NAH REE, ON THE INDEPENDENT PLANET OF LANOR

The rain had stopped, the sun peered down through a halo of mist, and a breeze found its way downriver and stirred the tall stately trees. They shivered, as if aware of their fate, and swayed from side to side.

The so-called spirit grove was located two miles upstream from the Transcendental mission—and consisted of trees planted more than a hundred years earlier during the reign of Emperor Pot Fas. Consistent with his belief in nature spirits, and the importance of maintaining habitat for them, thousands of such preserves still dotted the land. And, in spite of the fact that Naturalism had never really caught on, it was said that nature spirits could be quite vindictive. So, not wanting to take any chances, most LaNorians left the plantings alone.

So trees such as those that stood before Sergeant Zook remained untouched in spite of their considerable value as lumber and firewood. In fact, even now, with their lives literally on the line, the villagers were reluctant to disturb the spiritual status quo. But, with assurances from the Busso family and the certain knowledge that the Claw would attack again, they acceded. The trees, enough to construct twenty-two thirty-five-foot-long rafts, would carry them to safety. Or so they hoped.

Zook used his sensors to confirm that Sergeant Via and his squad were spread out along the southern edge of the grove and that the twenty-five person LaNorian work party was well clear of the fall zone. Satisfied that everything was as it should be the cyborg backed off to what he hoped was the correct distance. He'd never been called upon to cut a tree down, but Lieutenant Santana believed that he could, so Zook did too. He planned to harvest the trees that bordered the river first, thereby shortening the haul down to the water, and eliminating obstacles for the ones that were farther back.

Unsure of the right technique to use, and conscious of what one of the one-hundred-foot-tall trees could do to his body, Zook was careful to keep his distance. The legionnaire raised his right arm, saw the targeting grid superimpose itself over his normal "vision," and swung the appendage to the right. The crosshairs passed over the tree trunk, came back, and froze.

Zook ordered the energy cannon to fire, felt the recoil, and saw a flash of light as the bolt struck the target. Wood shattered, the tree groaned as if in pain, and toppled to the west where it clipped one of its brethren before finally hitting the ground. There was an explosion of broken branches and hundreds of circular leaves broke loose. They curled up into tight little balls, fell like green hail, and bounced.

The cyborg swore at his own incompetence, resolved to move south, where the impact of the bolt would be more likely to push the next tree toward the river, and signaled for the work party to move in.

Led by Hwa Nas and armed with Busso's chain saw, a dozen axes, and some machete-like knives, the LaNorians swarmed over the fallen tree, removed all its limbs, and stacked the larger ones in a pile next to the river. The rafts would need crossbraces, rudders, and shelters, all of which would require wood.

Then, once the branches had been removed, the resulting log was cut into three thirty-five-foot-long lengths, which were chained and made ready for skidding.

In the meantime Zook felled a *second* tree, this one landing much closer to the spot where he wanted it, not ten feet from the river's edge.

Then, while the LaNorians attacked the second trunk, the cyborg made use of his tremendous strength to haul the finished logs out into the river, where they were anchored side by side. That's where a team of raft builders, some of whom were carpenters, and some of whom had worked on the river prior to the coming of the railroads, went to work. They used hand adzes to fashion rudders, prepared standardized cross-pieces that would go on later, and used rope to bind the logs together. And so it went: As the sun rose higher in the sky, trees continued to fall and production accelerated.

Meanwhile, two miles downstream, preparations were under way to receive the rafts once they were completed. Conscious of the fact that it would be difficult if not impossible to anchor the rafts in the swift-flowing current that swept past the mission, successfully board something close to a thousand souls, and deal with the Claw at the same time, Santana had ordered that a breakwater be built.

The concept was to take a natural backwater, a place where the river started to curve, and the current lost its force, and enlarge the potential harbor by pushing a sort of jetty out into the main channel.

A difficult task but one made somewhat easier by the fact that the obstruction would be temporary and wouldn't have to last more than fifty-four hours. Or so Santana hoped.

As with the logging operation, the breakwater project would have been impossible had it not been for the second cyborg, who, thanks to her enormous strength was able to grasp boulders between her padded forearms, lift the rocks off the ground, and carry them out into the river.

The officer watched Snyder drop the latest boulder into place as a basket brigade comprised of two hundred LaNorians hurried to pour container after container of smaller rocks around their larger brothers. Later, after a reasonably firm foundation had been established, soil would dumped on top of the jetty and packed into place. Then, assuming everything went as planned, it would be time to bring the rafts into the newly created harbor, load them up, and shove off.

After that, well, who knew? Both Santana's map and the information provided by local fisherfolk were in agreement: The Gee Nas River flowed east, where it split into two tributaries, the Little Gee Nas, which turned toward the south, and the Jade, which passed through the city of Mys. The very place the officer wanted to go.

Santana remembered the night when he had walked Vanderveen home, when they had stood on the bridge, and looked down into the dark oily water. She had allowed him to place his arm around her waist, to taste the sweet softness of her lips, and invited him to come up to her apartment. And he, like the fool he was, had refused. Now it looked like both of them might very well die.

His radio operator, Lance Corporal "Bags" Bagano had managed to make contact with Legion HQ in Mys. The ensuing conversation was necessarily short, since there was increasing evidence that someone was providing the Tro Wa with illegal technology, and the last thing Santana needed was even more Claw on his back, but there was time enough to report that the team had arrived in Nah Ree and was making preparations to return.

Of more interest, from Santana's perspective at least, was the fact that Mys was under siege, a Drac shuttle had crashed into a densely populated area of Polwa, and more than a hundred people had been killed. The population, with encouragement from the Tro Wa, was up in arms. Not only that, but a full-scale attack had been launched against the city's North Gate, and only barely repelled.

All of which meant that even if Santana's plan was successful, and he managed to get the converts down the Jade River, he might very well deliver them into an even worse hell. One in which the person who meant the most to him might already lie dead.

He had told the Bussos that they and their entire flock might be jumping from the frying pan into the fire—and suggested that the missionaries might want to go only partway. Far enough to escape the local Tro Wa but not so far as to encounter the forces grouped around Polwa.

But the Bussos responded by pointing out that the converts would have no way to find food and shelter, that the Claw would almost certainly locate them, and that it was better to die trying to reach Mys than be sacrificed to the god of fire.

First, however, before Santana could worry about how to enter the city of Mys he had a more pressing problem to deal with. Still reeling from the losses suffered the night prior to the Legion's arrival, and unable to marshal a second attack, the Tro Wa had moved in to harass the compound during the night.

Drummers, working in relays, pounded their instruments throughout the hours of darkness. The females known as red lanterns paraded past, and, just to keep things interesting the Claw set off fireworks every hour or so. That forced the legionnaires and locals alike to open bleary eyes, rise from whatever resting place they had been able to make for themselves, and take up their weapons.

But there was no real attack; consequently, Santana ordered his troops to withhold their fire, or risk revealing both the unit's strength and its various positions.

The Tro Wa knew the off-worlders were present, the officer felt sure of that, but having no previous experience were unlikely to understand what they were up against. That's what the legionnaire hoped anyway—because the odds were that the intermission was about to end. Darkness would fall soon, and when it did, enemy scouts would reinfiltrate the area and the main force would move forward shortly thereafter.

Conscious of the fact that sunset was only a few hours away, Santana left the river and pursued a meandering course that allowed him to inspect the platoon's defenses without revealing exactly where the carefully camouflaged positions were.

Feedback if any could be provided by radio using call signs and military jargon that LaNorian eavesdroppers would find almost impossible to understand. Time passed and darkness started to fall.

But Santana wasn't the only individual who wanted to examine the battlefield before the sun dipped over the horizon. The terrain that lay between the village of Nah Ree and the point where the off-worlders continued to pollute the land was irredeemably flat. That meant that if Taa See wanted to get a look at the enemy objective prior to nightfall some ingenuity would be required.

The stilts were the tallest such members that any in the village had ever seen or that the regional commander had ever walked around on. Never in his wildest dreams had the Tro Wa leader imagined that he would one day use a childhood skill to scout an enemy position.

By ordering the village carpenter to paint the stilts green, and hanging them with all manner of vegetation, Taa See hoped to blend in with the background as he stumped up over a rise and paused on the forward slope. Then, having paused to ensure his balance, the Claw brought the off-world viewer up to his eyes.

Everything leaped close, *so* close that the rebel leader felt he was actually among the converts, helping them haul dirt out onto some sort of jetty. It didn't take a genius to figure out that it had something to do with the logging activities taking place upstream. The devils were up to something all right, something that it was his responsibility to stop.

Then, scanning from right to left, the Tro Wa leader took a long hard look at the camp's defenses. Having just arrived, and not having participated in the previous attacks, he had no personal experience to rely on.

Still, anyone could see that the moat and the berm that lay beyond it, were considerable obstacles indeed. Of course every lock has a key and Taa See had brought his along with him. Even now a contingent of fresh troops, some two thousand in all, were marching into Nah Ree.

Having used a pair of hot irons as the means to jog the previous commander's memory, Taa See knew that only his predecessor's squeamishness had enabled the off-worlders to live this long, and resolved to make no such mistake himself.

But even as the rebel leader spied on his enemy *they* spied on him. Private Bok Horo-Ba snuggled the .50 caliber sniper's rifle against an enormous shoulder and peered into the 10X scope. The stilt-mounted LaNorian was about 950 yards out—well within the weapon's 1,100-yard range. His voice was little more than a whisper. "I own the bastard, Sarge, over."

Cvanivich watched through her binoculars as the Tro Wa lowered *his* binoculars and allowed them to dangle from a strap. "That's a negative, Two Eight. You know the orders. Get some rest . . . You'll have more targets than you know what to do with tonight. Over."

The Hudathan knew better than to argue, pressed his transmit button twice, and fell back into his hide. It was homey, as homey as he wanted it to be, with a shelf for his spare magazines, a crate to sit on, and a reasonably dry floor.

Another just like it was located at the far end of the perimeter where Private Joan Fandel was busy taking a nap. Between them the entire sweep of the battlefield would be subject to fire from the long guns. The Hudathan smiled. Yao Che, who had volunteered to reload the legionnaire's empty magazines, shivered.

It had been dark for little more than an hour. Conscious of the tactics his predecessor had employed, and determined to utilize the element of surprise, Taa See gave no warning that he was about to attack.

There were no drums, no lanterns, and no fireworks to announce their coming as the Tro Wa crept forward. Just the whisper of fabric, the *click* of loose stones, and the sound of muffled whimpers as two hundred gagged noncombatants were prodded into motion and forced to precede the actual soldiers. Hands bound behind them, and fully aware of the manner in which their bodies were about to be used, the conscripts waited to die.

The cyborgs "saw" the vast smear of heat long before the Claw were within range and notified Santana who ordered everyone to hold their fire.

Having been sent out at dusk, the crab mines had established their fields of fire, dug themselves in, and gone to standby. Now, as the lead elements of the oncoming force entered the vicinity the mines awoke. There weren't that many, only fifty since a force the size of Santana's could not afford to carry more, but they were effective.

The officer broke radio silence. "Bravo Six to team—shut your eyes. Over."

The legionnaires knew what was about to happen and understood how it could impact their night vision. They closed their eyes.

Santana pulled the remote out of his pocket, punched the safety code into the keypad, and mashed the red button.

The officer could see the flashes through his eyelids. The explosions came in such quick succession that they merged into one gigantic roar. The ground shook as the conscripts plus the first rank of Tro Wa were torn to shreds.

Private Lars Hadley and two other members of Sergeant Cvanivich's squad occupied a fire pit at the forward edge of the curving moat. He felt something warm splatter onto his uniform, thought it was water, then realized the truth: It was raining blood.

Hundreds of yards south, toward the rear of the Claw troops, Taa See gave a grunt of disappointment. Not only had the attack been detected—the off-worlders had unleashed some sort of devil weapon.

What had become the front rank of the assault force paused. The second rank ran into them, as did the third. Taa See felt the shiver run back through his troops and raised the long thin razbul whip. It made a cracking sound as it touched a butcher four ranks forward. The meat cutter swore, lurched forward, and carried others with him.

Other leaders, all armed with whips, flogged the troops in front of them until the entire mass surged forward.

Santana slipped the first remote into his pocket and withdrew another. He entered a different code and sent another message. "One One to team . . . Snipers will fire at will—everyone else hold as long as you can. Over."

The officer pressed the red button and the RAVs opened fire. Located a hundred yards apart, and positioned so they would have overlapping fields of fire, the machines were equivalent to two crew-served weapons. Both robots had been dug in to provide them with as much protection as possible. Though not capable of independent thought, they were equipped with sensor arrays which could track movement and heat. The weapons mounted in their nose turrets operated with machinelike efficiency. The machine guns fired alternating bursts and the grenade launchers chugged as HE rounds arced out to explode in the midst of the oncoming mob.

Platoon Sergeant Hillrun ordered Private Kimura to fire a couple of illumination rounds. They arced into the air, made a popping sound, and drifted toward the ground.

Entire rows of LaNorians fell as the RAVs harvested them like wheat. The slaughter was horrendous and Santana felt sick to his stomach as the Tro Wa marched into his guns. But there was nothing the legionnaire could do except continue to fight, and judging from the fact that the Claw was teetering on the edge of the moat, he need to kill *more* of them not less.

Santana sighed. "You're up Five One, over." Snyder had been waiting for the order. The cyborg rose out of the moat like some sort of mythical monster, roared a primordial challenge, and opened fire. Scores of attackers fell as her bullets and energy bolts ripped them apart.

Santana watched in grim satisfaction as the enemy assault stalled once again. It would have been nice to have Zook defending the compound as well but the other cyborg was upstream where he and members of Via's squad were guarding the newly completed rafts.

Meanwhile, Horo-Ba stared into his light-intensifying scope and surveyed the possible targets. Santana had told both him and Fandel to search the *rear* ranks for the equivalent of officers, and sure enough they were using whips to drive their troops forward. Horo-Ba, who wasn't overly fond of officers, *anybody's* officers, licked his hard thin lips. Starting from left to right he took them one at a time. The process was simple: Lead the target, squeeze the trigger, and feel the recoil as the muzzle brake served to dissipate some of the gases, the bolt mechanism flew back, the casing was ejected, and a new one was fed into its place.

Thanks to the accuracy of the sixty-one-inch barrel and the power inherent in a .50 caliber round, the Hudathan could reach targets a thousand yards away. The sniper had fired eleven times, and killed ten enemy soldiers, before he was forced to release the first box-style magazine and seat another.

Yao Che, conscious of his duty as a loader, used loose rounds to reload the magazine and place it on the firing shelf.

With the exception of Fandel, who was working with Horo-Ba to thin the enemy's officer corps, Cvanivich and her squad hadn't yet fired a single round. But now, such was the pressure exerted by the officers at the rear of the oncoming mob that it bent out and around Snyder, threatening to flank her. The points were like two forward-thrusting horns. The RAVs beat at the horns, trying to break them, but lacked sufficient firepower to do so.

Then, as a mechanical malfunction took one of the robots off-line, the Tro Wa surged forward. Some of the oncoming LaNorians crossed the moats on planks passed forward from the rear, others found places where bodies bridged the gap, and still others made use of long sticks to pole-vault across. An innovation that made it possible for the Claw to leap the ditch at multiple locations. They screamed their bloodlust as they landed on the berm, fired down into the defenders, and jumped into the fray.

The legionnaires pushed up and out of their firing pits, leveled their assault rifles, and opened fire. The Claw were so close by then that the strobelike flashes produced by Cvanivich's weapon served to illuminate their faces.

That was when Frank Busso, along with three hundred

armed converts, rushed forward to engage the enemy hand to hand. Knives flashed, axes bit into flesh, and clubs thumped into heads. There was a scream as Private Dilley took an arrow through the neck and fell.

Corporal "Dice" Dietrich swore as his CA-10 carbine cycled empty, drew his sidearm, and rammed it into a LaNorian gut. The Tro Wa jerked as the noncom fired two bullets into his belly and fell away.

Doc Hixon shot one of the Tro Wa in the face, felt something pluck at her arm, and knew she'd been hit. Someone shouted "Medic!" and she ran toward the sound.

It had been difficult, but the off-worlders were going to die, and Taa See could *feel* it. The farmers, bakers, and tailors who comprised his army could feel it too and they surged toward the river.

The Claw leader gave an exultant shout, dropped the whip, and drew his sword. "Follow me! Victory is ours!"

Aghast at what was happening, but determined to carry out the task he had been given, Horo-Ba fired. The heavy slug whipped across the battlefield, passed through a schoolteacher's skull, and slammed into Taa See's chest. The rebel leader fell, was trampled by those around him, and buried in the mud.

That was when the Tro Wa paused. Not because of Taa See's death, but because the snipers had accounted for more than 60 percent of their leaders by then, and the only thing pushing most of them forward was their own momentum.

Santana sensed the hesitation and yelled into his radio. "First platoon! Advance!"

It was an ancient order that harkened back to the days of bayonets and muskets, an absurd order, but one the legionnaires understood. They shouted the name of the desperate battle that Danjou and his men had fought hundreds of years before, boiled up out of their muddy pits, and fired from the hip.

Then, with Snyder holding the center, and the snipers firing from both flanks, they pushed the enemy back across the moat.

Moments later, as the right RAV came back on-line, the rebels turned and ran. It was no easy task given the shadows cast by the flares, the bodies that lay in drifts, and the blood-slicked mud over which they were forced to travel but many of them made it.

The moment he was sure that the attack had been broken, and that the Tro Wa were unlikely to return, Santana ordered his troops to cease fire.

Two new flares popped into existence and floated toward the bloodstained ground as Frank Busso appeared at the officer's side. The civilian was bleeding from a scalp laceration but seemed unaware of it. He shook his head in sorrow. "What a waste. I feel sorry for them."

There were wounded on both sides and they began to moan. Santana searched inside himself for some kind of emotion but came up empty. There was no feeling of sorrow, no feeling of exultation, just a vast emptiness. Perhaps later there would be time to think, time to react, but war was his job. It wouldn't do to say that however so he nodded, said, "So do I," and went back to work.

11

Anyone who has ever led a small force behind enemy lines has been tested in ways that others can never understand.

Mylo Nurlon-Da
The Life of a Warrior
Standard year 1703

THE FOREIGN CITY OF MYS, ON THE INDEPENDENT PLANET OF LANOR

In spite of the fact that Empress Shi Huu's troops had lobbed cannonballs into Mys during the night, half the native quarter had been burned to the ground, and a Claw assassin had murdered a Thraki merchant in his sleep, it was a fine morning indeed.

That's the way Major Homer Miraby saw it anyway as he and an entourage that included Captain Drik Seeba-Ka, Prince Mee Mas, and a LaNorian whose job it was to carry the noble's recently acquired sword climbed the stairs that led up to the west wall. The reason that Miraby felt so good, and paused at the top of the stairway to inhale the coal- and woodsmoke-tinged air, was that he had been in combat.

The blessed event had taken place the day before when the Imperials attacked the city's North Gate. Immediately on hearing the news Miraby rushed to the top of the north wall, where he took over from Captain Seebo and assumed responsibility for his first battle. And it was from his vantage point over the gate that the legionnaire urged the Clones to do their utmost, emptied his sidearm into the oncoming mob below, and heard bullets whiz past his head.

Wonderfully, almost miraculously, there hadn't been the slightest trace of fear, only a sense of exultation as the attackers washed up against the gate and died by the dozen. Here, after all the years of sitting behind a desk was his *real* purpose, the moment for which he had been born. Never again would he be forced to sit silently by while others spoke of battles on distant worlds. Now *he* would have a tale to tell and an interesting one at that. Because somehow Miraby felt sure that when the siege was lifted, when the reinforcements finally arrived, it was he who would come forth to greet them. Bloodied perhaps (nothing too uncomfortable), but unbowed.

The fantasy vanished as Seeba-Ka touched his arm. "You might want to keep your head down, sir. Some of the Tro Wa snipers are good shots."

A parapet ran all the way around the top of the rampart, but it was only five and a half feet tall. A firing step provided shorter troops with a place to stand. Loop shaped apertures, each located at four-foot intervals, provided defenders with the means to fire on the surrounding countryside without exposing more than an eye to enemy sharpshooters.

Miraby, who was more than six feet tall, gave a snort of derision. "Good god, Captain, we can't be shy can we? What on Earth will the troops think? Well, come on, time to show the flag."

The Hudathan and the LaNorians followed as Miraby began his morning inspection. A bullet chipped the top of the parapet and was followed by the sound of a solitary gunshot as the officer turned and began his tour.

Since Santana was gone, and Miraby was in command, Mee Mas had decided to model himself on the major. That being the case he marched along the rampart fully erect until Seeba-Ka, who was careful to keep *his* head below the top of the wall, turned to glare at him. "What the major does is *his* business.

But you stick your head up one more time and *I* will take it off."

Mee Mas started to object, saw the look in the Hudathan's eyes, and thought better of it. He turned to his single retainer. "You heard the captain . . . keep your head down." The youth, a former scribe by the name of Non Noo, nodded meekly. He believed in Mee Mas and already thought of him as the Emperor.

Satisfied that the noble would obey Seeba-Ka turned and hurried to catch up.

Miraby had flirted with the notion of integrating all of the off-world military forces à la the Legion but quickly gave up on the idea as both politically and functionally impossible. Not only would the various diplomats oppose it . . . but so would his fellow officers. Therefore, each government having military forces on LaNor had been given one or more sections of wall to defend.

The Legion was responsible for the southern half of the west wall and all of the south wall. The assignment was dictated to a large extent by the fact that Ramanthians refused to defend anything other than the section of perimeter to the rear of their embassy.

The Thrakies, Prithians, and Hudathans had shared responsibility for the east wall, while the Clones had taken charge of the north, leaving the Ramanthians to guard the north half of the west wall.

So, as Miraby walked south, he passed through the troops directly under his command, and greeted most by name. Smoke drifted up out of the native quarter as the party crossed over the Jade River and looked down onto the destruction below.

No one was sure of exactly how the fire had started—although most people assumed that one of the hundreds of fire arrows fired over the walls during the night had landed on something flammable. Whatever the reason the misery was the same as now homeless LaNorians picked through the still-smoking rubble, salvaged what they could, and piled their finds on mats.

Miraby paused to look over the north–south street that most off-worlders referred to as 'Embassy Row.' It was there, about one city block north of the South Gate that Sergi Chien-Chu, with advice from Captain Seebo, had established a heavy barricade.

With a two-story tenement to the west, and an equally high row of warehouses to the east, the barricade turned that end of the street into a box. *If* the South Gate failed, *if* enemy troops managed to enter, the legionnaires behind the barricade, on the surrounding roofs, and the top of the walls would cut them down.

Though not supportive of the concept when Chien Chu first proposed it, Miraby liked the idea now, and had already incorporated the structure into his diary as an example of the many things accomplished under his overall leadership.

Bullets continued to ping against the breastwork as Miraby, his beret-clad head bobbing along like a target at a shooting range, continued his tour.

There was a deep and resounding *boom* as a cannonball hit one of the apartment buildings to the east and crashed through the roof. That's when it exploded and started a fire. Smoke boiled up through the hole as the already exhausted fire brigade struggled to respond to the latest crisis.

Miraby shook his head in exasperation, led the group onto the south wall, and paused to look out over Polwa. The response was nearly instantaneous. Dozens of bullets flattened themselves against the breastworks as snipers fired from the maze of roofs that stretched to the south.

Two members of the Claw paid the price for revealing their positions as the Legion's countersnipers squeezed their triggers and sent .50 caliber bullets through the crates, baskets, and other materials behind which the enemy sharpshooters had taken cover. Their deaths had a sobering effect on the Tro Wa irregulars and the incoming fire stopped for the moment.

Miraby nodded as if the entire sequence of events had gone according to plan—and continued his inspection tour. He crossed over to the south wall, took a turn to the left, and passed into what had become known as the Thraki sector.

With the exception of some lookouts, who used homemade periscopes to look out over the breastworks, the rest of the troops were lounging against the stone wall, sitting on the firing step, and in one case taking a nap.

There was no sign of Flight Warrior Garla Try Sygor, a somewhat diffident pilot who knew nothing about ground combat, but nonetheless served as their commanding officer. Miraby, who was outraged by what he saw as dereliction of duty, looked for someone to collar. L-7 Iturno had the misfortune to top the stairs at that particular moment and soon paid the price.

"You!" Miraby said, spearing the noncom with a blunt finger. "What's the meaning of this sloppiness? You're supposed to be soldiers damn your infernal hides . . . Act the part! If the Tro Wa plant a charge against the wall you'll be the first to die."

Cowed by the vehemence with which the human spoke Iturno ordered his troops to stand which all of them did.

Satisfied that he had put the situation right Miraby made a mental note to report the matter to Sygor and stomped past.

But when Mee Mas looked back over his shoulder a few moments later he saw that the Thrakies had already returned to the same slovenly postures they had maintained before. A phenomenon that served to teach the princeling about the problems contingent on the use of mixed forces, how important it is to have good noncoms, and the fact that while clearly brave Miraby lacked something Santana had. A quality that the LaNorian couldn't put into words but very much wanted to acquire.

Meanwhile Miraby entered the Prithian sector, where High Warrior Hak Orr came to flamboyant attention, shifted his plumage to signal a salute, and trilled a command. Most of his three dozen warriors were up on the firing steps, sniping at distant gun crews, but those who weren't went to a brace.

Miraby paused to compliment the Prithian on his troops, heard something whine past his left ear, and assumed it was an insect.

Then, still headed north, Miraby entered the section of the wall controlled by some fifty Hudathans, crack troops each and every one, and commanded by no less than the Hudathan ambassador himself who had been a warrior long before he became a diplomat, and would have preferred to charge the Imperials rather than crouch behind the defensive breastworks. His name was Dogon Doka-Sa. He nodded to Seeba-Ka *before* greeting the human. "Good morning, Major . . . Watch your head or someone will blow it off."

"They haven't so far," Miraby observed blithely. "It's good to see you and your troops up here. I have plenty of areas to worry about—but this sector isn't one of them."

The Hudathan inclined his head a quarter of an inch by way of an acknowledgment. He didn't really care what the human thought but had learned the value of such pleasantries.

Miraby turned onto the north wall, and ran into Sergeant Alan Seebo-21,112, better known as "Sergeant Twelve."

"Sergeant."

"Sir."

Miraby looked the length of the rampart and liked what he saw. The Seebos were alert and ready for action. "Nice show, Sergeant. Carry on."

Twelve nodded. "Sir, yes sir."

Sergi Chien-Chu and his crew of volunteers had constructed another box just inside the gate. This one had three sides, since there were no buildings to hem the potential invaders in, but the principle was the same. Contain the enemy, cut them down, and prevent them from entering Mys.

Then, having glanced out over the breastworks to where the previous day's battle had been fought, the officer rounded the next corner and entered the Ramanthian sector. The troops looked active enough, but the moment Seeba-Ka appeared, something changed. Not only had the Hudathan killed their commanding officer, it appeared that he would go unpunished, a possibility that made the soldiers angry.

Sensing their unhappiness, and fearful of triggering some sort of incident, Miraby hurried down the rampart, entered the area controlled by the Legion and heaved a sigh of relief. "So," Miraby said, as he turned to Mee Mas, "you can see how . . ."

But the sentence went unfinished as a 7.62 mm round entered the officer's brain through his left temple and blew the other side of his head out. Blood and brain tissue sprayed the air, the flat report arrived like a period at the end of a sentence, and the major toppled sideways off the rampart to thump into the ground below.

Eight hundred yards out, in a carefully prepared hide, the sniper's spotter lowered his telescope. "You got him, Pee Pas . . . that's one more bottle of beer that the commander owes you." The sniper gave a grunt of acknowledgment and began the long careful search for the next target.

Seeba-Ka looked down at the spot where Miraby lay and felt a moment of regret. Though pompous, not to mention hidebound, there was something about the officer that he had liked. Lieutenant Beckworth appeared at his elbow. "Damn . . . That's too bad."

"Yes," Seeba-Ka replied somberly, "it is."

Later that day, just before the tired-looking sun dropped down over the western horizon, Miraby joined the Thraki merchant whose throat had been cut the night before, a Seebo who had fallen prey to the same sniper, and seventeen LaNorians as the entire lot of them were lowered into a common grave.

But a legionnaire played taps, members of the embassy's staff cried, and Miraby would have taken a peculiar sort of pride in the entry which went on the company's rolls. "Major Homer Miraby, Killed in Action."

NEAR THE VILLAGE OF NAH REE, ON THE INDEPENDENT PLANET OF LANOR

It was a cold clammy morning. The sun was a distantly felt presence that peered down through multiple layers of cloud, fog and mist as if uninterested in the needs of those below. The bodies, *hundreds* of them, lay where they had fallen. Insulated as they were by those around them, many of the corpses were still warm, and steamed in the early-morning light. The river, still swollen with the rain that had fallen days before, raced past as if eager to keep its appointment with the Great Wet.

Fires had been built all along the beach, beacons of warmth for the cold bleary-eyed workers who waded and in some cases swam among the steadily growing fleet of rafts. Many paused just long enough to avoid hypothermia before plunging back into the water to fasten crosspieces in place, tighten final bindings, and secure newly made rudders.

Meanwhile, oblivious to the cold but exhausted by a lack of sleep, Zook and Snyder splashed from one raft to the next. The cyborgs lifted, pushed, and pulled thereby cutting hundreds of hours off the assembly process.

Santana stood on a slight rise and looked inland. When trouble came, as it eventually must, it would come from there. The Claw had suffered a defeat the night before—a terrible defeat from which it would take days to recover. That's what the legionnaire hoped at any rate but what if he was wrong? What if fresh troops were already on the way? Warmfeel and Fareye would provide some warning, hours perhaps, but not enough to restore the compound's heavily ravaged defenses.

Because rather than use hundreds of person-hours to fortify the very place he was trying to evacuate, Santana had chosen to put all of the group's energies into the rafts and gamble everything on a timely escape. That very evening if at all possible—or the following morning if it wasn't.

Santana's thoughts were interrupted as Platoon Sergeant Hillrun seemed to materialize out of the mist. Doc Hixon had cut the right sleeve off the noncom's shirt in order to bandage his arm. The Naa smiled. He had lots of white teeth. "Good morning, sir."

Santana was not only grateful for having such an experienced noncom as his number two—but enjoyed the legionnaire's unflappable personality as well. "If you say so, Sergeant. Personally, I think it leaves a lot to be desired."

Hillrun managed to look surprised. "*This,* sir? Why back on Algeron we would regard this as a fine summer day. The little ones would come out to play while their elders sat in the sun."

"No wonder you left," Santana replied dryly. "Perhaps the Legion should charge you for the privilege of serving on LaNor."

Both of them laughed. Hillrun jerked a thumb back over his shoulder. "We're about to launch the RAVs . . . Would the lieutenant care to witness the great moment?"

"The lieutenant would," Santana replied, "providing that the units in question remain afloat. Otherwise, the lieutenant will be filling out reports long after the sergeant has retired."

"Oh, they'll float all right," the Naa replied. "The question is for how long?"

It was a good question. Could the RAVs, which were weathertight, act as pontoons? If so, they would continue to offer some cargo-carrying capacity, the nearest thing the medics had to an intensive care unit, and some forward-firing offensive weaponry. Or, and this was all too possible, the first machine could sink like a rock.

What once appeared to be a great idea suddenly seemed a lot less exciting as Santana followed Hillrun up toward the point where the raft already dubbed the flagship, strained at the end of its tether some fifteen feet from the shore.

"There it goes," Hillrun remarked as Sergeant Cvanivich used a remote to guide the first RAV down the gently sloping beach into the relatively calm water upstream of the newly completed jetty. Corporal Carol Serka, straddling the robot like a razbul rider, waved as the machine waded out into the river.

A team comprised of both LaNorians and legionnaires waited to receive the RAV. They hurried to connect lines to the hard points located on various parts of the robot's anatomy, ran them through pulleys, and stood ready to pull as the water lapped at the machine's belly and eventually lifted it off its feet. "Now!" Corporal Serka ordered, and the lines sang through their blocks as the workers pulled on their various ropes.

The RAV started to roll as it was pulled sideways, threatening to throw Serka into the water, and expose the seal that ran around the top hatch to the full effects of the water.

But Zook was there, reaching out to stabilize the RAV, and prevent the machine from rolling belly-up. Then, with the lines taut, the robot was snugged into place alongside a six-log span. Later, after the first machine had been tested for leaks and potential malfunctions, the second robot would take its place on the other side of the raft.

Santana heaved a sigh of relief as the first RAV was secured, knew it was just the first of many challenges the day would hold, and glanced at his watch. Each second that ticked away was like an ally deserting his cause. Who would ready themselves first? The Claw, eager for revenge? Or the people they wanted to kill, desperate to escape? Only time would tell.

THE FOREIGN CITY OF MYS, ON THE INDEPENDENT PLANET OF LANOR

Vanderveen left the embassy through the front door, said, "Hi," to the heavily armed legionnaires who stood guard outside, and took a quick look around. The city had changed a great deal over the past few days—and so had the lives of those who lived there. It was crowded for one thing, a reality that hadn't hit home until the artillery fire began, and thousands of LaNorians were driven out of their hidey-holes and into the streets. Pitiful people who had chosen the wrong religion, gone to work for an off-world corporation, or simply been seen near one of the foreign "devils."

Such people had been entering Mys for weeks, and now, having been twice displaced, they stood, squatted, and lay as near the center of the city as they could get. A strategy designed to get them as far away from the areas where the vast majority of the shells landed as possible.

So now, as Vanderveen wound her way through their ranks, hundreds of hopeless eyes followed the diplomat out of sight, each hoping that she would turn and somehow pluck them out of their misery. But that was impossible since the FSO lacked the means to pluck herself out of the situation much less anyone else.

A flight of what the off-worlders had come to call screaming meemies roared up into the sky, seemed to sigh as their propellant gave out, and nosed toward the ground. The screaming noise was supposed to wear on the city's nerves which it certainly did. The rockets landed off to the west somewhere and presumably smashed themselves apart.

The sporadic sound of gunfire came from somewhere behind her. Though too busy to go up on the embassy's roof for a look Vanderveen had heard that the Imperials were massing for a second attack on the North Gate. Captain Seeba-Ka, now acting in Miraby's place, was doing what he could to disrupt the enemy's preparations.

Somewhere off to the east drums pounded as the Imperials dug trenches in toward the walls in hopes of moving their guns closer. Some even went so far as to suggest that the Imperials might try to tunnel in under the walls though nobody had seen any sign of that yet.

But, in spite of all the madness that surrounded her, Vanderveen had been sent home to prepare for a party. A social even that would help maintain morale. That was what Pas Rasha thought—and others agreed. So, during an evening when Vanderveen should have been working on the city's ever-worsening sewage problems, she would be in attendance at a reception the Ramanthians had agreed to host.

A nice gesture since the Strathmore Hotel's kitchen was being used to feed more than a thousand souls twice each day—and the ballroom had been converted into a makeshift hospital.

Still, Vanderveen thought she knew how to use the time profitably. There were a lot of things that LaNorian refugees were willing to tell Prince Mee Mas that they weren't willing to share with someone from off-world.

One such tidbit was the fact that the Ramanthian factories, all of which produced household products like molt picks, not only continued to run full blast, but were doing so without any interference from the Tro Wa! This while other foreigners were murdered—and their property destroyed. It didn't make any sense, not unless there was some sort of quid pro quo, which Vanderveen felt sure there was.

And of equal interest was motivation. Why, in the face of all-out war, were the Ramanthians so intent on producing the alien equivalent of combs? Something was very, very wrong. But to believe it was one thing and to prove it was something else.

That's why the junior FSO planned to slip away from the party, place a tap on the Ramanthian computer system, and drain it dry. Not then, while in the building, but later, from a safe distance away.

It was wrong, Vanderveen knew that, since diplomats were expressly barred from ". . . initiating, coordinating, or participating in any sort of intelligence-gathering activity regardless of purpose or intent." That's what it said in the regs and she knew that Pas Rasha would enforce them. But it needed doing, and insofar as she could tell, there was no one else to do it.

Her partner in crime, a young computer specialist named Imbulo, had reluctantly agreed to provide some much-needed assistance. Hopefully, given a little bit of luck, the two of them would pull the theft off.

Vanderveen hurried over the bridge, took the stairs that led down into the corporate sector, and made her way through the now-crowded streets. It seemed as though every square foot of ground had been claimed by someone, even if their chunk of real estate was no larger than a two-foot-by-three-foot mat.

Many of the homeless appealed to the diplomat for help, but Vanderveen forced herself to ignore their cries and kept on going. *If* she stopped, *if* she allowed herself to be drawn in, hours would pass and any chance of entering the Ramanthian embassy would disappear.

Vanderveen arrived to find that the building she lived in was on fire. It seemed that one of the incendiary rockets had landed on the northeast corner of the roof. The blaze was still relatively small, and it appeared that members of the fire brigade would soon succeed in putting it out, but the writing was on the wall. Even if the building survived the *next* attack, and the one after that, it would eventually go up in smoke.

The diplomat took a quick look around, spotted some likely-looking young males, and waved them over. "Would you like to make some quick money? Follow me."

The LaNorians followed the human up to her apartment and waited while she packed three suitcases. Food came first, followed by what few meds she had, and every container of lotion, soap and shampoo that she could find. It was a shame she would have to leave most of her possessions to the inevitable looters but that's how it was.

Then, having accounted for the most critical items, Vanderveen selected two sets of sturdy clothing, paused to grab her boots, and ducked into the bathroom to change.

The LaNorians blinked in surprise as the human emerged from the bathroom. None of them knew anything about human standards of beauty, but the dark blue cocktail dress with the gold buttons would have looked good anywhere, especially when worn by her.

After that it was a simple matter to look around, grab a few mementos, and stuff them into her bags. Then, having said a mental farewell to what had been her home, the FSO followed the three heavily laden LaNorians out into the evening air. The fact that Vanderveen wore a cocktail dress, plus heavy boots, and carried a hunting rifle cradled in her arms made her a strange sight indeed.

It took the better part of twenty minutes to reach the embassy, pass between the amused-looking sentries, and pay her bearers. Then, with help from one of the embassy's staff, the FSO hauled her luggage up to her office and dumped it on the floor.

Then, having traded the boots for a pair of dark blue slippers and checked to make sure that her makeup had survived the journey intact, the diplomat collected the data tap from her desk, stuck the disk into her cleavage, and checked to see if the device would show. It didn't. With that out of the way it was a simple matter to throw a LaNorian shawl over her shoulders, hurry downstairs, and exit the building.

Harley Clauson and his band had agreed to play, and their music could be heard from outside the Ramanthian embassy as Vanderveen approached.

No fewer than four insectoid troopers had been stationed outside the main entrance. One of them took a quick look at Vanderveen's ID and checked her invitation, but none of them took the ritual very seriously. It was the Claw that they had been ordered to be on the lookout for and this guest was human.

Typical of Ramanthian habitats everywhere, the interior of the embassy was warm, *too* warm, and Vanderveen was quick to shed her shawl.

Beyond, the heat, the thick odor of alien food, the oppressively low ceilings, and the warrenlike rooms combined to make the FSO feel claustrophobic. But Vanderveen forced herself to ignore that as she accepted a drink off a tray, paused to chat with a group of Clones, and eventually made her way over to where Pas Rasha stood talking to Fynian Isu Hybatha, the Thraki ambassador.

All three of them agreed that it was a shame the way that Ambassador Fas Domar and his staff had been killed, commiserated with each other regarding the steady erosion of their daily comforts, and wondered how Santana's mission was going. Everyone knew the relief force had arrived in the Nah Ree—but how would they make it back?

It was a question never far from Vanderveen's thoughts and it was depressing to hear others voice the same doubts she had.

Finally, when the FSO felt sure that her presence had been noted, she did what she thought of as a "diplomatic fade." Normally used for the purpose of escaping from boring functions early, the fade was best accomplished by going in search of a rest room, and never coming back.

However, before attempting to penetrate the subsurface levels of the embassy, where Vanderveen felt sure the Ramanthian computers would be, it was first necessary to create some sort of distraction. The diplomat dealt with that requirement by sidling up to one of the back tables, sticking one corner of a paper tablecloth into the flame under one of the food warmers, and walking away.

She was on the other side of the room by the time the first person hollered, "Fire!" around the corner by the time a smoke alarm went off, and standing near the top of the ramp as a half dozen Ramanthians shuffled up out of the basements below.

Then, careful to maintain the nonchalant pace of a woman searching for a rest room, Vanderveen strolled down the ramp into the hothouse conditions below.

There was no way to know exactly where the computer equipment would be kept, only the certain knowledge that the gear would be subject to the same laws of physics that governed electronics everywhere, which led Specialist Imbulo to believe that the room would be air-conditioned.

So, given the Ramanthian tendency to leave rooms open to each other, except where doors were required because of potential problems with fire, security, or toxic contaminants, Vanderveen's task was that much easier.

Conscious of the fact that she had very little time before the technicians returned from the floor above the diplomat hurried down a hall, looked into what appeared to be a series of office cubicles, and knew she had selected the wrong corridor.

The diplomat turned, ran back up the passageway, and paused. What felt like a pound of lead rode the bottom of her stomach. She could go left or right but which passageway to take?

Vanderveen heard voices from above, turned to the right, and sprinted for the opposite end of the hall. If someone saw the diplomat they would never believe that she was looking for the Ramanthian equivalent of a powder room but that was the chance she'd have to take. The diplomat's shoes hadn't been made for running and she almost fell. The FSO caught herself, saw some ductwork, and followed it to a door. Vanderveen turned the T-shaped handle, gave a door a tiny push, and felt cool air flow around her face.

Thus encouraged the diplomat barged in, took one look around, and knew she was in the right place. A cylindrical mainframe computer stood at the center of the room surrounded by a circle of lesser machines. Imbulo had predicted that communications between the machines would be wireless and that's the way it appeared to be since the floor was made of duracrete and there was no sign of overhead cable runs.

So, having made it to her goal, all Vanderveen had to do was attach the tap to any surface where it wasn't likely to be found. Data if any would be siphoned off from the transmissions that passed back and forth between the various computers.

Vanderveen had just removed the disk from her bra, and taken three steps forward, when the door opened behind her. The diplomat felt a second one-pound weight drop into her stomach, turned, and forced a smile. Having studied their culture, and dealt with Ramanthian diplomats face-to-face, she could see that the technician was surprised. "Hello!" the FSO said brightly. "Perhaps you could help me . . . I set out to find the rest room but wound up here."

"You are in a restricted area," the technician said sternly. His voice was rendered flat by the broochlike translator that Vanderveen wore but the no-nonsense tone was clear to hear.

"Oops! Sorry, about that," Vanderveen said. "Would you be so kind as to show me the way out?"

That's when the technician made a number of mistakes. He didn't notify his superior, he failed to ask for ID, and he turned his back in order to open the door.

Vanderveen, who had removed the backing by then, slapped the self-adhering device under the nearest countertop and followed the Ramanthian out of the room.

Three minutes later she was upstairs and back in the party. That's when she made a point out of finding the Ramanthian ambassador, told him about her error, and apologized for any inconvenience that she might have caused his staff.

Then, having waited for thirty long minutes, the FSO said her good-byes, hurried back to the embassy, and tried Imbulo's door. It was locked. Vanderveen knocked, saw a brown eyeball appear, and stuck her face up to the crack. "So? Did it work?"

"You bet it worked!" the technician replied enthusiastically. "Come on in."

Vanderveen entered, saw a screen filled with what looked like random numbers, and heard Imbulo lock the door. "What is it?" the diplomat asked, nodding toward the screen. "What does it say?"

"Beats the hell out of me," the specialist answered evenly. "It's in code."

"Code?"

"Yup. In spite of the fact that the Ramanthians were dumb enough to let you in—they weren't dumb enough to transfer data from one machine to the other without encoding it first. If we were on Earth we could crack it but doing so here would take more computing power than I have."

Something about the technician's demeanor and phraseol-

ogy caused a mental relay to close. Vanderveen's eyes grew
bigger. "Wait a minute . . . That tap thing isn't something a
Spec 3 would have lying around. Who do you work for anyway?"

Imbulo did her best to look innocent. "Why the same people you do . . ."

"Don't feed me that crap," the diplomat said angrily. "You
sucked me in! You work for one of the Intelligence outfits!"

Imbulo held her hands palms out. "I'll deny it outside of
this room, but yes, I had been hoping to get some sort of bug
inside their embassy, but never had an excuse to go in there.
You did. Not only that—*you* suggested it!"

Vanderveen shrugged sheepishly. "I can't deny that. So
you're suspicious of the factories too?"

"No, not till you brought them to my attention," the Intelligence officer replied honestly, "but I am now."

"And the information could be right in front of us," Vanderveen said ruefully, "except that we can't see it."

"That's about the size of it," Imbulo agreed, "unless we can
figure out a way to crack the code."

Vanderveen was about to comment on how likely that was
when the Tro Wa sent three wagons loaded with explosives at
the North Gate. The Clones used rocket launchers to destroy
two of the vehicles before they could come close enough to
cause any damage but the third got through. It exploded, killing both drivers and blowing the gate to smithereens. The
women felt the embassy shudder, dashed out of the room, and
ran for the roof. The second assault had begun.

NEAR THE VILLAGE OF NAH REE, ON THE INDEPENDENT PLANET OF LANOR

Though hopeful of casting off before nightfall, and moving his
charges at least five miles down river, a series of last-minute
problems prevented the group's departure.

The night passed with agonizing slowness as Santana waited

to see if his all-or-nothing gamble would pay off. Because if the Tro Wa attacked with the same ferocity they had before there was very little chance that his exhausted troops would be able to fight them off.

Knowing that, but also aware of the challenges that lay downriver, the cavalry officer placed even more chips on the table by making sure that every member of his platoon got at least six hours of sleep. That included the cyborgs who anchored both ends of the defensive perimeter and took turns going off-line.

The LaNorians, most of whom had been ordered to spend the night on the rafts, got as much as eight hours' worth of rest *if* they were able to ignore the noise made by squalling infants, the bone-chilling cold, and the way that the rafts bobbed and swayed.

If the Tro Wa attacked, *if* he had no other choice, it was Santana's intention to cut the rafts loose in hopes that at least some of the refugees would reach safety. It was all he could do. But finally, after what seemed like an eternity, the sky seemed to crack open, admitting a long ragged crack of pink-blue light off to the east.

Santana, who was certain that he was awake, discovered that he wasn't when Sergeant Hillrun touched his arm. "It's dawn, sir."

The officer, who sat huddled beneath a camouflaged tarp that someone had thrown over him, opened his eyes and tried to ignore the taste in his mouth. "Any sign of the enemy?"

The Naa shook his head. "No, sir."

"Excellent. Let's put some warm food into people's bellies and get the hell out of here."

Hillrun had already given the appropriate orders which meant that kettles of tea and soup were on the boil. It wouldn't be long until quantities of both would be transferred to the rafts by the only ones strong enough to lift the containers and carry them out to where the rafts waited in four or five feet of water: the platoon's hardworking cyborgs. There was no need to mention that fact however so the noncom didn't.

Now, as Santana stood, Private Pesta faded away. Unbeknownst to the officer six different legionnaires had voluntarily sacrificed one hour of sleep each to stand guard over him during the night. Pesta was the latest. Hillrun said, "Yes, sir. The food will be ready soon, sir," and disappeared.

Unaware of the efforts made to protect him from Claw assassins Santana wandered down to one of the cook fires, filled a mug with hot tea, and looked out toward the river. It was gunmetal gray and seemed to slide past.

The rafts, all twenty-three of them, tugged at their anchors as if eager to leave. Most, with the exception of the so-called flagship, were equipped with low A-frame-style shelters intended to give at least some protection from wind and rain. Simple meals could be prepared inside using small makeshift stoves. Fire was always a danger—but the use of fuel tabs in place of wood would serve to reduce the overall risk.

Of more concern, to Santana's eye at least, were the long sweep-style rudders mounted between pintles at each raft's stern, and the long poles that could be used to push things off or propel the vessels through shallow water.

Should a steering oar break, or a pole snap in two, it would be easy for one of the rafts to turn broadside into the current, or be swept into one of the rock gardens that were said to lie downstream.

In order to reduce the possibility of such a disaster the helmspeople were all handpicked, drawing on fisherfolk, and those familiar with the flat-bottomed scows commonly used for river transport. Extra poles, one per raft, had been issued as well.

Would the precautions prove adequate? There was only one way to find out. Santana poured the dregs out of his cup and went to the river to rinse it out.

One hour later, the last of the LaNorians had boarded their rafts, the platoon had been transferred to the so-called flagship, where Santana joined them by climbing out of a small fishing boat and onto the raft's stern. The anchor line was bar taut and

Hwa Nas made a last-minute adjustment to the rudder as Sergeant Hillrun pulled the officer aboard. "Welcome aboard Lieutenant . . . Or would 'Admiral' be more appropriate?"

Santana laughed. "Are you kidding? No admiral in his or her right mind would ride on this thing."

The officer followed the starboard aisle toward the bow. The center of the raft was dominated by a raised platform on which supplies were stored and up to ten legionnaires could sleep so long as they were exhausted enough to ignore the fact that it was damp and covered by nothing more than a loose tarp.

If the prospect bothered them the soldiers gave no sign of it as they checked lashings, cleaned weapons, or sipped tea. Santana exchanged greetings with many of them as he walked toward the bow.

The RAVs were roped to either side. While some of the supplies had been removed from the robots in order to improve their buoyancy, both carried a full load of casualties. Two privates had been assigned to assist the platoon's medics care for the patients within. Doc Seavy waved and Santana waved back.

Santana paused in the bow to look out at the smaller raft which had been designated as *Eyes-One*. It carried a crew consisting of Rockclimb Warmfeel and Suresee Fareye, both of whom would act as scouts, plus three LaNorians, all of whom had spent most of their lives on the river.

By sending *Eyes-One* down the river first the Santana would be assured of an early warning in case the advance team ran into navigational hazards or enemy forces. It was important to give them a healthy head start, which was why the lieutenant opened his mike. "Bravo Six to Bravo Two Seven. Time to cut her loose. Over."

"This is Two Seven," Warmfeel replied. "Roger that. Over and out."

Santana watched as one of the LaNorians cut the anchor line, a second put the rudder over, and the raft swung out into the current. Fareye waved and was rewarded by a barrage of catcalls from his fellow legionnaires. The river took command of *Eyes-One* after that-and it wasn't long before the advance party had disappeared from sight.

Now that the scouts were on their way Santana turned his attention to the cyborgs. Though not buoyant, both were capable of walking to Mys underwater if that were necessary, but it wasn't practical. Once the lines were cut the rafts would move much more quickly than Snyder and Zook could march on land much less the bottom of a river. Besides, the unit needed their firepower up on the surface, not below.

That meant the cyborgs would have to travel down the river like everyone else. The problem was how. They couldn't stand—the rafts weren't steady enough for that—and they weren't designed to sit. That seemed to leave either the prone or supine positions either of which would restrict their ability to fight.

The solution, one that Snyder came up with, was to create what she called horses, meaning carefully arranged bundles of logs the cyborgs could straddle and ride by themselves. A design which left their upper torsos completely unhindered.

A great deal of work had gone into coming up with the perfect configuration of logs and a pedal-operated rudder system that allowed the cyborgs to steer with their feet. But the effort had been worth it and the results were clear to see: Two powerful escorts waited in the shallows with their riders in place. Zook raised an enormous arm and Santana waved in return.

The lieutenant turned, looked for Frank Busso, and saw him talking on a radio. The missionary had agreed to ride on the flagship and relay messages to the rest of the fleet using radios contributed by ten of the legionnaires. That meant every other raft had a com unit, which though far from perfect, was a whole lot better than nothing. Santana waited for Busso to finish the latest transmission and smiled. "So, Frank, are we ready?"

"Ready as we'll ever be," the missionary said laconically.

"Okay. Remember, once I give the order to cut the stern

line, we want full three-minute intervals before the next raft departs."

Busso understood the need to keep the rafts spaced out and nodded. "No problem Tony, I'll call them one at a time. Captains of rafts that don't have a radio will wait for the folks in front of them to go, count to 180, and cut their lines."

"Good. Tell them to stand by."

Santana touched his radio. "Bravo Six to Bravo Five. Over."

Hillrun was positioned at the raft's stern. "This is Five . . . go. Over."

"You ready? Over."

"Affirmative. Over."

"Cut us loose. Over and out."

There was a cheer as Hwa Nas raised the axe high above his head, brought the razor-sharp blade down on the stern cable, and severed the rope with a single blow. The flagship was sluggish at first, as if unsure of itself, but soon picked up speed. Hwa Nas guided the raft out into the main channel, prayed to a god that Busso didn't believe in, and felt the river tug at the rudder.

The plan called for the flagship to precede the other rafts down the river, thereby putting the maximum amount of firepower up front. Should they run into trouble, Santana hoped to overwhelm the enemy *before* the passenger rafts could be fired on.

The cyborgs, who had pushed off by then, would fight from the water or beach themselves. Whichever made the most sense.

Then, should all hope be lost, the legionnaire could order the rest of the flotilla to ground themselves upstream of the threat and escape into the countryside. Not a pleasant prospect but some chance was better than none.

But those decisions lay up ahead somewhere. For the moment Santana was content to stand on the raft and look toward the east. Mys was under siege, and Vanderveen was somewhere inside.

THE FOREIGN CITY OF MYS, ON THE INDEPENDENT PLANET OF LANOR

That part of the basement that had previously served as a lounge for LaNorian staff had hastily been converted into a multi-purpose room for Ambassador Pas Rasha. There hadn't been time to put things away so boxes were piled along the walls, a jumble of furniture occupied one corner, and a rug lay unrolled off to one side. A funnel-shaped fixture threw a cone of light down onto the bana wood conference table as the diplomat and his staff stared at a large hand-drawn map. Red hatching had been added to show how much of the city had fallen to the Imperials with help from the Tro Wa.

The ambassador, along with Captain Drik Seeba-Ka, Harley Clauson, Christine Vanderveen, Marcy Barnes, Yvegeniy Kreshenkov, Dr. Hogarth and Willard Tran were still trying to adjust to the same horrible reality: The most recent attack had been all too successful. "My god," Clauson exclaimed feelingly, "the bastards took 25 percent of the city!"

Vanderveen, who had witnessed some of the battle from the embassy's roof, saw that her superior was correct. Everything east of Embassy Row and north of the Jade River was in enemy hands. That included the Drac, Prithian, and Hudathan embassies, as well as the warehouses located behind them.

Seeba-Ka, who had come to the meeting straight from the top of the wall, looked tired. "Yes," he said emotionlessly, "they did. Once the Claw managed to blow the gate the Imperials mounted a massed attack. The Clones, Hudathans and Prithians fought bravely, but there were too many of them. It appears that the enemy suffered something on the order of a thousand casualties. That would give pause to most military commanders but not to these.

"With no gate to stop them they pushed their way into the defensive box. The first waves were slaughtered, but more troops entered, until the Imperials were able to force a breach in the east barricade and escape into the area beyond.

"The good news, such as it is, was that we were able to hold them long enough to evacuate the Hudathan and Prithian embassies. Most of their food and munitions were saved as well.

"Given the fact that the Drac embassy was empty we planted charges inside and brought the building down."

"*We* did that?" Barnes inquired. "Whatever for?"

"So they couldn't use the building for cover," Pas Rasha said wearily. "The last thing we need is snipers firing down at us from across the street. Should I be unlucky enough to survive this mess the Dracs will no doubt petition the president to have me replaced."

The staff members chuckled . . . but knew it was true.

"So," Seeba-Ka said, resuming his report, "once the enemy seized the northeast quadrant of the city the next problem was to not only to hold them there, but keep them off the tops of the walls which our snipers continue to do.

"There was an attempt to cross into the corporate sector, using the footbridge to the south, but Prince Mee Mas and his irregulars were able to push the Imperials back."

Everyone had heard about the prince's adventures by then. With no other responsibilities, and a desire to help, the LaNorian had gone into the corporate sector, rallied a thousand Transcendental converts to the cause, and led them to the bridge.

Whether he had foreseen an attack on that location, or simply headed toward the sound of the fighting, wasn't known.

What *was* known was that the prince, with the faithful Non Noo at his side, led a charge over the bridge and into the face of the Imperial troops. He survived the fusillade of musket balls that felled many of those around him—and laid into the enemy with such energy that hundreds had been inspired to do likewise.

Steel rang on steel as Imperial swords met long curved blades. The brightly colored uniforms gave, broke into groups, and were smothered as peasants surged in around them. Shovels blocked spears, hoes parried pikes, and the Imperials fell back. Finally, having brought all manner of materials forward from the corporate sector, Mee Mas and his troops constructed a barricade at the north end of the bridge that served to confine the would-be invaders to the sector they already held.

It was a remarkable story and one which was already making the rounds. Strangely, through their attempts to reach Mee Mas and kill him, Shi Huu and Lak Saa had granted the youth the very thing he needed most: credibility.

"And that," the Hudathan finished, "is where things now stand."

"The captain made no mention of the importance of his leadership, or the valor of the legionnaires directly under his command," Pas Rasha put in, "so I must. Had it not been for Captain Seeba-Ka's presence in the critical moments after the blast the Imperials might have entered the west side of the city as well. I don't need to tell you what would have happened then. With the obvious exception of our Ramanthian friends his peers trust him and so do I."

There were nods and murmurs of agreement. Seeba-Ka showed no expression but was secretly pleased.

"So, that's it for now. Follow up on all the action items we agreed on—and I'll see you at the same time tomorrow. Christine? You wanted to see me?"

Vanderveen nodded but took her time circumnavigating the table. The others were gone by the time she arrived. Pas Rasha frowned. "If this is about the sanitation thing forget it. Someone has to deal with the sewage problem and you're elected."

"No," the junior FSO replied, "although I will admit that the assignment stinks. This is something else . . . something even more important."

The Dweller looked doubtful. "Does Harley know about this?"

"Yes, sir, he does. I have his permission to bring it up with you."

"You have *permission* but no endorsement. Is that correct?"

Vanderveen looked down and back up again. "Yes sir, it is."

"I see," Pas Rasha said unhappily. "You know how I feel about staff members going over their supervisors' heads . . . But if you must you must. Make your case but keep it short. I have a meeting with Ambassador Ishimoto-Forty-Six in ten minutes. He and his staff need somewhere to stay."

Vanderveen wasn't altogether sure that she could squeeze the entire story into the time allotted but resolved to give it a try. One word followed another and it wasn't long before the essence of her activities started to become clear.

Pas Rasha felt a rising sense of incredulity as a junior member of his staff confessed to entering a restricted area of the Ramanthian embassy, planting a data tap, and subsequently hijacking large volumes of encrypted information.

"So, let's see if I have this right," the Dweller said, his voice starting low, but consistently rising in pitch. "You violated Confederacy law, suborned one of my staff members, and want *me* to participate in your crime?"

"No," Vanderveen said defensively. "I didn't suborn Imbulo, she gets paid for spying on people, something *you* must have been aware of. All I'm asking you to do is help get the data off LaNor. What if the city is overrun? The information would die with us."

"As it should!" Pas Rasha said angrily. "There's a vast difference between intelligence-gathering activities carried out from within the confines of our embassy and planting taps on what amounts to foreign soil. Imbulo doesn't report to me but *you* do. I don't care who your father is. What you did is inexcusable. Once this is over it will be my pleasure to bring charges against you. Until that time you will destroy the data, return to the work you were assigned to do, and keep your mouth shut! That will be all."

The words came like physical blows. Vanderveen's face turned white. She took a full step backward and tried to speak. "But I . . ."

The normally undemonstrative diplomat brought a servo-assisted fist down onto the surface of the table. It jumped an eighth of an inch into the air. "Silence! You are dismissed."

There was very little that Vanderveen could do but say "Yes sir," and leave.

The FSO ran up the stairs, pushed her way through crowded corridors, and left via the back door. The sun hung low in the sky as a flight of screaming meemies passed over the diplomat's head. Vanderveen ignored the rockets *and* the people who called her name in order to walk toward the river. Was Pas Rasha correct? Had she been wrong? And what, if anything, should she do?

The river walk was still reasonably safe so that's where she went. The water swirled in through the West Gate, turned in circles, and fled east. Vanderveen stood there for quite a while, staring down into the water, and waited for inspiration. Finally, just as she was about to leave, an idea came. The diplomat slapped the rail, turned, and walked away. Maybe, just maybe, there was *another* way to get the data off-planet.

THE FORTRESS OF TOK RII, ON THE INDEPENDENT PLANET OF LANOR

The runner was the last member of a long-distance Tro Wa relay team comprised of six young males. His breath came in short well regulated gasps as he jumped a stream, landed on the other side, and scrambled up a rocky slope.

His name was Zho Zas, and even though he would have to run all the way up the hill at Tok Rii the youngster took pleasure from the knowledge that it was *he* who would place the message tube in District Commander Fuu Paa's hand. For to do so was a signal honor and something he could brag about for the rest of his life.

Unlike the market roads that meandered through the valleys, the trail that Zho Zas followed had been created by soldiers hundreds of years earlier, and ran along the high ridges.

That meant it was well drained and seldom used. Factors that combined to make for a good hard surface.

Gradually, as the sun drove the mist off the tops of the hills, the youngster's objective was revealed. The fortress was hundreds if not thousands of years old. It was circular in shape, and thanks to the sunlight that splashed the limestone walls, sat on the top of the hill like a well-burnished crown.

Originally constructed by a warlord, the citadel had later been seized by an Emperor long dead, and used to extract taxes from those who floated down the Gee Nas River. A purpose that it continued to serve, or had, until Fuu Paa's troops had taken the fort a week earlier.

That was a piece of news the Empress hadn't received as yet but soon would. Shi Huu would be furious, that much was certain, and send troops to take the citadel back. Then, assuming there were enough of them, and that they were well led, the fortress at Tok Rii would change hands again.

In the meantime there was no river tax—not at the point where the Gee Nas split into the Little Gee Nas and Jade Rivers. A fact which the Claw was using to illustrate the ways in which their efforts had improved everyday life.

Banners proclaimed this in the village below, as did the half-rotted corpses that lined the approaches to the ancient keep, their empty eye sockets staring at Zho Zas as he hurried up the seemingly endless limestone steps.

It wasn't long before the youngster was spotted and tracked all the way to the main gate where dried blood still splattered the walls and a squad of shabbily dressed Tro Wa lounged in the shade. Two of them knew Zho Zas, and having seen the message tube, were quick to take him inside. Given its age and the negligible amount of money that Empress Shi Huu was willing to spend on maintenance, conditions within the walls were understandably spartan.

There were lean-tos for the troops to sleep under, the same ones the Imperials had used, plus a well that marked the courtyard's center, and the one thing that made the fortress worth fighting for: a cannon, which even now lurked long and lean beneath the canopy rigged to protect it, and could shell the river below.

Zho Zas stared at the off-world weapon as the others led him past it. The original cannon, the one that had ruled the river for so long, had been referred to as the iron monster by those who served it.

But the monster had been replaced, rolled down the hill to the village below, and a new cannon had been lowered into its place. Not the old way, by hauling it up the steep side of the hill with ropes, but from the sky!

Everyone had heard about it, and while Zho Zas didn't pretend to understand all that a cousin had told him, he knew that the new cannon was called a howitzer, and could theoretically drop shells on his village ten sa to the south. A fearsome weapon indeed.

But Zho Zas was given no time to admire the off-world artillery piece prior to being ushered past a group of heavily armed ruffians and into the district commander's presence. Unlike thousands who called themselves Tro Wa, but knew nothing of the martial art from which the name had been taken, Fuu Paa was a true master and his morning workouts were legendary. He wore nothing beyond a loincloth. Muscles bunched and rippled as he twirled like a leaf and seemed to float over the ground.

Zho Zas watched in wonder as the rebel commander jumped, twisted, and slashed. The object of his attack, a sack filled with sand, spilled its contents onto to the ground. The youth had a good imagination. He winced as he thought of what such a cut would do to a *real* body—and hoped never to witness such a thing.

Though not especially handsome—Fuu Paa radiated strength. He turned, saw Zho Zas, and wiggled his ear fans. "And what have we here? An Imperial spy? String him up!"

Zho Zas felt something heavy fall into his stomach, and was

just about to plead for his life, when the Tro Wa laughed. "Had you going didn't I?"

Zho Zas smiled sheepishly. "Yes, Excellency, you certainly did."

"You have a message for me?"

The youth remembered the tube and handed it over. Fuu Paa broke the wax seal, pulled the wooden stopper, and shook the scroll out into his hand.

Then, turning so the light came in over his shoulder, the rebel scanned the text. He had never been very good at scholarly pursuits and his lips moved as he read.

Finally, he gave a grunt of anger, crushed the parchment into a ball, and held it under the youngster's nose. "You know what it said? No, I suppose you don't, so I will tell you . . . Upriver, at a village called Nah Ree, a fool named Taa See led two-thousand of our brethren against a ragtag group of villagers and off-world devils. Somehow, in spite of what should have been an overwhelming advantage, the idiot lost. Not only that, but the scum who defeated him are on their way downriver, and they want *me* to stop them."

"Surely that will be easy," Zho Zas said innocently. "You can kill them with the new cannon!"

"Perhaps," Fuu Paa said, his eyes wandering away, "*if* we can learn to fire it. The Imperials who knew how to fire the cannon were killed during the battle. None of my troops are familiar with such weapons."

The fact that Fuu Paa had allowed his subordinates to slaughter the Imperials without first learning all their secrets struck the messenger as somewhat incompetent but he was far too bright to say so. "Yes, Excellency, that was unfortunate indeed. Will you send a return message?"

"No," Fuu Paa replied, "not until the devils are destroyed. Then I will send you back with news so good that your feet will fly!"

"Pos Tuu . . . Give this lad something to eat! How complicated can the devil cannon be? Summon some ammunition!

This abomination will fire or someone will suffer!"

The first shell was fired later that morning. It arced out over the river and hit a tree off to the south. Fuu Paa swore as the resulting explosion blew a column of dirt, wood, and foliage up into the air.

The gunners opened the breechblock, slammed a fresh shell into the breech, and adjusted their aim. The cannon roared, the second shell missed the target, but not by much. A cheer went up as the Tro Wa celebrated the gunners' success and Fuu Paa allowed himself a smile. The devils were coming . . . and death would be waiting to greet them.

Santana felt the raft shift under his boots as Hwa Nas put the rudder over and swung the bow to starboard. A rock garden lay to port, visible where the water boiled around the half-submerged boulders, just waiting to pull the flagship in.

Though far from the first such obstacle the flotilla had encountered that day the rocks were a potent reminder of the dangers that seemed to lurk around every bend.

Worse, from the cavalry officer's perspective at least, was what he thought of as "the conveyor belt effect." The river was like an assembly line run amok, a nonstop conveyor belt that forced the helmspeople to make critical decisions based on very little data, and punished every mistake.

One raft had been grounded earlier in the day, forcing most of the passengers to disembark before floating free, while another hit a rock, spun around, and slammed broadside into a lone boulder. Thanks to some good luck, not to mention fast action by the males with the poles, the second raft had been freed but not before one person was crushed and another drowned.

On a more positive note the scouts aboard *Eyes-One* had proven themselves to be an invaluable source of intelligence as they fed information back to the fleet.

Now, as the flagship slid by within twenty feet of the right bank, a new report came in. The voice belonged to Warmfeel—

and was tight with tension. "Two Seven to Bravo Six . . . Over."

Santana touched his radio. "This is Six. Go. Over."

"We have incoming arty, sir. Something on the order of a 105 mm howitzer firing from the top of a hill. It looks like they have the main channel preregistered."

"Can we put anything on it? Over."

"Negative. It's out of range. Even for the borgs. Over."

"And it's firing on you? Over."

"That's the strange thing, sir. The cannon was firing *before* we came into sight . . . Like they were taking target practice or something. It looks like they're cycling faster now . . . You should hear it soon. Over."

All sorts of thoughts churned through Santana's mind. Keep going or beach the rafts? Those were his choices, or nonchoices, since the conveyor belt effect was such that it would take the better part of half an hour to beach the flotilla, assuming he succeeded, which was dubious at best. No, the legionnaire decided, the best thing to do was to keep going and hope for the best.

Decision made, the lieutenant passed the word to Busso and ordered the missionary to relay it to the others.

That was when Santana heard a loud *boom,* and the raft swung through a bend in the river to see the place where the point where the river split into two, the fishing boats that marked the village of Tok Rii, and the fortress on the hill above.

A puff of smoke drifted toward the north as the 105 mm shell made a sound similar to that of an old-fashioned freight train, and hit the water not fifty feet from *Eyes-One's* starboard side. The ensuing explosion produced a fifteen-foot column of white water some of which collapsed on the raft and nearly swamped it.

Santana raised his binoculars, watched data scroll, and scanned from left to right. Certain things became apparent. Not having any way to know which river their target would ultimately choose the gunners were dropping shells into the center of the main channel. That suggested taking evasive action that would force the enemy to swing the big gun right and left. No problem if the howitzer had a power supply and was computer-controlled but what were the chances of that? No, the officer concluded, odds were that the gunners had to muscle the gun around.

But could Hwa Nas and his peers pull it off? Owing to their size the rafts were difficult to control. There wasn't much choice however since the watery conveyor belt had the flotilla in its grip, and there wasn't a damned thing they could do about it.

Santana made his way to the flagship's stern, explained the plan to Busso, and watched while Hwa Nas put the rudder over.

Meanwhile, from the top of the hill, Fuu Paa watched the river through a telescope. The little raft was unimportant, but the big one, now *that* was a target. Especially given the strange things lashed to the raft's sides and the presence of at least fifteen foreign devils.

Fuu Paa's troops would have been surprised to learn that the rebel commander had never seen any off-worlders before, and based on the stories he'd heard, expected them to be much larger. But those considerations were thrust aside as the raft started to turn and Fuu Paa realized the importance of the movement. He started to yell, "Hold your fire!" but the lead gunner had been waiting, and pulled the lanyard the moment he saw the rebel leader start to speak. The howitzer roared, belched smoke, and jumped backward as a shell split the air.

Fuu Paa started to scream. "Swing the cannon right! Lead the target! Load and fire!"

A casing clanged onto the surface of the courtyard as the breechblock cycled open and a fresh shell was slammed home. Zho Zas, who had been inducted into the gun crew, ran to fetch another round.

The second shell, the one the gunner had fired prematurely,

struck the water right were the raft should have been, *would* have been, had it not been for the efforts of Hwa Nas. But it missed and the legionnaires swore and directed obscene gestures toward the top of the hill as cold river water rained down on them.

Santana felt terribly exposed as he forced himself to stand toward the bow hands clasped behind his back. The Tro Wa gunners would have corrected by then . . . but how good were they? A puff of smoke appeared high on the hill, the shell rattled through the air, and landed one hundred feet off the port bow! The bastards had missed.

How far could the gunners depress the big tube Santana wondered. And how would their commander react when the next raft rounded the bend? Would he take another crack at the flagship? Or swing back toward the flotilla?

"Fire!" Fuu Paa shouted. "Fire, damn you!"

The gun layer spun the wheel that controlled the howitzer's elevation, felt the mechanism hit its stops, and called to his commander. "The barrel is as far down as it will go, Excellency, what should I do?"

Fuu Paa swore as the raft loaded with foreign devils slid out of the kill zone and passed the long narrow sandbar that served to separate the Jade from the Little Gee Nas. "Sir!" One of Fuu Paa's lieutenants exclaimed, "Look!"

The rebel commander looked, saw the next raft appear, and ordered the gunners to shift. The gun layer had learned a thing or two by then, and rather than simply guess, put the sight on the spot where the near miss had taken place. Now that he knew which tributary the rafts would follow the whole thing became a good deal easier.

Fuu Paa continued to yell, but the gunner managed to ignore him, and waited until what he judged to be the perfect moment before jerking the lanyard.

Santana heard the report and held his breath as he looked back over the stern. But, rather than the column of water he hoped to see, the legionnaire saw a flash of light as the shell hit the second raft, and blew it apart. Splinters of wood and chunks of flesh floated high into the air, seemed to hang there for a moment, and fell into the river.

Then the scene was gone as the conveyor belt pulled the flagship past the village of Tok Rii and into the headwaters of the Jade River. Locals lined the riverbank, staring at the strange apparition that had appeared in front of them, and trying to understand what was going on.

Santana felt a wave of despair roll over him as the howitzer fired again. The rafts had been a horrible mistake . . . How many people had been killed by his incompetence? And how many more were about to die?

The officer had grown used to Busso talking in the background but paid attention when there was a sudden burp of static and another voice broke in. "Two Seven to Bravo Six . . . Over."

Santana forced himself to concentrate. "This is Six. Go. Over."

"We're beached on the sandbar," Warmfeel reported, "just above the village. They missed raft three . . . Four is coming around the bend. Over."

"Roger that," Santana replied thankfully. "Stay where you are—but watch your six. Over."

"Four One and Five One are providing us with security," the scout responded. "You can't get much safer than that."

Santana had lost track of the cyborgs during the recent action and was glad to hear that they were in the clear. "Roger, Two-Seven. Keep me informed. Over and out."

The legionnaire returned to the stern to find that though visibly shaken, Busso was back on the radio, and still working to coordinate communications. His wife and children were on raft three and he was relieved to hear that they were safe.

Santana turned to Hwa Nas. "We need a place to pause and regroup."

The LaNorian nodded. "The river is slow here. There's a place up ahead. The mud will cushion our landing."

"Good," Santana replied, "but be careful how you do it. We need to get the rafts off again."

The LaNorian's expression made it clear that such counsel was superfluous but he was too tactful to say so.

The howitzer continued to fire, and Warmfeel continued to provide sporadic reports as Hwa Nas guided the flagship over to the right side of the river, pushed in through a thicket of reeds, and skimmed the muddy bottom.

Then, once the raft came to a halt, the waiting began. The cavalry officer discovered that it was impossible to stand still and paced from one side of the raft to the other as the shelling continued.

Things went well for a while, as the howitzer continued to fire, and raft after raft passed through the kill zone without being harmed. But then disaster struck as a 155 mm high-explosive round landed squarely on top of raft 18 and blew the vessel to pieces.

Santana winced as the report came in and knew the total number of casualties had reached a hundred. How many more would die? And how would he manage to bear it?

Then, like a miracle sent from heaven, something wonderful happened: The firing stopped. Fuu Paa was nearly deaf by then, the result of standing too close to the howitzer without benefit of ear protection, so he had difficulty understanding what one of his lieutenants said. "What?" he shouted. "I couldn't hear you!"

"We're out of ammunition!" the Tro Wa replied. "*That* was our last shell."

It was bad news, terrible news, but Fuu Paa was tired, too tired to throw a tantrum. He nodded instead. Two rafts out of what? How many more were on the way. Four? Something like that.

It was poor shooting for a well-trained crew, and *good* shooting for an untrained crew, but would someone like Lak Saa make allowances for details like that?

The rebel commander sighed. He would, or he wouldn't.

All Fuu Paa could do was send Zho Zas cross-country with a message. The devils were intent on reaching Mys, that much was certain, and a force could be sent to block them.

Yes, the LaNorian said to himself, *if I double the number of rafts destroyed, and cut the total number by a third, a well-timed report should be sufficient to keep my head connected to my neck.*

Fuu Paa sent for Zho Zas, decided to dictate the message rather than take the hour required to pen it himself, and sent the youth on his way.

Even as Zho Zas left, the last raft entered the Jade River, and the rest of the flotilla pushed off again. The race was on.

12

Those who would hunt a man need to remember that a jungle also contains those who hunt the hunters.

Malcolm X
Autobiography of Malcolm X
Standard year circa 1960

THE FOREIGN CITY OF MYS, ON THE INDEPENDENT PLANET OF LANOR

It was raining. Not just raining but *pouring*, a fact which meant that the much-abused residents of Mys had an ally that soaked their enemies to the skin, made it impossible to move the large guns, and effectively forced a cease-fire.

Aware that the cessation of hostilities wouldn't last forever, the civilian construction brigade under the leadership of Sergi Chien-Chu, and with military advice from Captain Seeba-Ka, hurried to make repairs to the walls and to strengthen the barricades that had been erected after the loss of the northeast sector of the city.

And that's where Chien-Chu was, standing shoulder to shoulder with the mostly LaNorian construction workers as they labored to strengthen the wall of sandbags that started at the northeast corner of the Strathmore Hotel and extended north past the Clone and Thraki embassies to connect with the barricade that ran across Embassy Row near the North Gate.

Vanderveen, a black umbrella held over her head, watched

as the cyborg joined forces with one of the Legion's T-2s to lift an entire pallet load of sandbags up onto some heavy-duty scaffolding.

Chien-Chu saw the young woman with the umbrella, recognized her for who she was, and walked over. His clothes were soaked, water shot out from under his boots, and servos whined as he moved. "Ms. Vanderveen! It's good to see you. I was thrilled to hear of your safe return."

The diplomat smiled. "Thank you. Could I speak with you for a moment? It's very important."

Chien-Chu nodded. "Of course . . . Shall we get out of the rain? The hotel perhaps?"

Vanderveen shook her head. "No, Ambassador Pas Rasha might see me, and I'm in enough trouble already. How about the Clone embassy? We can stand under the overhang."

Intrigued, as well as concerned, the cyborg agreed. Why would his old friend's daughter feel it necessary to conceal her activities from Pas Rasha?

It was a short walk to the Clone embassy where they took shelter under the eaves. "So," Chien-Chu began, "what's on your mind?"

Vanderveen took a deep breath and launched into her story. She didn't know Chien-Chu, not personally, but she knew *of* him, and was careful to stick to the facts, even those that wouldn't necessarily make her look good.

Finally, after she had told the industrialist about her suspicions, the manner in which the illegal data tap had been planted in the Ramanthian embassy, the large quantity of potentially useful information that had been harvested, and Ambassador Pas Rasha's command to cease and desist, Vanderveen brought her narration to a close. "That's it I suppose, except for the fact that I believe Ambassador Pas Rasha is wrong, and rather than destroy the data I think it should be sent to the correct intelligence agency for analysis."

The cyborg raised an artificial eyebrow. "Even if it costs you your job?"

Vanderveen swallowed the lump in her throat. Her career was everything to her. Well, *almost* everything, excepting her on-again off-again relationship with Santana. "Yes, sir."

Chien-Chu nodded. "I respect you for that. So, given the fact that you believe this data is so important that you're willing to sacrifice your career to it, what would you have me do?"

"Take the data, get it off-world, and use your influence to force the right people to take a look at it."

"What makes you think I have the means to get the data off-planet?"

There was silence for a moment and even though Vanderveen knew the cyborg's eyes to be made of something other than flesh and blood she felt she could see the persona beyond. "Because, Mr. Chien-Chu, my father said that you are one of the most intelligent people he has ever met, and I find it difficult to believe that a person such as you would land on a planet like LaNor without having the means to leave when his work was done."

Chien-Chu chuckled. "Well said! And you are correct. A piece of information which I would prefer that you kept to yourself. The *Maylo* is too small to carry more than two passengers . . . but you can imagine how many people would like to accompany me."

Vanderveen nodded. "Of course. So you'll do it? You'll take the data to the right people?"

"Yes," Chien-Chu answered, "I will. In spite of the fact that I respect Ambassador Pas Rasha's strict adherence to the law, and the standards he sets for his staff, I know the Ramanthians extremely well. I've never been able to prove it but there's plenty of circumstantial evidence to suggest that their machinations were behind what has come to be called the Thraki war. The factories you describe *are* curious—as is the fact that the Tro Wa have chosen to leave them untouched."

"Thank god," Vanderveen replied gratefully. "Here it is . . . I urge you to depart as quickly as possible."

The industrialist accepted the small case and dropped it into a belt pouch. "I think we're doing the right thing Christine . . . but what if the data turns out to be something innocuous?"

The diplomat shrugged. "Then I'll be looking for a job."

"Come see me if that happens," the cyborg replied. "I happen to know someone who runs a fairly large company. She's always on the lookout for people who have both intelligence and courage."

Vanderveen started to say something but the industrialist was gone.

THE IMPERIAL CITY OF POLWA, ON THE INDEPENDENT PLANET OF LANOR

The water that hit the tiled roofs, trickled down into gutters, and gushed out of downspouts made a special kind of music that never failed to touch Shi Huu's heart and remind the Empress of her youth in the country where such storms were common.

Now, as she rose from the bed where her exhausted lovers still lay, she made her way to the window. It was late afternoon and the rain still pounded against the flagstones outside. Each droplet leaped back into the air, before surrendering to gravity, and starting the journey to the Great Wet.

The course of *her* journey was a good deal less obvious. The decision to cleanse the planet of foreigners made sense, especially given their refusal to surrender Mee Mas, but now she was starting to wonder. With more than half her army committed to the siege, and the rest tied up defending against the possibility of a Claw-inspired uprising, certain areas had started to slip.

Take the situation in the village of Tok Rii for example. Just that morning a messenger had arrived with news that the garrison had been slaughtered by the Tro Wa. Not only that, but the rebels had occupied the local fortress, and suspended the river tax. Just the sort of thing that made the Imperial government appear weak, encouraged civil unrest, and acted to place a strain on the royal coffers.

Worse yet was the fact that the troops who should have been marching on Tok Rii were camped outside of Mys, wallowing in the mud. Not to mention the fact that the continual state of hostilities had cut the Empress off from the Thrakies and the next step in the full rejuvenation of her body.

Shi Huu turned away from the window and walked over to a full-length mirror. Unlike those who claimed to serve her it never lied. The face was beautiful, miraculously so, but the body reflected every one of her sixty-plus years. The Empress made herself examine the wrinkled, sagging flesh, and felt something akin to revulsion.

How could her lovers force themselves to touch something so disgusting? Then Shi Huu laughed, because the Emperor was already old the night he took the Dawn Concubine into his bedchambers, and no one understood the finer points of sexual theater better than she did.

One of the twins stirred in response to the noise and Shi Huu made up her mind. Once the rain stopped, and the ground was hard, she would order her generals to redouble their efforts. The siege was taking too long—and must be brought to a successful conclusion soon. As for her body, well, the Thrakies could remedy that, and she would provide them with an opportunity to do so.

Satisfied with her decisions, and tired from her exertions, the Empress returned to bed. One of her lovers started to snore, the rain beat on the roof, and she drifted off to sleep.

WEST OF THE FOREIGN CITY OF MYS, ON THE INDEPENDENT PLANET OF LANOR

It was just after dawn as the legionnaires poled the flagship through the Jade River's calm, almost torpid, water. Though forced to pause during the night, lest they run aground on a mud bank, Santana had ordered the flotilla to get under way at first light. This particular part of the countryside was relatively flat, which explained the slow-moving water, and the meandering course of the riverbed.

Santana was seated near the bow, sipping a mug of tea, and watching the flits chase insects across the surface of the water as Busso arrived from the stern. "Mind if I join you?"

Santana didn't want company, not really, but couldn't think of a graceful way to say so. "Sure, pull up a crate."

Busso did so and discovered that the box belonged to his church. "It's a beautiful morning."

"Yeah," the officer replied, "it is."

The missionary raised his own mug to his lips. Steam fogged the view. "It wasn't your fault, you know."

Santana stared straight ahead. "Sure . . . whatever."

"No," Busso insisted, "I'm serious. More than a hundred people died yesterday . . . but more than seven hundred survived. Not in spite of you—but *because* of you."

Santana took another sip of tea. "No offense, Frank, but you talk a lot."

Busso shrugged and got up to go. "Sorry . . . I came here to get away from the life I had. That meant playing the part. Somewhere along the line I began to take the role seriously. Now I'm turning into a bore."

The missionary was two steps away when Santana spoke again. "Frank . . ."

Busso turned. "Yes?"

"Thanks."

Busso smiled. "It was my pleasure."

The morning passed slowly. The flat farmland was punctuated by the occasional bridge, a couple of small villages, fishing boats that rocked gently as the raft passed, and groups of excited youngsters who ran along the riverbank yelling and laughing.

Santana took a moment to wave at them—but his mind was elsewhere. His best guess, given the rather vague map spread out at his feet, was that the flotilla was approximately one day's travel west of Mys. The city had been surrounded, he knew that much, but how bad were conditions around the city? How many troops would the flotilla be forced to pass through? And how were they deployed?

There was only one way to find out. Knowing that no one could come to his aid, and concerned lest his radio transmissions be intercepted by his enemies, the cavalry officer had resisted the temptation to make the sort of reports that would be considered SOP under normal circumstances. But now, with the journey almost at an end, Santana needed information, and needed it badly. That's why he summoned Platoon Sergeant Hillrun and Lance Corporal "Bags" Bagano. Once both individuals were seated across from him, Santana outlined his plan. "Okay, here's what I want you to do . . . Bags, get HQ on the horn and ask for both Captain Seeba-Ka and First Sergeant Neversmile. The captain and I will speak with each other, but Sergeants Hillrun and Neversmile will translate our words into Naa, thereby providing one more layer of security. Questions?"

The legionnaires shook their heads. Yes, there was always the possibility that someone might have a translator loaded for Naa, but the language was relatively obscure, and rarely used on any planet except Algeron. That, plus the fact that the transmissions would be encrypted, made it very unlikely that anyone would be able to listen in.

The com link was established five minutes later, Seeba-Ka arrived ten minutes after that, and the officers provided each other with updates. Seeba-Ka was happy to learn that most of the platoon had not only survived, but had rescued the missionaries and were homeward bound.

Santana was sorry to hear how roughly 25 percent of Mys had been compromised, about the casualties which continued to mount, and the hardships suffered by those trapped in the city.

Then they got down to business. Both officers agreed that any chance of surprise had been lost. The Claw knew the refugees were coming via the river and would be waiting for them. As for the Imperials, there was no way to know how much information they had, so it seemed wise to assume that they knew as well.

With that in mind the officers formulated the best plan they could, realizing that the enemy held most of the cards, and would not hesitate to play those that they had.

Finally, as the conversation wound down, Santana sought to obtain one last scrap of information. "Given the casualties how is the diplomatic team doing? Is everyone okay?"

Many miles to the east Seeba-Ka listened to Neversmile ask the question and produced the Hudathan equivalent of a smile. "Tell the lieutenant that FSO Vanderveen is in charge of sanitation—but other than that she's fine."

Seeba-Ka had seen through the ruse with such ease that Santana felt his face grow warm as Hillrun passed the message along. "Okay, well that's it, I guess, you can sign off."

The Naa did as he was told, Bagano killed her radio, and both withdrew. Any member of the platoon who hadn't been aware of the lieutenant's interest in FSO Vanderveen would soon be enlightened. But Santana didn't care, not so long as she was alive, and somewhere in Mys. The river turned ahead—but his eyes were on the horizon.

THE FOREIGN CITY OF MYS, ON THE INDEPENDENT PLANET OF LANOR

The shaman droned on for the better part of an hour, burned sacred incense, and fastened bits of brightly colored cloth to various points within the tent. He meant well, but once the healer left, the eunuch felt no better than he had before.

For what seemed like the thousandth time Lak Saa wondered if he had done the correct thing and went on assure himself that he had. Rather than live in Polwa, and visit his troops the way the Imperial generals did, the leader of the Tro Wa insisted on actually living with his soldiers. It was the right thing to do, he knew that, but life was difficult out on the plains. There were bound to be has (evil spirits) wherever so many people had gathered—and one such being had taken the opportunity to invade his body.

Now, confined to his cot, and alternately shivering and sweating within the confines of his tent, Lak Saa felt worse than he had for many years.

Someone opened the tent flap. The mud stench entered along with him. Only weeks had passed since Lak Saa had demonstrated his prowess within the confines of the hodo but it seemed like a year. Now, having been promoted, the educator named Dee Waa had risen to the rank of assistant district commander. He spoke softly knowing how loud noises could enrage his superior. "A messenger has arrived, Excellency, with news regarding those who escaped from Nah Ree."

"Show him in," Lak Saa whispered, "and make him stand in the light."

The fact that the off-worlders had sent a column to Nah Ree was well-known. First, because the Ramanthians had told Lak Saa the moment they learned of it, and second because of the well-documented defeats that followed.

The messenger was the last of seven such individuals who made up the east–west relay team. However, unlike those who had run before her, *this* courier was female. A proud if somewhat muddy specimen who left footprints on the otherwise immaculate floor, took her place under the light, and met Lak Saa's gaze. Here was the sort of material from which the true generation would come forth. The eunuch smiled and used one of his long curved claws to beckon the youngster forward. "Come, my dear . . . I won't bite."

The female shuffled forward, offered the message tube with all the solemnity of a high-ranking official presenting a gift, and waited while Lak Saa broke the seal. He looked older than she had imagined—and very tired. The bedding smelled of urine and she wondered why.

Lak Saa shook the scroll out of the tube, read it, and called for Dee Waa. The teacher responded so quickly that it was obvious that he had been standing outside. "The foreign devils constructed rafts, loaded them with villagers from Nah Ree, and should arrive sometime tomorrow."

Dee Waa bowed. "Yes, Excellency. What would you have us do?"

"Line both sides of the Jade River with our troops. Tell them to prepare for battle and to show no mercy. Every person on those rafts must die."

"Yes, Excellency. And the Imperials? What of them?"

"They can stand and watch," Lak Saa replied, "while we show them how it's done."

It was dark at the bottom of the Jade River, very dark, which was good since the last thing diver-rigger Les Foro needed was for someone to see him and the hulking T-2s who plowed along behind. There were four of the cyborgs, all armed to the teeth, and eager to do something more than patrol the streets of Mys.

But first someone had to cut their way through the iron grate that filtered the Jade River as it flowed into the city from the west. Originally designed to thwart the smugglers who liked to float the river at night the grating was normally raised when the customs officials came on duty just after dawn. That routine had been interrupted by the siege however, which meant that the grating was not only locked into the down position, but couldn't be raised without producing a loud metallic squeal that would almost certainly alert the enemy to the fact that something unusual was going on.

That's why Seeba-Ka appealed to Chien-Chu, who polled his employees, to see if any of them would be willing to help. Foro, idiot that he was, had volunteered to cut a hole through the grate. Now, unable to use the lights mounted on his backpack, the cyborg "felt" his way through the murk via computer-enhanced sonar. In addition to the heavy layer of silt washed down from the interior, the river had long served as a receptacle for everything from raw sewage to worn-out household items, and construction debris. Stones from an old bridge lay across the riverbed like vertebrae from a prehistoric beast, a bronze cannon stuck its snout up out of the mud, and what looked like a huge kettle lay half-buried in the muck.

The riverbed was a nightmare world in which thick glutinous mud sucked at Foro's boots, his onboard computer painted diagrams of obstacles onto his electronic vision, and the current pushed against his chest.

Finally, having made their way from the riverside park, where they had entered the river, the cyborgs found themselves in front of the western water gate. The lead T-2 was named Hosakawa, and Foro spoke to him via short-range radio. "Okay, Sergeant, I'm about to go to work. Remember what I told you . . . The gate has been closed so long that a ton of debris has accumulated on the far side. Once I make a hole the river is going to suck that stuff downstream. You and your box heads need to position yourselves left and right of the grate. Stay there until the plug clears. Got it?"

The term "box heads" had a pejorative quality when used by bio bods, but being a cyborg himself, Foro was entitled to use it. "No problem," the noncom replied, "but what about you? Over."

"I plan to go flat on my back," the civilian answered, "so don't put one of your size fifties on my chest."

"Roger that, over."

"Okay, put your people in position, and notify Seeba-Ka. I'll start the first cut sixty seconds from now."

Hosakawa gave the necessary orders and switched frequencies. "This is Six Six . . . About fifty seconds from now . . . Over."

There were two *clicks* as the Hudathan acknowledged the transmission and the seconds started to tick away. Hosakawa started to count. He had just reach forty-eight when all hell broke loose.

Seeba-Ka, who was standing on top of the west wall, only slightly north of the water gate, watched the first mortar rounds fall into the no-man's-land that lay between the Imperial tents and the city. The shells blossomed like red flowers, strobed the plain with unexpected light, and threw great gouts of mud high into the air. Both the Imperials and the Tro Wa were familiar with how far the off-world weapons could reach and were camped well out of range.

But the true purpose of the barrage was not to inflict casualties, although Seeba-Ka could hope, but to distract the enemy long enough for Foro to cut his way through the grating undetected.

Meanwhile, at the bottom of the Jade River, the civilian triggered his torch. A bar of blue-green energy appeared—and the water surrounding it started to boil as Foro applied the tool to a horizontal rod. It was head high and approximately three inches in diameter. A full minute passed while the rigger completed the cut. One down and fourteen to go.

Lak Saa awoke from a troubled sleep to hear the *crump! crump! crump!* of exploding mortar rounds, and saw the flash of successive explosions through the material of his tent. The off-worlders had launched an attack . . . Why? To keep their enemies awake? Or for some other reason? Surely they were aware that the explosive rounds were doomed to fall well short of the Imperial encampments.

The eunuch swung his legs over the side of the cot, felt for his slippers, and pushed his feet inside. The material felt cold. Then, gritting his teeth against the pain in his temples, the rebel leader struggled to his feet. A wave of vertigo threatened to dump him on the floor, but Lak Saa waited for the dizziness to pass, and shuffled toward the door. The lantern threw a large misshapen shadow against the wall of the tent. The ground shook as the mortar rounds continued to fall.

Foro felt a sense of trepidation as he completed the final cut. Would he be able to back off quickly enough? Or would the current, plus the weight of the accumulated debris, push the grating down onto his head?

Metal groaned, the grating started to bend, and Foro threw

himself backward. The cyborg felt rather than saw the garbage surge over his head and allowed himself to sink into the ooze. The *first* part of his job was over.

Hosakawa waited for the plug to clear, stepped out into the center of the channel, and felt the grating give under his boots. "This is Alpha Eight . . . We're passing through the gate. Over."

"Roger," Seeba-Ka replied calmly. "Bravo Four One and Five One are waiting a hundred yards due west of your present position. Over."

"Roger that," Hosakawa replied. "Out."

Minus the sonar that Foro had used to pick his way through the stygian blackness, the noncom had little choice but to make occasional used of headlamps. It was dangerous, he knew that, but hoped the bad guys were too busy watching the fireworks to pay much attention to the river.

Dee Waa, who had been watching the bombardment along with other members of Lak Saa's staff, saw movement from the corner of his eye, and turned just in time to see the eunuch emerge from his tent. The ex-teacher rushed to the Claw's side. "Excellency! You should be in bed!"

Lak Saa swayed slightly as he surveyed the battlefield. He saw dozens of campfires, the flash of incoming mortar rounds, and the dark bulk of Mys beyond. By contrast Polwa glowed thanks to all the lights within. "Any sign of the rafts?"

Dee Waa was far too intelligent to ask "What rafts?" and shook his head. "No, Excellency, but we have troops stationed on both sides of the river. When the rafts appear they will open fire."

"On each other?" the eunuch demanded cynically.

"No, Excellency. The troops were briefed. They understand the importance of firing *down,* into the river, rather than straight ahead."

The ex-educator had all the answers, or so it seemed, and Lak Saa felt something akin to relief. He said, "Good, notify

me when the rafts appear," and turned back toward his tent.
There was something else, something having to do with the
mortar attack, but the rebel leader couldn't remember what it
was. The cot came up to meet him and darkness pulled the
eunuch down.

In spite of the fact that Sergeant Hosakawa didn't have sonar,
he did have heat sensors, and knew that the streaks of greenish
blue light that flitted through his field of vision were fish. He
turned his lights on every now and then, but there wasn't much
to see, so it was better to keep them off. There were times
when the cyborg was reduced to feeling his way upriver like a
child wearing a blindfold.

Those who followed behind had a somewhat easier task
since the heat produced by the noncom's electromechanical
body was clear to see and all they had to do was follow it.

At one point Hosakawa's fully extended arms encountered
something solid, and it was necessary to feel his way around
the obstacle before proceeding down the side of what was almost certainly a waterlogged barge. It was shortly after that
when Hosakawa saw the telltale glow of heat and activated his
radio. "Alpha Eight to Bravo Four One . . . I have visual contact. Confirm. Over."

There were two blobs now and one of them danced a clumsy
jig. Zook and Snyder had preceded the rafts downriver so they
could join the other T-2s in the combat zone.

Hosakawa smiled, or would have, had there been something
to smile with. "Nice try Four One . . . but you'd better keep
the day job. Cap? Do you read me? Over."

Seeba-Ka used a pair of light-intensifying binoculars to scan
the battlefield. The Claw had positioned troops on both sides
of the river. They clearly expected the rafts to pass through the
combat zone at any moment. "I read you . . . Get in position
and stand by.

"Blood Six to Bravo Six . . . Do you read me? Over."

"That's affirmative," Santana replied. "Over."

"Are you ready? Over."

There was a distant flash as a mortar round detonated and a sudden wash of light as more flares went off. Santana looked back over his shoulder. The rafts were hidden in the darkness. Were the refugees ready to pass through a hail of bullets? No, of course not. Neither was he. But there was only one answer the officer could give. "Sir, yes sir. Over."

"All right," Seeba-Ka said somberly, "bring them in. Once you enter the combat zone, notify Alpha Eight. Good luck. Over."

Santana hit the transmit button twice and turned to Hwa Nas. "Cut the line." He looked at Busso. "Pass the word. Cut the lines."

The missionary obeyed, the rafts drifted free, and the flotilla began to move downriver. It took less than fifteen minutes for the flagship to reach the edge of the plain and the point where the easternmost campfires burned. Santana waited for the inevitable cry of alarm but nothing was heard. It was just a matter of time however—and the platoon leader took one last look at his troops. They were positioned along both sides of the raft behind makeshift barricades. Each legionnaire carried a primary and secondary weapon, thirty magazines, and as many grenades as they could manage.

All of the soldiers knew the rafts would be forced to pass through what amounted to a shooting gallery and were determined to give as good as they got. The flagship continued to ghost along, seconds continued to tick away, and the battlefield seemed to hold its breath.

Seeba-Ka heard a boot scrape on stone and turned to discover that FSO Vanderveen had materialized at his side. She carried a scope-mounted hunting rifle which she proceeded to load with cartridges taken from her pocket. The Hudathan frowned. "No offense, ma'am, but what the hell are you doing here?"

"I'm going to shoot some members of the Tro Wa," the diplomat replied defiantly. "Do you have a problem with that?"

Seeba-Ka looked into the human's level gaze and was reminded of females like his grandmother who carried their husbands' weapons, guarded their backs, and tended their wounds. Santana, it occurred to him, was a very lucky man. "No, I don't. Try to hit their leaders. And be careful . . . The same sniper who killed Major Miraby is still out there."

Vanderveen nodded, found a place over the water gate, and waited for the killing to begin.

As chance would have it, it was Ply Pog, the same ruffian who had befriended Yao Che on his journey to Mys, who felt the need to pee and wandered down to the edge of the river. And there he was, busily adding *his* water to the Jade's steady flow, when the first raft sailed past. The Tro Wa saw it, pointed, and yelled. He was busy trying to stuff himself back into his pants when Private Joan Fandel put a .50 caliber round through the center of the Claw's chest. The battle had begun.

The cyborgs, all six of whom had been waiting for what seemed like an eternity, marched up out of the oily black water to take their places on the riverbank. Three faced north and three faced south. They were roughly a hundred feet apart and looked huge in the strange half-light cast by the flares.

The forward elements of the Claw had been stationed within twenty-five feet of the riverbank. They stared in horror as what looked like primordial monsters rose to confront them.

Muskets began to pop, an automatic weapon opened up, and the mortars put six illumination rounds up in the air. Suddenly the battlefield was bathed in ghostly light, the cyborgs opened fire, and the first raft passed behind their backs.

Snyder discovered that the targets were so thick that there was no need to aim. She, along with Hosakawa and a borg named Krisco, stuck their arms out and attacked like zombies. As they marched toward the north their machine guns harvested lives the way a combine cuts wheat. Rows of Tro Wa fell, campfires erupted into columns of sparks, and tents were torn to shreds. Energy cannons burped coherent light, a cannon toppled over onto to its side, and an entire squad of attackers was swept away. The LaNorians had never experienced anything like it before and many turned to run.

There were incoming rounds as well, *lots* of incoming rounds, and they made pinging sounds as they struck Snyder's armor.

But the cyborgs seemed to be indestructible, *were* indestructible, until Lak Saa stumbled out of his tent, stared at the mayhem, and ignored the line of machine gun bullets that dug divots out of the ground in front of him. "Where are the rockets? Bring me a rocket!"

Dee Waa would never forget what happened next as the eunuch grabbed one of the mysterious weapons, loaded a rocket into the tube, and brought the device to his shoulder. The sight of Lak Saa standing there, the breeze whipping the long white nightshirt out and away from his body, was an image that the educator knew he would never forget.

Then the SAM went off, except that rather than being aimed at an aircraft, it was targeted on a cyborg. The missile didn't care however. All it wanted to do was collide with the most intense source of heat available and the T-2 fit the bill.

Hosakawa's sensors warned him about the missile the moment that the head started to track, but it was too late by then, and the cyborg was just starting to think about evasive action when the warhead struck the center of his chest.

Snyder felt pieces of the noncom's body hit her armor followed by the sudden wash of heat. Her onboard computer provided the cyborg with coordinates for the probable point of launch and she sent death in that direction. It had been unwise to stack the SLMs like so much cordwood, but understandable given the Tro Wa's lack of training, and they exploded with a single earthshaking roar. The shock wave lifted Lak Saa off his feet, threw the eunuch into the side of his tent, and knocked a dozen rebels to the ground. Terrified by the monsters that had appeared out of nowhere, not to mention the force of the subsequent explosion, the remainder of the Claw turned and fled.

But the Imperials had been awakened by then, and while some were only half-dressed, they marched south toward the river as rebels passed back through their ranks.

Seeba-Ka swore as the regular army entered the fray, ordered the cyborgs to fall back toward the river, and waited for the Imperials to commit themselves further.

Though not exactly sure of who they were about to engage, each and every one of the Imperial officers wanted to distinguish himself, and ordered their troops to enter the line. As that occurred the left flank extended itself east and well into the range. "Hold," Seeba-Ka commanded his troops, "hold . . . Fire!"

Concentrated automatic weapons fire lashed out from the wall and the Imperial troops started to waver and fall. Entire ranks went down like dominoes as a storm of lead swept across the battlefield. Some of the Imperial officers attempted to turn their troops toward the incoming fire and were immediately marked down by Seeba-Ka's snipers.

Vanderveen saw one such individual, led him by a hair, and squeezed the trigger. The slug, punched a hole through the old-fashioned armor, and exited through the LaNorian's back.

Another officer stepped forward and the diplomat shot him as well, grimacing as her victim spun through a full circle, before falling to the ground.

Then, much to Vanderveen's horror, yet *another* officer appeared, this one in his teens. Tears ran down her cheeks as she forced the crosshairs onto the new target. The diplomat aimed low, hoping to merely disable the youngster, and pulled the trigger.

The Sycor Scout thumped against her shoulder, the officer tripped, and fell into the path of the .300 magnum bullet. It entered through the top of his skull and drove deep into his body. He went down and stayed there.

Vanderveen watched that particular contingent of Imperials

break and run toward the west where they collided with another group and shattered their formation.

Vanderveen swore as counterfire chipped the stone next to her head and sent a tiny fragment of rock into the side of her face. The diplomat ducked after that, partially to reload, but mostly to regain her composure. That was when Seeba-Ka happened by. He said, "Nice shooting! I'll take *more* diplomats if any are available," then continued on his way. New flares went off . . . and people on both sides continued to die.

Foro had cut through the lock and raised what remained of the grate by then. Something, Santana wasn't sure what, caused the officer to look up as the raft's bow slid under the archway from which the water gate was suspended.

And it was then, at that exact moment, that a flare went off and Vanderveen stood. Her face looked pale in the artificial light, like that of an angel, and the legionnaire waved as the flagship scraped the side of a quay and carried him into the city of Mys.

The diplomat ran to the other side of the walkway, returned the wave, and gave thanks that her payers had been answered. The rest of the rafts followed one after another until each of them had been accounted for—and every single refugee had been led off toward the Transcendental Cathedral.

There was something of a traffic jam at first, since it was necessary for all of the rafts to stop short of the bridge, or run the risk of taking fire from the northeast sector of the city, which was still infested with enemy soldiers.

But once the refugees were safely ashore Les Foro and a couple of his cybernetic buddies went to work dismantling the rafts and used dockside cranes to heave the logs up onto the bank where they could be used to reinforce the city's defensive barricades.

The patients had come through fine, but water had gotten into the RAVs, causing both to malfunction. One of the wooden riverside cranes was used to lift the robots out of the water on the chance that the techs could get one or both of them up and running again.

Later, as soon as it could be repaired, the grate would be reinstalled in an attempt to keep the Tro Wa from entering the city via the water gate.

Santana checked to make sure that all five of the surviving T-2's had made it into the city, thanked them for their efforts, and made a note to put every single one of the cyborgs in for a decoration.

Amazingly, almost unbelievably, Sergeant Hosakawa had been the Legion's only casualty. In fact, due to the fact that that the so-called flagship had been five feet below the top of the riverbanks, and the cyborgs had done such a good job driving the enemy back away from the river, most of the platoon leader's troopers never had the opportunity to fire their weapons. But the legionnaires were tired, *very* tired, and happy to make the relatively short journey down the south bank to the bridge, north along Embassy Row, and through the secondary barricade that had been established at the north end of the span.

Santana was amazed to see the ways in which Mys had changed during his absence. It was dark, but flares continued to pop, and bathed the area in their uncertain light. The trees that once marched down Embassy Row had been cut down and hauled away. Most of the buildings and other structures had been damaged by bullets, cannon fire, or incendiary rockets. The upper floors of the buildings had been taken over by snipers, counter-snipers, and counter-counter-snipers, who plied their deadly trade both day and night. Lower windows had been boarded up and blacked out. Bits of clothing, bloodied bandages, empty ration packs, scraps of paper, empty shell casings, and stray household items littered the streets. All within a thin fog of gray smoke, the reek of unprocessed sewage, and the stench of bodies that no one could reach.

It was like a stroll through hell, and Santana was happy to escape the street for the relative order of the now-overcrowded barracks. It had taken two hits, but still remained intact, and was surrounded by freshly stacked sandbags. They were made from fabric that Chien-Chu and his civilians had "liberated" from the hodos and given to the refugees to sew, which meant that the coverings came in a wild assortment of colors and designs.

There was no one to celebrate their return—the allied military forces were stretched far too thin for that—but Seeba-Ka stopped by to thank them, as did Ambassador Pas Rasha. Then, having cleared their weapons, the legionnaires did the one thing they wanted to do most: They went to sleep.

Clouds had moved into the area, and the first light was so weak, that it seemed as if night would never surrender to it. But finally, more as a result of persistence rather than any real conviction the sun managed to push a sickly yellow glow down through the intervening clouds.

Fynian Isu Hybatha, the Thraki ambassador to LaNor, left the embassy via the *back* door rather than risk the snipers who lurked on the other side of Embassy Row and eyed the two-wheeled cart. It was a dilapidated affair, which judging from the few remaining patches of paint, might have been blue once. Just the sort of vehicle favored by Polwa's less-prosperous merchants.

Hybatha hated the damned things but what choice did she have? The Empress had invited, no *summoned* her to the Imperial palace, and she had little choice but to go. The alternative, which was to surrender the subsea mineral deposits to Chien-Chu Enterprises, was too horrible to consider. Especially after all the effort dedicated to buying Shi Huu off.

Which raised an interesting question: Where was the human industrialist anyway? The cyborg had dropped out of sight a few days earlier. Some of her staff believed that he had taken refuge on the *Seadown*, where he could wait out the siege in relative comfort, but the diplomat had her doubts. Chien-Chu had never struck her as a person who was overly concerned about a little hardship. No, if the industrialist was missing there was a reason and Hybatha wondered what it was.

Flight Warrior Garla Tru Sygor cleared his throat. "Greetings. The ambassador's transportation is ready."

In spite of the fact that the nearest Thraki aerospace fighter was located thousands of light-years away, he had chosen to wear full flight gear. It looked absurd and the diplomat made a note to find out which one of her bureaucratic enemies had saddled her with the idiot and extract some sort of suitable revenge. First, she would have to survive the journey into Polwa however. Hybatha forced herself to be civil. "Thank you for stating the obvious. Now, should anyone ask any questions, you know what to say."

"Of course," the officer answered loftily. "The ambassador undertook a journey into Polwa in an attempt to negotiate a cease-fire."

"Exactly," Hybatha replied. "Pas Rasha won't like it . . . but so what? Let the skinny bastard stew."

The flight warrior nodded agreeably. "Of course . . . Can I send a detachment of troops with the ambassador to protect her?"

Hybatha sighed. "Yes, Sygor, and while you're at it, why not paint a target on the side of my cart? I have a pass from the Empress—not from the Claw. My only hope is to get through unnoticed."

The officer inclined his head but was otherwise expressionless as the diplomat climbed into the enclosed passenger compartment, pulled the musty side curtains into position, and rapped on the back of the forward partition. The driver, a LaNorian named Bok How, cracked his whip. The razbul gave a snort of indignation, passed a prodigious amount of gas, and plodded toward the south.

By passing to the rear of the Confederacy's embassy, Bok How hoped to avoid taking fire from Claw snipers who haunted the other side of Embassy Row, and weren't aware of the fact that he was a red. An allegiance driven more by the fact that the Tro Wa had kidnapped the teamster's family rather than a sincere belief in the rebel cause.

The cart turned toward the east, passed through the checkpoint that bordered the Confederacy's embassy, and headed south. A squad of Seebos ordered Bok How to stop in front of the bridge barricade, but Hybatha pulled the curtain back so they could see her face, and the soldiers waved the cart through.

Farther on, beyond the bridge, there was a great deal of cross-street traffic as hundreds of LaNorians, many carrying multicolored sandbags, streamed out of Dig Town headed for the Transcendental Cathedral. Bok How waited for a break, urged the razbul forward, and was forced to pause in front of the next barrier where a Thraki noncom stepped forward to confront him. It was no accident that Hybatha had chosen that particular hour to leave Mys. The L-8 saw the diplomat's face, came to attention, and delivered a salute as the conveyance passed him.

The next stop, at the gate into Polwa, was equally uncontested thanks to the Imperial pass which Bok How slipped through the slot in the heavily reinforced door. The barrier made a creaking sound as it was pulled open. A group of Imperial soldiers made as if to rush through the gap but stopped when their officer realized that it would be quite a while before reinforcements arrived, and thought better of the plan.

Bok How slapped the razbul with the reins, felt the cart jerk forward, and heard the gate close behind him. A persistent emptiness was gathering at the pit of his stomach. The threats had been quite graphic. One false move, one tiny mistake, and his family would die screaming. In contrast to Mys, the streets of Polwa bustled with life, and seemed completely unaffected by the horrors taking place only a hundred units away.

The Tro Wa operatives appeared from both sides of the road, jumped onto the cart's running boards, and blocked the doors.

Hybatha felt the impact, heard a noise, and peeked through

a curtain. A member of the Claw leered back at her, waved a well-honed knife, and gestured for silence. That was the moment when the diplomat knew that she had been hijacked.

Hybatha reached for her day pouch, fumbled for the pistol, and pulled the weapon out of the bag. The longer she remained on the cart the farther she would be from Mys and the possibility of a rescue. It wasn't clear whether Bok How had betrayed her, or was a victim himself, but it didn't really matter. The diplomat wanted the vehicle to stop, and there was only one way to make sure that it would.

The Thraki took aim at the spot where she judged the driver's back would be, fired two shots, and saw holes appear in the wood partition. There was a *thump* as Bok How pitched forward off his seat, inadvertently jerked on the reins, and brought the razbul to a halt.

Hybatha fired two shots through the left door, heard the Tro Wa scream, and was just about to do the same thing on the right side when a fist shattered the cheap window glass, fingers wrapped themselves around her wrist, and shook the weapon free. Then, careless of her struggles, the Claw pulled the diplomat across the bench-style seat, let go long enough to open the door, and slid in beside her.

It was only a matter of seconds before another member of the Tro Wa had replaced Bok How in the driver's seat, another ruffian had entered the passenger compartment, and the cart was under way again.

Hybatha, crammed in between two rebel warriors, thought about the radio in her pouch. The bag lay on the floor, only units from her feet, but might as well have been on one of LaNor's moons. The cart bumped its way over some sort of obstacle, the diplomat's heart started to sink, and the slums of Polwa closed in around her.

Lak Saa had been unconscious when Dee Waa found the rebel leader lying on top of the wreckage of his tent. Unsure of how to help him, the educator had the eunuch loaded onto a

stretcher and carried into Polwa via one of the rickety footbridges that spanned the Jade River. Now, lying on a richly
draped couch within the hodo that served as his headquarters,
the Claw was surprised to discover that he felt a good deal
better. Whether as a result of the battle, or in spite of it, his
fever had broken and he was hungry for the first time in days.
In fact, he was just finishing a happy bowl filled with chunks
of flavorful fish and nicely steamed kas, when a functionary
scurried up to foot of Lak Saa's bed and bowed. "A thousand
pardons, Excellency, but the prisoner has arrived."

The eunuch waved his spatula-like spoon as if it were a
scepter. "Bring it in."

There was a disturbance at the far end of the mostly empty
warehouse, a door slammed, and a pair of warriors appeared.
They were a good deal taller than Hybatha, which meant that
her feet rarely touched the ground as she was hustled from end
of the hodo to the other. She struggled to no avail. "Do you
know who I am? Put me down this instant! This is an outrage!"

The rebels came to a stop in front of Lak Saa's bed, allowed
the Thraki to stand on her own two feet, and awaited further
orders. Hybatha glared at the Claw leader as he continued to
eat. "And who are *you*?"

The eunuch continued to chew, took a sip of wine, and used
it wash the latest bite of food down. Then, having used a piece
of clean cloth to dab at his lips, he finally spoke. "Why did
the Empress send for you?"

Hybatha looked indignant. "*If* the Empress sent for me,
which may or may not be true, the nature of such a summons
would be private."

Lak Saa nodded to the onetime blacksmith who stood behind the diplomat. The tip of the metal rod was nearly white-
hot. Hybatha screamed as the LaNorian applied the instrument
to her right ear, felt her knees buckle, and fell into the void.
It was peaceful there but the sensation was short-lived.

A Tro Wa functionary threw a half bucket of water into the
off-worlder's face, saw her splutter, and nodded to the guards.

They jerked Hybatha up off the ground and held the diplomat by her arms.

"Now," Lak Saa continued, "I will ask again . . . Why did Shi Huu summon you to the palace?"

The Thraki tried to look back over her shoulder but the guards jerked on her arms. Her voice was less certain now—and the tone more conciliatory. "I don't know—honest I don't. It was a summons, an order to appear, but no reason was given."

Hybatha heard her flesh sizzle as the rod touched her left ear and the smell of singed fur hung in the air. She staggered, but was held erect, as another bucket of water was dumped over her head. Lak Saa selected a piece of fruit from a plate to his right, plopped the morsel into his mouth, and popped the delicate skin. Sweet juice flooded his mouth. "Let's try again . . . "Why did the Empress summon you to the palace?"

Ambassador Hybatha told the rebel leader about the subsea mineral deposits, the number of soldiers inside Mys, how much ammunition they had, and anything else that he wanted to know. Finally, having been spread-eagled at the center of the hodo, and tortured for many hours, the Thraki diplomat was forced to apologize for all the casualties inflicted on the Claw during the last twenty-seven hours, and disemboweled.

Later, just after the evening meal had been eaten, the Tro Wa used an old-fashioned catapult to lob the diplomat's head over Polwa's North Gate and into Mys. Ironically, it was the same noncom who had saluted Hybatha earlier in the day who retrieved her head.

The cathedral, the first and only such structure on LaNor, had been modeled on one back on Earth. Frank Busso wasn't sure which one, only that it was far larger than it needed to be, and that the money used to build it would have been better spent on the poor. To her everlasting credit Spiritual Director Abigail Abernathy had gone into one of the southern provinces on a rescue mission shortly before the siege began and hadn't been heard from since. There was the possibility that she had taken refuge somewhere, and would emerge when the hostilities ended, but the Bussos had very little hope.

Still, the missionaries knew what Abigail would want, and were determined to bring it about. There was no way to know what would happen to Mys, but the LaNorian converts would need protection, and the Bussos were determined to provide it. The civilian labor brigade started by Chien-Chu and furthered by· others had already built a protective wall around the church, but there was still work left to do, and no one understood the urgent need for such preparations better than Frank and Bethany Busso.

The missionaries, with help from converts like Yao Che, Pwi Qwi, and Hwa Nas, rolled up their sleeves and went to work. The logs taken from the rafts were difficult to move, but Yao Che took pleasure in the fact that they had been taken from the spirit grove near his home, and knew that once in position they would continue to protect the villagers of Nah Ree.

Garbage was a problem, a *big* problem, and all of it belonged to Vanderveen. Originally, before the siege, all manner of trash had been loaded onto a train of two-wheeled carts and taken out through the North Gate to a landfill located five miles north of Mys. That's where the noxious stuff would be dumped, "pickers" would sift through it looking for items of value, and the teamsters would take a break before returning to the city.

Now, with thousands of refugees to care for, Mys was producing even more trash but had no way to export it. So, faced with the choice of dumping the garbage into the much-abused Jade River, or starting what she thought of as a holding area, the diplomat had chosen to store the waste in the once fashionable residential area just north of the Transcendental Cathedral. The very place she had lived prior to the siege—but which had since been reduced to a collection of badly charred ruins. And that's where the diplomat was, watching as her convoy of filthy carts rolled past a burned-out apartment building, when she heard a noise behind her.

The diplomat turned to find Santana standing there, inexplicably neat in a fresh set of camos, his assault rifle slung over his shoulder. He grinned. "Hi. Captain Seeba-Ka tells me that I had my own guardian angel last night. I came to thank you."

Suddenly tears welled up in Vanderveen's eyes and the next thing the foreign service officer knew she was wrapped in Santana's arms, her face buried in his shoulder.

The legionnaire held her for a moment, glorying in the smell of her hair, and the way her body felt next to his. Then he pushed her away. Not far, just enough to wipe the tears away with the ball of his thumb, and kiss her on the lips. They were soft, and seemed to melt under his, as Vanderveen's hands came up to touch the back of the platoon leader's neck. Finally, as the kiss ended, she looked into his eyes. "Do you remember what you said? That there are times when nothing less than everything will do?"

Santana nodded soberly. "Yes, I do."

"Well," the diplomat said softly, "you were right."

13

ABOARD THE SYNDICATE VESSEL *GUERRO*, OFF RIM WORLD CR-9512

Captain Sari Hiko sat and stared out the viewport at the wreckage of Legion Outpost NB-23-11/E which co-orbited CR-9512 along with the Syndicate warships *Guerro* and *Ibutho*. Now little more than a half-slagged mass of metal, the outpost had once been part of the now-defunct Early Warning System (EWS), still under construction on the day that the Thrakies dropped into the system, destroyed the habitat, and went on to attack the Confederation itself. A war they subsequently lost.

But the ex–naval officer's mind wasn't really focused on the remains of NB-23-11/E—or the brownish planet that hung beyond her. Hiko had three problems: the need for critical spares, the idiot in command of the *Ibutho*, and a lack of agreement regarding what the two ships should do next. Of the three the last was the most urgent.

Fesker, the bozo who had been elected to command the *Ibutho*, disagreed with her. *He* felt that all the ships needed to do was roam the Rim, throw their weight around, and take whatever they wanted.

She knew that such a course would alienate the rimmers, the very people the Syndicate depended upon for intelligence reports, logistical support, and new recruits. Not only that but the sort of activities Fesker advocated would eventually stimulate reprisals by the Confederacy. Hell, the only thing that surprised her was the fact that the zoo they called a senate hadn't already authorized a punitive expedition.

But that would come, yes it would, and what then? Take on the Confed navy? Run like hell? Neither option made much sense. They would lose a pitched battle . . . and there was no place to run to. Not within explored space.

That was why Hiko, and those who supported her, favored a course that was diametrically opposed to that advanced by Fesker. She and her crew wanted to refit both ships, load them with supplies, and head out into the endless night. Because somewhere out there, beyond the Rim and the reach of the law, an Earth-like planet waited. One on which all of them could make new homes.

Yes, so-called civilization would eventually find the world, but not until the present generation were safely in their graves. The notion pleased Hiko and she smiled. Of course founding a colony was an iffy thing at best, especially with a single ship, which was why a deal was important.

Hiko's thoughts were interrupted as the intercom chimed. The voice was female and belonged to her adjutant. "Carly Prosser's shuttle just landed in the launch bay, Captain. She has two associates with her. Shall I send them up?"

"No, I'll come down. Go ahead and pressurize the bay. I want to see what they have. Oh, and send for the chief engineer . . . He'll want to be in on this, too."

"Yes, ma'am." There was a *click* as the intercom went dead.

Hiko felt a sense of anticipation as she headed for the lift tube. Fesker didn't know about the spares, and were Hiko to buy *all* of them, the other commanding officer would find himself in a tight spot. Fesker would have to accede to her wishes, find parts somewhere else, or risk a catastrophic failure. Yes, the *Ibutho*'s crew had voted Fesker in, but they could also vote the bastard *out*, which was exactly what Hiko had in mind.

Air had been pumped into the launch bay, which meant that Prosser, Booly, and Maylo could move about without the protection afforded by space armor. The samples had already been unloaded from the shuttle by the time Hiko appeared on the scene and Booly was nervous. More than that, he was tired of the act that he, Maylo, and the entire crew of the *Solar Princess* had been forced to put on during the trip from Nexus.

But the ruse had been successful and Prosser had led them to the Syndicate's lair. And not just them, but a heavily cloaked naval vessel, loaded with commandos.

Prosser went to meet the diminutive-looking pirate while Booly and Maylo waited to be introduced. The two women spoke for a moment before turning to approach the shuttle. Metal pinged as the drive tubes continued to cool. Prosser smiled. "Captain Hiko, I would like to introduce Lonny Fargo, and his associate, Ms. Star."

Hiko shook Fargo's hand, made note of the firm grip, and eyed his so-called "associate." Mistress was more like it, although the woman looked more intelligent than most arm candy, and somewhat familiar as well. Had they met before? No, Hiko didn't think so, but the impression lingered.

The ex–naval officer released Maylo's hand and gestured toward the open crates. "So, Carly tells me you have some spare parts for sale, let's take a look."

Maylo noticed that the other woman's black pageboy haircut would still pass a formal inspection, her insignia-free uniform had been freshly starched, and her shoes glowed with polish.

Though reluctant to bring all of the parts aboard lest the Syndicate simply steal them, Booly had allowed Prosser to talk him into bringing some samples. The *Guerro*'s chief engineer, a taciturn man named Gunther Womack, showed up just as they were about to inspect one of four actuator coils that Booly and Maylo had for sale. He had bushy eyebrows, a slash-shaped mouth, and a viselike grip. Though normally somewhat dour a single glance at the parts arrayed in front of him was enough to make his face light up. He lifted the coil out of its padding the way a mother might lift a baby. His eyes glittered with avarice. "Is she new?"

Booly noted that the part, like the ship it might eventually become part of it, had already been gifted with the female pronoun. He shook his head. "No, it's reconditioned, but just as good as new."

The engineer examined the actuator coil from every possible angle, gave what might have been a grunt of satisfaction, and lowered the device back into its shipping crate. "We'll need to run some tests . . . but she *looks* good."

The rest of the inspection took about fifteen minutes and culminated in a brief conversation between Hiko and Womack. Then, as the engineering officer marched away, Hiko looked to Prosser. "Gunther says the shift locks were in service before he was, and his techs need to run tests on the nav interface, but we can talk."

Prosser knew a bargaining position when she heard one, exchanged looks with Booly, and went to work. While the two women discussed the deal, the soldier tried to look interested, and examined the bay. It was big enough to accommodate the *Princess*. But, rather than unload parts, the freighter would disgorge as many commandos as Booly could cram into her hull, and they would take control of the bay.

Once the boarding party was in control, and had the doors locked into the open position, two dozen assault boats, all loaded with troops, would enter the *Guerro* and land. Meanwhile, the Confederacy warship *Kendo* would turn the Thraki-designed cloaking device off, and call on the *Ibutho* to surrender. The Syndicate ship would get *one* chance, and one chance only, before the *Kendo* opened fire. Under no circumstances would the renegade vessel be allowed to compute and execute a hyperspace jump.

It would have been nice to have two cruisers at his disposal, or *ten*, but there was no time to send for reinforcements. Nor any need assuming that everything went according to plan. Of course that was a big if since there were plenty of things that could go wrong.

"What do you think?" Prosser inquired. "Does that price seem fair to you?"

The legionnaire discovered that he hadn't been paying attention—and had little choice but to go along. "Sure, *if* we get half up front, and *if* we split your commission."

Prosser looked at Hiko. The renegade frowned. "Okay, but the samples stay *here*, and so does Ms. Star."

Booly was already forming the word "no," when his wife touched his arm. "Don't worry, hon, it'll be fun to be on a larger ship for a change. Maybe I can get my hair done." The message in her eyes was clear, General Bill Booly might be the kind of man who wouldn't leave his lover on a Syndicate ship, but Lonny Fargo definitely wasn't. Not only that, but she could handle the situation, or believed that she could.

The officer shrugged. "Okay, I'll be back in about eight hours, so don't get too comfy. How 'bout you Carly? Would you like to come with me? Or stay on the *Guerro*?"

"I think I'll stay," the go-between replied, "if it's all the same to you."

Booly was pleased but tried to hide it. He *liked* Prosser, in spite of the line of business she was in, and hadn't been looking forward to having her confined to the *Kendo*'s brig. "Sure, whatever. Now, if someone would so good as to bring me a large load of money, I'll get the heck out of here."

It took the better part of thirty minutes for the renegades to come up with the first payment and bring it to the launch bay. It consisted of some extremely rare minerals rather than seldom-used currency, but the truth was that the Syndicate could have paid him off with Drang jungle berries and Booly would have been happy to receive them. The hard part was saying good-bye to Maylo without saying any of the things that he wanted to. But Booly climbed the roll-up stairs, waved from the top, and entered the shuttle.

Fifteen minutes later, after the vessel had departed, Hiko spoke with her adjutant. She was an earnest youth who had been recruited *after* the great mutiny. Her name was Combi. She had serious eyes, bad skin, and wore a uniform that looked exactly like the captain's. The twosome stood in the traffic control booth looking out over the launch bay. A flight of interceptors were lined up for launch waiting for the final "go." Controllers murmured in the background. "So, Combi, did you take the pictures like I asked you to?"

"Yes, ma'am," the youth said earnestly, "and I sent the images to the folks in the data section. They compared them with all the news-related pix on file and came up with three positive hits. Here they are."

"Yes!" Hiko exclaimed as she accepted the hard copy, "I knew I had seen Star somewhere." The senior officer scanned the articles. Two of them included pictures, both of which showed a slightly younger version of the woman known as Star, though the captions identified her by a different name. Both agreed that she was Maylo Chien-Chu, president of Chien-Chu Enterprises, and a somebody in the world of business. A relative of the famous Sergi Chien-Chu perhaps? Yes, a niece according to the article, who ran the company's day-to-day affairs on behalf of her uncle.

Hiko frowned. So, what was the niece of some billionaire ex-politician doing with a piece of space debris like Lonny Fargo? Had she run off with him? Maybe. Half the people on the Rim were on the lam from something. "And Fargo? What about him?"

Combi shook her head. "Nothing in the news, ma'am."

Hiko sighed. The problem was that just about all of the stuff stored in the ship's computers predated the mutiny and the moment when the ship's original commanding officer ordered the long irreversible jump out to the Rim. Fargo could have been front-page news the next day, and Hiko would have no way to know.

"Okay, keep the Chien-Chu woman under surveillance and don't let her see anything important. Her boy friend will be back in about seven hours. Thirty minutes before he comes aboard I want her placed under guard and brought to me. Understand?"

Combi *didn't* understand, not really, but knew how to follow orders. She bobbed her head and used the same military lingo that the old-timers did. "Ma'am, yes ma'am."

"Good," Hiko said, pushing the matter from her mind. "Let's work on a message to Captain Fesker. He, along with the cretins who decided to follow him, can either get with the program or wait to see which type of major malfunction will transform their ship into a death trap. I can't wait to see the expression on the idiot's face."

It was uncomfortable inside the *Solar Princess*, very uncomfortable, but not for long. Fifty heavily armed Naa commandos, all dressed in space armor, had been crammed into the ship's small hull.

Would they be enough? Yes, Booly decided as looked forward over Captain Mort's shoulder, they would have to be. The heads-up display (HUD) was inoperative so long as his visor was up, so the officer checked the wrist terminal strapped on over his armor, and saw that twenty-eight minutes remained to touchdown. He thought about his wife, hoped she was okay, and tried to make time pass more quickly. It didn't.

Maylo Chien-Chu was on the run. Hiko was on to the operation, to some extent at least, something which had become obvious when the escort she had been assigned called her by her real name. A sure sign that her cover had been blown.

But the petty officer wasn't aware of his slip which gave the executive the opportunity she needed. They were about to pass through a hatch on their way to the ship's commissary when Maylo executed a reverse kick, felt her boot connect with the sailor's knee, and heard him grunt in pain.

The noncom landed on his butt, the business executive scooted through the hatch, and palmed a large red button. The emergency hatch slammed closed interrupting whatever it was that the crew member had been trying to say as he held his knee and rocked back and forth.

Maylo ran. The plan, such as it was, consisted of hiding until her husband retook the ship. They would be waiting for him, that much was obvious, but the Naa were tough. If anyone could secure the launch bay they could. But if the Syndicate had a gun to her head Booly might cave in. The thought both pleased and horrified her which was the reason why she needed to hide.

Working in her favor was the fact that the renegades had dispensed with their original uniforms in favor of whatever each individual chose to wear. That would enable Maylo to blend in—but not for long as the search became more intense.

Now, as she took a series of random turnings, the executive looked for a place where she could take refuge. The opportunity came when she saw a sign that read, CREW QUARTERS, FEMALE PERSONNEL ONLY," and followed a series of bulkhead-mounted decals into a communal lounge equipped with easy chairs, a large holo tank, and cubicles where women could tap into a broad range of on-line resources.

Half a dozen crew members were present but none of them even looked up from what they were doing as Maylo crossed the common area and entered the rack stacks beyond. The bunks were piled three high, padded to protect the occupants if the argrav generators failed, and equipped with privacy curtains. A sign cautioned QUIET! and the lights were intentionally low.

It quickly became apparent from the names posted over each rack, not to mention the personal effects stored within, that the bunks were assigned. Some appeared to be occupied by off-duty personnel although it was difficult to tell if the curtains were drawn.

That being the case Maylo looked for one that was unoccupied, prayed that its owner wouldn't come back anytime soon, and climbed inside. The executive figured that anyone presently on duty was likely to remain so once the attack started.

Maylo heard a commotion, guessed that a search was under way, and jerked the curtains. Then, having rolled over to face the pictures taped to the bulkhead, she pulled a blanket up over her clothes. And that's where she was, staring at a picture of a woman with two children, when someone knocked on the metal above her rack. Rings rattled as the curtain was pulled to one side. The voice was female. "Chief Hosker?"

Maylo answered without turning. "Yeah?"

"Aren't you supposed to be on duty?"

"Yeah, but I'm not feeling well. Some kind of bug."

"Okay, but be sure to log out next time."

"Sure, sorry about that. I had to barf, and it slipped my mind."

"No problem. We're looking for a stray . . . A Eurasian woman with hair like yours. Call security if you see her."

"Roger that," Maylo said, allowing the pillow to muffle her words.

"Good," the voice said, and Maylo heard the other woman continue down the corridor. The businesswoman looked at her watch. Her husband was due to arrive in the launch bay in about three minutes. Her heart beat like a kettledrum. She lay on the bunk and prayed.

The launch bay was open to space and armored crew members were still in the process of spilling out onto the deck when the *Solar Princess* swooped in through the widely yawning hatch. Booly knew the operation had been blown the moment he saw the heavily armed troops exiting the internal locks and forming up on the deck. Should he run for it? Leaving both Maylo and chance of success behind? Or risk everything and go for it? The decision had to be made in a matter of seconds and he made it. "Strafe the deck," Booly ordered grimly, "but don't destroy the locks. We need a way to enter the rest of the ship."

Though not known for his innovative leadership style Captain Henry Mort knew how to follow orders and did so. The *Princess* had two secondary weapons turrets. Dozens of renegades fell as both burped blue light.

Captain Hiko swore as she witnessed the devastation from her location in the Traffic Control Center. It had been her hope to capture the parts without firing a shot. "Close the outer doors! Trap the bastards inside! No heavy weapons! I want those parts intact."

"Aye, aye," the ship's master at arms acknowledged from the deck below, and went to work.

The *Solar Princess* had landed by that time and commandos were jumping down onto the steel plating. A group of renegades opened fire on them and they fired back.

"I'm about to bail out," Booly said, still addressing his comments to the ship's master. "The moment the last legionnaire clears I want you to place the ship directly under the port hatch. It's pretty obvious we won't be able to access the controls in the next few minutes and we have to block at least one door so the assault boats can get in."

"She'll be crushed," the retired naval officer replied, "those doors are heavy."

"So be it," Booly responded. "Maybe my wife can write it off somehow . . . Make sure that the crew gets clear."

"Roger that," Mort replied grimly. "There's four troopers to go. It looks like you'll be the last."

Booly took the hint, turned, and made his way to the lock. Energy bolts splashed the hull as he jumped, and his boots had barely touched the metal deck, when the spaceship rose on its repellors, slid across the deck and stopped under a blastproof door. It was halfway down by then which meant it was only a matter of seconds before durasteel met durasteel. There was no sound, not in a vacuum, but there was no mistaking the way the door knifed into the freighter's reentry-scarred hull and forced the metal to fold before eventually grinding to a halt.

The remaining opening was no more than fifty feet high. Large enough for a well-piloted assault boat to squeeze through? They would soon know the answer.

More renegades flooded out onto the deck, small-arms fire lashed back and forth, and Booly left that part of the battle to Lieutenant Hardkill, an extremely competent officer who definitely knew his business.

The more pressing matter, from Booly's perspective at least, was to secure at least one of the two locks that opened into the launch bay, both to gain access to the rest of the ship, and as the first step in finding his wife.

And that's where he was, watching a demolition charge being placed, when the first assault boat slipped in under the now-blocked door, completed a full circuit of the cavernous bay, and touched down off to one side.

Both the *Guerro* and the *Imbulo* were equipped with interceptors, at least fifty each, but so was the *Kendo*. Booly could only assume that there was one hellacious battle taking place outside the ship's hull and knew that each assault craft that made it through the gap had run a gauntlet of fire.

The commandos blew the lock as the third assault boat landed and a nasty compartment-to-compartment battle ensued. It lasted for the better part of two standard days and ended 257 lives before Captain Hiko finally agreed to surrender.

Fesker, who attempted to escape in an interceptor shortly after the battle started, had been captured by then, as was his heavily damaged ship.

All of which was nice but nothing compared to the moment when Booly found Maylo safe and sound, wearing someone else's space armor, and helping care for some of the *Guerro*'s casualties.

Things were busy after that as the Naa struggled to deal

with thousands of prisoners, prize crews were put aboard the recaptured warships, and plans were made to return the vessels to Earth orbit.

The better part of a week later, while headed for Legion headquarters on Algeron, there was time to talk. The *Guerro's* gig wasn't especially fancy, but it was spaceworthy, and that was all the couple cared about. Booly's bare chest made a pillow for Maylo's head. The NAVCOMP was piloting the ship and the gig was in hyperspace. The soldier stared at the nondescript overhead. "Sorry about your ship . . . but it made one hell of a doorstop."

"You mean *our* ship," his wife corrected him, "you married into money, remember? But I'll submit a request for compensation."

"You'll be an old lady by the time the Senate gets around to approving *that*."

"Probably," Maylo agreed, "so I won't hold my breath. In the meantime, there's plenty to do."

"Like what?" Booly inquired lazily.

"Like this," his wife replied, "and this, and *this*."

"Oh," Booly said contentedly. "*That*. We could certainly spend some time doing *that*. And they did.

PLANET HUDATHA, THE CONFEDERACY OF SENTIENT BEINGS

As if exhausted by the turbulence elsewhere the air around the castle was clear and still. There were clouds to the north, south, east and west but none over Cragmount, the castle built by Hiween Doma-Sa's ancestors more than a thousand years before and still guarded by members of the clan.

It was a large keep, perched on top of a crag from which it took its name, and accessible only by air or the long winding trail that originated in the fertile valley below. The path was so narrow that it was known as "the squeeze" and forced enemies to approach the fortress two abreast.

It was cold, *very* cold, and the Triad could see puffs of his own lung-warmed air as he stepped out onto one of the castle's many balconies to begin his morning workout. The sword called the *Head Taker* was nearly as old as the fortress itself having been born in the castle's forges hundreds of years before. As with all such weapons it had two edges, one straight, and one with razor-sharp teeth. The highly polished metal reflected shards of sunlight as it swept through the air.

Doma-Sa remembered the duel he had fought with the War Orno, one of Senator Orno's two egg mates, and the feel of the sword sinking into the Ramanthian's belly. *Head Taker* had gone hungry since then, and that was a good thing, since enough blood had been spilled. A new viewpoint, since there had been a time when Doma-Sa would have cheerfully murdered every alien he could lay his hands on but his attitudes had changed. For the betterment of the race? Or to its disadvantage? Only history would tell. Still, to practice the art of war was as natural to the Hudathan as breathing, and the puffs of vapor came more frequently as the Triad fought a file of imaginary enemies.

The War Commander sensed a presence behind his back, brought his right foot down, and used it to pivot. The page, a youngster of fifteen, stood absolutely motionless as the razor-sharp blade flashed through the air and stopped a finger's width away from his throat. Doma-Sa held the sword to the youngster's throat for a period of five heartbeats before allowing it to fall. "That was close . . . you could have been killed."

The youth shifted his weight subtly. "I was never in any danger, sire."

Doma-Sa considered the answer. Toro-Sa was correct, since he had no intention of killing his own son, but others of his rank were not so safe. Familial murder, especially in the pursuit of power, was an accepted tool in Hudathan society. The Triad offered an expression so subtle that only another member of his race would have recognized it as a smile. "No, son, you weren't. But don't grow lax. What do you have for me?"

"A message, sire, from Triad Infana-Ka."

Doma-Sa frowned. "From Ifana-Ka? That's unusual. What did he have to say?"

Toro-Sa activated a vocorder and held the device up so his father could hear. There was no mistaking the other Triad's gruff voice. "It's past midnight, and I have visitors. It seems that Hasa-Ba is here and wants to see me. Chances are that it's nothing, but if I turn up dead, don't believe whatever dra they tell you."

Typical of Ifana-Ka there was no good-bye—just a hard metallic *click*.

What felt like ice water trickled into Doma-Sa's veins. His voice sounded no different than it had before but Toro-Sa knew that his father was upset. He could see it in the subtle tightening of the clan leader's jaw. "Call the captain of the guard, put the entire complex on alert level one, and send the following message to Ifana-Ka: 'Are you alive? If so, prove it.' Do it *now*."

Toro-Sa knew that "now" meant *"now,"* and was gone in a flash.

Doma-Sa eyed the sky and wondered how many satellites, spy drones, and rock-crawling remote-imaging robots were watching him at that particular moment. An attack if any would almost certainly come from the sky.

But logical though the theory was the *real* danger had already passed the outermost ring of defensive sensors and was climbing toward the keep above. Not just climbing, but *running* up through the squeeze as if the narrow passage were level, never pausing to take a rest. That was because the entire assault force was comprised of Hudathan cyborgs all of whom were members of the Ba clan.

They were huge creatures each armed with an electronically driven six-barreled fully automatic projectile weapon plus a fast-recovery missile launcher. They were fast, they were armored, and they were mean. Something the humans had learned during the last Hudathan war. They were also barred from participating in military actions on Hudatha's surface—a prohibition that Hasa-Ba had chosen to ignore.

The captain of the guard dispatched a fast-reaction force that moved to block the invaders just as thousands had been blocked before.

But the defenders were bio bods, and the mechanized troops cut through them the way a hot knife cuts through dak, and the cyborgs continued to climb.

Doma-Sa was in the castle's Command and Control Center by then. Cameras mounted on the surrounding cliffs provided the Triad with an excellent view of what was taking place. Doma-Sa noticed that the third cyborg back was different from the others. A design he had never seen before. This particular unit moved on four feet rather than two, and carried a heavily armored rider.

Toro-Sa appeared at his father's side just as the lead borg fired his rocket launcher. There was an explosion as one of the many gates vanished in a flash of light. "A message arrived from Ifana-Ka, sire; he says he's fine."

"So," Doma-Sa said sadly, "they killed him. There was a code—and if Ifana-Ka was alive he would have used it. Their leader, the one riding the specially designed cyborg, that will be Hasa-Ba. It appears that he wants to rule alone."

Toro-Sa eyed the screens. "What will you do, sire?"

"Kill him," Doma-Sa said grimly, "because there is no other way."

The Triad turned to the captain of the guard. "Use the mines. Allow the first four units to survive. Kill the rest."

Meanwhile, a second contingent of defenders had emerged from a side tunnel, only to be blown away in a welter of flesh, blood, and bone. The wash of airborne biomatter splattered across Hasa-Ba's visor as his cybernetic mount galloped through the gruesome spray. He gloried in the moment, the way his force had penetrated deep into the Sa clan's territory, and could practically hear his ancestors as they shouted, "Blood! Blood! Blood!"

But the moment of combat-induced elation was terribly

short-lived as Doma-Sa ordered his captain of the guard to
selectively detonate the mines which lay not only below the
passageway's surface, but within side of the mountain.

The highly directional charges went off in sequence, starting just behind Hasa-Ba and rippling down through the
squeeze. The command-detonated mines exploded upward and
ripped into the cyborg's legs. And, even as that was taking
place, similar devices concealed within the mountain spewed
thousands of steel spheres out across the narrow trail. Some of
the troopers were cut in half, some were decapitated, and others
were thrown off the cliff that bordered that section of the trail.
It was a two-hundred-unit drop to the bottom of the sheer rock
face and none of those who fell survived.

By the time Hasa-Ba turned to look, fully 90 percent of his
assault force lay dead or wounded. The mines were a surprise,
a horrible surprise, and one that he should have anticipated.
Had he been stupid? Arrogant? Or both?

It hardly mattered, as all resistance seemed to melt away
and the Triad rode the highly specialized cyborg toward the
top of the mountain. Hasa-Ba was being herded, like an animal
bound for market, the difference being that he *knew* what
awaited him.

High above, still watching from the Control Center, Doma-
Sa gave further orders. "Kill the lead cyborg."

A technician eyed the screen in front of him, took the slight
time lag into account, and touched a button. The first cyborg
was literally lifted up into the air and pieces of him were still
falling as the surviving units passed through a rain of debris.

"Good," Doma-Sa said matter-of-factly. "Take the last one
now."

Hasa-Ba felt rather than saw the explosion that took the life
of the cyborg immediately to his rear. The resulting shock wave
nudged him in the back and he cursed Doma-Sa with every
obscenity that he knew.

Then, just as the only remaining escort neared the castle

itself, he too was killed leaving only the four-legged mount
and its gore-drenched rider to proceed alone.

Gates slid up and out of the way, weapons tracked the lone
invader, and Hasa-Ba was admitted to the keep's central courtyard. The strange-looking four-legged cyborg was heavily armored but had no offensive capabilities of its own. That meant
Hasa-Ba had been left with nothing other than a sidearm with
which to defend himself. The Triad dismounted, drew the
handgun, and waited to die.

The courtyard, which had been the site of any number of
betrayals, murders, and executions during the last thousand
years was empty. Everywhere the Triad looked he saw nothing
but gray stone, reflective windows, and closed doors. A voice
issued from loudspeakers mounted all around the ancient en-
closure. "Drop your weapon."

Hasa-Ba eyed the galleries above him. "I know you're there
Doma-Sa. If you want my weapon come and get it. I challenge
you to single combat."

The energy bolt seemed to come out of nowhere. It sliced
Hasa-Ba's hand off at the wrist, cauterized the wound, and sent
the weapon clattering to the ground.

Hasa-Ba wanted to scream, managed to restrain himself,
and settled for a grunt instead. He cradled the stump as a door
whined open and Doma-Sa entered the courtyard. The War
Commander held *Head Taker* so that the blade rested on his
right shoulder. He circled the other Triad as if examining a
prize cax. "So you murdered Ifana-Ka, attempted to kill me,
and think you are entitled to single combat. That's the most
absurd thing I've ever heard . . . Now, tell me about the rest
of the plot, *all* of it."

"There is nothing more," the other Triad lied. "I tried to
seize control of the government and failed. Do with me whatever you will."

Light flashed as *Head Taker* swept through the air, nicked
the back of Hasa-Ba's neck, and drew blood. The Hudathan

lurched forward, managed to catch himself, and swayed from side to side.

"Have it your way," Doma-Sa said. "As the sole surviving member of the Triad, I will outlaw your clan, erase the name 'Ba' from all of the historical records, and reduce your castle to rubble."

Had Doma-Sa threatened to torture Hasa-Ba, or members of his immediate family, the Triad would have laughed. His life was over, and as for his relatives, they could look after themselves. But the erasure of his clan, of thousands of years' worth of achievements, *that* was unbearable.

"All right," Hasa-Ba said through clenched teeth, "there's no need to punish the dead. I cut a deal with the Ramanthians, with Senator Orno, to steal part of the Sheen fleet. I urge you to honor that agreement, to take the alien ships, and restore Hudathan sovereignty. You'll be a hero, the people will honor you, and your clan will celebrate your name."

"But *how?*" Doma-Sa demanded. "The Sheen vessels remain under heavy guard."

Hopeful that his plan might live on beyond his death Hasa-Ba hurried to explain. He felt dizzy and it took all of his strength to remain standing. "Senator Orno smuggled the parts required to construct a bomb onto the *Friendship*. When it goes off every naval vessel in the Arballan system will rush to the rescue. That's when the Ramanthians, along with forces under my command, will make their move."

Doma-Sa felt movement behind him, heard Toro Sa yell "Father!" and turned in the direction of the threat. Though unarmed the cybernetic steed had a mind, an identity, and a set of loyalties. The enormous electromechanical beast reared up on its hind legs, took three steps forward, and brought its front feet downward. They were shod with steel and could easily crush the Triad's skull.

Doma-Sa stepped in past the metal hooves, shoved the ancient blade up through the cyborg's lightly armored abdomen, and saw as well as felt a bright blue electrical discharge ripple along *Head Taker*'s length. The resulting shock knocked the Hudathan off his feet, which was just as well since a half dozen energy beams converged on the cyborg, and it crashed to the ground.

That was the moment when Doma-Sa heard the single gun-shot and rolled over to discover that Hasa-Ba had recovered his handgun. But Toro-Sa had seen the move and fired his weapon first. The top of the other Triad's head was missing along with any additional information that might have been contained there.

A strange sort of silence descended on the courtyard as Doma-Sa struggled to his feet, discovered that his right arm was completely numb, and that he couldn't grip the sword. It remained on the ground. The Triad looked up, toward the galleries above, and Toro-Sa looked back. The single nod was both a gesture of thanks and respect—a moment the youth would never forget.

It took the better part of three days to mobilize Doma-Sa's supporters, establish an alliance with Ifana-Ka's clan, and take Hasa-Ba's lieutenants into custody.

Then, confident that the interim government he had put in place could hold long enough for him to visit the *Friendship*, Doma-Sa boarded the fastest ship available. He knew who was involved in the plot, and he knew how they planned to execute the theft, but the question was when. In a day? A week? A month? There was no way to be sure. All he could do was head for Arballa, get there as quickly as possible, and hope for the best. The ship lifted, broke free of the planet's gravity well, and entered hyperspace. There was nothing the Hudathan could do but wait.

PLANET ARBALLA, THE CONFEDERACY OF SENTIENT BEINGS

In spite of a passion for privacy there were times when it paid to be well-known, which was why Sergi Chien-Chu had chosen to leave the muscular "Jim James" body on his yacht and wear what the industrialist thought of as the "political" body, a vehicle very similar to his original biobod.

The face had a rounded slightly Asian cast, the torso had some extra padding, and the clothing was extremely plain. It was a nondescript body, but one that was familiar to billions of sentients, including those who trod the *Friendship*'s corridors. Many waved and called the ex-president by name. Chien-Chu nodded politely, and paused to speak with those he knew, but kept a close eye on the time. The industrialist had been aboard the massive ship for sixteen hours by then, been granted a meeting with President Nankool, and had his worst fears realized.

In spite of the fact that the urgent requests for reinforcements had arrived from LaNor more than a week before, no action had been taken, and the matter was still under discussion. It seemed that while the relief forced had been assembled, and stood ready to jump, the so-called peace coalition, which was led by the likes of Senator Alway Orno, was essentially holding the relief force hostage while they argued in favor of downsizing the military.

Now, given Chien-Chu's arrival, and familiarity with the situation on LaNor, those who favored both the relief force and a healthy defense budget hoped that the impasse could be broken. Such was the closed world on board the *Friendship*, and the buzz that accompanied Chien-Chu's testimony, that the Senate was packed by the time the industrialist arrived. The ongoing animosity between the ex-politician and Senator Orno was well documented, and no one wanted to miss the fun.

The Ramanthian, who was well aware of the way his peers were watching him, had used a tool arm to preen the areas to either side of his parrotlike beak. The last few weeks had been extremely difficult. First there had been the need to act as if everything was normal, which explained why he had led the effort to downsize the defense budget and worked to stall the relief force.

Second, there was the need to finalize the necessarily complex arrangements by which Ramanthian forces would coordinate with the Hudathans in order to hijack the Sheen fleet, a task that involved scores of encrypted communications, not to mention some secret face-to-face meetings.

Third, and most wearing for him personally, was the task of assembling the bomb deep within one of the *Friendship*'s cavernous holds. A task that he could entrust to no one else . . . yet bore tremendous risk. What if he were discovered? Or, worse yet, accidentally triggered the device?

Yes, it had been an extremely wearing time, and now as his old nemesis Chien-Chu entered the Senate chambers, Orno prepared to make one more sacrifice on behalf of his people. The relief force could be delayed no longer, the Ramanthian knew that, which meant that Chien-Chu would be seen as the victor in the ensuing confrontation.

The resulting loss of face would be nothing less than humiliating, and other senators would sneer at him behind his back, but there was one consolation: Soon, within a matter of days, most if not all of them would be dead.

Chien-Chu was both surprised and embarrassed by the rattle of applause that greeted his arrival in the Senate chambers and even more flustered by the standing ovation that followed. The fact that President Nankool had not only requested that Chien-Chu be allowed to testify regarding the situation on LaNor, but that the chief executive had agreed to introduce the cyborg, gave his testimony that much more weight.

The applause faded as Nankool took the opportunity to remind those present of Chien-Chu's many accomplishments. Then, as the industrialist mounted the riser and took his place at the podium, the senators came to their feet once more.

Chien-Chu motioned for the politicians to take their seats and cleared his throat. "Thank you for the warm reception . . . I won't let it go to my head however. There have been times over the years when at least half the beings in this chamber would have cheerfully blown me out of the nearest lock."

The senators laughed, snorted, and hooted, all according to their various physiologies.

"But those days are in the past," the cyborg said, his eyes sweeping the audience. "Because the matter I wish to put before you today is one that I believe all of us can agree on—the urgent need to send a relief force to CR-9765 otherwise known as LaNor.

"What I'm about to show you is video taken weeks *after* the initial message torps were sent. Conditions had deteriorated a great deal by the time I left as these pictures will make clear."

The ensuing presentation included hundreds of images captured through the cyborg's high-quality optics and stored in his onboard computer. The industrialist provided a running narration as his audience looked through his eyes to the encampments beyond the city's much-abused walls, walked among the bullet scarred buildings, and labored to build defensive barricades. They saw families camped in doorways, the blood-spattered triage center that occupied the Strathmore Hotel's lobby, and stacks of bodies sitting in what had once been a flower garden.

One member of the audience, a high-ranking diplomat named Charles Winther Vanderveen, saw something else. He saw a young woman dressed in a filthy jumpsuit, standing on a pile of rubble, directing some sort of work project. Christine was alive! Or had been a few weeks before. His chest swelled with pride and he fought to hold back the tears that threatened to spill down his cheeks.

For weeks Vanderveen had been struggling to obtain the support necessary to release the relief force and here was proof that he'd been correct about the urgency of the situation on LaNor. But would the beings around him listen? Or were they so lost in the labyrinth of political gamesmanship that they would allow the entire population of Mys to be slaughtered? The next few minutes would tell.

"And so," Chien-Chu concluded, as the final picture faded to black, "I think you'll agree that the situation qualifies as desperate. It's my understanding that this matter will be subject to a vote in the next hour or so—and I urge all of you to come together in a unanimous show of support for the diplomats, soldiers, and citizens now trapped on LaNor. Thank you."

Charles Vanderveen was heartened by the round of applause that followed the cyborg's testimony and continued even as he left the chambers. But applause was one thing—and votes were another. Though due back in his office the diplomat resolved to wait and see what would happen next.

The woman who headed the Confederacy's Department of Intelligence (CONINT) was a very busy person, but then-President Chien-Chu had promoted her out of obscurity back during the second Hudathan war, and she had never forgotten that. That's why she had agreed to scrub an extremely important conference to meet with the industrialist in the privacy of her office. Chien-Chu arrived as he always did, right on time, and they embraced. "Maggie, it's good to see you."

Margaret Rutherford Xanith, better known to friends and enemies alike as "Madame X," smiled. It made her look younger. She had a head of carefully coifed salt-and-pepper hair, a largely unlined face, and bright inquisitive eyes. Once the smile faded away her features returned to a look of perpetual disapproval. The lighthearted form of address took Chien-Chu back to his days as chief executive. "Hey, boss, it's good to see you, too. Nice job this morning."

Xanith returned to her high-backed chair as Chien-Chu took his place on the other side of her metal desk. It supported a comp screen, a palm pad, and a stylus. The rest of the surface was bare—as were the walls of her office. Artifacts of Xanith's private life, assuming she had one, were clearly kept somewhere else. "So, you were there?"

The official shook her head. "No, I watched from here, but the view was fine. I predict that the relief force will be in hyperspace by the end of the day."

"I sure hope so," Chien-Chu replied fervently, "because a lot more people will die if they aren't."

"So," Xanith said tactfully, part of her mind on all the other things she had to accomplish that day, "you had some sort of input for me? Something from LaNor perhaps?"

"Yes," Chien-Chu answered, "although there's a chance that this data might have a bearing on the overall strategic situation, not just LaNor. One of the embassy's junior diplomats, a young woman named Christine Vanderveen became suspicious regarding Ramanthian activities on LaNor, and managed to place a data tap in their computer room."

Xanith's eyebrows shot upward. "*Christine* Vanderveen? As in Charlie Vanderveen's daughter?"

"Yup," the industrialist answered, "one and the same."

"And she did this by herself?"

"No, she had some help," the cyborg replied. "From a Spec 3 named Imbulo. One of your folks perhaps?"

"Maybe," the Intelligence boss allowed evasively, "and maybe not. What Ms. Vanderveen did might be construed illegal—and my people have strict orders to stay within the boundaries of the law."

Like any successful bureaucrat Xanith was "playing to the walls," governmental shorthand for the process of never saying anything that could be recorded and used against them, but Chien-Chu saw a distinct twinkle in the official's eyes and felt sure his old friend knew all about Spec 3 Imbulo and her mission on LaNor.

"Of course," the industrialist responded smoothly. "Should it turn out that Ms. Vanderveen somehow exceeded the limits of propriety, I'm sure that her superiors will find the means to ensure that no further transgressions take place. In the meantime, given the urgency of the situation on LaNor, I wondered if you would have your staff take a look at this."

So saying the cyborg slid the small container that Christina Vanderveen had given him across the surface of Xanith's desk.

She accepted the package, nodded, and raised an eyebrow. "Where will you be?"

"Right here," Chien-Chu replied grimly, "until we know what we have."

Senator Always Orno was elsewhere when the question of the relief force came up for a vote and was unanimously approved. The reason for his absence lay partly in his pride, and a desire to avoid the humiliation attendant on what he viewed as a loss, but there was a pragmatic component as well.

For even as the political community focused its attention on the vote, the Ramanthian was down in one of the *Friend-ship*'s least-visited holds, installing the assembly which would trigger the subnuclear bomb.

Positioned as it was directly below the Senate chambers, and adjacent to one of the vessel's mighty ribs, Orno hoped to eliminate most if not all of the Confederacy's key political leaders, while simultaneously breaking the warship in two. If all went well some of the crew would survive, call for help, and draw the navy away form the Sheen fleet. That was when the Ramanthian forces would strike, thousands of ships would be stolen, and he would return home having revenged the War Orno *and* established his position for all time.

The thought of that made Orno happy, very happy, and the trigger assembly made a positive *click* as it mated with the bomb. It didn't matter what did or didn't happen on the planet called LaNor—the *real* action was going to take place thousands of light-years away.

14

Allies, much like a double-edged sword, have the capacity to cut both ways. Only a fool would trust them.

Grand Marshal Nimu Wurla-Ka (ret.)
Instructor, Hudathan War College
Standard year 1957

THE FOREIGN CITY OF MYS, ON THE INDEPENDENT PLANET OF LANOR

It was still dark when the once renowned Imperial Archers were ordered to march into the heavily cratered no-man's-land that separated the besiegers from the besieged, raise their long-bows, and send hundreds of arrows over the city's walls. His unit was an anachronism, the commanding officer knew that, but still took pride in the way the shafts whispered into the darkness.

Then, having fulfilled their mission, the archers executed a neat about-face and marched back toward the Imperial lines. They were halfway to safety when the flare went off and bathed the battlefield in harsh green-blue light. Most of them made it but six fell to off-world sniper fire.

Santana heard the rush of disturbed air as the arrows passed over his position followed by a wild clatter as they fell inside the city. A legionnaire swore as one of the steel points pene-trated his thigh, and a noncom yelled, "Medic!"

Private Alice Hixon responded, slapped some sealer around

the point of entry, and called for stretcher-bearers. It would require surgery to removed the barbed point and the doctors would be waiting. Ten minutes later the trooper was in the lobby of the Strathmore Hotel having the shaft removed.

Santana was at the wall, watching the last of the archers march out of range, when Sergeant Via appeared at his elbow. "Lieutenant, take a look at this."

The noncom squatted under the protection of the wall while the officer lowered his binoculars and knelt next to him. The noncom played a small flashlight across the arrow as Santana rotated it between his fingertips. A single glance was sufficient to establish the fact that a piece of parchment had been wound around the shaft and secured with a blob of wax. The platoon leader used a thumbnail to break the seal, allowed the paper to unwind, and freed it from the arrow. Text had been printed onto the parchment. Santana eyed the LaNorian script and activated his radio. "Bravo Six to Bravo-Five . . . Have someone find YC and send him to the top of the west wall. Over."

It didn't seem likely that either the Claw or the Imperials had the means to monitor the Legion's radio traffic—but they weren't supposed to have SAMs either. That was why Santana used Yao Che's initials rather than his name. Assuming the youth was fortunate enough to survive there was no point in putting him on someone's hit list.

"This is Bravo Five," Hillrun replied. "He's on the way, over."

The LaNorian arrived five minutes later. He was out of breath as if he had come from a long distance away. "You wanted to see me, Lieutenant?"

"Yes," Santana replied, handing the parchmentlike scroll to the youth. "What does this say?"

Sergeant Via aimed his flashlight at the paper and Yao Che read the words out loud. "To the residents of Mys . . . This is your last chance to take up arms on the side of righteousness. Rise up against the foreign devils, open the gates, and release the cleansing flood. Those who heed the call shall be blessed—

those who ignore it shall suffer the fires. Consider carefully before you choose to align yourselves with defeat."

Via groaned. "Great . . . that's all we need."

Santana met Yao Che's eyes. "Take this to Captain Seeba-Ka. Tell him what it says."

The youngster nodded, scooted along the walkway, and soon disappeared.

The legionnaires stood—careful to keep their heads behind the wall's protective crenellations. "Arrows," Via said, "what will they throw at us next?"

Then, as if in answer to the noncom's question, the wall shook, and a loud boom was heard. "Well," Santana answered dryly, "how 'bout some rather large cannon balls?"

Lak Saa was feeling better, *much* better, and stood with a telescope to his eye. The sun, which had just started to peek over the eastern horizon, provided just enough light to confirm the initial hit. The arrows were intended to have a psychological impact on the aliens, rather than the LaNorians, but who knew? Perhaps some brave soul would open one of the gates. Not that it mattered much since every LaNorian still within the walls would be executed once Mys fell.

In the meantime, with the aid of sympathizers within the Imperial Officer Corps, Lak Saa hoped to create his own door. The point chosen for the breach lay immediately south of the western water gate. A hole there, with a nice pile of rubble on which to climb, would enable Imperial troops to enter the already damaged southwest quarter of the city, the area the devils often referred to as Dig Town," and used as a stage for their drunken revelries. Then, once the Imperials had sacrificed themselves in the breach, Claw warriors would stream into Mys where the true slaughter would begin.

The key to success was the long east–west trench that had been driven in toward the city during the hours of darkness. There were other trenches as well, two of them, which was why the troops called them the triplets, but the others had been dug more to draw attention away from the one in front of him rather than to achieve any particular objective.. The effort to dig the trenches had taken three days and cost sixty-seven lives.

Now, safely ensconced behind a berm of earth and wood the cannon was positioned to pound the western wall into submission. Lak Saa knew enemy shells would rain down on the trench at any moment—but hoped that an attack on the city's North Gate would serve to divide their fire. Could the offworlders repel the new attack? While simultaneously silencing the cannon? He didn't think so. The Thraki ambassador had been most forthcoming during the many hours of torture she had been subjected to, and while the devils had a considerable quantity of small-arms ammunition, there were certain categories of ordnance where their supplies were limited, especially the larger stuff. Time would tell.

Lak Saa brought the Ramanthian-supplied radio up to his lips and squeezed the pincer-friendly side grips. "Start the attack now."

His morning chores completed, the Tro Wa leader retreated to his tent, performed his morning calisthenics, and ate a hearty breakfast.

Though aware of the intermittent *boom* of a cannon off to the southwest, Captain Jonathan Alan Seebo-1,324 had his own problems, and swore as stared out through his binoculars. The Imperials camped opposite the North Gate were in the process of pulling up stakes in order to make a channel through which a phalanx of densely packed troops could pass. The newcomers were still too far away to make out any details regarding their equipment or weapons but there was no doubt regarding their intent: Force the North Gate, join the forces still occupying the northeast sector of Mys, and attempt to break into the rest of the city.

Still looking north, the Clone spoke out of the side of his mouth, knowing that the NCO called Sergeant Twelve would hear. "Put a call into Blood-Six . . . Tell him we have what looks like at least two thousand hostiles incoming from the north. Request support from the heavy weapons company and permission to engage."

Twelve made the call, got a quick response, and turned back to his CO. "Captain Seeba-Ka is on his way. He requests that we feed coordinates to the tube team but hold fire until he arrives."

The officer nodded. "Make it happen . . . and notify the Hudathans. We're going to need more firepower here on the wall."

The Hudathans, under the command of their ambassador, were on a four hour sleep cycle. Seebo hated to wake them up but knew his force of fifty-eight soldiers wasn't going to be able to stop two thousand attackers no matter what kind of technological superiority they had going for them.

It was only a matter of a few minutes before the Hudathan had made his way up onto the wall via the stairs at the northwest corner of the city.

Seeba-Ka paused to acknowledge Captain Seebo's wave, raised his binoculars, and peered out through one of the firing loops that the clones had drilled through the rectangular crenellations. A bullet spanged off rock, and chips flew as a Tro Wa sniper attempted to put a bullet through the four-inch-wide hole.

The legionnaire forced himself to ignore the incoming fire and let the oncoming troops fill his lens. They were closer now, but close enough, so he touched the zoom control. Faces leaped forward, but rather than the hard-core combatants that he expected to see, Seeba-Ka found himself looking at rows of terrified females. Some carried infants, or were trying to deal with the youngsters who clung to their pants, all propelled by what? A hatred of the foreign devils? Or something less obvious?

The Hudathan switched loopholes in an effort to throw the snipers off, reacquired the mob, and tilted the glasses upward. Data scrolled down the right side of the screen as the officer boosted the magnification to max. And there, right where Seeba-Ka expected them to be, were three ranks of males, Claw judging from their clothing, forcing the females forward. The mob was just that, a mob, intended to serve as cannon fodder. The clanless bastards *wanted* him to slaughter the civilians but why? For propaganda reasons? Or something else?

The *boom* of a cannon impinged on Seeba-Ka's consciousness and then he knew. It was a trick! A way to split the mortar fire so that less would fall on the newly active east–west trench! The Hudathan activated his radio. "Blood Six to Charlie Six. Hold your fire! Ignore the civilians at the front and put your snipers to work on the cadre toward the rear. When the mob breaks let the noncombatants escape. Confirm. Over."

Seebo could see the civilians by then and understood the plan. "That's affirmative, Blood Six. Over and out."

New orders went to the tube crews, bombs bracketed the east–west trench, and another cannonball struck the western wall. A cascade of stones fell, the Imperial artillery team cheered, and the battle of attrition continued.

THE CITY OF POLWA, ON THE INDEPENDENT PLANET OF LANOR

The palace was chilly, which accounted for the fact that the Empress Shi Huu had once again decided to spend her morning on the fire throne, where the heat produced by the three coal-fed fires would help warm her old bones. More than five hundred candles burned, their light playing across the mural that wrapped the room, adding their heat to that produced by the metal stoves.

The Empress had chosen to deny the dictates of her seasonal wardrobe and caused quite a stir when she insisted on wearing a summer sheath. It was black with elaborate gold embroidery and fit like a glove. A beautiful dress to be sure, but one which wasn't scheduled to enter the royal rotation for another sixty-seven days, when a crisis was sure to develop. What would the Empress do her retainers wondered? Wear the dress she should have worn earlier? Wear the black dress for a second time during the same year? Or demand something new? It was no small problem and the clock had started to tick.

Now, having dealt with the matters placed before her by Dwi Faa, the Empress inclined her head. "Please clear the court."

Grateful to escape the now-considerable heat, the courtiers bowed, and took turns backing out of the room.

Finally, when only Dwi Faa remained, Shi Huu said, "Thank you, that will be all. Please instruct my majordomo to admit the first guest."

The minister, who would have dearly loved to know the identity of those with whom the Empress was about to speak, bowed low. "Of course, Majesty. Thank you, majesty."

The eunuch had been gone for little more than the time it took for Shi Huu to check her makeup in a tiny finger mirror before the first informant entered the throne room. As with of all his kind the spy wore a hood pierced with eyeholes to protect both his identity and his life. The head covering was made from nondescript brown cloth, as were the clothes he wore, and the rags wrapped around his feet. He bowed, to which Shi Huu responded with an impatient hand. "Yes, yes, please get on with it . . . What little morsels did you bring for me today?"

The informer, who served as third assistant soup chef for one of Polwa's most prosperous merchants, launched into an extremely entertaining account of the manner in which his employer's wife had betrayed her husband with a handsome spice monger from the west. Once the tale was complete Shi Huu opened the wooden box she kept at her side and addressed the spy by the code name she had assigned him. "That was entertaining, my little soup ladle—but essentially worthless. I need information—hence the title *informant*. Did you hear that booming sound? That was a cannon, one of *my* cannons, firing on the west wall. Interesting, isn't it? Especially since I was never consulted in the matter. That, my dear, is the sort of thing an informant should report on.

"So, assuming you wish to please me, which I'm sure you do, focus your efforts on matters of substance. Still, I am generous if nothing else, so here's something for your trouble."

The spy crept forward, accepted a coin, and backed out of the room. A second informer entered seconds later. This individual was notable both because his disguise hung all the way to the floor and because the body within appeared to be badly misshapen.

"So," Shi Huu began, "you come once more. It has been some time since your last visit."

"My duties, plus the hostilities, make it difficult to break free," the informant explained, his words muffled by the hood that he wore. "Still, I have news for Your Majesty, and came as quickly as I could."

The Empress was interested but did what she could to look bored. "And your efforts are appreciated. Please proceed."

Coal black eyes stared at her through the holes in the spy's hood. "The Thraki ambassador attempted to respond to your summons but was intercepted before she could reach the palace."

Shi Huu leaned forward. Here was an informant who not only knew his business, but understood *her* priorities as well. She had been very disappointed when Fynthian Isu Hybatha had failed to appear. There were rumors that the Thraki diplomat had been murdered—but there were rumors that her long-dead husband had been seen walking the streets of Polwa as well. What she needed were facts. "Tell me more . . . Who intercepted the off-worlder—and what became of her?"

"It was Lak Saa," the spy said with certainty, "or those operating on his behalf. The foreign devil was tortured, disemboweled, and beheaded."

"Trust Lak Saa to make sure of his work," the Empress said sarcastically. The lightness of her words belied the way that she actually felt. The loss of Hybatha was a blow, a cruel blow, since it meant any possibility of rejuvenating her increasingly ugly body was now lost. Odds were that the eunuch knew about her new face, had anticipated her desires, and killed the off-worlder out of spite. Assuming the report was true that is.

She eyed her visitor. "Is there any proof of what you say?"

"Yes, Majesty," the informant replied. "The Claw used a catapult to launch the ambassador's head into Mys. Here is a picture of what the Thrakies recovered."

There was a shuffling sound as the informant moved forward. His hand was encased in a black mitten. The photo was held by one corner.

Shi Huu accepted the offering, looked at the print, and marveled at the off-world technology. It was Hybatha all right, or part of her, and the Empress felt a twinge of regret. Not regarding the diplomat's death . . . but the loss incurred by *her*.

"Yes, well, your proof is adequate. It seems that my old friend Lak Saa has lost all sense of propriety. I will find a way to make him pay."

"Of course, Highness," the spy said. "Perhaps I could be of assistance."

"Really?" Shi Huu inquired. "How?"

"Much as I might desire to offer the information as a simple gesture of loyalty—there are other issues I must consider," the informant replied tactfully. "Simply put, once I share what I know, it will no longer be possible for me to return to Mys."

Shi Huu's ear fans twitched in annoyance. "What do you want?"

"I would like a land grant, Majesty, privileges commensurate with noble rank, and the right to recruit and train my own bodyguards."

"How many bodyguards?" the Empress asked suspiciously.

"Five hundred warriors would be sufficient, Highness."

"Done," Shi Huu replied, "*if* I deem the information you provide to be worthy. If not, I shall have your head as recompense for this unseemly haggling. Now divulge what you know."

If the threat bothered him there was no sign of it as the spy spoke. "The Ramanthians have factories out in the country, factories which though completely unguarded, have yet to be touched."

Shi Huu felt a rising sense of excitement. Though aware that the factories had been constructed—she had assumed that the Tro Wa had long since burned them to the ground. "How interesting . . . tell me more."

"In return for protecting their factories, and Lak Saa's assurances that they will be spared in the aftermath of the city's fall, the Ramanthians supplied the Claw with off-world weapons and communications devices. Therefore, if you strike at the factories, you strike at Lak Saa."

It made sense, good sense, but Shi Huu was cautious. "I need proof."

The informant felt a sense of frustration but managed to keep it in check. "The factories remain untouched—and the Tro Wa have off-world weapons. Your military should be able to verify both assertions. The rest is obvious."

"Thank you," Shi Huu said sincerely, "Minister Dwi Faa will handle the administrative aspects of your reward. I suggest that you pay close attention to the discussions, or you could find yourself living on a large chunk of unproductive desert."

"Thank you for the advice, Majesty."

"However," Shi Huu said sternly, "there is one more thing . . . *All* of my nobles are known to me. You must remove the disguise."

There was a pause, as if the spy was hesitant to remove his robes, followed by the rustle of black cloth. It swirled, fell, and puddled on the floor. The Ramanthian bowed. "Specialist Poth Dusso at your service."

The Empress was far from surprised. "So you believe that the off-worlders will lose?"

"Yes, Highness, I do."

"And Lak Saa?"

"Once the Tro Wa enter Mys, they will slaughter everyone, including the staff at the Ramanthian embassy. That's why I chose to leave. However, *if* you destroy the factories, and *if* you cut Lak Saa off from further off-world support, he will be weakened. Order your military to turn on him *now*. Wait, and it will be too late."

The words were more assertive than what Shi Huu was used to, but they rang with truth, and continued to echo long after the Ramanthian had left.

THE FOREIGN CITY OF MYS, ON THE INDEPENDENT PLANET OF LANOR

It was dark, or would have been, had the glare of the generator-powered work lights not pushed the darkness back. Captain Drik–Seeba-Ka stood next to FSO-5 Christine Vanderveen as both stared at the inside surface of the west wall. The entire day had been spent trying to shore up the wall but to no avail. Even as the twosome watched the Imperial cannon boomed, another iron ball struck the severely weakened structure, and workers ran to escape their own falling timbers, an avalanche of stone, and rock fragments that scythed through the air.

"My ancestors fought like this," the Hudathan said somberly. "First you surround the city, then you select a weak point, and put the artillery to work. The inhabitants attempt repairs, but can't keep up, and the breach becomes practical. Counterfire is an option of course, but the defenders must have plenty of ammunition, or the attackers will fire unopposed."

Vanderveen tried to remember the last time she had heard outgoing mortar fire . . . the closest thing the allies had to artillery. She looked up at the legionnaire. "We ran out of rockets, didn't we?"

"They're normally referred to as 'bombs,'" the officer said impassively, "but yes, we fired our last round at 15:32. The cannon had been blown off its carriage by then, but repairs were made, and the battery was back in operation by 1900 hours."

Vanderveen looked at the wall. What remained of the scaffolding that her people had worked so hard to put in place was tilted and appeared ready to fall. The wall, which had appeared intact only thirty minutes before, was cracked. Not only that, but a small hole had appeared at a point roughly fifteen feet off the ground, and would soon grow bigger. "So, what should we do?" the diplomat asked, her voice hard and determined.

"We'll have to pull out of the southwest quadrant," Seeba-Ka said grimly, "cede Dig Town, and try to keep them contained. We still command the top of the walls and that will help."

The diplomat tried to visualize the resulting grid, one in which each side controlled two diagonally opposed quarters of the city, and the manner in which the off-world forces would be cut off from each other. It didn't look good.

"Pull your workers," the legionnaire continued, "and do it *now*. The wall could go at any time and I don't want any civilians in the area when it does."

The cannon fired, the projectile struck the wall very close to the existing hole, and flying rubble sprayed the area within. A LaNorian screamed, one of the work lights crashed to the ground, and the retreat began.

It was dawn on what promised to be a beautiful day. The sky was clear, the sun was out, and a city waited to be conquered. Lak Saa drew the cold morning air deep into his lungs and released it. It felt good to be alive. Thousands of troops, many of whom would be dead by the time the sun arrived at its zenith, stood in hushed silence. The eunuch could hear the gentle *clink* of metal on metal, smell their unwashed flesh, and feel their tightly coiled energy. There was something magical about that, something powerful, something which fed the fire in his soul. Within a matter of minutes, the cannon would fire one last time. This particular shot would have more symbolic than real value because the breach had been practical for hours by then.

However, unlike Lak Saa's troops, who delighted in fighting at night, the Imperials preferred the full light of day. A time when their often poorly trained troops were less likely to march in the wrong direction, open fire on each other, or fall victim to evil spirits. Ah well, the rebel leader consoled himself, given the fact that most of the soldiers in the first few waves were likely to be cut to shreds they should be allowed to die at whatever time they preferred.

The cannon fired, the ball struck the pile of rubble that had accumulated in front of the breach and bounced up through the hole. A signal rocket went off, the Imperials shouted some sort of nonsense about death and glory, and ran toward the breach. That was when the machine guns started to chatter — and the brightly clad LaNorians began to die.

But there were *thousands* of Imperial troops, all of whom had been waiting for weeks with nothing to show for it, and were eager to be the first through the breach. Partly for the glory of it, partly because they had been ordered to do so, but mostly because Mys was rumored to be rich with potential loot. The troops wanted to get their hands on the hodos filled with supplies, the wealth of prosperous refugees, and the weaponry that gave the devils their power.

That meant that even as Santana and his legionnaires fired their automatic weapons there was little that they could do beyond force the oncoming troops to pay for the privilege. And pay they did falling in waves as members of the heavy weapons platoon, sent to the top of the wall for that very purpose, swung their crew-served .50 caliber and 7.62 mm machine guns back and forth.

However, horrible though the slaughter was the LaNorians had more bodies than the off-worlders had bullets, and it wasn't long before a handful of brave Imperials staggered up over the pile of rubble to enter the breach itself. They screamed their victory, staggered under the impact of more .50 caliber slugs, and died as Sergeant Carlos Zook, Corporal Norly Snyder, and two additional T-2s detached from Beckworth's platoon stood on what had been one of Dig Town's busiest streets, and poured fire into the gap. The cyborgs couldn't remain for long, however, not in an area that would clearly be overrun, and backed down the thoroughfare toward Embassy Row and the barricades intended to keep the invaders from flooding into the city.

That's where Mee Mas, along with his increasingly effective force of three hundred irregulars, waited to provide covering fire. Though armed with a hodgepodge of off-world as well as LaNorian weapons, the Freedom Brigade as the prince had named them, had been drilled by none other than First Sergeant Neversmile himself, and were fairly reliable by then. "Hold your fire!" Mee Mas commanded his troops. "Wait for the cyborgs to pass through our lines!"

The LaNorian knew that the T-2's armor would protect them from a few rounds fired from behind, but took pleasure in the fact that discipline held, and all four of the off-world creatures were safely behind the barricades when his newly minted officers gave the orders to open fire.

The Imperials continued to flood in through the breach. They were well mixed with the Tro Wa by then, who rather than pouring into the city as they imagined, found themselves trapped in a killing zone. The weapons on the top of the wall had been turned inward by then, and while free to enter the southwest sector of the city, the invaders had no place to go.

Having been caught win an overwhelming cross fire those fortunate enough to survive did the only thing they could, they hid in the half-burned-out remains of Dig Town's tenements, shops, and hodos, fired on targets of opportunity, and searched for things to eat.

Confident that Mys would fall by early afternoon, and that their troops would feast on the food stored in the city, the Imperial officers had sent their soldiers into battle with no more than a single canteen full of water, four cold kas balls apiece, and a hundred rounds of ammunition. Though successful, the attack had stalled, and the siege continued.

Lak Saa was disappointed by the failure to end the siege, very disappointed, but far from depressed. Progress had been made, the devils had been denied yet another sector of the city, and forced into a pair of boxes which remained linked, but only tenuously so, where their corners touched.

Yes, all things considered the morning could be described as a success, and that was the Tro Wa's state of mind when the Imperial messenger arrived.

Lak Saa accepted the baton, broke the seal, and withdrew the message. It seemed that Sha Nef, one of Shi Huu's more competent generals, wanted to meet with him during the early afternoon. Casualties had been heavy, but the combined assault had been successful, and there were further matters on which the two groups could cooperate. A rather sensible suggestion—and one with which Lak Saa concurred.

Was Sha Nef positioning himself for a position within a Lak Saa-led government? Yes, quite possibly, but so what? All that indicated was that the general was possessed of good sense.

Buoyed by success, as well as the possibility that key military leaders might be interested in joining his cause, Lak Saa sent his reply. Yes, he would be willing to come, and looked forward to doing so.

The messenger departed, the Tro Wa returned to his tent, and was halfway through a sponge bath when the second runner arrived. This one was a member of the Claw, and so dire was the news that he carried, that Dee Waa felt it necessary to interrupt his leader's absolutions and show the youngster into the Lak Saa's tent.

Both visitors stared aghast as Lak Saa stood before them nude, with only a pucker of badly mangled flesh left to mark the spot where his genitals had once hung, soapy water streaming the length of his body to collect in a pan at his feet. The eunuch, who seemed oblivious to their horror, rubbed a rag over the surface of his paunch. "Yes? What could possibly be so urgent that you would need to interrupt my bath?"

Dee Waa, who had obtained a pretty good idea of what the message was likely to say from the youth who bore it, gestured toward the tube. "May I, sire?"

"Please get on with it," the Claw leader said grumpily, applying soapy water to his groin.

The ex-teacher unrolled the parchment and read the text out loud. "The commander of the Hokla District is sorry to inform the supreme commander that the devil factories were attacked by Imperial troops, put to the torch, and destroyed. Local elements of the Tro Wa attempted to stop the Imperials, but were badly outnumbered, and went down to defeat."

Lak Saa swore. Shi Huu! It had to be Shi Huu . . . The old lizard had informers, plenty of them, at least one of whom had figured out the special relationship he had with the Ramanthians. Shi Huu, eager to punish him for killing her pet Thraki, had ordered the factories destroyed.

But wait, the LaNorian thought, the message had other implications as well, some of which were quite unpleasant. If the Empress had decided to move against the factories, it was logical to suppose that she was ready to move against him generally, which meant that the meeting with Sha Nef was likely to be a trap!

Lak Saa snatched a towel off the back of a folding chair, used it to dry his chest, and started to issue orders. The alliance, such as it was, had ended.

Ambassador Pas Rasha's exoskeleton whined intermittently as he made his way into the basement lounge that now served as a multipurpose room and paused to look around. The gray concrete walls, sketchy refreshments, and haggard-looking diplomats were in marked contrast to the pleasant room, heavily loaded buffet table, and well-rested faces that had once defined such occasions.

Not only that, but certain faces were missing, including that of Fas Doonar, who had been killed when the rebels had blown his shuttle out of the sky, and Fynian Isu Hybatha, whose ill-fated peace mission had ended with her head being flung over the south wall and into Mys. Pas Rasha sighed, said,

"Good morning," even though it wasn't, and heard the usual pro forma responses as he took his seat.

Those present included Ishimoto-Forty-Six, the Clone Hegemony's ranking diplomat, Dogon Doko-Sa, who had left his troops long enough to attend to the diplomatic aspect of his job, Sea Sor, the Prithian ambassador, and Regar Batth, who represented the Ramanthians and appeared especially glum. There was a dull *thump*, as an explosion of indeterminate origin shook dust off the light fixtures, causing them to sway gently. Ishimoto-Forty-Six frowned. "What the hell was that?"

"Who cares?" Batth replied gloomily. "The outcome is certain. Mys will fall."

"Really?" Pas Rasha said primly, "I hadn't heard that . . . The last time I looked we were holding our own."

"They have the native quarter," Batth responded. "The rest will follow."

"Not necessarily," the Dweller replied calmly. "Captain Seeba-Ka did a masterful job of containing the damage. It's true that a combined force of Imperials and Tro Wa now occupy the city's southwest sector, but they are largely contained. The clock continues to run."

"Which raises the following question," Sea Sor put in. "Where is the relief force? It should have been here by now."

In spite of the fact that Pas Rasha asked himself the same question at least a hundred times a day he did the best he could to put a good face on the situation. "These things take time, which is why we need to hold, and refuse to give in."

"Nice in theory," Batth said heavily, "but the reality may be different. We might be able to get halfway-decent terms if we surrender now. But later, after the city falls, we'll have no leverage whatsoever."

"What about the civilians?" Doko-Sa inquired, his voice rumbling like an engine in low gear. "Do you seriously believe that the Claw will leave them unharmed?"

The Ramanthian hunched his narrow shoulders. "Who knows? Perhaps not, but most of the civilians are here because they believe in a human-conceived religion, which means that Earth should look out for them. I have my staff to consider."

And yourself, Pas Rasha thought cynically, *which always comes first*. The diplomat was tired, so tired that he was about tell the Ramanthian where he could shove his defeatist crap, when Vanderveen slipped into the room and signaled from the doorway. "Excuse me," Pas Rasha said. "I'll be right back."

Only a few seconds passed as Vanderveen whispered into her superior's ear, he nodded, and returned to the makeshift meeting room. Pas Rasha paused by the back of his chair. "Good news! Nobody knows why, but based on recent troop movements, it looks like some sort of schism has developed between the Imperials and the Tro Wa. Thousands of irregular troops have left the battlefield and are pulling back toward the west."

Ishimoto-Forty-Six led the light applause. "That is good news indeed! We'll take anything we can get at this point."

Batth remained silent—but his mind was racing. A schism? Why? And how might that affect Ramanthian interests? The situation was changing, he could feel it, but lacked sufficient information. Specialist Dusso was supposed to provide that, not to mention liaison with the Claw, but hadn't been heard from for days. Had the eggless bastard deserted? Been murdered in some dark alley? Or found himself trapped outside the walls? There was no way to know.

"So, what would you suggest?" Sea Sor asked. "What should we do?"

"Hold," Pas Rasha said simply as he took his seat. "Hold, hold, and hold some more. Captain Seeba-Ka is concerned about the rather fragile connection between the two sectors that we still control and would like to reinforce the cathedral the moment that darkness falls. Prince Mee Mas is there, along with his irregulars, but they lack experience. An injection of off-world troops would go a long way toward strengthening the corporate sector's defenses.

"Oh, really?" Batth inquired sarcastically, "and how are we

supposed to accomplish that? The corridor into the corporate sector is iffy at best—and subject to unrelenting sniper fire."

The Dwellers weren't a warrior race, they never had been, just one of the reasons why their culture had produced so many excellent diplomats. But Doko-Sa, who *was* from a warrior race, knew a predatory look when he saw one, and that was a fair description of the expression that stole over Pas Rasha's features.

"You are absolutely correct," the diplomat said softly. "It *is* dangerous to make the journey across the river and into the corporate sector. Fortunately for us, however, we have not one, but *two* different military contingents capable of flight, one of which belongs to *you*. For that reason Captain Seeba-Ka requests that twelve Ramanthians and twelve Prithians be placed under High Warrior Hak Orr's command and transferred to the cathedral."

Ambassador Sea Sor was proud of the fact that Seeba-Ka was willing to entrust such an important responsibility to his senior military officer and the brightly colored feathers around his neck rose. "Please inform Captain Seeba-Ka that the Prithians would be proud to participate in the corporate sector's defense."

Pas Rasha nodded. "Thank you. Ambassador Batth? Can the captain count on your forces as well?"

Batth was trapped. There was nothing he could do but offer a grunt of assent, wait out the rest of the day, and make his final decision later on.

"Good," Pas Rasha said, "I appreciate your time. It has been a good meeting—and I remain confident that we can hold out until the relief force arrives. Please do everything in your power to bolster morale. All of the people, off-world and indigenous alike, take their cues from you. Let's be careful what kind of messages we send. Now, if you'll excuse me, I have some funerals to attend."

And that's where Ambassador Pas Rasha was, standing next to an open pit, listening to an all-too-familiar burial service, when an Imperial soldier stationed out beyond the west wall accidentally triggered his weapon. The slug stalled and fell two seconds later. It plunged straight down, struck the top of the diplomat's unprotected head, and took his life. The exoskeleton served to hold Pas Rasha's body upright—and nearly five minutes had passed before anyone realized that he'd been hit. The Dweller was buried along with those he had come to mourn.

The Strathmore Hotel's once beautiful ballroom had been transformed into a large hospital ward. FSO-2 Harley Clauson lay in bed 43, not far from the stage on which he and his band sometimes played, and next to a Hudathan trooper who made horrible gurgling sounds as he struggled to breathe.

Christine Vanderveen nodded to Dr. Hogarth, as she passed what had once been a bar but now served as the nurse's station, and wound her way back through the maze of hotel beds. The air was thick with the combined odors of alcohol, vomit, and fecal matter. Attendants, most of whom were LaNorian, moved from bed to bed in an attempt to keep the patients clean and comfortable. It was a difficult and for the most part thankless job.

Clauson felt someone brush the covers on his bed and opened his eyes. Vanderveen's face was dirty, but he thought she looked angelic nevertheless, and managed a smile. "Hey, Christine, what are you doing? Goofing off again?"

The younger diplomat nodded. "Exactly. How did you know?"

Clauson shrugged. "Bosses know these things."

"Here, I brought you some of those lozenges you like."

There was only one place on LaNor where that particular type of lozenge could be obtained—and that was in the lower-right-hand drawer of Clauson's desk. So, given the fact that the diplomat's office was on one of the upper floors, Clauson knew Vanderveen had risked sniper fire to retrieve them. She unwrapped one and slipped it between his lips. "There . . . How's that?"

The coffee-flavored drop tasted wonderful. "Thank you," Clauson said feelingly, "but don't go up there again. You could get killed."

"I won't have to," Vanderveen said brightly. "I brought your entire supply down to ground level—and locked it in the embassy safe."

Clauson laughed, but the motion made his leg hurt, and his hands went down toward the stump. The incoming artillery shell, one of dozens lobbed over the wall on that particular day, had exploded as he crossed Embassy Row. The lower part of his right leg had been severed below the knee. One of the Legion's medics had put a tourniquet on long enough to stem the worst of the bleeding, slapped a battle dressing onto the stump, and allowed the built-in coagulant to seal the wound. Assuming the relief force arrived soon the limb could be regrown or, failing that, replaced with a bionic prosthesis. In the meantime it hurt like hell. Vanderveen frowned. Should I call for a nurse?"

The diplomat shook his head. "No, they have enough to do. Besides," he said, glancing at his wrist term, "the med cart is due by in five minutes and twenty-six seconds. Not that I'm keeping track."

Vanderveen nodded. "Good, but I'll check in every once in a while, just to see if there's something you need."

"Thanks," Clauson replied sincerely. "So, how's the boss? Has he managed to hold the menagerie together?"

Vanderveen bit her lower lip. This was the moment she'd been dreading. "I'm sorry, Harley, but a spent bullet fell out of the sky, and struck the top of the ambassador's head. We buried him earlier this afternoon."

Clauson felt a sense of disbelief. Pas Rasha? Dead? It didn't seem possible. In spite of the Dweller's fragility, he'd always seemed to be above it all, as if subject to a completely different set of rules and therefore invulnerable. "And Madam Pas Rasha? How is she?"

"Devastated. Cerly is trying to comfort her—but she's taking it hard."

Both diplomats were silent for a moment. Clauson was the first to speak. "You know what this means . . . Given the fact that Pas Rasha is dead, and I'm out of commission, that makes *you* the ranking diplomat on LaNor."

Vanderveen nodded mutely. The reality of that was still sinking in. The Confederacy was big on protocol, it had to be in order to hold so many diverse cultures together, and nowhere was that more true than in the area of diplomacy.

In spite of the fact that individual governments were free to send representatives to worlds such as LaNor their portfolios were supposedly limited to areas such as economic development, agricultural programs, and cultural exchanges. It was the Confederacy's diplomats, who on behalf of the president, dealt with matters such as treaties, technology transfers, and military alliances.

All of which meant that while diplomats like Sea Sor, Regar Batth, Ishimoto-Forty-Six, and Doko-Sa might be senior to Vanderveen in both rank and years of experience, it was she who was in charge. A sobering thought. "So," the no-longer-junior diplomat asked, "do you have any advice?"

Clauson considered the question for a moment, then nodded. "Yes, I do. Don't dither, delay, or be too deferential."

Vanderveen grinned. "The three D's."

"Yeah," Clauson replied thoughtfully, "I guess so. Just grab ahold of the situation and don't cut any of our honorable colleagues any slack."

Vanderveen nodded. "That's what I figured."

"Good," Clauson replied. "Now get out there and hold this mess together. The relief force should arrive anytime now— and it would be nice if there was someone left to greet them."

Vanderveen smiled, squeezed the other diplomat's hand, and turned away.

There weren't any trumpets to announce her coming, but it was the new ambassador to LaNor who stepped out into the afternoon sunlight, and started to make her rounds.

Darkness had settled over Mys by the time that the Prithian warriors had formed up at the southeast corner of the parade ground. That was the point from which they and the Ramanthians were scheduled to depart for the corporate sector where Mee Mas and his irregulars were all that stood between the LaNorian converts and the mixed force of Imperials and Tro Wa dug in on the west side of Embassy Row.

There was the gentle murmur of voices, plus the occasional *clink* of metal, as Prithian officers forced each warrior to jump up and down. Any gear that clinked, rattled, or squeaked was identified, resecured, and tested again. The whole idea was to make the trip from the parade ground to the roof of the cathedral undetected so that subsequent flights could be used to ferry critical supplies.

Seeba-Ka watched impassively as the Prithians made ready, but kept an eye on the time and finally ran out of patience. Santana and his platoon were stationed on the west wall not far from the Ramanthian embassy which explained why they were chosen. "Blood Six to Bravo Six. Over."

Santana ducked below the top of the wall. "This is Bravo Six. Go. Over."

"Take a squad and check on Golf Six. He and his detachment are late for dinner. Over."

The platoon leader could guess what "dinner" referred to, and pushed the transmit button twice. Then, switching to the platoon frequency, Santana gave the necessary orders. "Bravo Six to Bravo Two Six and Bravo Three Six. Two, take your squad and meet me at the base of the wall. Three, cover the resulting gap. Over."

The officer listened for two sets of affirmative *clicks,* heard them, and moved toward the stairs. It was relatively quiet at that particular moment, blissfully so, with only the blare of a distant trumpet, the occasional gunshot, and the pop of a flare to mar the otherwise peaceful night.

Once on the ground Santana spotted Sergeant Bonnie Cvanivich, pointed toward the Ramanthian embassy, and used hand signals to direct the squad forward. It was a strange thing to do, given that the Ramanthians were allies, but Santana couldn't bring himself to trust them. Not after his experiences on Beta-018 . . . and the march to Ka Suu.

As usual it was Private Rockclimb Warmfeel who led his teammates toward the dark one-story building. The Naa seemed to float over the ground like an animated shadow. Pausing to look, listen, and feel, pushing ahead, then pausing again.

Santana felt a vague uneasiness transform itself into something akin to fear as the legionnaires closed with the building. Where were the normally territorial bugs anyway? The squad should have been challenged by then.

In the meantime Warmfeel had sidled up to the building, announced himself, and received no reply. Consequently, the scout slid along the wall, arrived at the embassy's back door, and made an amazing discovery. Not only was it hanging open, and completely unguarded, but the smell of smoke hung in the air. Not the normal stuff, typical of both Mys and Polwa, but a more acrid odor reminiscent of burning plastic. The Naa looked for Santana and was quick to motion the platoon leader forward.

The officer sprinted across a patch of moonlit duracrete and arrived at the other side of the door. The Naa hooked a thumb toward the interior. "Not a bug in sight, and it seems like something's burning, sir."

Santana swore and mashed his transmit button. "Bravo Six to Blood Six. It looks like Golf Six ran away from home . . . or decided to hide under his bed. I'm going in to see what we can find. I suggest that you put the Quick Reaction Force front and back until we know what we have. Over."

"This is Blood Six," Seeba-Ka replied. "Roger the QRF. Report in five. Over."

Santana sent two *clicks*, checked to ensure that Cvanivich and her squad were ready, and followed Warmfeel inside. What illumination there was emanated from their helmet lights and what Santana thought of as "footers" because they were mounted at the base of walls and spaced roughly six feet apart. Having been in the building before, the platoon leader knew that the primary lighting was off and the footers were emergency backups.

Cvanivich used a series of jerky hand movements to direct members of her team down side corridors and through open doors. Their helmet lights played across walls, glinted through glass, and wobbled across the floors. All were back within a matter of minutes. They shook their heads and fell in behind.

Santana located the ramp that led down into the basement, made note of the fact that the smell of smoke had grown even more intense, and followed his nose. They hit the bottom of the incline and paused. More squad members were dispatched and it wasn't long before Hadley returned with news. "We located the fire, sir. It looks like someone used thermite grenades to destroy their computers."

Santana nodded. The new piece of information suggested that the Ramanthians had left on their own although there was no way to be absolutely sure of that. His concerns continued to deepen. "Sergeant, let's keep everyone together for the moment, I don't like the way this place feels. I want good spacing between the troops . . . and a clean line of retreat."

Cvanivich nodded and passed the word. Santana followed the main corridor toward the back of the building. The farther the legionnaire went the warmer it became. Beads of perspiration dotted his forehead, ran down into his eyes, and forced him to wipe them away. The atmosphere grew steadily more oppressive, the air thickened, and the officer released the safety on his CA-10 carbine. Something was wrong, *very* wrong, but what was it? There were no Ramanthians, dead or alive, yet the city was surrounded . . . Where had the bugs gone?

The answer came with horrifying suddenness as a LaNorian

screamed and the lead elements of an Imperial assault force poured out of the darkness. Santana fired his weapon on full automatic, saw a wild-looking face shatter as his bullets tore it apart, and yelled at the top of his lungs. "Pull back! Pull back! The bastards tunneled their way in!"

They backed onto the ramp. It was only about four feet wide which meant that contact was limited on both sides. Cvanivich and Warmfeel stood shoulder to shoulder with their platoon leader and fired into the oncoming mob. Santana felt a steady stream of hot shell casings hit his left shoulder as the noncom fired her weapon, fell over backward, and went down with what looked like a crossbow bolt protruding from the center of her forehead. Corporal "Dice" Dietrich moved forward to take her place. Dietrich was considered to be something of an artiste where grenade launchers were concerned and used his weapon to send a steady stream of high-explosive (HE) rounds down the corridor.

The objective was to relieve the pressure on Warmfeel and Santana and grease as many of the digs as he could without getting killed by one of his own projectiles. A very real danger in such close quarters.

There was a series of bright flashes as the grenades went off, shrapnel cut the Imperial troops to shreds, and the walls were drenched with blood.

Santana felt his weapon cycle empty, hit the magazine release, and had just seated another when someone used his combat harness to jerk him back off his feet. The platoon leader fell backward, hit the deck, and had the impression of something huge stepping over his body. "It's the QRF!" Bagano shouted into his ear. "I was afraid Zook might step on you."

"Thanks," Santana said, struggling to regain his feet. "Please feel free to deck my ass whenever you see fit."

All further conversation was rendered impossible as the T-2 squeezed his way down the ramp, arrived at the bottom, and opened fire. It took the cyborg less than three minutes to clear the corridor all the way back to the point where the

LaNorian tunnel connected with the rear of the Ramanthian embassy. Two hours later, having plugged the tunnel with one of the reconditioned RAVs, the perimeter was secure once more.

A close look at the LaNorian bodies revealed that while the invaders had been dressed in Imperial uniforms, many wore metal claws, or had Tro Wa symbols cut into their ear fans. Based on that it appeared that members of the Claw had been disguised so they could pass through Imperial lines. One more indication that the earlier alliance had come apart.

No one knew where the Ramanthians were, except to say that they were outside the walls, where it was assumed that the Tro Wa would give them sanctuary. A possibility that made Seeba-Ka's blood boil. It didn't take a genius to figure out that Regar Batth believed that Mys would fall, that the entire off-world population would be put to death, and that safety lay in surrender.

However, much as Santana wanted to get his hands on the Ramanthians, he wanted sleep even more. In spite of the fact that he had been forced to share his room with one of the corporate types, the businessman had volunteered to be part of the city's extremely active fire brigade, and was presently on duty.

Santana slipped into the room, took a quick shower, and fell into his bed. Sleep had already reached up, and was in the process of pulling him down, when the door opened and someone slipped inside. The platoon leader was reaching for the sidearm on his nightstand when a hand covered his and a fall of soft blond hair brushed his arm.

The legionnaire felt Vanderveen slip into his bed, knew he should do something about the fact that she was fully clothed, but couldn't quite muster the energy.

The diplomat whispered into the soldier's ear, he whispered into hers, and then, locked within each other's arms, they drifted off to asleep.

15

Our best ally is surprise.

Ramanthian General Jawa Harl
Standard year circa 1245

PLANET ARBALLA, THE CONFEDERACY OF SENTIENT BEINGS

Even if Sergi Chien-Chu's body didn't require any rest, his brain did, and it was asleep when the com started to chime. The cyborg mumbled, "Com on," and struggled to make sense of the words that spilled from the speaker. "Whoa," the industrialist said, "hold on. Who is this? And what's the problem?"

It wasn't the first time that Analyst 5 Sikora had been asked to start over again so she hurried to apologize. "Sorry, sir. This is Clarice Sikora. It's about the disk you gave us—the one from LaNor. Could you come see me? It's very important."

Given the nature of the ship's purpose the *Friendship* was literally crawling with thousands of electronic bugs. So that meant Sikora couldn't tell Chien-Chu why she was so excited but there was no need to. The Ramanthian code had been broken, a translation had been made, and the results were interesting. *Damned* interesting judging from the urgency in the analyst's voice. "I'll be there in fifteen minutes," the industrialist assured her, and broke the connection.

The corridors were busy as usual, but Chien-Chu knew the ship better than most, and arrived in the Intelligence section a scant twelve minutes after having left his cabin. Clarice Sikora was there waiting for him, as was her boss, Margaret Rutherford Xanith.

No one was allowed to bypass security, not even an ex-president, which meant that the women had no choice but to wait while Chien-Chu was forced to produce ID, scanned for bugs, and "sniffed" for explosives. Finally, having been cleared through the checkpoint, he was ushered into a sterile-looking corridor.

Other than her bright intelligent eyes, the rest of Sikora's features could only be described as plain, as was her unrelieved beige clothing. In fact the only thing that hinted at the non-professional aspect of the analyst's personality was the extravagant fall of shiny black hair that hung all the way to her waist. It was held together by a silver clasp located at the nape of her neck, the sort manufactured by Prithian silversmiths, and prized for the quality of their craftsmanship. "Wait till you see this stuff!" the analyst said excitedly. "This is the intelligence coup of the century!"

Chien-Chu glanced at the woman known as Madame X, and she nodded soberly. "Clarice is correct, but that doesn't mean that you're going to like it, or that we aren't in a whole heap of trouble."

The cyborg winced. "It's that bad?"

"Yup, I'm afraid so."

Chien-Chu was about to ask for a summary, a one-line synopsis of what they had learned, when the women guided the cyborg into a vacant conference room. "Have a seat" Xanith suggested, "and take a look at this . . . Once the code was broken we had the contents translated. There were reams of administrative garbage, the sort of stuff the Ramanthians would get if they pulled the same stunt on *us*, but right there, buried in the middle of a production report from the bug in charge of a LaNorian factory, is the equivalent of a hundred-megaton bomb. What you are about to look at was written by an administrator named Akko Seda—and addressed to a bigwig named Suu Norr. And he, if memory serves, heads the Department of Civilian Affairs on Hive."

The use of the pejorative term "bugs" was far from politically correct, but neither Chien-Chu nor Xanith made an effort to correct her. Sikora flipped a switch and a block of text appeared on the conference room's wall screen. The words began to scroll and Chien-Chu followed along. ". . . during the last quarter of the year. So, barring any unexpected production problems, I believe that we will be able to do our part in providing the 5 billion new souls with the basic everyday tools necessary for them to lead civilized lives." Chien-Chu paused at that point and went back to read the same words over again.

"That's right," Xanith said, her eyes following the cyborg's, "the report says '5 *billion new souls.*' "

"But that's absurd," Chien-Chu replied skeptically. "It must have been a typo."

"I don't think so," Sikora countered, and used a remote to change the text on the screen. "Here is an abstract from one of their production reports. Look at the unbelievable number of pumice stones, molt picks, and containers of wing wax they're cranking out . . . Enough to supply the existing population for the next hundred years!"

"And that's not all," Madam X offered evenly. "What sometimes seemed like irrational political activity starts to make sense when you consider it within the context of a Ramanthian population explosion. Think about all their efforts to acquire new real estate, to partition the Sheen fleet, and destabilize the government. All of it fits.

"My god," Chien-Chu said feelingly. "The bastards will outnumber the entire Confederacy."

"Far from it," Sikora said with the certainty of a professional fact checker, "but it's worrisome nonetheless."

"Did you inform the president?"

"No," Xanith replied, "not yet. I thought we would go together."

"He's not going to like what we have to say."

"No," the Intelligence chief agreed, "but then neither do I."

The *Friendship*'s launch deck was a very dangerous place to work. Not only because the cavernous bay was open to space 90 percent of the time, but because of the constant flow of incoming and outgoing fighters, shuttles, and supply ships, not to mention the movements of deck tugs, robo hoses, landing drones, security sleds, maintenance bots and hundreds of brightly suited personnel.

One such individual, a Ramanthian named Hodo Buak, had been assigned to the maintenance crew, a position he enjoyed both because of the wide range of duties involved, and the fact that the job allowed him to spy on the ship's many comings and goings. Something that he, as an intelligence operative, was paid to do.

That's why Buak, who had been assigned to repair the crash cage that protected the Number 16 fueling bay, pulled his torch away from a section of cracked tubing long enough to eyeball the distinctively shaped ship that swooped in for a high-priority landing.

The operative was fairly sure that he knew to whom the ship belonged, and who was likely to be aboard, but it was important to be sure. Especially in light of the fact that the Triad named Hasa-Ba was an important ally.

Buak killed the torch, put in a request for a bio break, and shuffled his way across the deck to one of the kiosks that provided access to the ship's computer systems. Maintenance workers didn't rate wireless access but it was a simple matter to jack in and use a series of voice commands to access the information he wanted. He was soon able to confirm that the recently arrived ship was the property of the Hudathan government, but, rather than the name he expected to see on the passenger manifest, the Ramanthian saw "Hiween Doma-Sa" instead. A rather alarming state of affairs since Triad Doma-Sa was supposed to be dead! Buak wasted little time notifying an intelligence officer named Ruu Sacc, who understood the danger, and put a call in to Senator Alway Orno.

The Ramanthian politician was neck deep in a soothing sand bath when the call came in. Should he ignore it? It was tempting, and he might very well have done so, had it not been for the fact that the stutter beep indicated a high-priority call from a member of his own staff. The politician tried to keep the annoyance out of his voice but failed. "Yes? What is it?"

It took Ruu Sacc only three sentences to bring his superior up and out of the sand bath. The orders came in short staccato bursts. "Prepare my ship for immediate departure. Dispatch a Protocol Three message to all embassy personnel. Send order six-point-one to the fleet. Execute."

Communicators buzzed or vibrated at various locations throughout the ship, more than two dozen Ramanthian staff members consulted small backlit screens, and all saw the same words: PROTOCOL THREE.

Some were frightened, others felt pleased, but all reacted in the same way. They disengaged from whatever they were doing and headed for the flight deck. Personal belongings, along with office files, furniture and other items were left behind. None of the Ramanthians mentioned the order to each other or to acquaintances who happened to greet them in the halls.

Meanwhile, as his staff filtered toward the launch bay, Orno had important things to do. The first was to get dressed. Having donned his robes, the diplomat went to his desk, grabbed what looked like a cylindrical piece of decorative art, and turned the top and bottom in opposite directions. There was distinctive *click* followed by a *whir* as two half-round panels retracted to expose a pair of rubber grips. Orno used a tool pincer to squeeze both grips at the same time, saw an LED start to blink, and knew that all of the embassy's files were being overwritten. An unnecessary precaution given what he planned to do next but it was best to be careful. Take Hasa-Ba for example . . . Rather than kill Doma-Sa the way he was supposed to, the stupid shovel head had botched the job, and probably been killed himself.

Had he revealed the nature of the plan? Including the bomb? Yes, it seemed safe to assume so, which was why Doma-Sa had come. Not to inform the government of his peer's un-timely death, but to warn them about the bomb, and the raid on the Sheen fleet.

But it's too late, Orno thought to himself, *as my enemies are about to learn.*

The bomb's trigger resembled a handheld computer. All the politician had to do was punch a code in via the Raman-thian squeeze keys, hit enter, and repeat the code for a second time. A steady tone served to confirm that the bomb was op-erational and that the timer had been activated. Sixty standard minutes, that was how long he and his staff had to clear the ship, and the blast that would follow.

Satisfied that things were well under control, the Raman-thian took one last look around his cabin, grabbed a holo stat of the War Orno, and slipped out through the door. It locked behind him.

President Marcott Nankool bit off a piece of apple. He had gained some weight over the last year and the fruit snacks were part of his latest effort to lose a few pounds. He chewed but barely tasted the food. His mind was elsewhere.

Doma-Sa had encountered Chien-Chu and Xanith in the alcove outside the president's office, and such was the nature of the relationship between the industrialist and the Hudathan leader they held a whispered conference. That's when both the industrialist and the Intelligence chief learned of Hasa-Ba's death, the possibility of a bomb, and the raid on the fleet. Then, alarmed by the sum of the information that they possessed, the threesome barged into Nankool's office, apologized to a startled official, and ushered him outside.

Then, even as Xanith used her communicator to contact the *Friendship*'s commanding officer (CO), the other two took the opportunity to brief Nankool.

Now, having consumed the slice of apple, the president struggled to assimilate what he had learned. "So, let's see if I have this right . . . For reasons we don't understand yet the Ramanthians are about to add 5 billion souls to their overall population. In order to provide for their new citizens, they plan to steal the Sheen fleet, and use the ships to move the excess population to the worlds they received as war reparations."

"That's correct," Chien-Chu said impatiently, "but with one important addition. Just before he died Triad Hasa-Ba told Triad Doma-Sa that the Ramanthians have constructed a bomb on board this ship. Now, assuming the plan remains in effect, they plan to detonate that device as a way to pull navy vessels away from the Sheen fleet."

"No offense," Nankool replied, "but the whole thing is preposterous. Why would Senator Orno blow himself up? We need to do some research, find out what's going on, and . . ."

"Excuse me," Madam X interrupted, "but I'm on the horn with the captain, and traffic control confirms that the Ramanthian shuttle *Hive Spirit* departed from the bay five minutes ago. She's large enough to carry Orno's entire staff. The master at arms is still searching but it appears that all of the Ramanthians have left the ship."

Nankool might have been political, but he was no fool, and made the necessary adjustment. "Tell the Arballazanies that we have a situation here—and ask them to bear with us. Notify security regarding the possibility of a bomb. Tell the CO to announce an unscheduled drill. Note the word 'drill.' Let's keep the lid on to avoid any possibility of panic. I want every member of the government off this ship and I mean *now*. Pull the navy in and warn them to expect guests."

"That's what Orno *wants* you to do," Doma-Sa cautioned.

"The moment you pull those the ships the Ramanthians will pounce on the Sheen fleet."

"What would you have me do?" Nankool demanded angrily as he rose from his chair. "Allow the entire government to die? Who will oppose the bastards then? Our lifeboats are just that, *lifeboats*, and there's no place for them to go except those ships. I have no choice. Xanith, tell the CO to warn whatever force that remains with the fleet to expect an attack. Perhaps they can save at least some of the ships.

"Now, if you don't mind, I need to be seen. There's going to be a whole lot of pissed-off politicians roaming the halls, and someone has to cool them down."

"This is the captain," a calm unemotional voice said via one of the speakers built into the overhead, "all personnel will stop what they are doing, assemble by their assigned lifeboats, and prepare to embark. This is an Alpha, repeat *Alpha* drill, which means that all boats will launch. Estimated duration of the exercise is three, repeat *three* hours, assuming we don't run into any problems.

"We apologize for any inconvenience this may cause but know that both the ship's crew *and* our guests understand the need for realistic emergency exercises. We are running a clock on this so please proceed to your station in a brisk and efficient manner. Thank you."

"You heard the man," Nankool told his guests. "I can't afford to lose even one of you. Get to those stations *now*. That's an order. We'll sort the rest of it out later."

In keeping with regs, and the procedures required for an Alpha drill, a squad of legionnaires arrived to escort the president through the halls.

The others went their separate ways while the timer continued to run. Teams of specially trained naval personnel were searching for the bomb—and they had twenty-seven minutes and thirty-two seconds left in which to find it.

• • •

The Sheen fleet, more than six thousand vessels in all, occupied an orbit very similar to the planet Arballa's which put the ships only hours away. A temporary arrangement until the Senate could determine what to do with them. Once controlled by an artificial intelligence known as the Hoon, the vessels were presently on standby, their propulsion systems pumping out barely enough power to keep their shields up and protect the hulls from meteorites and other debris. That meant that the glow or "sheen" by which the ships were known had been reduced to a dull silvery glow.

Still, there was something unusual about the vessels, a sort of brooding quality, that caused Vice Admiral Enko Norr to give orders quietly, as if the ships might hear and awake from their slumbers. Carefully, conscious of the risk of collision, the Ramanthian guided the destroyer class *Pincer of Freedom* through a shoal of gigantic gray hulls.

Though not privy to *why* the Confederacy's naval vessels would leave the fleet largely unguarded, the naval officer had been assured that they would, and the prediction had come true.

What hadn't come true was the promise that ten shiploads of Hudathan commandos would arrive to assist his forces and take their share of the fleet. Not that Norr cared, since he hated the ridge heads, and was glad to be rid of them.

It had taken the better part of ten Hive days to bring the flotilla in to the very edge of the solar system, activate the cloaking devices purchased from the Thrakies, and close with the mothballed fleet. Now, thanks to the fact that the vessels under his command remained undetected, and the majority of the patrol vessels were headed in toward Arballa, the fleet lay at his mercy. Countless hours of training had been spent preparing for this moment and all was ready. He glanced at a display on the console to his right, waited for the final seconds to tick away, and gave the next order. "Tell Ship Commander Joss to engage the enemy."

Thousands of units away three Ramanthian ships revealed

themselves, fired on an unsuspecting destroyer, and a brand-new sun was born. It expanded briefly, radiated light, and collapsed. Two-hundred and fifty-six sentients died.

Only six ships had been left to defend the fleet. They raced to avenge themselves on the attackers who, rather than fight, immediately turned and ran. Unaware of what was happening elsewhere the navy ships followed.

Meanwhile, relying on classified documents provided by no less a personage than Senator Orno himself, Vice Admiral Norr directed his raiders inward. Because of the fact that the Sheen ships were, and always had been, robotic, there was no need to put crews on all of them. Instead, thanks to sophisticated electronics obtained from the Thrakies, all his personnel had to do was place command modules aboard certain vessels and turn them on. Then, assuming what he'd been told was true, other ships, sixty-six per "raft," would lock on to the so-called Alpha ship, and follow it wherever it went.

And a good thing too since the Ramanthian lacked sufficient personnel to crew thousands of ships. Though hopeful that Orno's plan would succeed the Queen had placed definite limits on the resources available to him, pointing out that should he fail Hive itself would come under attack, and the Ramanthian navy would need all of its resources to defend the home world.

The flagship shuddered as it made lock-to-lock contact with one of the Sheen Alpha ships, pressures were equalized, and the Ramanthians took their first prizes.

The temporary command post had been set up on Echo Deck. It consisted of some man-portable screens, what looked like an enclosed food cart, and a cluster of personnel wearing specially designed suits and equipped with satchels full of sophisticated equipment. Once the bomb was found it would be their task to disarm it, but none of the so-called det-heads had anything to do except watch their CO sweat. Lieutenant Commander

Murdo was a big man with ginger hair, green eyes, and eternally flushed cheeks. The officer wore a dark blue ship suit, a billed cap, and a world-class frown.

From his position behind the hastily set-up screens, Murdo could monitor the precise location of every single person or machine but it didn't mean squat. The *Friendship* was an extremely large vessel, so large that looking for a bomb inside her hull was like searching for the proverbial needle in a haystack. Not only that, but the det heads and their electromechanical assistants didn't have the foggiest idea what they were looking for. Assuming the bomb was real, how big was it? How much did it weigh? And what did it look like? No one knew—and that was driving him crazy.

He was trying to find out though, and that's why sentients raced through the halls, opened inspection panels, and ran scanners over every surface they could find while specially designed robots spidered through the vessel's air ducts and searched for the slightest hint of radiation, chemical residue, or unmapped heat. Anything that might betray the presence of an explosive device.

Even worse was the fact that the bomb might be on a timer, and if so, could go off at any moment. Assuming the threat was real, what had the timer been set for? An hour? Two hours? And how much of that time was left? The brass seemed to be of the opinion that one of the politicos had set it, but they weren't saying how they knew that. Why? Politics that's why—and the reality of that sucked.

A radio operator appeared at the officer's elbow. She belonged to the Legion and was one of the 136 sentients who had volunteered to remain aboard and help some three hundred robots search for the bomb. If she was scared their was no sign of it on her face. Tactical communications were being routed through the ship's Command and Control Center and from there to other ships if necessary. "I have the boss on the horn, sir, and when I say the 'boss' I meant the *big* boss."

Murdo made a face. Looking for the bomb was tough

enough without having the president looking over your shoulder. "Terrific . . . Just what I need."

The radio operator grinned and slapped the handset into the officer's beefy palm. "Lieutenant Commander Murdo, sir."

Nankool's voice was calm, cool, and collected. Just the way he wanted to appear. "This is the president, Commander. While I appreciate everything that you and your people are trying to do it's too damned dangerous. I want you to pull out and that's an order."

Murdo felt wildly conflicting emotions. On the one hand he wanted to get his people off the ship as quickly as he could. On the other hand it was *his* ship that someone was trying to blow up—and that pissed him off. He wanted to find the device and disarm it. "Yes, sir," Murdo replied, "but I would . . ."

Nankool, who had been taken aboard one of the navy's cruisers by then, never got to hear what the naval officer would like to do. The timer hit zero, the bomb exploded, and the ex-battleship was destroyed in a single eye searing blast.

In spite of the fact that it had been Orno's intention to blow the vessel in two, leaving at least some of the crew alive in both halves, the explosion managed to penetrate two of the ship's six magazines and triggered the ordnance stored there. The results were catastrophic.

As chance would have it both Chien-Chu and Doma-Sa were with Nankool at that fateful moment and witnessed the tragedy firsthand. Light found the wardroom's viewport, was electronically dampered to protect those within, but still packed sufficient intensity to strobe the bulkhead behind him. "My god," Nankool said in wonderment, "what was that?"

"*That,*" Chien-Chu said grimly, "was the first shot in a new interstellar war. Having tried to eradicate our government, and having destroyed our capital, the Ramanthians are in the process of stealing a fleet."

"Not to mention the fact the bugs are about to hatch 5

billion new citizens," Doma-Sa said darkly, "about 1.6 billion of whom will be raised as warriors."

Nankool's legs felt weak. The afterimage of the explosion was still floating in front of his eyes as he collapsed into a chair, an officer arrived, and announced what they already knew: The *Friendship* was gone. One moment he had been talking to Murdo—and a fraction of a second later the naval officer was gone. He could hardly believe it. His voice was little more than a whisper. "Whatever will we do?"

The industrialist stared into the blackness of space. There wasn't much point to it, but the reserve admiral knew that SAR (Search and Rescue) units had already been launched, and would comb the newly created debris field looking for survivors. His voice was hard and unyielding. "We'll do the only thing we can do. We'll bury our dead, reconvene the government, and prepare to fight."

And it was only a few minutes later, with a dozen naval vessels closing in on his position, that Vice Admiral Norr gave a single somewhat terse order and 3,213 ships disappeared into hyperspace. More than 3,000 of the space craft were prizes. The Ramanthian navy had doubled its strength in a blink of an eye. Everything had changed.

16

Rare is the craftsperson who has all of the materials that he or she might desire. Build what you can, construct it to last, but know that nothing stands forever.

Author unknown
Aaman-Duu Rotes for Hatchlings
Standard year circa 250 B.C.

THE FOREIGN CITY OF MYS, ON THE INDEPENDENT PLANET OF LANOR

There was a deafening roar as tons of gunpowder exploded, the buildings along both sides of the wall rocked as if locked in the grip of an earthquake, and the once impregnable South Gate simply disappeared. No one was expecting it, especially at five in the morning, not even the Imperial officer in charge of driving the tunnel under the gate, excavating the chamber, and packing it full of explosives.

What had occurred? There was no way to know. A spark probably, generated by some idiot who had chosen to use a metal pick rather than a wooden one, or engaged in a similar folly. It didn't matter though, not really, since the offender had already paid the price for his stupidity, and the whole idea was to destroy the gate. An objective that had been fully met.

The officer stood in the center of the street that led from Polwa into Mys, gave thanks for the fact that his breakfast had been served late, and stared in wonder at the huge column of smoke and dust that pointed up at the sky.

The wind was already in the process of pushing the dark pillar to the west, but the Imperial would never forget the sound of the explosion, the way the earth had moved, or the destruction left behind.

Others, the officers who had to lead troops into Mys, cursed the engineering officer as they struggled to round up enough troops to launch an attack before the devils could throw a barricade across the still-smoldering entryway. But he, still mesmerized by the extent of the destruction he had wrought, simply stood and smiled.

Meanwhile, about two miles away, Captain Seeba-Ka peered at the destruction through his binoculars. He spoke from the side of his mouth. "Tell High Warrior Hak Orr and Prince Mee Mas that they can expect an infantry attack in the very near future. Order them to pull back inside the walls and inform me the moment that the gates are closed."

Lance Corporal "Bags" Bagano, the captain's RTO for the day, nodded and passed the message along. She received a double *click* from Hak Orr, plus a paragraph of completely unnecessary commentary from Mee Mas. The LaNorian had come a long way, but still had a tendency to run his mouth.

Thanks to the time required to prepare the assault the allied forces had retreated inside the cathedral's newly strengthened walls by the time the LaNorians launched their ground assault. It was easy at first, almost too easy, as Qwa Was led fifty troops into the gap, and prayed that the devils would miss. His mother had given him a spirit bag to wear around his neck, a powerful amulet which was supposed to render him invulnerable to bullets, a claim he had no desire to test.

But the off-worlders had run away rather than face his soldiers, that's the way it appeared at any rate, and Qwa Was felt a tremendous sense of exultation as he took his soldiers north along Embassy Row. The ragged remnants of the force that had entered Mys via the western breach came out of hiding, waved red banners, and shouted happy slogans. The Imperials ran to embrace their much-put-upon comrades and congratulate them on their bravery. Though relatively inexperienced, Qwa was intelligent, and knew that the impromptu celebration was a bad idea. The officer was already shouting at his troops, trying to make them disperse, when the QRF appeared at the far end of the street.

There were four T-2s, all standing shoulder to shoulder, their weapons at the ready. Qwa Was spotted the danger, started to yell an order, and saw something wink. The energy pulse cut the officer in half, killed a group of four celebrants, and splashed the side of a half-burned-out hodo.

The Imperials began to run after that, seeking shelter any-place they could find it, but it was far too late. Snyder, Zook, and two cyborgs from Lieutenant Beckworth's platoon opened fire with everything they had. Machine-gun bullets cut the LaNorians to pieces, energy cannon pounded the pieces to bloody slush, and the street ran red with blood. Survivors, a couple of hundred or so, took shelter in the ruins where they would attempt to regroup.

Satisfied that he had forestalled the assault, Seeba-Ka ordered the cyborgs to pull back and used his binoculars to scan the area. There was nothing to be seen except smoke, devastation, and the sky beyond. *How much longer* he wondered? *How much longer?* The wind tugged at the sleeves of his jacket but offered no reply.

THE CITY OF POLWA, ON THE INDEPENDENT PLANET OF LANOR

Literally thousands of workers were required in order to maintain the palace and the elaborate grounds that surrounded it. However, rather than house the workers within the walls during the night, where their presence might give offense to the Empress and represent a threat to her security, the vast majority of the gardeners, carpenters, and other craftspeople required to keep the Imperial household functioning were herded out into Polwa's noxious streets at six each evening.

Now, even as the dust continued to settle from the massive

explosion off to the north, a long line of ragged-looking workers were queued up to enter the so-called inner city. But some of the workers, a group totaling nearly a hundred, and sprinkled through the crowd like spice on kas, were not what they appeared to be.

In fact some, such as Ambassador Regar Batth and two dozen of his Ramanthian soldiers, weren't even *LaNorian*, much less skilled craftspeople, in spite of the fact that they possessed credentials that claimed otherwise. The diplomat, who feared that the foul-smelling hood and robes, which nearly dragged on the ground, couldn't possibly disguise his alien physiology, was terrified.

Not only was his decision to sneak out of Mys, and throw his lot in with the Tro Wa starting to look a bit premature, it now left him at the mercy of Lak Saa, an individual who *had* no mercy and was quite possibly insane. Something which had everything to do with the diplomat's present predicament.

Having lost some real as well as political ground over the last few days, and aware that *more* off-worlders could arrive at any time, the Claw leader had decided to risk everything on a single audacious plan. *If* he could reach Shi Huu, and do so with a large enough force, it would then be possible to seize the palace from within, and with it the power he had sought for so long.

Were that to take place, and were the rest of the off-worlders put to the sword *before* the relief force could arrive, then Batth would be in a position to sell them on his own highly edited version of history. That's why he had been convinced to come, that's why the plan had to succeed, and that's why what felt like cold lead rode the pit of the Ramanthian's stomach.

Forward of the diplomat's position in line, but dressed just as humbly, Lak Saa eyed the guards ahead. They were members of the household guard, an elite organization known for its loyalty to the royal family, and the intelligence of those who served in its ranks. But monotony can dull even the keenest mind, and rather than rotate the guards from one activity to another, the unit's officers had a dangerous tendency to assign the same soldiers to the same duties day after day. That's why the guards were less alert than they might have been.

Claw spies had made note of the fact that they seemed more interested in checking to see if the heavily embossed disks that each worker wore were genuine, rather than focus their attention on the equally important question of who was carrying them. It was a tendency Lak Saa hoped to exploit.

The line jerked forward and the eunuch followed. He was larger than the average LaNorian and was careful to slouch. His hands, including the long lethal fingernails, were concealed in wide funnel-shaped sleeves. A grubby hand reached out to grab the disk that dangled from Lak Saa's neck and a pair of well-trained eyes scanned both the front and back to ensure that the code stamped into the metal was authentic.

Not something the rebel leader was concerned about since every medallion issued to the force of Tro Wa cutthroats and off-world devils who accompanied him had been obtained from an actual craftsperson. Some had surrendered their livelihoods willingly—others lay dead in one of Polwa's stinking alleyways.

The guard, who in addition to his role as security officer was also expected to monitor the workers' physical cleanliness, detected the faint odor of urine. "Do everyone a favor and take a bath tonight," the soldier said, and allowed the disk to thump against the eunuch's chest.

Lak Saa felt a tremendous sense of relief as he bobbed his head and shuffled forward. The soldier's face was burned into his memory. The Empress could employ fools if she chose to— but *he* would insist on a higher level of talent. A great many people would die during the days that followed his ascension to the throne and the guard would be one of them.

And so it went as dozens of LaNorians and Ramanthians were admitted to the inner city. But that kind of luck couldn't last forever, and came to an abrupt halt as one of the guards noticed a medallion that had a familiar-looking dent in it, looked up ready to greet his uncle, and found himself looking at a stranger instead. The soldier grabbed the imposter, summoned help, and the guards threw the offender to the ground.

Lak Saa, who was pretending to tend some plantings not far away, waited to see what would happen. Would the prisoner give his companions away? Or follow instructions—and allow himself to be arrested?

It soon became clear that rebel had a clear head and would pretend to be a cutthroat and thief who was intent on stealing whatever he could lay his hands on. He would be sentenced to death, but the executioners had a three-day backlog, and there would be plenty of time in which to free him. Having frisked the imposter and confiscated both a knife and an off-world pistol, the guards hoisted the miscreant to his feet and led him away.

Then, rather than become even more vigilant as Lak Saa might have imagined they would, the guards seemed to be even *less* attentive, as they commiserated with the soldier who had lost an uncle, joked about how stupid the imposter was, and placed bets on how long the thief would dangle before death finally claimed his spirit.

Ten minutes later the last Tro Wa cleared the check point and entered the inner city. Lak Saa licked his lips, used a Ramanthian-supplied whisper mike to marshal his forces, and led the way toward the palace. Every step the eunuch took, every odor that invaded his nostrils, every sound he heard reminded him of his youth. *Hard* memories, *cruel* memories, all of which were about to be avenged.

THE FOREIGN CITY OF MYS, ON THE INDEPENDENT PLANET OF LANOR

Having blown the South Gate, and infiltrated more than two hundred troops into what had been the corporate sector, the Imperials wanted to finish the job.

High walls surrounded the cathedral, but everyone knew it was packed with converts, not to mention the devils them-

selves. To leave such a place untouched would be a failure of
will, an affront to the spirits, and a surrender to evil. After all,
everyone knew that the devils loved nothing better than to
rape LaNorian females, and sacrifice their babies to off-world
gods.

Though not privy to the Imperial plans those within the
walls didn't have to be. They knew the attack would come; the
only question was when. A special noon service was held. Hundreds of candles, something the defenders had plenty of, filled
the cathedral with an ethereal glow. As Frank Busso led his
followers in prayer the sound of their individual voices blended
together to form a rich harmony that lifted spirits and caused
sections of richly carved wood paneling to vibrate in sympathy.

The sound was so loud, so strong, that the Imperials heard
it as well, many of whom covered their ears lest the haa (evil
spirits) invade their minds and take control of their bodies.
Finally, once the service had ended, Busso retrieved his rifle
from a corner, kissed his wife on the cheek, and told her he
loved her.

Bethany looked up into his face. "Are you sorry?"

Busso shook his head. "No. I was at first . . . but not anymore."

"Me, too."

"I'll see you later."

"Promise?"

"I promise." Busso kissed her forehead, but the words rang
false, and Bethany doubted that either of them would live to
see the next dawn much less each other.

The shelling started a scant thirty minutes later. The first
shell landed outside the wall, the second on top of it, and the
third blew a crater in the courtyard. Shrapnel cut a work party
to shreds. It was just a matter of time before the LaNorian
gunners dropped a shell through the roof of the cathedral.

The purpose was obvious. The Imperials hoped to soften the
place up prior to attacking it. And, since the off-worlders
didn't have any artillery of their own, they had no choice but

to hunker down and wait. That's the way it seemed anyway, until High Warrior Hak Orr asked for three volunteers, and his entire detachment warbled a response.

Busso watched in disbelief as the Prithians spread their wings, launched themselves off the wall of much-abused cargo modules, and soared over the desolation below. Rather than the gunfire the missionary expected to hear, there were screams as the seemingly supernatural off-worlders glided out over the eastern wall, and the superstitious Imperials dived into whatever holes they could find.

The cannon fired, a shell whistled over Busso's head, and crashed into the main gate. It knocked a timber loose but failed to explode. Foro, the same cyborg who had volunteered to cut through the western water gate, hurried to disarm the unexploded shell. There was silence for a moment, followed by an explosion, and the rattle of gunfire.

The Prithians returned a few minutes later. Each carried two or three LaNorian ear fans which they submitted to Hak Orr as proof of their valor. He trilled a quick series of notes to which they responded in kind. The warriors returned to their sectors and Busso approached Hak Orr. "What did they say?"

"I asked them about the cannon," the officer said evenly. "They blew it off its carriage. It won't bother us until the enemy can come up with another one."

"Will they bring more artillery to bear?"

The Prithian cocked his head to one side. "Of course . . . but that will take hours."

It was said as if hours were equivalent to weeks—and it certainly felt as if weeks were passing as the day wore on.

Denied their cannon, the Imperial infantry withheld their attack and used other methods to prepare the way instead. Message arrows fell like rain, some found flesh, but most clattered off the cathedral's walls, or shattered on the flagstones below. The messages they bore urged the converts to rise up against the "devil masters," promising mercy to those who did. Each arrow and piece of parchment was saved for use as fuel for the cook fires.

Then came the catapult-launched fire pots, iron kettles filled with hot burning coals, each lobbed from the relative safety of Polwa. The coals exploded as they hit, sprayed sparks in every direction, and started numerous fires.

Then, even as many defenders were drawn away from the walls to fight the flames, trumpets blew and the long-awaited infantry attack was launched.

Mee Mas and his irregulars were responsible for the vast majority of the wall, and he walked it much as Major Miraby had, though careful to keep his head down. He heard the yells, knew what they meant, and said the same things over and over as they circled the perimeter. "Wait for them to come in range . . . Make every bullet count . . . Kill their leaders . . . Wait for them to come in range."

Steadied by the prince's presence, and confident after days of combat, the irregulars obeyed. Not a single weapon was fired as ragged lines of Imperials appeared and charged the walls. They advanced in groups, all holding newly made ladders over their heads, intent on placing them against the walls.

The Prithians, conscious of how important their fully automatic weapons might become if the Imperials found a way in, held their fire as well.

The irregulars waited for the assault teams to enter what Mee Mas and First Sergeant Neversmile had taught them to think of as the "killing zone," and opened fire. The leaders, made conspicuous by the fact that they weren't burdened by ladders, went down first. Many, distant as they were, seemed to trip and fall.

Then, having switched their fire to the ladder teams, the defenders aimed for the lead individual in each file. When he went down those behind him were not only forced to shoulder more of the load, but to walk over his body, which caused some of them to trip. Mee Mas watched in grim satisfaction as one entire ladder team went down, tried to get back up, and were slaughtered on the ground.

However, in spite of the defenders' best efforts, three ladder teams managed to reach the walls, and tried to climb their ladders. A team of civilians led by Busso made use of long forked poles to push one ladder over backward. The Imperials fell, tried to regroup, and were killed with a homemade grenade.

Hak Orr sprayed the second team with machine-gun bullets, even as the third team actually topped the cargo modules, where they fought hand-to-hand with a party of irregulars prior to being killed and thrown off the wall.

That's when the trumpets blew, and like a wave that has already thrown itself high onto a beach, the Imperials pulled back into the ruins. Piles of brightly uniformed bodies lay along the high-tide mark—evidence of their unfortunate valor.

Mee Mas felt a strange sense of exhilaration, knew it was somehow wrong, but couldn't help himself. The battle had been exciting, no thrilling, and he had enjoyed every moment of it. Conscious of what an officer like Santana would do, and intent on quenching his own thirst for battle, the prince made his rounds.

Busso, tears running down his cheeks, sat at the base of the north wall and held Yao Che's bloody body. The youngster had been there, pushing on a pole, when an Imperial bullet had taken him in the throat. Now, as the brave youngster's life ran out onto the flagstones, there was nothing the human could do but grieve.

Hak Orr, his weapon slung over his shoulder, was busy preening his feathers when a subordinate approached and offered a radio. "It's Captain Seeba-Ka, sir. He wants a report."

The Prithian made no effort to accept the radio but looked out over the compound instead. They were still counting the bodies but it appeared that at least a hundred beings of various descriptions were dead. How many more attacks would they be able to repel? Two? Three at most? It didn't look good.

"Tell him that the enemy attacked, that we fought back, and that the cathedral stands."

The warrior looked at the officer, decided that he wasn't going to say anything more, and passed the message back.

Meanwhile, the sun climbed higher, the air grew warmer, and the bodies started to rot. Defeat, or the possibility of defeat, hung heavy in the air.

Well aware of how bad conditions within the city were, and concerned lest all the records of what had transpired be lost when Mys fell, Vanderveen had gone up to Pas Rasha's office, and was sorting documents on the floor, when salvation crashed through what remained of the window, hovered, and did a full 360.

The far side of Embassy Row was infested with enemy snipers, and Private Bok Horo-Ba, who had been stationed in the office in order to keep the largely Tro Wa sharpshooters under control, saw metal flash through his peripheral vision, tried to bring the forty-seven-inch-long rifle around, but couldn't do so in time.

The recon ball fired a stun pulse, the Hudathan fell over backward, and his rifle clattered to the floor. "Sorry about that," the cyborg said to one in particular, "but I'm allergic to .50 caliber slugs."

Vanderveen felt her back touch the wall and tried to scoot toward the door. The machine, if that's what it was, appeared to be about four feet in diameter and made a soft buzzing sound. The ball rotated slightly, extruded what looked like a gun barrel, and said, "Hold it right there . . . I'm looking for Ambassador Pas Rasha, Major Homer Miraby, or both. You wouldn't happen to know where they are would you?"

"They're dead," Vanderveen said shakily, still unsure of who or what she faced.

"I'm sorry to hear that," the cyborg replied. "Who is in charge if I may ask?" FSO Clauson perhaps?"

"No," the diplomat replied, "*I* am."

"And you are?"

"FSO Christine Vanderveen."

The recon ball took a moment to consult his onboard computer, confirmed that a diplomat fitting her description was listed as part of the embassy's staff, and made note of how junior she was. The situation was bad, *very* bad, much worse than he'd been led to expect. "Yes, well it's a pleasure to make your acquaintance, Ambassador, although I'm sure we both wish it was under more favorable circumstances.

"My name is Hawes, Colonel Jack Hawes, not that rank means much in my line of work. You'll be happy to know that the relief force that you've been waiting for has arrived."

Vanderveen looked at the cyborg in astonishment. "They sent you down rather than send a message by radio?"

"All sorts of people have radios," Hawes replied, "and discretion truly is the better part of valor. Why warn everybody? Now, we have aerospace fighters, a detachment of quads, and two thousand legionnaires who are just itching to shoot the place up. The only problem is that it's hard to tell the good guys from the bad guys in situations such as this one. Maybe you and your staff can enlighten us."

There was a loud clang as one of the Tro Wa snipers tried to put a bullet into the strange apparition that had seemingly materialized out of nowhere.

The cyborg turned, fired his energy cannon, and blew a hole through the sniper, the wall behind him, and the wall beyond that.

The ball rotated again. "Impudent beggars, aren't they? Well, the Thirteenth DBLE will soon put an end to that . . . Now where were we? Oh, yes, the political situation. What say we retreat to more hospitable surroundings and talk things over?"

Vanderveen made as if to crawl over to Horo-Ba's unconscious body.

"Your Hudathan friend will be fine," the officer assured her, "except for a serious headache. He should come around in about ten minutes or so."

Thus reassured, Vanderveen made for the door, the recon ball followed, and it wasn't long before the besieged city felt the first stirrings of hope.

THE CITY OF POLWA, ON THE INDEPENDENT PLANET OF LANOR

The Empress Shi Huu had already risen, completed her makeup, and allowed herself to be wrapped in silk. This particular dress was gray, like the sky on a cloudy day, and decorated with cheerful ola blossoms. A fitting choice for a morning that would start on the air throne.

But even as Shi Huu and her retainers were clattering through the maze of hallways, passageways, and corridors designed to protect her from assassins, the very person she feared most had already entered the palace, and thanks to his intimate knowledge of the structure's layout, was on his way to the same destination that she was.

Lak Saa had chosen a circuitous route however, one that would allow his force to engage and neutralize a significant number of bodyguards *before* an alarm was sounded, thereby reducing the level of response that would come later on.

The key to Lak Saa's strategy was Nu Ga Su, or "the way of silence," just one of the many subdisciplines that every third-level Tro Wa was required to master.

That was why the rebel leader had structured his force so that he along with ten level-three masters led the way, followed by thirty-five level-twos, the entire party of Ramanthians, and a rear guard comprised of ten level-threes, ten level-twos, and four level-ones. It was a configuration designed to cut through opposing forces, maintain control over the aliens, and create what Tro Wa literature referred to as the two-headed snake, meaning a column that was equally prepared to go in either direction.

The entire party was armed with knives and off-world pistols but had been forbidden to use them until specific permission had been granted. Heavier weapons would be obtained from the defenders themselves.

The slaughter began immediately. The outer ring of sentries, all of whom were young, barely had time to issue their challenges before Lak Saa and the other Tro Wa were upon them. Blood splattered the walls as the Claw slashed their throats, took their weapons, and passed them toward the rear of the swiftly moving column.

There was a great deal of blood, and even though Regar Batth would have preferred to leap over the puddles, there was no opportunity since he and his warriors were continually pushed from behind. *His* boot prints, plus those made by the rest of the column, created a long red snake that followed them down the corridor.

The so-called second wall was comprised of more seasoned soldiers, all of whom took one look at the blood-spattered Tro Wa, and immediately raised their weapons. Unfortunately their safeties were on, a wise precaution under normal circumstances, but one which cost them their lives.

Lak Saa nodded to his companions who used the one-second-long interval to throw their double-edged knives. All but one of the weapons found their marks, and four of the guards went down with slivers of steel protruding from their throats.

The fifth managed to deflect the incoming knife with his rifle, shot one of the Claw in the stomach, and used his arm-long bayonet to spit another. Even as his opponents fell he blew three short blasts on his whistle and prepared to fire again.

Lak Saa spun, slashed the guard with a long, curved nail, and wished there had been a way to spare him. Such soldiers were rare—and he would have need of them.

The soldier was still clutching his neck, still trying to staunch the flow of blood, when Batth edged past. Although the War Batth would have been comfortable with such sights they made the diplomat uncomfortable. The pace picked up after that as Lak Saa and his fellow Tro Wa masters started to run.

Having been summoned by the whistle a squad of guards appeared at the far end of the corridor, saw the blood-drenched assassins, and did what they had been trained to do. Three of the soldiers knelt, three continued to stand, all of them fired.

Four out of the six bullets found their targets. Two of the Claw were snatched from their feet. A third felt something hot slice the outside surface of his left arm, and the fourth fell as a slug punched its way through the meaty part of his thigh.

The guards, all of whom were armed with brightly chromed off-world hunting rifles were in the process of working their bolts when the flying column collided with them. They fell in a welter of blood and were literally trampled as the "snake" passed over them and continued on its way.

Now, as the invaders wound their way toward the inner guardroom, the place where the majority of the ready reserves were likely to be, most of the lead Tro Wa stepped off to either side, allowed the Ramanthians to advance and fell in behind them.

Lak Saa, along with his most trusted lieutenants, remained at the head of the column. He smiled in anticipation. Besides their potential usefulness as shields, the aliens represented a critical part of his plan, and the means by which he would pass through the "third wall" to penetrate the throne room.

Batth, who understood at least part of the role that he and his soldiers were slated to play, began to shed his disguise. The medallion, hood, and robe all fell to the floor. The rest of the Ramanthians rid themselves of their LaNorian garb as well.

The result was what appeared to be a phalanx of has, devils such as the household guard had never seen before, and would almost certainly scare the hell out of them. The plan worked even better than the Claw leader had hoped as a full company of soldiers, all summoned by the sound of gunfire, rounded a corner and spotted the oncoming Ramanthians. The officer who led them skidded to a halt, a pair of soldiers slammed into him, and someone yelled the key word: "Has!"

That was all it took. Convinced that evil spirits had some-how managed to invade the palace, and scared out of their wits, the Imperials attempted to run.

But the Ramanthians were ready for that. Rather than the sidearms that the rank and file Tro Wa carried, *they* had ma-chine pistols, which the aliens fired in short, three-round bursts. The bullets caught what had been the front end of the column first, forced the retreating soldiers to dance, and plowed ahead, sometimes taking as many as three lives before lodging themselves against bone, or becoming trapped in mus-cle.

The slaughter took less than thirty heartbeats to accom-plish—and left a charnel house of bodies through which Lak Saa was forced to pick his way.

Some of the soldiers were still breathing, so pistols were used to finish them off, even as their weapons and ammunition were added to supplies captured earlier.

Shi Huu had already entered the throne room by then, passed under the transparent dome, and climbed the four steps that led up to the throne. Though muted by many intervening walls, and therefore rendered unidentifiable, the gunshots were out of the ordinary and sufficient to elicit a royal frown.

Ever solicitous of Shi Huu's comforts the minister Dwi Faa hurried off to identify the culprits and have them punished.

But the culprits found *him*, and Lak Saa, who had known the other eunuch since the age of six, was the one who seized Dwi Faa by the throat and lifted him up onto his toes. "Well, well, look what we have here! Shi Huu's favorite Dar Tu (pup-pet person.) I have waited a long time for this moment."

Dwi Faa, who had been instrumental in sowing the seeds of doubt and suspicion that eventually undermined Lak Saa's position and forced him into exile, blanched. "Please, Lak Saa, I beg of you . . ."

However, much as Lak Saa would have enjoyed stretching the moment out, time was of the essence, and the *real* prize lay in the room beyond. Having already used his left hand to hoist the more diminutive Dwi Faa up off the ground—the Tro Wa used his right to open the eunuch's belly.

The cut felt like nothing at first, but that was before Dwi Faa's abdominal cavity opened like a tired envelope and dropped his intestines onto his feet.

"Why don't you gather them up," Lak Saa suggested kindly, "and go seek help? Perhaps a seamstress could sew you up."

Dwi Faa looked down to see that his robe had been split open as if by scissors, only to give birth to a mass of dark, dangling flesh.

The Tro Wa laughed uproariously as the minister gathered his entrails into his arms and shuffled up the hall.

Shi Huu had just completed her breakfast, but was still sipping her tea, when a small group of invaders burst into the throne room through three of the six possible doors. Her bodyguards turned, raised their ceremonial pikes, but fell as each was riddled with bullets.

Then, with gun smoke still drifting through the air, Lak Saa entered the room. He bowed formally, as he had so many times before, and offered the usual greeting: "Hoso poro, (good morning) Your Majesty, I see all the rumors are true. The full beauty of your youth has been restored."

Shi Huu was so startled, so taken aback by the sudden violence, that she sat frozen with the delicate teacup halfway to her lips. She was frightened, *very* frightened, but more than sixty years of training enabled the Empress to hide what she felt. The teacup completed the journey to her lips, she took a sip, and put the container down.

"If it isn't my ex-minister Lak Saa—what an interesting surprise. You never were one to worry about appearances—but that outfit falls beneath even *your* standards."

The eunuch bowed once more. "My apologies, Highness, but at least the blood I wear is honest blood, shed by those who died trying to defend you. But the blood on *your* clothes, though a good deal less visible, is real nonetheless."

Shi Huu laughed. "This *is* amusing. To hear *you*, he who has slaughtered thousands of those he claims to fight for, make a claim of moral superiority. Enough of this nonsense . . . What do you want?"

"That which is mine," the eunuch answered. "The throne you sit on."

"Don't be absurd," Shi Huu replied contemptuously. "You can't *take* the throne, you must be *born* to it, and though of noble birth you were never in line for the throne."

"Those are the *old* rules," Lak Saa answered evenly, "and I'm here to introduce some *new* rules. I am more intelligent than you are, and stronger than you are, so the throne is mine."

The foot pedal had been installed *after* Lak Saa's banishment—and was concealed by the carpet under Shi Huu's feet. Now, as the eunuch took one step forward, she pressed down with her right foot.

Lak Saa felt the slight give as the trapdoor started to fall and threw himself forward. Perhaps one in a thousand could have reacted quickly enough to initiate the necessary move, and perhaps one in *ten* thousand could have landed on the palms of his hands, only to push his entire body up into the classic gund do, or "kick the sky." But the eunuch was one such person and made the move look easy.

And so it was at that moment, just as Lak Saa's left "claw" broke off near the end of his middle finger, that both feet struck the bottom of Shi Huu's jaw. Her head snapped back, an audible snap was heard, and the Dawn Concubine was dead.

Lak Saa held the position for a fraction of a second, allowed himself to bend, and was soon back on his feet. Even as the sound of intense fighting could be heard from out in the halls, the eunuch grabbed hold of the good luck amulet that hung from Shi Huu's neck and used it to jerk the corpse off the throne.

The still-yawning hole in the floor seemed like the ideal place to dump the body, so Lak Saa did so. Then, unwilling to deny himself a pleasure so long delayed, the eunuch sat on the throne. A smile claimed his face, and for the first time in many years, Lak Saa was happy.

THE FOREIGN CITY OF MYS, ON THE INDEPENDENT PLANET OF LANOR

The three aerospace fighters started out as specks in the east, nearly invisible against the still-rising sun, but quickly became more substantial as they roared over Mys only a hundred feet over the roof tops. Engines screamed, sonic booms rattled the few remaining windows, and the diplomatic community cheered. Though still conscious of snipers, they had turned out to see the display, and were understandably jubilant.

Vanderveen, the person who had engineered the show of power, yelled with all the rest, jumped up and down, and waved at the pilots.

Then, even as the fighters came around for a low-altitude pass over Polwa, the political situation started to change. Some of the Imperial troops ran every which way, alternately firing their weapons at the aircraft, and looking for a place to hide. Others, those who were more disciplined, formed up into the equivalent of companies, and marched off the plain. Though lacking orders, the senior officers knew they couldn't fight the flying machines, and saw no reason to commit suicide.

The Tro Wa troops, however, many of whom had started to gather at the far edge of the plain awaiting orders from Lak Saa, were a good deal more belligerent.

A few had SAMs which they proceeded to fire at the invading aircraft. That was a mistake, a *horrible* mistake, as the pilots proceeded to show them. The fighters ejected both chaff and flares. The SLMs went for the false targets and were quickly drawn away.

That was when the planes wheeled, lined up on the group that had fired the missiles, and opened up with their rockets. The surface of the planet seemed to boil as the missiles hit, exploded, and killed more than three hundred troops in less than thirty seconds.

No further demonstrations were required. The Imperials continued to withdraw, the Claw seemed to melt away, and thousands streamed out of both cities to trudge across the plain. Ordinary citizens didn't know much, but they knew one thing, the devils had been tortured for many weeks, and would want their revenge.

Nobles rode on palanquins carried by slaves, merchants bounced along on wagons heavy with inventory, craftspeople pulled carts loaded with their worldly goods, laborers pushed wheelbarrows piled with what few possessions they had, and the poor and elderly walked out through Polwa's gates with what they could carry on long poles or in packs on their backs.

First, upon leaving the cities, those refugees who chose to go west or east were forced to find their way through a virtual wasteland of craters, trenches, and abandoned weapons pits. Then, once that was accomplished they had to negotiate the shanty town which the Tro Wa had built just out of rifle range. A squalid place full of windblown trash, stinking latrines, and fat nar rats. There were ad hoc graveyards as well, areas where dozens of bodies had been buried, where rotting limbs protruded from the dirt, as if to flag the refugees down.

Sniper fire had all but disappeared allowing the off-worlders to mount the walls. Seeba-Ka examined the exodus through his binoculars before turning to Vanderveen. "Well, Ambassador, it looks like your plan is working. Are you sure about this? I don't know much about the law as it applies to situations such as this, but engineering a planetary government might be illegal, and could get you into a lot of trouble."

Vanderveen managed to look surprised. "I'm not sure I follow you, Captain. Based on information received by Prince Mee Mas, the Empress was assassinated, which makes him the Emperor. I agreed to escort him into Polwa and to serve as an advisor until someone more senior can relieve me. What's wrong with that?"

Hudathans can't smile, not the way that humans do, but Vanderveen would have sworn that the officer produced something akin to a grin. He knew that the so-called information available to Mee Mas was actually little more than an unsubstantiated rumor, and that the diplomat had every intention of sending Shi Huu into exile if she could. Not only that, but Colonel Hawes had turned a blind sensor to the plan, hoping she would be able to pull it off. And if she didn't? There was very little doubt as to who would take the fall—and it wouldn't be Colonel Hawes.

The officer nodded. "Thank you, I stand corrected. Good luck with your mission. I put Lieutenant Santana in charge of your escort . . . Will that be satisfactory?"

Vanderveen silently cursed the Hudathan's rather ponderous sense of humor, managed what she hoped was a noncommittal shrug, and said, "Thank you. It's been my experience that the lieutenant is quite competent."

It took the better part of two hours for the heavily armed party to assemble, make its way through the still-dangerous streets, and pass into Polwa. That's where both of the extra T-2s Seeba-Ka had sent as escorts dropped off, leaving the platoon on its own. Two squads of legionnaires, plus a couple of T-2s, didn't constitute much of an invasion force, but the addition of approximately fifty of the prince's irregulars helped make the force look a little more impressive.

Santana would have preferred to have even more bodies, but the digs were all Hak Orr could spare until the relief force landed, and the entire area was secured.

Still, the cyborgs were worth a squad each, and helped clear the way. For even as the mixed party of LaNorians and offworlders made their way toward the inner city, the fighters continued to overfly Polwa and send thousands of new refugees out into the streets. People shouted, infants cried, animals squealed, dust rose to fog the air, the sun seemed to grow dimmer, and everything looked brown and gray.

A whip cracked as a merchant attempted to force his wagon through the mob. But, rather than give as they normally might have, half a dozen refugees jumped up onto his heavily laden vehicle and pulled the merchant off his seat. Both he and his wife were thrown to the ground and trampled as the crowd overwhelmed the four guards. The screams lasted a few seconds and were mercifully cut off. The entire city was in chaos and no one was safe.

Santana had insisted that Vanderveen and Mee Mas wear nondescript clothes and remain at the center of the first squad now under the command of *Sergeant* "Dice" Dietrich. But they were still extremely vulnerable, something that would have troubled Santana under any circumstances, but worried him even more given the way he felt about Vanderveen. However that was something the officer couldn't allow himself to dwell on, not while he had a job to do, and they were in what amounted to enemy territory.

The crowd had started to close in behind the T-2s. Not in a threatening way, but simply because of the number of bodies on the streets, and a shortage of space.

Santana opened his mike. "Bravo Six to Bravo Two Six. We need some elbow room. Put some smoke along both sides of the column. Over."

Dietrich, who was armed with his trademark grenade launcher, answered with two *clicks*. The launcher made a soft *ka-chunk* as the noncom fired nonlethal smoke grenades to either side.

The orange smoke had the desired effect and caused the crowd to pull away. It also had unintended consequences as the mob turned on itself, children became separated from their parents, and wails of anguish were heard.

Vanderveen heard Santana swear, knew he was upset with himself, and was thankful when the Imperial city appeared off to the right. The concept was one thing—but the reality of what she had set in motion was something else. Had she been correct? Would Mee Mas govern more fairly than his aunt? Or would the whole effort end in disaster? Something that felt like a cannonball rode the pit of the diplomat's stomach and made her want to throw up. Excitement was evident on Mee

Mas's face as he grabbed Vanderveen's arm, pointed to the right, and yelled at Santana. Over there, Lieutenant! That's where we want to go!"

Santana nodded, gave the necessary orders, and led his platoon through the gates of the inner city.

A fighter passed over the palace, momentarily blocked the sun, and rattled the transparent dome over Lak Saa's head. Contrary to all common sense, contrary to Regar Batth's advice, the LaNorian continued to occupy the throne. The only thing that had changed were his formerly blood-soaked clothes. They had been exchanged for a clean robe brought along for that purpose. All the attempts to retake the throne room had ended soon after the aerospace fighters first appeared. That left the self-proclaimed Emperor free to flee, if only he had the sense to do so.

"Listen to me," Batth said desperately. "Troops will land soon and take control of Polwa. Take the throne with you, leave the city, and take refuge in the countryside. You can rule from there."

Lak Saa's ear fans went back against the sides of his skull. "You will request permission to speak. Then, assuming that permission is granted, you address me as 'Majesty' or 'Highness.' Failure to do so will result in death. Do you understand?"

The Ramanthian swallowed. "Yes, Majesty. May I speak?"

"No. I have heard enough. You, like so many of those who while away their lives at court, have your outcomes confused with *mine*. Fact: The Empress is dead. Fact: The Confederacy needs a government with which to negotiate. Fact: The Confederacy was willing to tolerate Shi Huu—so the Confederacy will tolerate *me*.

"*You* have betrayed your kind, *you* fear possible retribution, and *you* want to run.

"That, however, is stupid since I am in a position to protect you. Remain at my side, provide what counsel I may require, and all will be well."

There was a great deal of truth in what the LaNorian had to say, or so it seemed to Regar Batth, and he felt a sudden surge of hope. Rather than end by being sent back to Hive in disgrace, or tried for war crimes, perhaps he could emerge as the Emperor's sole off-world advisor. A potentially powerful position that would not only enable him to restore the burned-out factories, but lock up LaNor's mineral wealth and eventually colonize the planet!

The diplomat was still enjoying his theoretical rise to power when one of the Tro Wa burst into the throne room. "Your Highness! Devil machines have entered the inner city! And there are troops as well!"

Lak Saa raised a permissive hand. "Do not worry. This is to be expected. You may admit their leader plus a reasonable number of bodyguards."

The Claw was careful to bow before he withdrew from the room.

A good fifteen minutes passed as Regar Baath wove the story he would tell, Lak-Saa filed the stump of his broken fingernail into a razor-sharp point, and another flight of fighters passed over the palace.

Finally, when Batth had started to wonder if the relief force would ever arrive, there was a commotion out in the hall. Then, entering the throne room as if he owned it, came Prince Mee Mas.

Even though Pas Rasha had befriended the young noble as a way to counter Shi Huu, the ambassador had been killed, and the Ramanthian was surprised to see Mee Mas. So was Lak Saa, who looked at the princeling, and frowned. "When you enter the throne room it is customary to bow."

Mee Mas, who had been psychologically prepared for a confrontation with his aunt, struggled to change gears. He forced his voice to sound steady and stern. "That is where you are mistaken. No LaNorian is required to bow to a common criminal.

"Lieutenant Santana, take this *thing* into custody, and secure both his hands and feet. He is extremely dangerous."

Santana had entered the room by that time, along with Vanderveen, Hillrun, and Dietrich. He looked at the diplomat, saw her nod, and took a single step forward.

The Ramanthian recognized the human as the same individual who was indirectly responsible for the War Batth's death and felt a surge of anger. "Wait!" the diplomat said, terrified that the source of his power was about to be removed. "By whose authority are you arresting this individual?"

"By *my* authority," Vanderveen said grimly. "Prince Mee Mas is next in line to take the throne. It's as simple as that."

Lak Saa, who had been silent till then, stood and held out his hands. "The human is correct. I believed Prince Mee Mas to be dead. Come, Highness, take your throne, and include me among those who serve you."

Santana shouted, "No!" but it was too late. Mee Mas stepped forward, the trapdoor opened, and the youth screamed as he plunged down into the darkness below.

Lak Saa, confident that the off-worlders would underestimate his abilities, launched himself into the air. But no one is faster than a bullet, especially one fired by someone who is extremely skilled with a gun, and the first slug hit the eunuch's shoulder. That might have handled the job, but Santana had plenty of ammo, and continued to fire. Every single slug hit home; the body crashed onto the floor and slid across the highly polished floor.

Vanderveen took an instinctive step backward, or started to, when a viselike grip closed around the circumference of her left ankle. She was carrying the Sycor Scout, had been from the beginning, and tilted the barrel downward. The .300 magnum bullet passed through Lak Saa's brain, smashed into the marble floor, and caused it to crack.

"Nice job," Santana said approvingly, and was just about to head over to the hole in the floor when something slammed into his thigh.

The legionnaire was already falling by the time the noise

registered on his brain as a gunshot; Regar Batth had shifted his aim to the dome above, and empty casings were arcing through the air. The glass shattered and shards fell like rain. Even as they did so, the Ramanthian spread his seldom-used wings, jumped high into the air, and flapped toward freedom.

Hillrun raised his assault weapon but Dietrich shook his head. "Save your ammo, Sarge, I'll handle the bug." The Naa nodded but kept his weapon raised just in case.

Dietrich tilted the launcher up, waited for the Ramanthian to beat his way up through the opening, and pulled the trigger. The stubby weapon was loaded with HE, and the solitary round exploded slightly above Batth, tore his wings to shreds, and peppered his body with pieces of shrapnel. The Ramanthian crashed through a section of unbroken glass, smashed into the floor, and green blood oozed out to stain the white marble.

Dietrich ambled over with a pistol held down along the side of his right leg, kicked the diplomat in order to get his attention, and looked him in the eye. "The grenade was for me—and this is for the lieutenant." Vanderveen was about to object when the pistol went off, Batth jerked, and the diplomat was dead.

Santana grimaced as Hillrun slapped dressings onto both the entry and exit wounds, heard laughter as his legionnaires pulled Prince Mee Mas up out of what amounted to an underground sewer, and felt a cascade of blond hair brush the side of his face. Vanderveen knelt by the legionnaire's side and held one of his hands. "Thank you for saving my life. *Again.*"

"Sorry about the ankle thing . . . I'll try to do better next time."

"Promise?"

"Promise."

"They'll probably fire me, you know."

"Maybe, but maybe not. You bent some rules, but you also brought the whole thing to a successful conclusion, and there's nothing like success to put the critics in their place."

"Will we see each other? After this is over?"

"Even if I have to crawl," Santana answered, "or hop on one leg."

Vanderveen frowned. "What you need is bed rest, a lot of it, somewhere up in the hills."

Santana smiled. "But what about my leg? How will I get a glass of water? Or something to eat?"

"Oh, your nurse will take care of that," the diplomat assured him, "and she'll take care of your other needs, too. *All* of them."

"That sounds nice," the soldier replied, "*very* nice." And it was.

Author's Note

For More Than Glory was inspired by, and very loosely based on, events that took place during the Boxer Rebellion of 1900 in China.

While most of the characters in the book are entirely fictitious there are a few that were inspired by real people. The dowager Empress Tzu Hsi (also known as the Dawn Concubine) made a fitting model for the evil Shi Huu, and may have been even more heartless than her fictional counterpart.

The gallant messenger Yao Che is based on the real life Yao Chen-Yuan and other Chinese, who took terrible risks on behalf of the foreigners and often paid with their lives.

The Tro Wa (Claw) were based on the Boxers, who were even more cruel than the individuals portrayed in this book, and just as superstitious.

Although they weren't from some other planet, the Americans, British, French, Germans, Italians, Japanese, and Russians were just as contentious as the Clones, Dracs, Hudathans, Prithians, Thrakies, and Ramanthians depicted in this book, and in many cases just as brave, often fighting against overwhelming odds and doing so without benefit of cyborgs to help them.

And, while the foreigners (nine hundred western men, women, and children plus thousands of Chinese Christians for whom they became responsible) did combine forces to hold Peking's diplomatic quarter against a combined force of Boxers and Imperial troops, that unanimity was shattered only a few years later when World War I broke out in Europe.

By the time the conflict was over tens of thousands of Chinese lay dead, the days of dynastic rule were numbered, and China's worldview was forever tainted.

For anyone who would like to learn more about the Boxer Rebellion, I recommend *The Boxer Rebellion* by Diana Preston.